The Nyctalope
vs. The Antichrist

IN THE SAME SERIES

Jean de LA HIRE

The Nyctalope
vs The Antichrist

translated by
Michael Shreve

BLACK COAT PRESS

ISBN 978-1-64932-266-1. First printing: January 2024. Published by Black Coat Press, an imprint of Hollywood Comics.com, LLC, P.O. Box 17270, Encino, CA 91416.

TABLE OF CONTENTS

Jean de La Hire

Introduction

The Nyctalope vs. The Antichrist was first serialized in France under the title *La Captive du Démon* [The Demon's Captive] in the newspapwer *Le Matin* from 28 January to 21 April 1927. It was then reprinted as two slim volumes respectively entitled *La Captive du Démon* and *La Princesse Rouge* [The Red Princess] by publisher Arthème Fayard in 1931

For those who have just joined us, their protagonist, Leo Saint-Clair, a.k.a. The Nyctalope, had previously appeared in three books: *Le Mystère des XV* [tr. as *The Nyctalope on Mars*] (1911), *The Nyctalope vs. Lucifer* (1922) and *L'Amazone du Mont Everest* [The Amazon of Mount Everest] (1925), plus another novel, *L'Homme Qui Peut Vivre dans l'Eau* [The Man Who Could Live Underwater] (1909), which featured a Jean de Sainte-Claire who could only be Léo's father. An updated bibliography of all the Nyctalope novels and related books was included in our previous volume in this series, *The Nyctalope and The Master of Life*.

Jean de La Hire, the creator of the Nyctalope, was born in Banyuls on January 28, 1878, into a relatively obscure, aristocratic family which had long been impoverished by various social upheavals. His birth name was Adolphe-Ferdinand Célestin d'Espie de La Hire. His family claimed descent from one of the knights who fought with Jeanne d'Arc, although its most famous member was the mathematician and astronomer Philippe de La Hire (1640-1718), who has a theorem and a lunar mountain named after him.

La Hire began his literary career with high ambitions, selling his early work to Fernand Xau, the editor of *Le Journal*, and to the humorous periodical, *Gil Blas*. He worked for a while as secretary to Colette's husband, "Willy," and wrote a brief memoir of that time.

La Hire's first successful serial was *La Roue Fulgurante* [*The Fiery Wheel*] (1907)[1], the extravagant account of an alien abduction by a spacecraft which appears to anticipate the now common notion of "flying saucers."

His most enduring creation, the Nyctalope, was one of the first modern superheroes—a crime-fighter who can see in the dark and, as it was later revealed, also sports an artificial heart and is seemingly gifted with an unusual vitality and longevity. To modern readers, the Nyctalope is bound to seem rather feeble next to the likes of Superman and Spider-Man, but he compares well to Doc Savage or The Shadow. His powers are ultimately less important than his symbolic status as a paragon of moral and scientific enlightenment.

---

[1] Available in a Black Coat Press edition, ISBN 978-1-61227-217-7.

After World War II, La Hire was arrested in May 1945 for having collaborated with the Vichy régime and was tried in December; the judgment confirmed his permanent exclusion from the world of French publishing. He escaped from custody in February 1946 while being transferred to a hospital, but was condemned *in absentia* in 1948 to ten years' imprisonment and the loss of his citizenship rights. He never returned to serve his sentence, and was still in disgrace when he died on September 6, 1956.

Then, the Nyctalope and its creator fell into literary oblivion, until, after an absence of fifty years, the character returned in our anthology series *Tales of the Shadowmen*, where he proved to be immediately popular. Thanks to the indefatigable Brian Stableford, ably succeeded by Michael Shreve, several translations of the original works have since followed, and today, the Nyctalope has reclaimed his title as one of the pioneers of superhero fiction.

New readers may be surprised by some *Harlequin*-like aspects of the story. One should remember that, in the United States and England, pulp magazines were bought mostly by men. However, in France, a daily newspaper like *Le Matin* had a sizeable female readership, often comprised of secretaries, salesgirls, etc. Therefore, it was important for any author of *feuilleton* fiction to incorporate both adventure and romance in their serialized novels.

Finally, La Hire is not always clear in the text if the eponymous "Antichrist" is Leonid Zattan himelf, or someone yet to come—in which case Zattan would be the "Ante-Antichrist", so to speak. For the sake of simplicity, and in light of the villain's clearly evocative patronym, we have chosen to interpret it as Zattan being the Herald of the Second Coming.

Now, read on!

Jean-Marc Lofficier

THE NYCTALOPE vs. THE ANTICHRIST

PART ONE: THE DEMON'S CAPTIVE

CHAPTER I

On Saturday, March 13th, 1926, the Cannes post office sent the following telegram:

Have the honor of informing you cargo will leave on Taurus *tomorrow March 14. Planned route. Will be on board. Your servant S. M. D.*

The next morning, Mademoiselle Sylvie Mac Duhl, a young woman, an orphan and French despite her Scottish name, got on board the big sloop *Taurus* anchored in the small port of Villefranche near Nice.

The day before departure, since the deck boss Fidly had fallen sick, they had to leave him in the Nice hospital and Master Allen, the captain, furious but with no other choice, hired a sailor who claimed to have disembarked from a Spanish vessel laid up because of old age and irreparable damage. The "new guy" was called Pedro Tchicoz and he hit it off right away with the sloop's shipwright, Pizano, a mixed-blood Spanish and Indian, who, like Tchicoz, was born in Mexico. But they didn't hang around much with the other two sailors on the *Taurus*, both Scottish like the captain, who were the first mate Jackson and the cook Willis.

Sylvie was put in Master Allen's cabin and the captain moved into Jackson's, which had two bunks just in case.

They were first towed out by a dinghy and then they put up the sail to profit from the land breeze. When the sun had set, the wind died down but kept the same heading, which was northeast.

Clear skies lit by a colony of stars, not a cloud in sight, a steady ocean swell—fair weather. On the second night watch Master Allen withdrew to his cabin, leaving Pizano at the helm.

Tchicoz, who was apparently sleeping on the deck at the bow, in a pocket hollowed out of the rigging, got up and came silently up to the wheel.

"Hey, Pizano," he whispered.

"Hey."

"Can we talk?"

"Sure, why not?"

"Bueno." After a moment of silence the deck boss asked, "You know what they're carrying as cargo?"

"Sure I do," the mestizo growled with a mute laugh. "I helped load and stow it, pal. Bins of bitter orange rinds to make curaçao."

The two faces were lit from below by the lantern in the compartment. Pizano saw the apish jaw of Tchicoz come right next to his own and whisper, "Is that all you know?"

"What else is there?"

"This—listen up, amigo. I did a little digging, me, and I started a while ago. It wasn't easy but I didn't give up... and in the end I found out. So, I got myself on this boat. You want to know why?"

"Sure I do."

"Be careful, Pizano! Be careful because it'll mean death for you if don't do go along me. And what I'm going to do is a once in a lifetime chance with the risk of hanging! You want in?"

"Sure I do!" he barked back.

"Listen up, then," Tchicoz continued in the same low, sinister voice. "Listen, you hate Master Allen, I can see it in your eyes when his back is turned and you're glaring at him, right?"

"I hate him. He humiliated me in front of a woman one godforsaken day... and I'm waiting..."

"I know what you're waiting for," Tchicoz snickered. "Payback. Yeah? Yeah, well, I'm offering it to you. You still want in?"

"I want in! Talk, bandito."

"Here it is." He lowered his voice even more, whispering directly in the shipwright's ear. He said slowly, "The *Taurus* is not going to Barcelona, but it's making the trip around Gibraltar and it won't stop, God willing, ho, ho, until it gets to Ushant off the tip of Brittany. You know where that is?"

"Sure."

"A rowboat will come out at night and they'll pick up the cargo to bring it back to land under cover of darkness."

"Aha."

"Hold on. We're carrying orange rinds, right? But in the back of the hold are other bins stowed there on the night Master Allen gave you leave, since you're not Scottish, and you went and got drunk in a Villefranche dive."

"And these bins?" Pizano hissed.

"Full of gold—100-franc coins from Monaco. And pearls, diamonds, rubies... and gold, millions in gold! Which makes ten or twenty times more in paper money, in cash. Plus the diamonds, rubies and pearls..."

Tchicoz stopped talking and Pizano said nothing in reply. The two men just looked at each other. The light dancing on their brutal faces made their black eyes sparkle. The silence lasted a good three minutes. In the end, Tchicoz spoke up.

"Nobody knows about the gold and precious stones except Mademoiselle Mac Duhl and her Japanese friend, plus the captain, the first mate, the cook... and me! I saw it all and heard everything. So..."

"So?"

"Well, now there's only the captain, the first mate and the cook."

"Yeah, them three. And then no one else knows the secret..."

"Except the Japanese, but he's long gone.

"And the Mac Duhl girl."

"I'll take care of her," Tchicoz assured him. "We won't kill the pretty thing, at least not right off. During the crossing... Get it? You get it?"

"I get it," the other said.

So, Pizano held out his right hand and Tchicoz grasped it with his. Their fingers bent and squeezed and the two men spit hard on the deck, each to his left. Then, for a long time, they discussed how best to carry out the three murders that they figured were absolutely necessary. For the fourth, they would worry about it later."

The first killed was Willis the cook. Luck alone was the deciding factor. No doubt suffering a bout of insomnia, he showed up on deck, coming out of the big hatch only five minutes after the two conspirators had finished plotting. He went to the back and opened his mouth to say something when he got a fist full in the face that knocked him for loop and made him stagger. But he didn't fall. The thump of his falling body would have been heard by the captain or the first mate whose cabin was just underneath. As he was about to keel over, Tchicoz caught him in his arms, lifted him up, scooted to his left and simply tossed him overboard. The splash in the water was barely audible.

"One down!" Tchicoz chuckled.

"It might not be so easy with the other two," Pizano grumbled but was satisfied. "At dawn Allen and Jackson will come up together as usual. Even when they're not sleeping in the same cabin, the first one to open his eyes goes to wake up the other with a slap on the back."

But Tchicoz' brow was furrowed and he didn't answer right away. With his head lowered he seemed to be consulting the compass. At last, he looked up, shot a fierce, menacing look at his partner and sneered, "I killed one, pal. The two others are yours. I hung a six-shot rifle on my bunk. It's short and handles easy. Leave me the helm and go get it. Then hide wherever you want and do your part like I did mine."

"I was going to suggest that, pal," Pizano groaned. "Didn't I say I wanted to get revenge on the captain?"

There was a cool breeze. Speeding through the water, the sloop was pitching slightly as it jumped smoothly from one wave to the next, almost without a jolt. The milky whiteness of dawn was already breaking through.

Down at the foot of the mast, by the hull of the upside-down rowboat, Pizano was sneaking around. He turned and stopped, rifle in hand.

Other noises could be heard besides the wind whistling through the yardarms and rigging: the water grating over the bow as the ship churned through the sea; and sometimes a thud against the starboard beams from a rogue wave. Daybreak came from the southeast by swiftly turning the whiteness of dawn into a rosy pink.

All of a sudden, Tchicoz at the helm and Pizano by the mast, both of them at the same time heard a noise that drowned out all the usual noises of sea and ship—a rheumy cough under the deck. Tchicoz leaned on the wheel while Pizano stiffened, straightened up, already raising the rifle.

Master Allen was the first to come out. His big, white and red head, his bare neck, his broad shoulders that half covered the turned-down collar of the soft shirt, his powerful chest and huge arms: all this surfaced progressively out of the hatch... Then, up jumped the lower body. And immediately afterward, first mate Jackson emerged, alert and chipper, skin and bones, hatless and shaggy.

Was the mestizo at the foot of the mast trembling with hatred, anger or fear? Three shots were fired without Allen or Jackson being brought down. The captain howled as his ear was blown off and blood ran down his neck and shoulders. The other let out a dreadful gasp as he stumbled back against the starboard gunwale. He held his chest with his right hand while the left waved in the air, blood-spattered.

"Ho, ho!" Tchicoz yelled, the veins in his neck popping out, his whole body craning toward Pizano but not letting go of the rudder.

"You rats!" Allen hollered as the truth dawned on him. And he jumped back to the hatch, probably to get a weapon, but a fourth bullet hit him. Then a fifth. The captain raised his arms, spun around and fell on his side, lifeless.

"Oh ho," Tchicoz yapped, snickering and twitching, diabolically, bent over the cabin with his arm stretched out to hold the wheel. "Ho, Jackson! In the sea with you! In the sea! Jump!"

"Yeah, yeah, jump, Jackson!" Pizano shouted, with his back against the mast now.

Obviously not seriously wounded in the chest, the bullet probably deflected by a rib, first mate Jackson stood up straight and got some crazy idea in his head because he started running toward the bow so fast that he sped right past Pizano before he had time to react. And he hopped onto the boom, jumped out and hung onto the jib stays. Now he was at the tip of the sloop as it bounded over the waves. With his feet held together on the thin shaft that formed the stay there, he kept his balance only by the strength of his hands, all his muscles straining to the utmost. And when his head turned back, his face wore an expression of ghastly horror.

The murderers were horrified, too. Together, with demented rage, they started screaming, "Jump, damn you! Jump, Jackson! To hell with you! Jump!"

And dropping to one knee and bracing his elbow, Pizano took aim and fired the sixth and final shot. Hit or not, Jackson jumped, dropped and disappeared under the bow in the foam of the parting waters.

In the cabin where, after the tiring day before, Sylvie had been fast asleep, she was woken up only by the last shots. She thought they were the sails flapping in a gust of wind. But the bright daylight filtering through the porthole led her to believe that the sun had risen. After a quick morning wash-up, she climbed up to the deck. She got there just as Tchicoz and Pizano were lifting the bloody body of the captain to heave into the sea. She stood stupefied, petrified with horror, still not understanding what had happened. But Tchicoz saw her.

"Hold on," he groaned and he dropped the corpse that Pizano kept holding by the arms.

He ran up to the girl, pulled out of his pea coat a big Browning and threatened her, "You, stay calm! Go to the rudder and steer her straight for Spain. And watch out, Jackson and Willis are dead and in the water. The captain's corpse is going after them. Make sure the coast is always clear. If you don't want to join the crew in the sea, do as I say."

As Sylvie, in a flash of revolt, looked ready to run back to the cabin, probably to look for a weapon, Tchicoz grabbed her arm and sneered, "No need to go down there. Yesterday I checked both cabins and took the bullets out of all the guns. So, no way to fight. Now to the helm! Go! And no funny business. I know the coast that we should always be in sight of. Day after tomorrow, if the wind is good, we'll be by the Spanish Pyrenees. And I know where to land. As for you, I repeat, your life depends on your obedience."

The monster was sincerely tempted to hug the girl and kiss her hard on the lips, but his prudence was stronger than his passion. After waving his Browning at her, she looked submissive and went to take the wheel. Tchicoz went back to the corpse, which he and Pizano tossed into the water. Then they got busy cleaning up the deck to erase any evidence of foul play.

They sailed all day long. Night fell. Sylvie didn't refuse to eat the bread and cold meat Pizano brought her. She didn't want to drink the wine but she accepted several glasses of water.

Since the breeze turned really cold after sunset, the two murderers secured the sail. Tchicoz went to the helm and threatened to kill Sylvie if she left the wheel. Then he and Pizano went down to the hold because they wanted to get a look at the gold. It had been haunting them all day. They could resist no longer.

Feverishly, silently, half-dressed, they worked like madmen. They had to lift all the bins full of orange rinds, carry them out of the hold and line them up so they could put them back later to cover up the secret cargo again.

They had lit a lantern because it was the middle of night when they finally got to the last row of bins. Bundles of orange rinds surrounded and hid the wooden boxes and thick canvas sacks. They sliced open one of the bags with a sword and gold came pouring out. They both spent a few minutes digging their hands into the gutted bag and groping the gold.

The boat rocked and threw them against each other. They fell on the bags of gold, hitting the lantern, which toppled over and went out. Now they were lit only by the pale moon casting its dull rays through the covered hatch. In an instinctive gesture of greedy brutes, the two men stuffed their pockets with gold and felt their way back up to the deck.

The wind was raging, the clouds racing through the moonlit sky. Pizano and Tchicoz tightened the rigging on the two jibs and reefed the mainsail.

Then, while Tchicoz went over by the helm and sneered at stone-faced Sylvie who was lit eerily by the lantern in the cabin below, Pizano went to the galley and was soon back with an armful of food and drinks.

Sitting on the helm, the two men drank and ate heartily, laughing all the while. Tchicoz gave a bottle, a biscuit and an open can of food to Sylvie who ate, still stone-faced and somber, and drank calmly, never letting go of the wheel. But a swell heaved and the sloop lurched. The two men rushed off to deal with the sails while the young lady stayed at her post.

Hours passed like this until daybreak when all of a sudden, a storm broke out. The sloop was so battered and so aslant that the two liquored up men went rolling over the deck and smashed into the port side railing where foamy water was sloshing through the scuppers. They fought, accusing each other of being clumsy. Then Tchicoz guffawed. He had an idea that he shared right away.

"After all, what's the point of you living. I can very well put down the girl and spend the gold all by myself."

And brandishing the knife he had pulled out of his pocket, he lunged at his accomplice. The other tried to use the revolver he had kept on him, managed to draw and aim it, but it was too late. The knife slit his throat and he staggered back to the helm where he collapsed, still gripping the revolver.

Sylvie had observed the unexpected fight between the two rogues with passionate interest. When Pizano fell dead near her feet, she no longer cared about the dangers of a boat left rudderless in a storm-tossed sea. She abandoned the wheel and jumped on the corpse, trying to pry the gun out of its hand.

At first, a little stunned by his quick and easy victory, Tchicoz stood there for a few seconds unsure of what to do, struggling to keep his balance on the reeling boat. But on seeing Sylvie bend over Pizano, he understood and rushed at her with his knife raised. Just when he was about to pounce on the girl, she snatched up the gun and skidded away, agile and alert, and escaped the bandit's blade.

But a gust of wind hit the unpiloted sloop, which spun around 90 degrees and ripped the mainsail.

Sylvie realized the peril and ran to grab the wheel with her left hand. With her right she kept the revolver aimed at Tchicoz and ordered, "Get to work, you wretch, or I'll kill you."

He was too smart and too quickly sobered up not to see that duty was calling if he wanted to live. For a few minutes there was a united battle of the young lady and the salty dog against the storm. The former struggled to keep the boat leeward and the other pulled down and threw overboard the ripped sail that was flying and flapping dangerously in the wind. He succeeded, but with the immediate danger averted, he dove down into the forward hatch.

"Ah, the wretch," Sylvie snarled. "He's going to get a gun."

With the erratic state of the storm in which gales were blowing from all points of the compass, the wheel could not be abandoned and an eye had to kept on the sails, someone had to be ready to do the necessary maneuvers.

Braced against the wheel and putting all her strength into her left hand to hold it steady, Sylvie leaned over to look into the holds, both closed now because after jumping down Tchicoz had shut the hatches to keep the water out. Sylvie was ready to shoot first if the man popped up out of either hatch.

But already from the crew's quarters Tchicoz had grabbed a rifle, the same one Pizano had used to kill Allen and Jackson. He loaded it, put some extra ammunition in the right pocket of his peacoat and got ready to climb the ladder out of the hatch. Since he first had to slide open the cover, however, he figured that if the "girl" was on her toes, he could easily be greeted with a bullet from the Browning when he showed his head. Therefore, he stood there on the ladder in a quandary.

After a moment's reflection he went back down and over to the porthole that was high above the waterline and even higher over the sea when the boat was leaning in the other direction. This porthole was right where an anchor hung. After opening it, Tchicoz leaned out and saw, as he hoped, that he could grab onto one of the arms of the anchor, shimmy up the shank and hoist himself over the ring to reach the gunwale. Then he just had to sneak up to the foredeck.

"I'll be hidden by the rowboat stowed on deck" he told himself, "and then I can just show the girl the barrel of the rifle while I make my demands."

And that was what he did. The acrobatics were hard, especially with the turbulent pitching of the *Taurus*, but in the end, with the rifle slung over his shoulder and all his muscles straining, adroitly, boldly, determined to succeed, Tchicoz managed to get on deck. He was soaked from head to toe, but he didn't care.

Kneeling behind the rowboat, in a voice muffled by the wind and waves, he yelled, "Mademoiselle Mac Duhl! Mademoiselle Mac Duhl!" Protecting both his head and arm, he raised the rifle barrel over the rowboat. To make sure he was understood, he pulled the trigger.

The shout and the shot got Sylvie's attention. She understood and she winced a little. "I'm lost," she said. But right away reacting against the desperate threat she blurted out, "No! No!"

An instinct made her look at the sky, the sails and the sea. She frowned, hesitated a few moments, then smiled defiantly.

"The wind is less strong," she said in a low voice, "the sea a little calmer. Besides, the *Taurus* isn't loaded enough to sink. The worst that can happen is a gale will blow down the mast and sails and the sloop will turn into a pontoon. These waters get busy and now that the storm is passing, a boat is bound to pass by. I'll have to kill this guy. I've got more to fear from him than from the sea."

She had finished her internal monologue when Tchicoz spoke again, faintly in the wind blowing against him, but still clear enough. He shouted, "Throw your gun into the sea or I'll shoot, got it? Throw your gun into the sea or I'll shoot!"

With amazing speed, Sylvie fastened the wheel with a rope hanging nearby and dropped down behind it to protect herself. It was a good thing, too, because when Tchicoz saw her tie down the wheel, he took quick aim and fired.

The bullet cut clean off one of the handles but Sylvie had already left her refuge. She was sneaking behind one of the piles of rigging, then, keeping hold of her gun, she ran toward the middle of the boat. Tchicoz couldn't see what was happening but wanted to, so he risked a peek over the dinghy. Out of Sylvie's Browning flew a bullet that grazed the keel of the rowboat, a hair's breadth from the man's head.

Thus started the perilous game of hide-and-seek.

With the mainsail and the boom sail now gone, the sloop was sailing with only the jibs and the staysail, catching the wind from all quarters. But with the wind dying down and leveling off, the boat ran no risk of being cast adrift since the rudder was solid and, for the time being, correctly positioned.

On deck, now that the hatch was closed, the only shelter was the low deck-house on the stern, the foot of the mast, the base of the cockpit and the ship's wheel. There was also the upturned, solidly fastened rowboat and a few coils of rigging.

Now the boat was listing to starboard and frothy water was gurgling in the scuppers.

Sylvie figured that if she could hold out as long as possible against the port side, she could keep an eye on all the visible parts of the deck. She spied a coil of ropes between her and the wall, big enough for her to crouch behind and so providing her with an excellent shield against gunfire as well... She watched the rowboat and when the sloop was tossed hard enough that Tchicoz in his hideout certainly had to grab onto something to keep from tumbling overboard, she made her daring leap. She calculated her momentum perfectly—she dropped directly inside the rigging, got on her knees and hunched over.

"I'm good here in this hole," she figured. "I'll just stay put."

16

She rearranged the top coils of the ropes a little to create a kind of narrow, horizontal slit. Wedged in against the sudden jolts of the boat, protected against enemy fire, she observed the rowboat.

But she was thinking, "The sea was rough. The thug had to worry about not falling overboard and couldn't have seen me jump in here. He must think I'm behind the deckhouse. I'll wait and see… let him find out for himself…"

On her left wrist she had a watch set in a strong leather bracelet. She checked it. The hands showed 8:42. At 8:50 her hunch proved correct: Tchicoz used a lull in the wind and sea to creep around the side of the dinghy. He crawled on his knees with his left side hugging the rounded hull of the rowboat, holding the rifle with both hands.

Sylvie felt her heart racing. A kind of smile twisted the pretty features of her slightly thinned face. "He thinks I'm behind the deckhouse. If I was really there, the bulge of that boat would still be hiding him from me. If he has one atom of common sense, he'll stay there… Good, he stopped. He has some common sense, but unfortunately, this time, it will do him no good."

While Tchicoz was cautiously sticking his head out to verify the distance to the starboard side of the deckhouse, Sylvie Mac Duhl braced her legs, took careful aim and fired…

"Demonios!" Tchicoz swore.

The keen eyes of the young warrior woman saw the effects of her shot right away: the man wasn't hit, but his rifle was in two pieces, the butt on one side and the barrel on the other. The magazine was bent, the weapon useless.

Sylvie stood up straight with her Browning raised. "Your knife—in the sea!" she shouted.

He knew "the pretty girl" now. He knew that she would kill him like a rabid dog if he didn't obey. So, he obeyed instantly. His big pocketknife went overboard.

"To the helm!" she ordered. "And stay there! And watch out because the slightest false move and I'll kill you. Anyway, I have an idea. Get going!"

With that balancing talent that sailors have on the deck of a ship tilted 45 degrees and bobbing through the waves, Pedro Tchicoz passed by Mademoiselle Mac Duhl, who stepped after him. When they were at the wheel, she gave him cold and somewhat scornful orders.

"Unfasten the wheel… Give me the rope. Keep your hands on the wheel if you want to live."

She was behind him. She kneeled down. Keeping a wary eye on him, she quickly and skillfully attached the rope tightly to his left ankle, then to the right, leaving only 10 or 11 inches of play. Then she tied it to an iron ring bolted to the deck about three feet behind the man.

When this was done, and done well, she got up and in the same cold, scornful voice said, "It'll take you at least five minutes to untie all this. You'll have to let go of the wheel first, and step away… If you do this, I'll kill you as soon as I see it. I warn you, too, that I won't stay more than three minutes down below when I have to get something to eat or drink…"

She stopped talking, pondered for a moment, then stared straight into the shifty eyes of the man who was captured but not crushed.

"You know the Spanish coast really well, you said?"

"Yeah, yeah," he grumbled.

"If I'm not mistaken, that's the Cap de Creus over there?"

He turned his head in the direction indicated by the white hand holding the black gun. He squinted to see better and farther. Over in the cloudy, tragic sky, a black line was jutting out into the gray sea.

"Cap de Creus," he grumbled.

"Spain," she muttered. "Spain when the *Taurus* ought to be sailing east of the Balearic Islands."

She pondered for a moment, instinctively staying on guard.

Then she said, "If I were sure I could reach Barcelona alone, I'd kill you, Tchicoz, because you've earned more than your share of death. But I can't sail this sloop alone in bad weather. So, I need you. The two of us will make a pact and I'd untie you so that we can both get some sleep, but I don't trust you on your word. You'd betray me and run the boat aground on the coast even if it meant leaving behind some of the gold."

"I swear that…"

"Be quiet. I'll never believe you, so I'll keep you like this. I give the orders and you obey, or else I'll kill you no matter the consequences. Behind the Cap de Creus is the Bay of Roses, which is well sheltered. Let's go. We'll drop anchor there. We'll put up the spare mainsail and then we can head to Barcelona where I'll hire a new crew. I'll worry about getting through the formalities and I'll spare your life. But I'll bring you with me to drop you off where I know we're going to land. In the meantime, however, I'll lock you in a secret compartment on the sloop where you'll stay bound and gagged while I go ashore and afterward until I kick you off the boat. I'll be bringing you food at night and dealing with any problems you might have. It'll be utterly detestable because you disgust me, but I can do anything to accomplish what I set out to do. There you have it. Now you know what I want. Obey or you die."

He mumbled like he knew he was beaten, "I'll obey, but I…"

She cut him off, "No need to say anything. Do it if you value your life." And after a brief pause, "So, to the Bay of Roses."

"We're on our way, mademoiselle."

But fifteen minutes later the wind shifted from east to west. They had to tack hard. The Bay was far. The sloop didn't get there until nightfall. The lights from the town were scattered over a low hill. Not a boat was in the wide, deep bay because the fishing boats in these areas were brought to shore at night.

As tough and tenacious as she was, Sylvie Mac Duhl was worn out. She had been up for two days and one night, fighting or guarding, without an hour of sleep, without a minute's rest. She had to make painful efforts to drop anchor. Then she ate and drank and brought food and drink to Tchicoz, who was still attached to the iron ring at the helm.

When he had his fill, he lowered his head and said, "Mademoiselle, I'm sleepy."

"Wait!" She fetched a mattress and blanket, threw them at his feet and barked, "Sleep!"

He lay down.

She checked that his ropes were still tight and thought, "If I bind his hands as well, I can get some sleep." She ran off to find a suitable rope and came back. "Your wrists!"

He understood, sneered, but held out his hands crossed. She didn't let go of the Browning as she very deftly wrapped the wrists and pulled tight. Then calmly, putting the gun in her pocket, she fiddled with the improvised handcuffs to secure them.

"Go to bed now... and sleep."

Still standing, she mulled it over. All of a sudden, "No, I'll never sleep knowing you're out here in the open. I've known people to get free from harder shackles than these. But I have to sleep too. Otherwise, tomorrow I'll nod off for sure. You're going to get up, Tchicoz."

During the day she had buckled on a holster for her Browning and strapped a sword around her waist as well. The blade was sharpened on one edge. Sylvie used it to cut the ropes around his wrists and ankles in three quick strokes. Tchicoz got up, slowly, as if he felt stiff.

"Walk in front of me," she ordered, "and go into the deckhouse."

He obeyed. But as he was slipping around the wheel, he jumped to the side, bent down, spun around and like a whiplash sprang up and over the gunwale. Two shots rang out. Then there was a splash. Sylvie leaned overboard and scrutinized the calm water that was as dark as the sky where a low dome of clouds loomed... Trying to control her racing heart and the blood rushing to her head, she listened... To see him, just hear him, then shoot and kill him... Because she had the very clear impression that she had missed when he jumped... Would she have to chase him in the water...

But she saw and heard nothing that broke the monotonous rumble of the surf on the distant beach and against the rocks...

"Could I have killed him? Wounded him? Did he sink?"

She stayed there for more than an hour, ears pricked up and eyes zeroed in. Finally, the silence and the monotonous lullaby of the surf, the gentle rocking of the boat in the soft, rolling waves and the fatigue, the immense fatigue, the irresistible need to lie down, close her eyes and sleep, sleep... Almost unconscious, Sylvie staggered over to the mattress she had brought up for Tchicoz and collapsed onto it, stretched her limbs, sighed... and immediately fell into a deep sleep.

It could not have been more than an hour and a half, all was calm, the sky heavy, the sea black, the land invisible, the boat motionless, Sylvie Mac Duhl out cold...

All was calm except for Tchicoz and five other men. They were in a rowboat that had shoved off from the shore and was nearing the *Taurus*. Four of them were manning the oars slowly in a lazy, soundless rhythm. Two were in the back. The one with the rudder in his hand was Tchicoz. The other with his sombrero pulled down and wrapped in a cape was completely incognito. He was listening to what Tchicoz was whispering. But soon he stopped talking altogether. Without breaking the silence any more than would a wisp of straw on the current, the rowboat pulled up under the jib-boom, a couple of feet from the bow. Hanging from the stay, Tchicoz reached the boom, swung up on deck and crouched down. After him came the man with the sombrero. Then two rowers, leaving the other two in the rowboat.

The four goons crept down along the deck. When they shouted out, Sylvie Mac Duhl woke up with a start, but her feet were already bound. She fought and they held her to tie her hands behind her back. Someone stuffed a silk scarf into her mouth. Two men picked her up and carried her off. An authoritative but even-tempered voice spoke calmly. The young lady knew Castilian. She heard and understood:

"Tchicoz, go get some sleep. I'll take care of the rest with my men. Tomorrow we'll continue our conversation."

But first, Tchicoz showed the two men to the cabin that the late Master Allen had relinquished to the young lady. The Mexican led the way with a pocket flashlight. In the cabin he struck a match and lit the candleholder hanging from the ceiling. Only then did he leave, snickering as he went, "This time, Mademoiselle Mac Duhl, I am going to sleep well for sure. I hope you can too."

The two men dropped the girl on the bunk, covered her with a blanket, made sure the porthole was closed, unhooked the candleholder and left. The prisoner heard them lock the bolt from the outside... and leave the key in the lock...

Before the Great War, all the inhabitants of Monte Carlo knew George Mac Duhl. Perhaps the best but certainly the calmest and most regularly gratified of gamblers. Whether at roulette or baccarat or trente et quarante, the noble Scotsman never played for more than two hours in the afternoon and an hour after dinner. And he always left with winnings that varied between 10 and 1,000 louis. Mr. Mac Duhl had become legendary from Menton to Cannes. A few well-informed gossips knew that this mild, dependable and very rich favorite of Lady Luck lived in Cap Ferrat in a small Italian château deep in the wild woods full of pine trees, cork oak, eucalyptus and cypress trees—it was known in that region as the Château des Nopals.

He made the roundtrip between Cap Ferrat and Monte Carlo on a regular basis in his four-seater torpedo sports car, fast and powerful, which was driven by his Japanese mechanic, named Gnô, a curious man, servant and factotum, with a rare and remote dignity, unwavering discretion and the impassivity of the buddha.

And the cleverest professional informants could say nothing more about the "Scotsman" Gregor Mac Duhl, the lucky gambler.

At the start of the Great War, Gregor didn't change his habits. Six afternoons and six nights a week, routinely, he could be found in a casino. But suddenly nobody saw him, not at all, not for an hour, not for a minute, not for an instant. He had vanished as completely as if he had died.

Since most of the former staff was in the war and the players had dwindled by two-thirds, almost totally different people than before August 1914 as well, the sudden disappearance of the legendary Scotsman made nobody particularly concerned or curious. Besides, so many men were disappearing in those Apocalyptic times!

Nobody even remarked on this one thing, a peculiar and very strange coincidence. Nobody, really? Yes, one man, only one...

Destiny has some dreadful quirks. A man was observing out of simple curiosity. In a flash of inspiration, a man recognized the coincidence that was if nothing else weird and, in any case, memorable: It was that the Scotsman stopped showing up in Monte Carlo on the day when officially and permanently the 100 franc gold pieces with the figure of the Prince of Monaco were replaced at the tables by simple chips and at the cashiers by paper money.

The man who noticed this coincidence, the only man, was neither exceptionally intelligent nor unusually observant. Just an average man really, whose vague and vacillating will doomed to bad luck and, if the opportunity arose, to shady affairs and even to crime.

This man was Pedro Tchicoz. He was Mexican, in his forties and worked as a mechanic in a garage in Monte Carlo. He had lived in the Principality since 1907. A gambler and a rake, he loved his job, however, with a kind of passion and he gained experience, skill and an uncommon ingenuity. His boss, who treasured this top-notch worker, paid him very well. But more than the exorbitant wages, it was the gambling kept Tchicoz in Monte Carlo. He played every night, sometimes winning, sometimes losing, which kept him going without ever being too discouraged or satisfied. And this Mexican took a lively interest in Gregor Mac Duhl who had been in Monte Carlo since 1900...

People who don't believe in destiny can say, "It was this daily and longstanding interest that made Tchicoz take note of the coincidental disappearance of the Scotsman and the gold coins at the same time."

Whatever the case, Pedro Tchicoz was struck by the coincidence. He spent three days and two nights thinking about it after waiting a week to verify it.

Then, with cold determination and something savage, mean and ruthless deep down inside the man, he told himself, "I want to clear up this matter."

What was he thinking? What did he suspect? What was he planning? Nothing precise, nothing that could be put in words, but he had the irresistible desire to clear up the matter, as he kept repeating to himself...

And he took the tramway to Cap Ferrat one evening, the evening—and not another, surely—that was stamped by destiny.

That day, in the dining room of the Chateau des Nopals, when the midday meal was over, Gregor Mac Duhl stood and said spoke seriously to his daughter. "Sylvie, today is your 21st birthday. Come down to the cellar with me."

Sylvie Mac Duhl was a pretty young lady whose face and demeanor would lead you to believe that she could endure great emotional upheavals without losing her spirit or strength. Not that she looked manly! She was gorgeous and charming—her unfathomable blue-green eyes with dark pupils and her dazzling golden hair, everything about her showed a young lady turning into an exquisite and seductive woman, but an athletic young lady and a woman of character as a result of physical training and moral education, the two enemies of all weaknesses.

And it was this amazon (the word is fitting for anyone seeing her riding her black steed on the roads between the Alps and the sea) who blushed at her father's words. Then she turned a little pale and leaned against the oak wainscoting and in a choked voice stammered, "The cellar, you say? The cellar..."

The Chateau des Nopals was rectangular, flanked by two square towers. Under the entire extent of these three buildings the architect had installed three tanks to catch all the rainwater that fell on the vast surface of the roof: a wise precaution because there was no spring on the property and drilling for a well at 100 feet around had proved futile.

In May, 1899, Gregor Mac Duhl, coming from Scotland, had moved to Villefranche and got his French citizenship. He bought the Nopals property. It had been abandoned and left to rot. The new occupant organized and directed the work that in two months made the chateau comfortably inhabitable. The tanks, for instance, had been drained, cleaned and refurbished. While waiting for the first heavy rain in the fall, a small tanker truck came every day with a supply of water for Nopals.

But when the rain started, only two tanks were catching the water from the roofs—the middle one and the one to the east. As for the one to the west, Gregor and Gnô had cut it off, either by plugging up or rerouting the pipes. But they had put in a pipe connecting the west tank to the middle one with a double valve closure. With this, it would take only a few minutes for the dry tank to be flooded three quarters full of water. In Gregor's bedroom they had carefully hidden the operating lever.

Moreover, the inspection window and access door of the dry tank had been fitted with a very thick, solid-wood panel with a strong, secret lock. The ground-floor room of the tower where the door opened in the tile, was transformed into a plush and formal office-library. And Gregor's huge American desk was placed over the door to hide it from view. Plus, they nailed a thick rug on the door and then laid a carpet over it. All this work was done by Mac Duhl and Gnô themselves in secret during the month of August, 1901, when they were alone. Then Gregor left the Japanese there and went to Paris. He came back at the end of September with Madame Mac Duhl, a very pretty French woman, along with two servants: a cook and a chambermaid. Three years later, the young woman died in childbirth. She left behind a daughter whom Gregor baptized Sylvie and whom he loved with all his heart and soul. He alone took responsibility for educating, training and refining her mind and body.

Nevertheless, the young Mac Duhl knew nothing about the existence of a secret cellar until she had turned 19.

On her 19th birthday, at 10 o'clock sharp, Sylvie went into her father's bedroom as usual to kiss him good morning, prepare the tea and toast for his breakfast and talk with him privately for twenty minutes or so. But when she was about to leave, for the first time in six years of this daily routine, Gregor held her back. Very gravely he revealed to her the existence of the cellar, the lever, the trapdoor and explained the simple but secret trick to open and close it.

Then he concluded, "If ever I die, my dear, before I've reached my goal, you will go into the cellar after reading my will, which I've handed over to Monsieur Aubépin, a notary in Nice, and you follow the instructions I've laid out. Promise me."

Emotionally touched, she promised.

But her father said nothing more, ever, on the subject. And the young lady lived for two more years without knowing what was in the cellar or what her father and Gnô were doing down there every Sunday afternoon. See, she had found out—oh, not on purpose since she had too much self-respect to be indiscreet—that every Sunday, between 2 and 3 pm, Gregor and the Japanese spent around forty minutes in the mysterious cellar.

And it was in this cellar that she was being invited to see today on her 21st birthday! Over the past two years Sylvie had thought so much about the cellar. Whenever she did, she felt deeply anxious. And now she was about to go down there! The mystery was about to be revealed to her!

But the source of her emotional affliction was not the revelation in itself. No, it was that she was living through a prediction made to her in total secrecy by a very mysterious friend of her father, an odd man who lived all year long on Ushant Island off the farthest tip of Finistère and who came to Nopals once only for one day: that Gregor would die in the year he revealed the mystery of the cellar to his daughter…

The prophecy came true.

Three months to the day after bringing Sylvie down to the cellar, Gregor died suddenly of an embolism.

And that was when Sylvie Mac Duhl started to really live since she started to advance, with her moral character and physical strength, on the extraordinary path laid out by the mysterious will of her father.

Gregor had died on Friday, March 13th, 1925. He was buried on the 14th in the small cemetery of Villefranche. On Sunday the 15th Sylvie spent all day with Gnô making a kind of inventory of papers left behind by the deceased, filing some of them away but burning most of them. On Monday the 16th, accompanied by Gnô who left the car at the door in Julien's care, Sylvie went to Monsieur Aubepin's office to hear her father's will.

After that, she lived at Nopals, served by Gnô and her young chambermaid, another Japanese called Mâh, and an old Italian cook. She lived alone and quiet, beautiful and somber, staying away from people, avoiding curiosities, doing things just for herself, playing the organ in the big salon, racing her horse at breakneck speed, speeding over the roads on the Côte d'Azur in her father's car with herself or Gnô at the wheel or making short trips across the Mediterranean in her sloop the *Taurus*.

But on March 13, 1926, the first anniversary of Gregor Mac Duhl's death, Gnô went to the Cannes post office with this telegram:

Have the honor of informing you cargo will leave on Taurus *tomorrow March 14. Planned route. Will be on board. Your servant S. M. D.*

The next morning, Sylvie got on board the *Taurus*, which was anchored in the small Villefranche port, while Gnô and Mâh took the car to Brest. A second valet and the cook stayed at Nopals to guard and maintain it.

Three days later, in the Bay of Roses in Spain, Sylvie Mac Duhl, the *Taurus* and her cargo fell into the hands of the crook Pedro Tchicoz and five mysterious cohorts.

CHAPTER II

Around Ushant Island, which is the westernmost point of France, the currents are strong, the reefs plentiful and the fog frequent and heavy, which all make for dangerous waters abounding in shipwrecks. The island itself was a craggy land overlooking the turbulent sea. No trees grow there. Few people live on it because the men are almost always sailing on long voyages. The women who do live there look proud and wild with their long hair left free in the wind.

If there is a region on Ushant that is more savage and dreadful and cursed than any other region on the tragic island, it is certainly the arid, rocky, desolate land that forms the long and wide headland that juts out into the immense ocean ending at Créac'h Point. Over a mile long east to west, no man had ever built his home on the Créac'h Headland where the women with flowing hair only venture during good weather, which happens rarely. But in 1899 an Englishman landed on the island, bought two acres of land on Créac'h Point and marked it off with a low, dry-stone wall. Then, at great price and thanks to a contractor from Brest with his crew, he built a house right in the middle of his property, a veritable fortress but fortified against the elements rather than against man: thick walls, huge buttresses, double roofs of herringboned slates, double windows with massive shutters, low doors with rounded arches, iron-braced gates with roll-up doors inside. Furthermore, the house was very broad and very low. Only one story, but 100 feet of façade at the four cardinal points, which made it perfectly square. And the basement and cellars excavated from the rock with dynamite...

The people of Ushant wondered, "What was this Englishman doing here?"

They never knew because exactly seven days after he moved into the finished and comfortably furnished house, the Englishman was killed by his Irish servant during an argument after too many glasses of strong whiskey. When he was arrested the murderer killed himself in the Ushant jail. Locked up by the authorities, the house never saw a visit from any English heirs from Birmingham.

Why did the owner-builder get the funny idea to call it "The Chalet", Swiss style, instead of "house", "cottage" or "castle"? A mystery.

But it didn't take long after the death of the extraordinary gentleman for the men and women of Ushant to call the weird fortress-house the "Ghost Chalet" because henceforth, every Friday and Saturday night when they dared to pass by it on their way to the lighthouse, they saw light filtering through a cracked shutter and they heard shrieks and groans inside the Chalet.

A year passed. The folk in Ushant convinced anyone willing to listen that not a Friday or Saturday night went by without the light and shrieks and groans manifesting.

But this didn't keep the Ghost Chalet from being bought in the spring of 1900. On May 1st, with good weather and a calm sea, a steamship moored in Lampaul Bay. Four dinghies unloaded 58 very heavy crates, each three feet square. Two men and a woman followed these crates into the Ghost Chalet and settled in with the help of a sailor from the steamship. When it weighed anchor three days later it left behind a gas-powered whaler, long, wide, solid and well balanced, which was called *Nostradamus* and was registered in Conquet, the only port on the coast of Finstère that had regular contact with Ushant. The sailor who had helped set up the new occupants was the owner of the whaler and he lived in the Ghost Chalet. His name was Ephrem Lluch, an uncommunicative Catalan around 30 years-old, born in Collioures in the Roussillon. They knew this because he registered himself, as he should have, with the Marine Commissioner in Conquet.

Within a week Ushant also knew that the buyer of the chalet was Mathias Lumen, that his associate, a kind of secretary and partner, was a Parisian named Placide Bonnard, that the woman, a servant and cook, was called Sidonie. But that was all they could find out. When a letter addressed to Monsieur Lumen, labeled him the "chemical engineer", they knew the profession, real or fake, of this man who never left the house except at night to stroll around the property and whom the gossips in Conquet nicknamed the "Hermit of Ushant".

Years passed. Once a week the steamship came back, dropped anchor in Lampaul Bay, unloaded 3-foot square crates, weighed anchor and left. Once a week in the whaler Ephrem Lluch ferried the secretary Placide Bonnard to Brest. Silent and severe, Sidonie did the daily shopping in Lampaul—few things really because when the whaler *Nostradamus* returned from Brest, it was always loaded with canned foods, meat, vegetables and fresh or dried fruits.

Years passed. The Hermit sometimes went to the mainland and wasn't seen for days or weeks.

And the Great War broke out. Placide Bonnard and Ephrem Lluch were mobilized and sent off, but nothing changed at the Ghost Chalet except that they no longer received the mysterious crates every six months because from 1914 to 1918 the ship didn't dock once. The whaler still went to Brest every week, but with the deep respect of the Ushantans, it was Sidonie who piloted it, as slick as an old Breton sea dog in the channels and currents.

In November, 1918, Placide Bonnard and Ephrem Lluch came back to Ushant, pretty the same as they had left, except Lluch was minus one eye and wearing a Military Cross and Placide Bonnard had a limp in his left leg and on the lapel of his overcoat was the thin, red ribbon of the Legion of Honor. When Sidonie brought them from Brest, the men and women who saw them disembark in Lampaul gave them an honorable salute.

Then it was exactly like before the war at the Ghost Chalet. It had been a long time since the curiosity of the Ushantans had petered out. When they saw Sidonie or Lluch or even "Monsieur Bonnard" out shopping or on a therapeutic stroll, they greeted them respectfully and a little fearfully. Many of them crossed themselves if they happened to pass by Créac'h and saw "Monsieur Lumen" ambling around his property with his hatless head lowered as his bony hand stroked the long waves of his white beard.

On March 14th, 1926, at eleven in the morning, Mathias Lumen was sitting in an upstairs room in the chalet, attentively reading a long, narrow, yellowed parchment when Bonnard brought him the bundle of mail from Brest. On top of the bound letters, leaflets and newspapers lay the blue rectangle of a telegram.

"Hello, Sir," Placide said.

"Hello, my friend," and Lumen took the telegram.

The mysterious man might have been 50 years-old. Tall, broad-shouldered and muscular, with white hair and beard, gray-blue eyes surprisingly youthful but very majestic and unbearably penetrating, a strong, slightly hooked nose, a pale, weathered face with a high, broad, turbulent forehead, he was the very image of an Olympian Jupiter... But if he smiled, with all his shiny white teeth intact between those lips that would take on color, he could have passed for God the Father. His voice was incredibly nuanced, from the most charming gentleness to the most chilling sternness... Standing before him, Placide Bonnard, who "showed" his age of 35, was the contrast in his skinny, nervous body, short, alert, with hazel eyes, short, brown hair and clean-shaven.

The huge room they were in—it took up three quarters of the upstairs— also showed astonishing contrasts. Lit by three bay windows facing east, south and west, it was a chemistry and physics laboratory on one side with its kilns, retorts, and various instruments and machines; on the other side was the library with its shelves full of books, two big globes, tables piled with files, leather chairs and oak stepladders. On the library side, the parquet floor was covered with a sumptuous, very thick carpet; on the laboratory side you walked on galvanized plates. A heavy, split curtain, both sides secured by gilded brass tiebacks, could be drawn between the two sides of the room to isolate them completely from each other, at least from sight.

When Bonnard had entered, Mathias Lumen was in his library on a couch. He was wearing a white flannel shirt with a very open, turned-down collar, wool pajamas and his bare feet were slipped into leather sandals. His thick, curly, very long, white hair made a bright halo around his face. And this majestic face lit up with a smile on his lips and a sparkle of joy in his eyes when he read the telegram.

"Good news, Placide," he said emphatically in his clear, lilting voice. "Yes, good news indeed. Read."

With blue slip in hand Bonnard read out loud softly:

Have the honor of informing you cargo will leave on Taurus *tomorrow March 14. Planned route. Will be on board. Your servant S. M. D.*

But while he was reading, Lumen's eyes narrowed a little, looked pensive, severe, his face almost frozen. His voice sounded harsh and hollow.

"Placide, the time is near to accomplish the most mysterious and most troubling, in its tremendous clarity, of all the prophecies of Nostradamus... The woman is coming with the fateful gold for us. But where is and who is the man?"

Like his master Placide Bonnard had turned serious and solemn. A shiver ran through his body. The work that was more than titanic, the work that was in a way divine, in which he was collaborating—how insignificant he was!—appeared once again in all its infinite grandeur, in its enigmatic and tragic reality. Bolstered by his intelligence and unshakeable faith he responded simply, his voice trembling a little with uncontrollable emotion.

"The man will reveal himself since Nostradamus asserts it and since the predestined woman is coming."

Mathias put the unfolded telegram on the corner of the table where the rest of the mail was stacked. The two men stared silently at the blue paper for a long time. Finally, with his eyes lost in meditation, he murmured:

"In the name of Scotland and orphaned of all
"Golden maiden with love will bring to life
"In the time one and nine and twenty-six
"Great brown-haired male with divine attributes.
"If stone and gold by chance more than enough
"Fill the well that in Ushant Englishman made
"Death wretchedly by blade to the throat
"Against the Antichrist the male is opposed.
"Victorious will he be if the woman gives birth
"Otherwise, the Time will be long delayed
"Blood over one and nine and twenty-six
"With the dead in dreadful piles."

And also meditative, Mathias Lumen pronounced, "Within a year, I hope, the well will be filled with the gold that is coming to me, that will come from all my gambling halls around the world. Right now Sylvie Mac Duhl is on her way, the golden-haired maiden of Scottish stock who is an orphan and has no relatives, not even a distant relation in Brittany!"

But he shuddered, stood up, took a few steps toward the laboratory, came back and spoke normally, "In fact, Placide, what day might Sylvie Mac Duhl be arriving?"

"We can only have a very rough estimate," Bonnard replied as he, too, stood up.

The secretary walked over to a globe, spun it with a finger, then stopped and traced a slow line from Nice to Finistère.

"The distance from Villefranche to Ushant is roughly 1,700 nautical miles. I know the *Taurus*. I was onboard it from Monte Carlo to Alexandria. Master Allen is an experienced, skilled and bold sailor. But still, we can't give the sloop of the late Mac Duhl an average speed in excess of 10 knots an hour. That

28

makes 170 hours for the voyage, meaning seven or eight days. Moreover, we have to factor in bad winds that will force them to tack, storms that might force a layover in some a sheltered cove, and dead calm that could slow them down or even stop them."

"Well," Mathias Lumen said, "let's say fidteen days. We'll expect Sylvie Mac Duhl in the second week of April. But as was agreed, Gnô Mitang and Mâ Ito will leave tomorrow from Cap Ferrat by car. They'll arrive in Brest the evening of the 17th or early the 18th. You'll go pick them up on the 18th. Don't forget to remind Lluch. You can leave early as long as the sea isn't too rough."

"Very well."

"Let's see the rest of the mail now."

The chemist and his secretary (his student, assistant and collaborator) sat down again, the former on the couch and the latter on a stepladder next to the table with the stack of mail. He untied the bundle and the stack collapsed. Quickly he slit the envelopes with a slender letter-opener, pulled out the paper, unfolded it and scanned through, placing it to his right if it needed an answer or to his left for the rest. The envelopes dropped into a basket he had pulled between his legs. For every letter he stated who signed it, where it came from and summarized what was written. For a long time Mathias Lumen listened, bent over a little, his face impassive, not saying a word, his lovely, sober eyes abstractedly watching the movements of Bonnard's hands.

When he pronounced "Ramon Bastos, Port Bou..."

The master looked straight at him and stiffened.

After a quick glance at the correspondence, Placide perked up.

"I'll read the whole thing, master:

"*Port Bou, March 12th,*

"*Dear Colonel, I am relieved to finally inform you that I am on the trail of J.C. Coming from Paris where he was seriously compromised under the name of Zakopane and on the verge of being arrested for spying on behalf of two powers, he entered Spain via Irun on March 1st. He went to Madrid where he met a delegate of Leonid Zattan, then to Barcelona where he got in touch with cell 33, which I note in passing had been increased by four Mexican 'tourists' from Monte Carlo.*

"*I saw J.C. I talked to him. He pretended to be a Parisian painter of the new school of Montparnasse. He was doing a 'study' of the sea rocks when I approached him and sincerely praised his talent. I'm convinced he'll be at Roses for a few weeks, meaning until the affair that forced him out of Paris has blown over.*

"*What should I do with J.C.? I respectfully await your orders.*

"*I am as always, my dear colonel, your ever faithful, devoted, grateful,*

"*Ramon Bastos.*"

"Very well," Mathias Lumen said. And as simply as could be, "Answer to-day. Use the Spanish code. Tell Bastos to kill or rather execute Jacques Cervier—since it'll be a just execution and not a murder."

"Master, this will be the first time that Bastos..."

To this potential objection, the master replied, "All the more reason! It will also be the first time that Ramon Bastos will have the opportunity to prove his gratitude, devotion and faith. He knows the crimes of Jacques Cervier. He won't balk. And we will be rid of a traitor who so often got in our way, damaged the holy cause and who has been the infernal collaborator of Leonid Zattan since the armistice."

"Very well, master, I'll write to him today."

"Yes, and I'll sign it."

Bonnard put Ramon Bastos' letter to his right and continued going through the mail. There was no other letter that drew Lumen out of his silence. The newspapers, journals and leaflets were sorted to be registered in the catalogue and put in one of the eight libraries in the house or were set aside to be read after lunch.

Nothing else remarkable happened at the Ghost Chalet on March 14th. Mathias Lumen and Placide Bonnard worked as usual on their mysterious undertaking, which drove them from the library to the laboratory and then into the cellars and finally each to their own office on the ground floor where the secretary typed the letters in duplicate and the master examined the records, made notes and revised them, then between 5 and 6 pm signing the letters he had asked for in the morning. And this signature was made with an M and an L intertwined, under which Bonnard used a tiny stamp for Mathias Lumen's seal—impressed on the verso and embossed on the recto: a seven-flamed torch held in an iron fist and crossed with a sword that a bare fist wielded.

At 6 pm it was, no matter the weather, time for Lumen's therapeutic stroll on the grounds and the no less therapeutic trip for Bonnard to the post office on the island where he mailed the daily correspondence by regular or registered mail, the former for simple letters in simple language, the others containing more important missives in a secret language... Between them, the master and his student knew almost all the languages of the civilized world and, in fact, they had correspondents from all nations and of all races. But the postal workers in Ushant, Conquet and Brest were no longer surprised. Mathias Lumen was well known now on the island and the coast as a very rich scientist who wrote to all the scientists around the world.

They knew that at the start of the war the police had taken a look at the mail of the Hermit of Ushant. The investigation, legitimate in the state of war, had turned up nothing against the chemist in his physical retirement from the world, except epistolarily. And since his secretary Placide Bonnard and his sea-faring servant Ephrem Lluch had been honored and decorated by the army, the owner of the Ghost Chalet was not bothered by the police. He was even admired, discreetly venerated, after the summer of 1916 when the police got information from notes written and signed by Mathias Lumen, the genius colonel in retirement, which led them to the discovery and arrest of a gang of Bulgarian-German spies living under false names with perfect French accents in the middle of Le Havre where they had set up a Franco-Swiss transit house.

It was natural, therefore, that Mathias Lumen, his secretary and his servants had become deservedly accepted in Ushant and instead of suspicion or curiosity they raised only a respectful sympathy.

The days from the 15th to the 17th pass like so many others in the Ghost Chalet without incident. The 18th and 19th saw them disappointed and a little worried at not finding Gnô Mitang and his travelling companion at the hotel in Brest. They didn't arrive until the 20th. An accident on the road had stopped them in Tours for a major repair to the car, which had been hit by a badly driven truck. The former factotum of the late Gregor Mac Duhl, who had become the steward of Sylvie, knew the Hermit of Ushant and household well. It was different for Mâh Ito, the maid, who was coming to the island for the first time. But nothing surprised the Japanese woman. She reached an agreement right away with Sidonie to take on some of the work. As for Gnô, he was immediately brought to the lab by Bonnard.

After the customary greetings, Gnô spoke in a low voice with a strange, boyish tone, but with a calm that made it sound deceptively indifferent.

"Master, in the *Taurus* there's 58 million in gold, in coins of 20, 40 and 100 francs and in precious stones, diamonds, rubies and sapphires, that add up to hundreds of millions. It was all acquired either directly from gambling or through trades made by Gregor Mac Duhl. But the trading was only done with the players in the casinos from the cash that my master had stashed away. That was what he asked of me on his death bed, to tell you this because it isn't written down anywhere."

"Very well," Mathias said, unruffled by the catalogue of his wealth. "When do you think the sloop will get here?"

Gnô answered directly, "At the earliest, March 25th. At the latest, April 8th, unless the gods..."

For, the Japanese believed in the eternal battle of rival gods, one being the principle of good, the other of evil, but he was unable to say which of them was more powerful.

"Very well," Mathias said again. He opened a file on his table, thumbed through it, took out a piece of paper and handed it to Gnô. "Read this letter. You know both Ramon Bastos and Jacques Cervier. The letter is from the former. It talks about the latter. Mull it over while I go with Bonnard to open today's mail. Then you can tell me what you think."

Gnô bowed, took the letter and started reading. Mathias and Placide went to another table... and work went on as usual.

31

For fifteen minutes nothing interrupted the work of the master and his secretary, reading and registering, with hushed comments, the good and bad news of the day.

But all of a sudden, one piece of news had the effect of setting off a powder keg during the monotone whizzing of fireworks. Bonnard's hand, holding the letter, started trembling and his voice, while reading the letter, faltered.

Mathias Lumen shouted, "Is it possible? Gnô! Gnô Mitang!"

And the Japanese walked over.

"Placide, read, read it!" Mathias ordered. "Start from the beginning."

Bonnard read, a little louder than the first time and more assertive:

"Roses, March 18, 2 am.

"My dear colonel, I am writing to you at this unusual time because I've just learned some things that seem to me too serious to wait and that I judge it better to tell you without delay. As soon as I finish this letter, I will jump into my car and go to Figueras. When the post office opens, I will send it registered mail to leave with the first delivery of the day.

"Here it is: yesterday morning in Port Bou, I received your letter of the 15th containing the supreme order. I kissed your signature while saying, 'I will obey!' And I left for Roses right away, determined to carry out your order in the way long ago agreed, at the first favorable opportunity, which I had decided to create within 48 hours if it didn't present itself naturally.

"Now, wanting beforehand to take precautions and leave nothing to chance, I slipped in at nightfall to the small courtyard behind the isolated house where J.C. lives. I knew he wasn't alone because several men from the gang had entered the house. I'd been at this lookout point for around an hour and had heard only banal conversations (the men were smoking and gabbing about all kinds of news) when I heard hard knocking at the front door on the other side of the house. The knocks followed a code I recognized. It was, therefore, a member. But why knock so hard? The newcomer must have been in a hurry, impatient, worked up...

"The courtyard inside had very high walls but I had the key to one of the gates, which I'd left open on my way in so I could get away quickly if necessary. I ran out and around the house and peeked around a corner to see the front just in time for the door to open and spill light on the nocturnal visitor.

"I was astonished as well as very agitated. The stranger was panting, disheveled, soaked despite the dry air on this starry night, and blood was dripping from his left ear, which looked cut half off. He was barefoot, dressed in pants rolled up like sailors do and a sleeveless shirt. I saw and I heard:

" 'Oh, Tchicoz,' a voice in the doorframe said.

" 'Tchicoz!' another voice, that of J.C., repeated. 'Get him in here, quick!'

"The man rushed in and the door closed. In a jiffy I was back at my post. And I listened. It would be too long, colonel, to write down here everything my

ears heard and my memory, I'm sure, recorded word for word. But what you are about to read is the exact summary, complete although succinct, of what I heard.

"Tchicoz had come swimming from a sloop anchored in the bay. A sloop named the Taurus! *Some tragic event had bloodied the ship whose entire crew, except Tchicoz, had perished and drowned. Tchicoz was the cause and key player in the tragedy but was afterward defeated by a young lady, the owner of the sloop, whose name I couldn't really make out, either Sylvie or Lydie. But Tchicoz got lucky and jumped into the sea, while being shot at by the girl who hit his left ear. Tchicoz had assured them the sloop was loaded with gold pieces and precious stones worth an incalculable sum.*

"He had come to J.C. to bring him back to the sloop right away, but J.C. wanted more details. I didn't hear why because just then they all left and went into the next room, which was the kitchen and dining room. But they left the door open, which meant I didn't have to move even though I could only hear snatches of what was being said. Then suddenly everything went quiet. I thought maybe the whole gang had left the house.

"Right away I left courtyard again and went around the house. This house is outside the town itself, maybe 200 yards from the seashore. The coastline there is made of sandy and rocky beaches. On wooden runners was a dinghy that J.C. had rented for three months. I saw six men running together towards this dinghy. The land is completely out in the open, so I took a firm and steady gait like I was out for a casual evening stroll. If they tried to stop me, I was determined to kill J.C. with my revolver even at the price of facing all his men. Once the idea popped into my head, it wouldn't leave. I had to kill him! If he reached the sloop, he'd slip out to sea and maybe escape me forever!

"I didn't know and still don't know if the Taurus *has any bearing on your work, colonel, but I had the feeling that I had to try the impossible in order to obey you and to try it all the more so since if I didn't kill J.C., taking over the sloop might increase his power, which you are battling against.*

"So, I walked forth, not too fast, my right hand gripping the revolver in my coat pocket. But I couldn't run if I didn't want to make J.C. suspicious and sic his men on me before I got close enough to get off an accurate shot. Suddenly I realized that I wouldn't make it in time if I didn't run. They were already untying the ropes and sliding the dinghy down the waxed planks. So, I ran and my pounding footsteps caught their attention. A quick order was given in a language I didn't understand and right away a pole hit my legs, which I saw later was the rudder from the dinghy. I fell and rolled down the sloped beach. When I got to my feet, the dingy was in the water and the four oars were rowing it quickly away. In my fall I had hit my elbow and dropped the revolver. I scurried around looking for it.

"When I finally found it, the dinghy was out of range. I had failed.

"I send you my deepest regrets, colonel. As a result of my failure, my debt to you has doubled. I beg you, let me serve you more than ever.

33

"Distraught and hopeless, I stayed on the shore. The moon had just risen. It was still huge because the full moon was only three days earlier. It lit the bay. I could clearly see the dinghy approach the sloop and the men climb aboard by the boom. Less than fifteen minutes later, the big sail was hoisted along with the staysail, the foresail and the jib, the whole shebang. The dinghy was used to tow the sloop to the point of the bay not protected by the hills from the offshore wind. And the sloop set off, leaving the dinghy to float away empty.

"No one but me saw the scene. The solitude gave me the idea to search the house. I went back right after the wind had filled the sails of the Taurus. *The door was firmly closed, but with the rudder pole they'd thrown at me, I broke a rotted shutter in one of the downstairs windows without too much noise. Another blow to the glass, a quick turn of the hasp and I was in.*

"I went through the house meticulously, in and under the beds, through the closets and cabinets, broke some furniture, but I found nothing except in the ashes of some scraps of paper almost completely burned. I've included them in the other envelope.

"And you must know that my bungling failure is causing me tears of shame, regret and anger, but please know also that I will always be grateful, devoted and loyal to you, colonel.

"Ramon Bastos."

This moving letter was read without the slightest comment or interruption from Mathias Lumen or Gnô Mitang. Unruffled, the first like Michelangelo's Moses, the second like a mask from his country, the powerful and mysterious Israelite with the inscrutable and respectful Japanese, listened silently until the end.

And yet, every sentence hit the two men like a mighty blow. At present, for both of them, Sylvie Mac Duhl and the *Taurus* were the most precious things in the world, first and foremost!

Worse, the gold and the girl were in the hands—not of some random bandit—but, horror of horrors, in the hands of the traitor Jacques Cervier, the damned soul of Leonid Zattan, who was the herald and lieutenant of the Antichrist—if, however, Leonid Zattan, or the formidable man whom hundreds of initiates from two enemy sides knew under this name, was not himself destined to become the Antichrist!

When the four syllables "Ramon Bastos" fell from the trembling lips of Placide Bonnard, Mathias Lumen looked at Gnô Mitang. And Gnô stood up, bowed, straightened up and spoke in a calm voice, so oddly cold and enigmatic it was as if his whole being were speaking through it:

"Master, great woe has befallen. It will be the death of me if it is fulfilled, meaning if Sylvie Mac Duhl and the *Taurus* disappear from the Mediterranean. Before the sloop reaches the southern coast of Turkey, we have to get to it and save the girl. Then I'll go after Tchicoz and make him suffer countless tortures before he dies."

"You know this Tchicoz?" Lumen asked softly.

"I've seen him twice for a total of maybe three minutes. He's from South America. Master Allen hired him the day before the *Taurus* shoved off from Villefranche because the deck boss Fidly got sick, which makes sense now to blame on Tchicoz. But I will find him again or die trying. But first, the sloop!"

Mathias Lumen got up. He was majestic and divinely solemn. He looked at the Japanese and said, "The loss of Sylvie Mac Duhl and the *Taurus*, if it spells our death, Gnô, would mean an abominable misfortune even worse than death for me—the destruction of my Faith! All the prophecies of Michel Nostradamus, added to those of our own prophets but more precise in time and place, have been fulfilled so far. The prophetic verses concerning the battle of the new Messiah—man, the son of man and not the son of God!—against the Antichrist—he, too, a man, son of man, but possessed by all the forces of evil, these verses can be obscure, understood in different ways, apparently meant for man's free will... Until today, Gnô, the battle between me and Zattan has been limited to preparatory generalities, a secret battle, vast but obscure, a battle of waiting because the 'Golden Virgin with the Scottish name', in fact, had not yet set out toward her destiny.

"The Virgin has finally set out but the enemy has seized her at the very start. The real fight, personal, physical and explicit has now begun, Gnô! And it is the supreme war between the principles of good and evil. This is the first battle of the war at the end of which either men will experience the glorious and immortal peace under the rule of the messianic king or else they will put an end to the human species by going through a hell in which the earth will be transformed by the Antichrist.

"Nostradamus said:

"In the name of Scotland and orphaned of all
"Golden maiden with love will bring to life
"In the time one and nine and twenty-six
"Great brown-haired male with divine attributes.
"If stone and gold by chance more than enough
"Fill the well that in Ushant Englishman made
"Death wretchedly by blade to the throat
"Against the Antichrist the male is opposed.
"Victorious will he be if the woman gives birth
"Otherwise, the Time will be long postponed
"Blood over one and nine and twenty-six
"With the dead in dreadful piles."

"Well, Gnô, we need Sylvie Mac Duhl for the messianic male to oppose the Antichrist..."

Mathias stopped talking. Calmly Gnô said simply, "We do need it."

"Very well!" the master concluded. Then with poise and the voice of a captain of industry giving orders to his employees, "Placide, prepare five checks of

400,000 francs each made out to Gnô Mitang." And to the Japanese, "Will that be enough?"

"Yes."

"You have a definite plan, I imagine?"

"Very definite."

"Can you tell us?"

The Japanese bowed and this reverence was one of the reasons why Mathias felt such brotherly affection for him. The Japanese replied immediately.

"In the port of Nice is a big-engine yacht, the *Fulgur*. It cruises at 30 knots. It was armed, I know, to transport resistance fighters whom its owner, Edgard Countil, had sent to the Arabian coasts. Lord Edgard Countil died last month and the *Fulgur* is for sale. For three more weeks his crew will be on it for maintenance. Then the sailors will get off and the ship will be guarded by only three or four men. At Brest I'll hire my own crew and, if necessary, finish up in Marseille. I'll buy the *Fulgur* for a million francs. Then I'll go after the *Taurus*, searching blindly of course, but if I pass by it, which is probable, I'll wait for it between Cyprus and Rhodes. At sea Sylvie Mac Duhl is in no danger from Cervier, Tchicoz or the others because Cervier will want to get glory and profit out of delivering her unharmed to Leonid Zattan. But I'll stop Cervier before reaching the Turkish coast and I'll take the *Taurus* and free Sylvie Mac Duhl... or else I'll die wrenching out the last breath from Tchicoz."

He ended there.

Half an hour later, in the whaler piloted by Lluch, Gnô Mitang went back to Brest. In his pocket, besides the personal checks worth 200,000 francs, he also carried four checks adding up to two million. Mâh Ito was with him.

All these astonishing things took place in the Mediterranean on the one side and in Ushant on the other, in France in the year 1926, preludes to other, more astonishing things that would happen there and elsewhere and the whole world was ignorant of these events on which hinged the destiny of humanity.

CHAPTER III

Elsewhere…

In central Asia, in the mountains of Tian Shan in the middle of the bleak regions enclosing Mongolia, Turkestan, Afghanistan and Pamir, lies the lake Issyk-Kul with its craggy, wild coasts cut deep and jagged.

On one of the rocky spurs that juts out into the deep water stands four square towers and the keep of the Issyk Castle. Huge, crenellated walls with arrow slits connect the towers. The ones to the south and west have their walls flush with the sheer rocks that drop directly into the lake. The cliff is 100 feet high, the tower 65; a watchman looks out onto 150 feet of surface of the watery abyss.

Three sides of the quadrilateral are thus surrounded by water. The fourth side, flanked by the east and north towers, faces solid land. It is separated from it by a wide, deep moat that can be filled with lake water if the owner wishes and whose bottom is barbed with sharp, iron spikes. Sometimes men are impaled there, thrown from atop the walls—that is justice at the castle. A gigantic drawbridge controlled by two turrets and a balcony with battlements hung by double chains creates a bridge over the moat. Inside the quadrilateral, in the middle of a vast courtyard, are the living quarters that have a triangular keep in their center, which is fifteen feet higher than the four towers.

As for Lake Issyk-Kul, it is one of the strangest little inland seas in the world. Located within an amphitheater of gigantic mountains whose peaks are much higher than Mont Blanc, it lies at an elevation of over 5,000 feet above sea level. It is ten times bigger than Lake Geneva. Sailing on its waters is extremely dangerous because of the terrible winds that blow out of the deep mountain gorges and blast the lake with brutal violence. Lake Issyk-Kul never freezes, even in the coldest winters. Its name literally means "warm lake". It owes its temperature—truly extraordinary in the region—to hot springs that gush out of the rocky cliffs and pour into the huge basin. The water is incredibly clear, turquoise blue near the shores and darker azure over the unfathomed depths farther out, which extends as far as the eye can see into the ring of tall mountains with their eternally snow-covered summits.

All around is almost complete solitude. Except for the castle, there are only a few small fishing villages tucked into the rare hollows provided with a beach and forming a short, narrow valley. The city of Karakol, which is a really just a big village inhabited primarily by shepherds and hunters, is almost 15 miles away in one of the wider zones of prairie land within the steep mountaintops.

Especially since the fall of the last tzars and the splitting up of the Russian Empire—which Issyk-Kul was part of—the region has been left to itself under

37

the exclusive control of the castle owner, who is a like a feudal lord and whose sovereignty is the only recognized authority.

In 1926, this lord was Leonid Zattan, the only son of old Yark Zattan, who, in 1917, had massacred the Russian garrison in Karakol and thus secured his absolute rule over the whole region of Issyk-Kul.

In 1922, the Soviets had sent a Bolshevik commissioner from Moscow and armed men in order to "sovietize" Karakol and take down Zattan's feudal dynasty. When he had learned of the Moscow delegate's arrival, Yark Zattan had died of a fit of rage. The very next day, with the blessing of the population and followed by all the fishermen around the lake who formed part of the troops, Leonid had captured the Bolsheviks, delivered the soldiers over to fishermen's harpoons and, with his own hand, cut off the ears, nose and tongue of the commissioner.

Since then, Leonid Zattan had been master, lord and king of Issyk-Kul and the inhabited valleys of the Tian Shan mountain ranges. What an extraordinary man, this Lord of Issyk Castle!

He was 35 years-old. From the age of 15 to 20 he had studied hard in Paris, foremost at the Lycée Voltaire, then the preparatory courses at the Ecole de Saint-Cyr and finally at the Ecole Polytechnique for university—all at the same time. Endowed with exceptional intelligence, an iron will and mental energy equaled only by his health and physical prowess, he had astonished and frightened both his fellow students and his teachers.

At 20, he had left Paris and accompanied by a personally chosen private tutor, a former captain of the artillery devoted to philosophy and the occult sciences, he had traveled through England, Germany and Italy—not without quite a few adventures due to his violent passions and that had always ended with him unscathed, either because of his fortune or intelligence or courage.

At 28 years-old, after seeing most of Europe, he had gone alone to America, then Japan and China, Persia and Asia Minor, not returning to his paternal domain, to Issyk Castle, until 1922.

Starting in September of that year, he had waged guerilla warfare against the Russians at the head of a small army of Kurdish horsemen and had become famous from the Caspian Sea to the Mediterranean, from the Caucasus Mountains to the Syrian desert, for his invincible courage, his infernal cruelty and his insatiable voraciousness. Every month he had sent armed caravans back to Issyk Castle loaded with everything he had pillaged from the massacred soldiers and the terrorized people. Among the booty were always two or three of the most beautiful young girls.

In 1922, he had returned to Issyk for good, summoned by his father who was being menaced by the Bolshevik government in Moscow. Six months later he had inherited everything from old Yark and with great laughter had himself crowned "Prince of Issyk-Kul, King of Karakol, Emperor of Tian Shan". On the day of his coronation he had organized a magnificent feast at the castle in which the "climax" was the execution, by candlelight, of the earless, noseless, tongue-less commissioner. The executioners were the thirteen women of his harem and on his order the instruments of death were solely to be tortoise shell combs with sharpened teeth. The agony of the poor man lasted 57 minutes!

Such was Leonid Zattan. Such was the man whom Mathias Lumen in Ush-ant spoke of only with sacred loathing and divine horror. Such was the master to whom, on one tragic, passionate, mysterious night that might someday be made known, a professor of mathematics, lieutenant in the reserve, a deserter and trai-tor, sentenced to death in absentia, the Frenchman Jacques Cervier had commit-ted himself.

So, on March 21, 1926, at 2 pm, Leonid Zattan happened to be smoking a nargileh and reading the January issue of *Revue des Deux Mondes* in his "stu-dio" in the castle. It was a huge, square room taking up the entire ground floor of the south tower. Wall hangings, sumptuous tapestries, paintings of the masters, carved bookshelves full of finely bound books, thick carpets, couches, stuffed chairs, ebony stepladders inlaid with ivory and mother-of-pearl, countless cush-ions, two massive tables of carved ebony, a grand piano, flowers in gold and sil-ver vases and on a low table supported by a silver trolley with rubberized wheels was a telephone, a panel of electric buttons and the horn of a telephonograph with a microphone.

The first day of spring was beautiful. Through two of the four huge bay windows to the veranda sunbeams and fresh air from the lake poured in, cheer-ing up the room, which was rather severe because of the somber tones of the furniture hardly lightened by a few bright colors in the tapestries and the fresh-ness of some of the paintings from the French school called "impressionist".

Leonid Zattan, sunk into the cushions on a couch with legs stretched out, was dressed in red silk pajamas. Bare-headed with his closely shorn hair, there was something Mephisthophelian about his face even without a moustache or goatee and even though his flat eyebrows looked drawn in Chinese style. His face was Kalmyk with high cheekbones and his black eyes had red tints because the whites were always injected with blood at the slightest flare-up of anger or the least fit of passion. Tall, rather thin, nervous, muscular—it was the body of an athlete.

The clock built into the ebony frame of a thermo-barometer read 2:07 when the quiet buzz rang on the electro-telephonic table. Leonid leaned over a little, pressed the ivory buttons, sat back and spoke in his normal voice—dry and commanding but extremely clear and resonant.

"Hello. Speak!"

The official language in Issyk Castle was French. The captain of the guards and his officers, the steward, the butler, the chief eunuch, the lieutenant-secretary, the master horseman and the troop leader, finally the personal valet and the three stenography maids—everyone among the "higher domestic staff" at Issyk wrote and spoke French very well. It was in French, therefore, that a distant voice, made to sound normal through the telephone mic said:

"Hello, prince, greetings! From the Balearic Islands, by direct mail, came the following message that Woldski just deciphered: *Hello, March 19. From 17 to 3. Captured sloop* Taurus *loaded with gold and precious stones bound for Ushant. Held prisoner is owner Sylvie Mac Duhl, alone on board after crew murdered. With new and reliable crew I'm sailing to the Gulf of Adana. Averaging eight knots. Farewell!*"

On hearing the number 17, Leonid Zattan had jerked his head in attention. But when he heard the name Sylvie Mac Duhl, he tossed away the *Revue des Deux Mondes* and the nargileh tube, jumped to his feet and bent over the speaker horn, devouring it with his eyes as if he could see the face of the man who was talking more than 3,500 miles away from the castle in the Balearic Islands.

It must be noted here once and for all that through a private wireless telegraph, more or less secret, or through the public post office where he had contacts thanks to a healthy monthly contribution, Leonid Zattan could be almost immediately in touch with hundreds of his agents stationed all over the world. These agents were all appointed numbers. 17 was Jacques Cervier. The number 3, the ultimate cabalistic figure, the image of the hermetic triangle, symbol of divine and demonic trinities, designated Zattan himself. In the system, there was no number 1 or 2—Zattan was both 1 and 2 together, therefore 3.

"Sylvie, Sylvie," he growled to himself, clenching his teeth to keep from verbally expressing his secret thoughts, his elation, his tremendous emotion. "Sylvie Mac Duhl in the hands of Cervier and so in my power! Sylvie, the golden-haired virgin bearing a Scottish surname, an orphan with no other family. Sylvie, the only girl whose personal and family characteristics answer to the ambiguous prophecies of Nostradamus! Sylvie, whom other prophecies from this same seer forbid me from deliberately snatching from 'her own.' And that's why I never gave the order to watch her and I never, in any way, interfered in her life... I even managed to wipe her out of my thoughts. But Cervier is bringing her to me, a captive, by some trick of fate, utterly unforeseen, when my thoughts and willpower, my whole being was otherwise occupied... Sylvie has been 'snatched from her own'. It's been done and the prophecy forbidding my personal involvement has not been violated. Now I can act in place of Cervier. I can and must. Yes, I must because Lumen can't be warned. He'll go into action and try to free Sylvie, the protective icon of his cause, the instrument of divine action, the eventual host of the man who will be the enemy of the Antichrist. And if I let Lumen act, even though he's probably already mobilized some of his fanatics, Sylvie Mac Duhl will be freed and Cervier killed! There're also the millions from the old Scot that are nothing to sneeze at, but again the interpretation of the prophecy had forbidden me from coveting. Now that they're there, that they're bringing them here, I'll take them. I can never have too much gold! All right, enough thinking, it's time to act!"

This silent monologue had taken only half a minute. The microphone was still resonating with the "Farewell" that had ended the prodigious message. Short and fast was Zattan's response:

"Arm the *Aquilon*. For mechanic, Ivitch. We leave in fifteen minutes."

The *Aquilon* was a monoplane with an electric motor invented by Petrus Ivitch, a kindly scientist who had rebelled against the tsar and been exiled, then against the Bolsheviks and was almost shot to death. Petrus Ivitch called himself "the enemy of the human race." He served Zattan and had put his body, mind and genius at his disposal because the Lord of Issyk had convinced him that the most terrifying enemy of the human race was himself, Zattan. The inventor was 55 years-old but the fire of the spirit in his small, skinny body burned with a vitality, a vigor that belonged to youth. In the castle, Petrus Ivitch answered to nobody but Zattan.

The electric motor of the *Aquilon* was supplied with fluid from a battery of accumulators that used special devices (which were the real invention) to continually capture and store electricity from the atmosphere. Thus, the plane didn't need to carry fuel or recharge its batteries. Oil for lubrication, food, weapons and ammunition were the only freight.

Also, barely bigger than a Blériot monoplane from those already legendary times, the *Aquilon* could carry six people including the pilot and mechanic. The part of the cabin provided with the six bucket seats was a convertible body that opened and closed as needed.

The electric plane reached speeds up to 200 mph. The only sound it made was the hum of the propellor and the whir of air along the wings and body...

"Hello!" the distant voice answered. "The *Aquilon* and Ivitch will be at your service in fifteen minutes. Is that all?"

"That's all."

The telephonic conversation ended.

Leonid Zattan pressed an ivory button. A minute later a door slid open and a man stepped in, young, clean-shaven, intelligent-looking, dressed in black pants and a red and yellow striped vest, in his shirt sleeves with his bare neck showing from his turned down collar. He was the personal valet, a Turk by the name of Ali Soud.

"Ali, I'm leaving by plane in ten minutes."

Ten minutes later an elevator dropped the Prince on the ground floor. A man was waiting there, dressed in black with red leather, knee-high boots. He gave a military salute and said, "The *Aquilon* and Petrus Ivitch are ready."

"Very well, Woldski. Follow me."

As they walked down the vaulted corridor lit by electric lights Leonid Zattan gave his orders.

"The envoy to Moscow should arrive tonight or tomorrow. You'll meet him. You'll get him drunk. You'll make him talk. If he doesn't drink, if he can't drink, if he stays silent, watch him, meaning don't leave him alone for a second and make sure he doesn't talk with anybody but you. He'll have to wait for me. If he refuses and wants to leave without seeing me, punish his pride by cutting off his head and send his head back to Moscow by regular post with a letter relating the orders I'm giving you except for the part about getting him drink and making him talk. Understood?"

"Understood, Prince."

"Perfect. For the rest, stick to the regular routine."

"Goodbye, Prince."

"Goodbye, Woldski."

The two men had arrived in a huge, square room with a ceiling made of big tiles supported by iron beams. A multitude of electric lights lit the space. In the middle of the room, standing on its landing gear was the slim but solid *Aquilon*.

Without another word Leonid Zattan left his lieutenant-secretary and climbed up the short ladder into the plane, immediately followed by Ali Soud who had run up carrying coats and a suitcase. Ali closed the door to the plane. The ladder automatically disappeared into a special compartment. While Ali and the coats and suitcase settled into the back of the plane, the prince went to sit in the seat next to the pilot.

The pilot was a man with blank, somewhat crazed eyes and a clean-shaven, oddly chubby face. His grumpy lips muttered a brief greeting to which Zattan replied with a wave of his hand. He glanced around the cockpit for a quick inspection before talking.

"To Malta, non-stop. We're doing the flying ourselves."

The pilot, who was none other than Petrus Ivitch, gave a short nod, then unrolled a map showing the Issyk-Baku section. In his weird, high voice he said, "We'll pass over Tashkent and Baku, then probably by Smyrna and Athens."

"Right," Zattan agreed.

"Around 3,500 miles," Ivitch continued, "19 hours flight time…"

"Got it! Let's go!"

Ivitch pressed a button and a bell rang. Right away, in front of the airplane, a whole section of the wall split open vertically. Beyond was daylight. It was shining on a vast terrace with no railing at the far end, then it came flooding into the hangar room. Immediately afterward, the wheels of the plane started rolling, quickly picking up speed and launching the plane into the air at the end of the terrace with the propellor already spinning fast enough for a perfect takeoff.

A few minutes later the electric bird was out of Woldski's sight as he stood at the end of the terrace.

CHAPTER IV

Now, Gnô Mitang and Mâh had left Ushant on March 20th. They slept in Brest and spent the whole next day in the city. This was enough for the Japanese to recruit two-thirds of the crew for the *Fulgur*. Putting his men under the command of a young, long-distance captain named Paul Guennec, he set up a rendezvous for three days later in Nice. Then, he went to Paris with Mâh.

He spent the 22nd there, got a letter of credit from the bank but kept only a few thousands in francs on him, then left that night for Marseille. In a cabaret of the old port he recruited the last third of his crew. On the morning of the 24th he was in Nice.

Right away he paid a visit to the *Fulgur* and was thoroughly satisfied. He talked for a long time with his captain, a strangely anglicized native of Marseille, Marc Ayol. He was 45 years-old, wiry and black, tall and thin, with all his teeth capped in gold and clean-shaven but a heavy five o'clock shadow turning half his face dark blue. He had very lively, black eyes deeply set under huge eyebrows. His curly hair had not one strand of white and was probably a great source of pride.

With all this, the sailor had one of the best service records in the world. During the war he commanded a patrol ship that sailed over all the seas of the globe. Legion of Honor, Military Cross, a few English and Italian medals, five different scars on his body—a hero! And a first-rate sailor.

Having listened to Gnô, who trusted revealing to him some secret matters, Marc Ayol agreed to remain captain of the vessel "through thick and thin" as he swore in his resounding voice that had an oddly British accent. Paul Guennec would be his lieutenant, the second-in-command and the crew, now counting twenty-five men hired in Brest and Marseille would be accepted by him without discussion.

It took Gnô Mitang the whole afternoon of March 24th to finalize the purchase the *Fulgur*. On the morning of the 25th the entire crew was on board. By common consent Marc Ayol and Paul Guennec assigned the ranks, posts and duties of the men. The night before they had loaded the coal, the provisions and other necessities. Because of the original purpose of its previous owner, Lord Edgard Countil, the *Fulgur* was armed with all kinds of weapons, from machine guns to cannons (which numbered four).

On the morning of the 26th the *Fulgur* weighed anchor and cast off.

In theory, they should have headed for the waters southwest of Sicily through the Strait of Bonifacio. In order to give everyone time to think, Gnô Mitang, who had explained the situation to Captain Ayol and Lieutenant Guennec, had likewise decided that they should not give much consideration to the problem of the itinerary until they were at sea. Consequently, an hour after the *Fulgur* left the port of Nice, Gnô and Guennec joined Marc Ayol on the bridge.

Lord Countil's yacht was hybrid, meaning the sails with most of the rigging of the brig could replace the steam if needed or just increase the speed with wind power. Since it was blowing strongly from the northwest, the captain had flown the sails and the *Fulgur* was soon up to almost its maximum speed limit.

It was a joy to see it bounding over the waves, slicing through them with amazing gracefulness and poise. For a minute, the three men enjoyed the boat's handling, but their thoughts were too burdensome for their contemplative silence to last long.

"Captain," the Japanese suddenly spoke up, "you've thought about it, so, any ideas?"

"Oh," Marc Ayol shrugged his shoulders, "a cabin boy would come up with the same thing. Since you're right to suppose the *Taurus* wants to get as quickly as possible to the Gulf of Adana or Alexandretta and since it took off from Roses, the shortest route with the wind that's been blowing for days now on the Mediterranean is obviously to pass by south of Sardinia, hug the southern coast of Sicily, then head straight for Crete, then Cyprus…"

"That's unquestionable," Paul Guennec said.

"I think so, too," Gnô agreed.

"You say the *Taurus* can't really sail faster than 10 or 12 knots and it left Roses the night of March 17th … It's the 25th, so it's got around a 90-hour head start on us. But it's far from Roses to Cyprus. I made two calculations. One, the *Taurus* might've run into shifting winds or a storm south of Sardinia from what I read in the papers lately. And a little boat is at the mercy of the slightest change in weather, so if it has to tack in the winds, its average speed is reduced by three fourths. On the other hand, we're going fast. The wind doesn't bother us. It's either favorable or of no account. It would take a major storm to slow down the *Fulgur*, which is by far the best ship I've been on as far as seaworthiness… I think can catch the *Taurus* around Sicily. What do you think, Guennec?"

"I think so, captain."

"Of course," Ayol went on, "it's one thing to be in the same waters as the *Taurus* and another thing to actually find it. We might pass by 1,000 miles off from it and never suspect a thing. At night we risk missing it completely even if we're a stone's throw away since the bandits on board won't be having any lights on after sunset. Really, it'll be pure luck…"

"But captain," Gnô hazarded, "don't you think that when we get between Sicily and Tunisia we could tack during the day to explore a wider swathe of the sea?"

"Sure, no doubt. But if the Taurus was strong and got far ahead of us… I repeat, we have to count on luck. Just imagine! A sloop somewhere on the vast extent of the Mediterranean… Any ideas, Guennec?"

The Breton replied, "What I think, I believe Monsieur Mitang already expressed it yesterday when we talked for the first time about this whole adventure—the best would be to sail as fast as possible to the Gulf of Adana and cross between Cyprus and the southern coast of Asia Minor before them. We'll certainly pass by the *Taurus* and will have a good chance of picking it up when it gets into the Gulf or if it goes into the Gulf of Alexandretta, into the straits that separate Cyprus from the big cliffs on the continental coast..."

"Yes," Mitang said, "but I've thought more about it. I know that our enemy, Leonid Zattan, has at his disposal a small fleet made up of some very modern, very fast ships docked in certain ports of Asia Minor and Palestine or anchored in the rocky inlets around Cyprus. He also has an airplane that the reports from my agents confirm has an electric engine that harnesses the fluid from the atmosphere itself..."

"Wow," Guennec gasped.

"Damn," Marc Ayol swore. "So, he could send a ship or a plane out to meet the *Taurus* or even be waiting for it at a precise meeting point."

"Yes, that's possible," Gnô Mitang said worriedly. "We know enough about the extraordinary, meticulous organization of Zattan's secret service to know that all over the world but especially in the Mediterranean they have posts set up with wireless communication. In the Balearic Islands, Sardinia, Sicily, the *Taurus* could've contacted a point on the shore where there's a Zattan ally and immediately communicated with him... The lake and castle of Issyk-Kul are a long way off but distance doesn't matter to wireless. You see, the problem has no easy solution."

"I'll go back to what I told you before," Marc Ayol stated coldly. "Luck. We've got to count on it. So, let's do all we can to make sure luck is on our side. For the moment there's only one thing for us to do: get to the south of Sicily as fast as we can and from there every ship we sight we get close enough to identify. We have excellent binoculars and from what I can tell, some of our crew are pretty keen lads. I suggest you offer a big bonus to the first guy who spots the *Taurus*. I'll put it in the daily log and I guarantee you that day and night there won't be anybody sleeping on board more than necessary."

The conversation went on like this for a few minutes, the three men proposing and worrying and turning the cold eye of reason on all that was said. After some false starts and dead-ends, they finally decided on what had already been said: go fast, keep constant watch, lie in wait at the mouth the Gulf of Adana which leads to Alexandretta.

And the *Fulgur* sped off. At 7 pm on March 25th, it spotted the headlands of Favignana that marks the westernmost point of Sicily. Just like in the morning, Gnô Mitang, Marc Ayol and Paul Guennec met on the bridge. The weather reports seen in Nice had indicated to the Japanese and his partners that during the day, in all likelihood, the *Taurus* had rounded the southern point of Sardinia where the region had been hit by a kind of cyclone. The possibility of the *Taurus* having perished in the storm was not even considered. Gnô Mitang knew that the gang around Jacques Cervier included fine sailors. Moreover, since Sylvie was on board the sloop and she knew her vessel inside and out, her kidnappers would not fail to use her in case of danger and the young lady would be smart enough to escape the storm and find shelter in some hole on the Sardinian coast or on the rugged Algerian coast between Béjaïa and Annaba.

But one thing was sure: the bad weather had slowed down the *Taurus*. Seven days after leaving Roses, the boat might very well be within range of where the *Fulgur* was sailing southeast towards Malta with both steam and wind power driving it on.

What in all these assumptions was true? They were based on one single certainty: the *Taurus* had left Roses on the night of the 17th. To this was added a conjecture that logically could only reflect reality, which was: the *Taurus*, under the command of Jacques Cervier, was headed for the Gulf of Adana or Alexandretta or at least somewhere in the eastern Mediterranean where it could join up with one of the ships or the electric airplane of Leonid Zattan.

Except for this certainty and this probability, Gnô Mitang knew nothing…

And yet, so far, so many terrible things had happened! As soon as Jacques Cervier and his cohorts had been brought by Tchicoz to board the *Taurus* on that fateful night of the 17th, Sylvie Mac Duhl had been nabbed in her sleep, since she could not stay awake. Incapacitated, her hands tied behind her back, a silk scarf stuffed in her mouth, she was carried into the cabin she had made her own and Tchicoz had left her there alone after lighting the candleholder hanging from the ceiling and snickering as he left, "This time, Mademoiselle Mac Duhl, I am going to sleep well for sure. I hope you can too."

On the bridge, Jacques Cervier was giving orders. During the Great War, although a simple lieutenant in the colonial infantry of the reserves, at first in service and then a deserter, he had sailed enough and observed enough to be able to realize right away that in the light of the stars and with the lanterns quickly lit up the sloop's rigging was in sorry shape.

He shouted, "Del Campo!"

From the group of men who had come with him from the house in Roses one guy stepped out. The light from a lantern cast Rembrandt shadows over his hard, stern face. His body was a little bigger than average, on the thin side but obviously athletic, with weird eyes of indistinct color and oddly intense, a short, black moustache and, bizarrely, two sideburns keep trimmed but extending down almost all the way to his lower jaw. He was wearing a light-colored, tailored business suit but no shirt, just a sailor's red jersey, and his bare feet were in espadrilles.

"What do you want, boss?" he asked in Spanish. His voice was sharp and very cold.

46

"Take command of the ship. Since you were captain of a merchant ship before, you know all about sails and navigation better than any of us. What do you think of this boat?"

"Fifteen minutes of work," Del Campo said curtly. "If there are extra sails and rope, no problem. The jibs and foresails are holding, so there's only the topmast and the mainsail to hoist. The other damage is nothing... Tomorrow during the day the men can fix it all."

"Good," Cervier said. "Where's Tchicoz?"

At that moment the Mexican was just stepping onto the deck after locking up Sylvie Mac Duhl.

"Yeah, what do you need?"

"Are there extra sails and ropes?"

"Sure."

"Very well. Everything on deck. Del Campo is in charge. Follow his orders like he's following mine."

"Where are we headed, boss?" Del Campo asked.

"The Balearic Islands. You been there?"

"Yes."

"Well then, in the cove of Porto Cristo. You know where that is?"

"Yes, southeast of Mallorca."

"Right. The boat is yours now."

A quarter of an hour later, all sails to the wind, the *Taurus* was heading south. Pedro Del Campo intended to pass between Mallorca and Port Mahon and take the shortest route to reach Porto Cristo. His sailing skills were so assertive, so precise, so self-confident that everyone, including Jacques Cervier, bent under his authority, which was very strict and diligent. There were five of them carrying out the orders. They were more or less used to seafaring matters and formed a competent crew on the Taurus in every way.

When everything except for the carpentry, which had been put off until the next day, had been satisfactorily arranged on the sloop as it ran swiftly southward, "Captain" Del Campo ordered, "You, boss, and you two, Tchicoz and Geronimo, go to bed. Sleep until we come get you. You'll be on the morning shift. You, Ramuz, take the helm. You've been a pilot so I won't say anything else since you know where we're going. And you, Barbone, lookout on the bow. You're a sailor, that's enough."

"And you?" Cervier asked.

"Me, I'm going to sleep like you. If anything happens, Barbone, come get me. I'll be in the crew's cabin with the deck boss and the others."

All of Del Campo's orders were carried out immediately. In the crew's cabin hammocks were hung and Del Campo climbed in just like Cervier, Tchicoz and Geronimo. A few minutes later, surrendering to fatigue since all the men had just spent many long hours of work, worry and woe, they fell asleep.

All four of them? No, only three. After twenty or twenty-five minutes of silence and stillness disturbed only by the snoring and swinging of the hammocks, one of those men slowly raised his head. It was Pedro Del Campo. In the flickering light of the lantern hanging from a beam, he watched his comrades. He was sure they were truly, soundly asleep. Quietly and agilely, he slipped out of the hammock and stood there barefoot for a second. Then he left the cabin.

When he'd gone down, he'd seen a key hanging on the wall by the stairs and he caught Tchicoz showing it to Cervier. He grabbed it, climbed up just enough to peek out to make sure Ramuz was at his post and Barbone still at the bow. Reassured, he went back down, sneaked along the corridor to the cabin door that he recognized right away. He used the key to open it, entered, closed it and left the key in the lock inside. Then he walked over to the bunk.

Sylvie Mac Duhl was lying down, eyes open, limbs bound, breathing heavily through her nose because of the silken gag that was soaked with her saliva and therefore swelled up in her mouth and half choking her.

Pedro Del Campo leaned over with a smile that instantly erased all his usual gruffness. In French, with the delicate Parisian accent, he said, "Mademoiselle, have no fear of me. I'm a friend. I hope I can save you. I'd tell you I will save you but it's always unwise for a man to promise the future because the future sometimes bites back and gets its revenge."

While talking he had very gently parted the clenched jaws of the young lady and removed the suffocating gag.

"Are you bound too tight? Does it hurt?"

"A little," Sylvie replied.

Hastily, he loosened the ropes around her ankles and wrists so the prisoner could stretch out a little and lie more comfortably on her side.

"I can't untie you completely," he said, "because it'd be stupid. I'll even have to put the gag back in when I leave, but I'll ball it up tight so you can push it against a cheek if it bothers you too much."

"Who are you?" she asked.

"Ah, well, thinking of you, I wondered whether I should tell you who I am. I'm not vain but it seems to me impossible that you don't know my name and this name alone, with no other information, should be enough to give you confidence."

A moment of silence.

"I am Leo Saint-Clair."

"The Nyctalope! My God!" the young lady exclaimed. "The hero of the Black Forest where you fought the human monster they called Lucifer![2] The heroic explorer of the planet Mars![3]"

---

[2] *The Nyctalope vs. Lucifer.*

[3] *The Nyctalope on Mars.*

"There, there," he said with a mocking kindliness. "Enough with the heroics, mademoiselle, please. The important thing is that you believe who I am."

"Oh, I believe," she said. "Eyes like yours right now can't lie. Besides, who would dare assume such a name?"

"You're going to make me blush with embarrassment, mademoiselle, and regret it."

She wasn't listening to anything but her own thoughts. "But how did you get here?"

"It was very simple or, if you prefer, providential. It's true that when Providence gets mixed up in human affairs, it rarely likes things complicated...

"A month ago I was in a hotel room in Madrid. I was smoking and thinking next to a wood-burning fireplace. In the wall was an air vent that the old architects used to use sometimes to control drafts. My left ear was only 20 inches from the grill of this vent... I was smoking and thinking... I heard nothing, not a sound. It was 3 am. Everyone, except for the guards at the royal palace, was asleep.

"But I was not the only one awake because all of a sudden, I heard voices. They were not coming down from heaven, but maybe they were drifting up from hell—which was represented this night by the room located directly beneath mine. The voices of two men speaking in French. They said things so profoundly interesting that I instantly broke my train of thought, as pleasant as it was, and I let my cigar go out, as exquisite as it was. And it was a result of what I heard there through the acoustic pipes of the air vent that I am here with you today."

"It was about me?" she asked.

"Not at all. It was about a certain Leonid Zattan and Mathias Lumen, people I had a little acquaintance with during the Great War. It was about a rather extraordinary undertaking, about the prophecies of Nostradamus and then about a bunch of other things far from ordinary. They were so alluring to me that after disguising myself, getting close to them and telling a story, which I'll fill you in on, I became one of the henchmen of Jacques Cervier, a former lieutenant in the colonial infantry, a deserter, a traitor, sentenced in absentia and for the moment one of the major players in a drama whose director lives in a remote castle in Issyk-Kul."

"I know nothing about any of this," the young lady muttered.

"It doesn't matter," he said. "Besides, there's no proof that the current adventure in which you and the *Taurus* are victims has any connection to what I heard in Madrid. Still, I can be of help to you and at the same time learn a little more about this game of Cervier that's been pretty obscure to me so far. But enough talking. Has it at least put your mind at ease a little and given you some confidence and renewed courage, which I'm afraid is going to be indispensable?"

"Oh, yes," she replied. "But listen to me. It can all be over in a few minutes. Free me and the two of us, with some weapons that should be easy to get hold of, will take back the *Taurus* in no time. I'm sure the men are out there drinking or sleeping. Couldn't we take them by surprise?"

"Of course," the Nyctalope nodded and smiled. "But excuse me, mademoiselle, for not putting you first in my thoughts. I'm looking ahead. I'm asking you now to be my partner, my ally in the work I've undertaken. I plan to save you, you and the *Taurus*. I plan to give you complete liberty to take your ship and finish the trip on which you fell victim to such a detestable criminal... But Cervier is going somewhere with this ship and he's going to do something. So, I've got two questions: where and what? I have to find out! And for this we have to continue, you and I, on this little journey we've undertaken. When I've got everything I need, I'll let you know and then you'll be my priority. Do you accept?"

"Yes, I accept!" she cried out. "But let me tell you something that should greatly interest you."

"I'm listening."

"You heard them talk about Mathias Lumen in Madrid and you just said you didn't know whether there's any connection between what you overheard and my own adventure... There is a connection."

"Indeed!"

"Monsieur, the connection exists and it's undeniably strong. You won't doubt it when you hear it: The *Taurus* is carrying more than 100 million in gold and a great deal of precious stones. This fortune is meant for Mathias Lumen, for a secret project whose enemy is Leonid Zattan."

"Oh, oh," Saint-Clair was jolted. "Talk. Keep talking. What else can you tell me?"

"Nothing else. When my father, before dying, entrusted me with the mission of transporting the gold and precious stones to Ushant Island where Mathias Lumen lives, that's all he said." And she recited, " 'This fortune is meant for a secret project whose enemy is a man called Leonid Zattan.' That's all I know. Gnô Mitang, a Japanese confidant of my father, when I asked him about it, told me he'd sworn on the souls of his ancestors to never tell me more until he was released from his vow by the only man who could do so—Mathias Lumen."

"And you overheard nothing else? Caught nothing? Guessed nothing?"

"Nothing."

"So be it! But all the more reason for us to follow Jacques Cervier until time or circumstances puts your life in imminent danger. And to save you we'll jump ship if necessary, we'll kill Cervier if we have to and forget about following him alive to the goal of his journey here. But please, hang in there as long as possible. Force yourself not to be afraid. Don't allow your imagination or your nerves to exaggerate the dangers you might be facing. I'm here, me, the Nyctalope, and I'll risk everything to save you when the time comes that your life is seriously threatened."

The big, blue eyes of Sylvie Mac Duhl had a charming expression of child-like abandon. She said, "I trust you. I'll be brave and strong and do whatever you say."

"Perfect. My first order is this: get some sleep, mademoiselle. Good night. Now open your mouth."

He gently tucked the balled-up scarf into her mouth. Then, he gave her a little wave goodbye, turned his back, left the cabin and closed the door quietly. He went to hang the key by the stairs before going back to the crew's cabin where he saw that the others were still sleeping. He climbed into the hammock, lay down, sighed with relief and almost immediately fell asleep.

Afterward it seemed that, except for purely nautical matters, the *Taurus* would sail without incident to reach the destination that Cervier had set for it. In Porto Cristo on the island of Mallorca, they moored in the small bay that faces the entrance to the famous Caves of Drach. Cervier got taken ashore in the dinghy and stayed for an hour. He had told no one on board what he was going to do there. When he got back, he was as reticent as when he'd left. He just gave orders to lift anchor and get back to sailing.

"Where are we going now?" Del Campo asked.

"A little far. Let's consult a map of the Mediterranean basin."

"As you wish," Del Campo said coolly.

On board the *Taurus* all conversations were carried out in Spanish. The former lieutenant, deserter and traitor spoke the language very comfortably and almost fluently. As for Del Campo and the rest of the crew, they were or pretending to be Spaniards from Europe or the Americas.

However, when the expedition leader and the ship's captain were in the map room next to the cabin where Sylvie Mac Duhl was held prisoner and were standing over the map laid out on a table, since these maps were French-made, Jacques Cervier automatically fell back on his native tongue.

"See here," he put his finger on the map. But he looked up and asked, "You understand French?"

"Yeah, sure," Del Campo answered and with an exaggerated Spanish accent added, "I even speak it pretty good."

"Fine," Cervier gave it no more thought. "South of Sardinia, south of Sicily, south of Crete, the Gulf of Adana... You follow me?"

"I follow," Del Campo said curtly.

"How many days do you figure?"

"Ah, well," the other replied, "better ask the sky and the sea and the winds. If we had steam or a gas engine, since this boat seems solid enough and well balanced, I could tell you after two or three hours of testing the speed—this many miles to cross at this many knots, it'll take us this many days... But with sails on this small boat, I'll tell you again, it depends on the weather and the sea."

"Fine, but if all goes well?"

"Oh, if all goes well, let's say eight, ten, twelve days."

And the provisional captain of the *Taurus* waved his hand, shrugged his shoulders and his eyes turned lifeless, which he knew how to do when he wanted to conceal his true thoughts.

"Good!" Cervier exclaimed. "Let's hope the weather and the sea are smiling on us. Plus, we have to make sure we have enough provisions."

"I checked," Del Campo said. "There's enough for a 20-day voyage. Even figuring on long delays, it seems more than enough to me. Plus, we can always lay up for a few hours in a port on the southern coast of Sardinia or in Agrigento in Sicily or on Malta. And finally we've got Crete. There's plenty of places to restock."

"Very well, very well," Cervier said.

He folded up the map, put it back in the cabinet and the two men went back on deck because the sea was calm and the weather very nice.

After a quick check on the men who were all, except for the pilot, already busy on the repairs to the damage done by the storm three days ago in the Gulf of Lion, Jacques Cervier left Pedro Del Campo to the bridge while he went down below deck. On his way he grabbed the key to Sylvie's prison and a minute later was sitting in the cabin at the foot of the bunk on which the young lady was lying.

They had ungagged and untied her a few hours earlier when they'd brought her food and drink. She was calm, her eyes open and her hands crossed behind her neck. When the visitor entered, she didn't move but she stared at him unblinking.

Jacques Cervier was a short man, a bureaucrat, and would have become obese long ago if it weren't for his life on the go. Still, he was pudgy and a little weasel-like too. He exuded something slimy. His gray, shallow eyes looked shifty and naïve at the same time, but deceptively naïve, which never fooled anyone for long. He was wearing a shabby beige suit, threadbare at the knees, with a cheap tie, cuffs and a celluloid collar peeking out. In short, at first sight, everything about him looked pretty dull.

And this was much more deceptive than his apparent naïveté. For, in truth, he had a vast and profound intelligence, unfortunately spoiled by greed and an unquenchable thirst for pleasure. Vulgar pleasures to boot—gambling, fast women and fine dining. This man, who could have been an excellent desk or staff officer, a remarkable organizer and a boon to his country, had been turned into a rogue by greed and lust, a deserter, a traitor and for the moment one of the damned souls of Leonid Zattan.

Now, thanks to Tchicoz, in possession of the (for him) immense fortune of the secret cargo of the *Taurus*, presently master of the pretty and charming young lady Sylvie Mac Duhl, Jacque Cervier had spent hours debating with himself whether he should steal the girl and the gold.

On the one hand, he knew that there was no place in the world where he could hide safely from Leonid Zattan if the master was determined to know the reason and circumstances for one of his main agents disappearing. On the other hand, for the double theft even to be possible, it would be necessary for his five accomplices who made up the present crew of the *Taurus*, including Tchicoz, to be murdered, which would be tough, or to run away from Zattan with him, which was highly doubtful.

Consequently, Cervier's mental debate had concluded that he be faithful to the Lord of Issyk-Kul. That was why he had sent a wireless telegram to Porto Cristo to announce the capture of the *Taurus* and Sylvie Mac Duhl.

Such was the individual whom Sylvie was glaring at with her blue eyes and frowning at without trying to hide the disdainful disgust she felt.

And he looked her over, this young lady, from head to toe. The short, fat, traitorous reptile shuddered with desire. But he knew that satisfying this desire, more than any other, was strictly forbidden by Zattan because he was unforgiving about his privileges as absolute master.

Without being clued in on the causes, the means or the goals of the battle going on between Leonid Zattan and Mathias Lumen, without knowing anything or having the slightest hunch about the prophecies of Nostradamus, Cervier was, however, aware of the great and priceless value the Lord of Issyk-Kul placed on Sylvie Mac Duhl. He was aware that Zattan had made a point not to get personally involved in the capture of the mysterious girl. But he knew that if Zattan had ever cherished one desire in his life, it was to capture this girl without having had anything to do with the capture.

To wrap up all this rationalizing and ruminating, Cervier told himself, "Without a doubt, Leonid Zattan won't give me a share of Sylvie and the *Taurus* equal to what they would mean to me if I kept them for myself. But he's generous. He's going to be deliriously happy. I'll surely get two, three, maybe even four or five million from the 100 or 200 million that the cargo's worth. My new riches will be added to the rest I've got stashed in New York. And when I'm finally at 100 million, I'll quit Zattan. I've got the right to. Too bad I'm not there yet." Then, with a snicker he added, "Little fish will get big as long as God keeps him alive."

"Mademoiselle," he said aloud in a falsely sweetened voice, which he used when he wanted to appear nice, "please excuse the somewhat harsh treatment my men put you through. It was the only way to make sure your bravery didn't get you in trouble. In a fight, you would've been badly bruised or seriously wounded, if not killed. I would never have forgiven myself for that. I ordered the sailor in charge of you, his name's Geronimo by the way, to be especially considerate and get you whatever you wish, provided it's within reason, of course, considering you're our prisoner. But oh, that's something else I can't do anything about, you being our prisoner!"

He stopped. She didn't deign to pronounce a word. Seeing in her hard, blue eyes and her tight, scornful lips that she wasn't going to reply, at least to his opening speech, Cervier went on:

"In case you're not you're not satisfied with the treatment you're receiving, you can tell me. I'm Monsieur Cervier. Anything you want, don't hesitate... I'm here for you and I'll do everything in my power to get what you need."

Sylvie Mac Duhl didn't even seem to hear the man. She stared at him with the same expression and her pretty face, by now a little thinner, remained impassive. He got irritated and spoke less sweetly.

"You're wrong, mademoiselle, to get haughty and hostile with your glare and your silence, which will get you nowhere. Understand that I am the master of your fate, the absolute master, in fact, and I..."

"Enough!" the young lady shouted, springing up and uncrossing her hands. She sat there, her whole body wound up like she was ready to spring. And this was so clear to Cervier that he jumped up, stepped back and instinctively got into a defensive position like a boxer.

At this Sylvie burst out laughing. Then, with boundless contempt in her voice, "I said 'enough', monsieur because all your talk is useless. But don't be scared that I'll fight you. I'll tell you right now that with no other weapon but your fists, you're a lost cause. I'll knock you out in the first round. Or better, because I'm more French than Scottish, I'll put you down with my first punch. But that's not the issue. I have a question for you. Will you answer?"

"It depends, mademoiselle," Cervier said coldly.

"Let's try anyway. You said I was a prisoner. I see that. But I also see that you're lying when you say you're the absolute master of my fate. Whether I know or not who you are is none of your business. But here's my question: where are you taking me and to whom?"

"I have no luck at all," he whispered back. "The only question you ask me is the only one I can't answer."

"Very well, monsieur," Sylvie said as she lay back down. "Our conversation is over. I won't keep you. But I will say that I'll be very grateful if you stay away from me from now on. And please, on your way out, be a gentleman and open the porthole because after your presence the room needs to air out."

As used to contempt and rejection as he was—for a man like him got it constantly—Jacques Cervier was taken aback this time. This girl's courage and character, even though he really wanted to be in control and use her as he wished, this girl's courage and character was so assertive that he was speechless, defenseless. All he could do was bow clumsily and go the porthole to open it... After which, he hastily left the cabin. But as happens sometimes the physical movement alone gave him back his self-control. He snickered to himself, turned around, went back into the room and in a low voice, strangely imbued with subtle violence, he declared:

"Defy me all you want. Enjoy it while it lasts. I'm bringing you to some-one who will avenge me for your insolence and how! Anyway, I won't take back anything I said. We're here for you, for whatever you need. Plus, you're free to go on deck. At your age, with your personality, people don't commit sui-cide, so I'm not worried that you'll jump overboard. For everything else you'll be watched closely even though we won't bother you. Don't forget, Geronimo will get what you want but it's me who, if possible, can get you more and better. I am respectfully at your service, mademoiselle."

He bowed deeply, walked out without locking the door behind him, and went up on deck.

Life on board the *Taurus* was, to all appearances, very simple, but with some very serious, underlying complications since Pedro Del Campo was in re-ality Saint-Clair the Nyctalope and Sylvie Mac Duhl knew it.

Half an hour after her conversation with Jacques Cervier the young lady went on deck. Nobody seemed to pay attention to her. Tchicoz and Barbone were working on repairs, Geronimo was busy in the kitchen and storeroom, Ramuz was at the helm, Del Campo was on the bridge and Cervier was coming and going with his hands behind his back and a big, fuming cigar clenched be-tween his teeth. But Sylvie realized very quickly that Cervier never lost sight of her and through the two open doors of the kitchen and storeroom Geronimo was always watching her.

She set her own mealtimes. She was served either in her cabin or on deck as she wanted. At night her cabin was locked but at 7 am Geronimo brought her coffee and toasted biscuits and when he left, he didn't lock the door.

Things went on like this for 48 hours. Then suddenly everything changed because the pleasant northeasterly wind turned into a storm. They left Sylvie free on deck and even Del Campo let her help the sailors with handling the boat. But they couldn't stay on course. The storm was so violent that they had to out-run it. Heaving to and standing by was too dangerous because the sloop might not have been sturdy enough to withstand the strong waves bashing it.

After a terrible night and almost as terrible morning of sailing, the sea was in complete turmoil and the boat more and more battered, even starting to let in water. Del Campo had to decide to find shelter.

He found it in a cranny at Cap Roux a few miles west of Tabarca, Tunisia, and he stayed there without being able to leave until March 25th! On the morn-ing of that day, with the storm abruptly died down in the night, the sea was man-ageable once again.

Consequently, on the advice of Del Campo, Jacques Cervier gave orders to set off again. When anchored the men had worked on caulking the interior seams of the *Taurus*, on drying the bottom of the hold and on repairing all the damage, really not very serious, caused by the storm. And the sloop left its crev-ice turning east-northeast to round the northern point of Tunisia and then veer off to pass between Sicily and Malta.

Likewise on the of the 25th the yacht *Fulgur* was speeding away from Nice toward the Ionian Sea.

And again on that same day, the electric airplane *Aquilon* was taking off from the outer harbor of Valletta to make its third reconnaissance flight between Malta and Sicily.

Leonid Zattan and Petrus Ivitch had left Issy-Kul on the 21st and in less than 24 hours at an average speed of 170 mph had crossed the 3,500 miles that separated the castle from Malta. They'd rested after landing comfortably in the harbor until the 23rd. the two long reconnaissance flights they had made that day and the next did not find the expected sloop. But Leonid did not lose patience. He knew that his search could last all week. He was sure it would end in success.

Having explained everything to Ivitch, he had concluded, "The *Taurus* has to pass between Malta and Sicily. As long as the current wind conditions keep up, the sloop won't make enough headway, even if it sails at night, to slip by us a few miles to the east. And my luck might hold for it to sail during the day."

Like the two precious days, the Aquilon headed first toward the east on the 25th. It went from Malta to the southeast point of Sicily, making a wide curve. With binoculars to his eyes, Zattan examined every boat sailing eastward or tacking on the sea. Four-masts, three-masts, schooner, brigs and tartanes sailed on without a second glance from him. But if a cutter or a sloop was spotted, quick orders were given to Ivitch and the *Aquilon* spiraled down, closer and closer.

After meticulous examination Leonid would say, "It's not the *Taurus*." And the plane was pulled up by its two propellers connected to the electric engines that were inexhaustible, indefatigable and silent.

Until noon the sun rose in a clear sky over a deep blue sea, but then clouds showed up in the west, multiplied, spread out, gathered together and attacked the sun, which disappeared as if it had been swallowed up. The sea was white. The wind turned cold. But the *Aquilon* didn't stop its shuttling between the coasts of Sicily and an ideal trajectory traced on the map from Malta to Cape Bon.

The two clocks on board showed 2 pm sharp and Cape Bon was clearly visible to the southwest when Zattan shouted his favorites curse word—a profanity that made sense in no known language:

"Kirakef! This time I'll be burned alive if that's not him! 48 degrees to the left, Petrus… That white spot there. A sloop! It's the first time in three days that I feel sure of it. The sea's getting rough so it'll be hard to board. But who cares! I'll jump in and swim if I have to. Be careful! Try to land downwind from the boat. I'll have the stern in sight any minute and see the name… Anyway, if it's him, Cervier will know it's me and stop the boat right away."

Zattan reached out with his left hand and pressed a button numbered 6 on a panel that had twelve. A sharp click was heard over the humming propellers and the whistling wind. Halfway between the plane and the surface of the sea a kind of harmless bomb exploded, sending out six red flares and six plumes of white smoke.

The Aquilon was less than 700 feet altitude, making wide circles around the small boat that was being hauled through the sea by its unfurled sails. Petrus Ivitch piloted stoically, attentive to every word and gesture of his dreadful master who was watching the sloop with his naked eye.

Two minutes after the signal flare had gone off and the order it represented was starting to be obeyed—some pygmies ran across the deck of the toy boat and the sails were pulled in.

"That's it, it's the *Taurus*... At last!" the Lord of Issyk-Kul muttered. And his black eyes sparkled for a few seconds with red flashes of diabolical joy or maybe satanic anger.

While the sloop brought itself to a full stop, stalled in the water and only drifted slowly on the waves, the plane landed. Even though the sea was getting rougher, the waves becoming monstrous, the landing gear allowed the huge bird to keep its balance on the water. Only a big swell or a stampede of stormy waves could have kept it in the air. Still driven by its propellers spinning at a relatively slow speed, it bounced lightly, marvelously stable, closer to the boat, as close as the most basic caution allowed.

Finally, sloop and airplane were only a stone's throw away from each other.

Leonid Zattan had a tiny bullhorn that amplified the range and volume of his voice. "Ahoy, sloop! Number 17!"

A voice less loud and less clear but still audible to the men in the plane answered directly, "Ahoy! Exactly! Number 17! What are your orders?"

Zattan commanded, "Don't risk a dinghy. Throw three moored buoys into the sea. Get towels and warm clothes ready for me. Right?"

Three minutes later, dressed in a swimsuit, Leonid Zattan dove into the water. The plane had come close enough that its left wing almost grazed the sloop's stern. Swimming, grabbing a buoy, winding it around his waist then sitting on it while the men hauled him in and then heaved him up—it was child's play for the versatile athletes of Issyk-Kul.

On the back of the *Taurus*, Jacques Cervier was visibly moved as he bowed before his master who had jumped on the deck, dripping wet. The air was cold and the wind lashed them under the dark clouds.

Without a word, after a deep bow, Cervier went to the deckhouse, opened the door, bowed again, stepped aside and closed the door. Standing at attention, he waited. The five others at their posts were waiting, too, as if hypnotized. They knew that Prince Leonid Zattan, Lord of Issyk-Kul and Tian Shan, had the power of life and death over them. They had never set eyes on him before this extraordinary moment when the swimmer had let go of the buoy and leaped onto the deck. They were about to see him again but dressed like them because the clothes waiting for him were from the stock of shirts, pants, sweaters and pea coats found on board. They were about to see him again, to hear him, experience the fascination of his eyes and the sovereign authority of his voice.

Now, one of these five men, frozen, attentive and excited, looking like a young sea dog called Pedro Del Campo was none other than Leo Saint-Clair, the Nyctalope! Standing on the bridge at his post of interim captain of the *Taurus*, he pretended to be just as excited as Barbone, Ramuz, Geronimo and Tchicoz. But he'd had a second secret meeting the night before with Sylvie Mac Duhl. He'd overheard all of the conversations between Tchicoz and Cervier and remembered what he'd caught in Madrid through the air vent in the hotel. Adding logical hypotheses to the certainties he'd learned, the Nyctalope could imagine why the mysterious and formidable Lord of Issyk-Kul was here in the afternoon of March 25th in the middle of the sea off the coast of Tunisia and Sicily on board this sloop.

And Leo Saint-Clair the Nyctalope knew now. While waiting for the right time to go into action, he was more than ever the seafaring adventurer Pedro Del Campo, captain of the boat carrying a fated young lady and millions in gold and precious stones.

Cervier and his five men didn't have to wait long. Seven minutes after disappearing into the deckhouse, Leonid Zattan stepped back out on deck. Comfortable and natural in his old shoes of straw and gray wool, in his white linen pants and blue knit sweater and heavy woolen pea coat left open at the neck, clean shaven, black hair slicked back, he leaned casually back against the closed door and with a slight smile spoke in French, a little modestly.

"Cervier, introduce the crew of the *Taurus* to me. I want to know the names of these men. Destiny has handed them the greatest chance of their lives. Soon they will know what this chance is worth. Introduce them first, Cervier."

From the top of the poop deck to the stern crane he could be heard. The men were shivering with excitement. Cervier obeyed and shouted.

"Ahoy, all here! And you, captain Del Campo!"

Starting with the "boss", the introductions were made by name, each followed by some appropriate remarks. Cervier was no dummy and he knew how to flatter the men while giving his master relevant information.

Zattan knew how to observe and judge men, to go beneath the surface of their eyes, to read the lines, the features, the marks on the face. Five times his eyes glared and sparkled. But without knowing it he failed himself because he saw nothing in Pedro Del Campo that seemed any different from the others: shady pirates, fairly clever brutes, sailors who knew their trade. But he himself was being sized up by Leo Saint-Clair and the Nyctalope knew the Lord of Issyk-Kul was no one to be trifled with.

Once the inspection was over and the five men had gone back to their respective posts, Zattan told Cervier, "It's fine, I accept Del Campo as the ranking captain of the *Taurus*. I'll get him a bigger boat later. Tchicoz, Geronimo, Ramuz and Barbone will follow him on the new ship. You, Cervier, will be more than satisfied with my plans for you. But first, we've got to get this sloop to a safe harbor, meaning to dock 2 in the Gulf of Adana. You'll wait for my cargo planes to transfer your freight. Then you'll be given my written orders regarding the *Taurus*, the crew and yourself. Done. Now, take me to Sylvie Mac Duhl."

Luckily, Saint-Clair had overheard the recent conversations between Tchicoz and Cervier, so he knew about this rendezvous on the sea with the electric plane from Issyk-Kul. He'd spent part of the night preparing the girl who promised to follow the Nyctalope's advice with courage and self-control, with hope and patience.

Sylvie Mac Duhl, therefore, was not surprised by the appearance of the plane in the cloudy sky. Cervier hurried to lock her up again in the cabin. Although she had no clue about the immeasurable, imponderable, mysterious and prophetic value she held in Zattan's eyes, she figured that the enigmatic enemy of Mathias Lumen would make her his prisoner for reasons she might learn one day but that for the present she could only guess or glimpse. She knew she had a role to play in a high-stakes game, but apart from being a woman, a very pretty girl, a passionate virgin, she didn't think her role was any more important than, say, the huge fortune lying in the hull.

She was not surprised to see Jacques Cervier come into her room like a butler to announce the arrival of a lord, then stepping aside, bowing deeply and saying, "Prince, this is Sylvie Mac Duhl."

"Leave us," is all the man said. When the door closed, the noble Kalmyk spoke with majestic simplicity. "Mademoiselle, I am Prince Leonid Zattan, Sovereign Lord of Issyk-Kul and Tian Shan. Events beyond your control but in which you are called to play a vital role have forced me to keep you as my prisoner for now and the unforeseeable future."

He stopped talking. She was sitting on the bunk and hadn't moved since the two men had entered. She watched Zattan with a calmness that was both naïve and severe. Her beautiful lips didn't even part. Not once did her pure face twitch. She was clearly waiting for him to finish what he had to say. He did just that.

"Mademoiselle, I came from Issyk-Kul by airplane. It is slowly circling the *Taurus* adrift. I have to bring you along. If you have anything here you want to keep, tell the guy I'll send in here. He'll pack them up or help you to do so. As for you, will you willingly accept to take, with me, the unpleasant but necessary plunge in the sea? Or should I tie you to a buoy and have to fight you when you resist or refuse to budge. As you want. But willingly or not, I'm sorry to say that you will be moving from the *Taurus* to the *Aquilon*."

He stopped again. His voice, not very sharp, almost gentle, stayed even-pitched. His wretched face even cracked an almost peaceful smile. His eyes were mellow, though domineering. What strength of character must it have taken for this man to control and curb and hide all the passion that had been his driving force for so long and that could have, if unleashed, pounced on the girl like a wild beast on its prey!

The young lady didn't know enough to have the slightest hint of the astounding victory Zattan was currently accomplishing over himself. More than ever she had the feeling—like so often in her life—of being swept away by Fate, like a piece of driftwood carried off by a stream through lazy waters turned into a raging river, then into stagnant pools that are quickly stirred up and driven over waterfalls into other lazy streams... But she knew that this particular driftwood had the superiority of being living, thinking matter capable of independent action...

And the young lady was too intelligent not to understand that in the present impasse, any sudden movement against the current dragging her along would not throw her onto a safe harbor but into a deadly maelstrom.

Very calmly but with no less scorn than she had shown Cervier, she responded to Zattan. "You have the upper hand, monsieur, for the moment. Besides, I don't understand anything that's happened to me over the past ten days. So, I'd rather follow you willingly than be forced since I can't avoid going."

She stood and continued.

"I do, in fact, have some things here that I'd rather not part with. I'll put them in that light, aluminum chest. It's waterproof so my things won't get wet. But can you tell me why going to the plane will require us to jump in the water? There are two dinghies on board and the sea isn't too rough."

Zattan replied in the same calm and casual voice, "It's true, mademoiselle, but it's still a risk for the little boats and for the plane, which I prefer not taking. I think it's easier and quicker and safer to swim with the buoys. A buoy for each of us and a third one for your chest, which will be tied to yours. Just some skillful handling of the plane, which we'll be boarding on the side, between the floats in the middle and the one behind—it's a little inconvenient is all, a short bath... please put on a bathing suit."

"Why not..." the young lady resigned but her lips scowled.

He bowed, smiling, and wrapped up, "A change of clothes, a fur cap and some scarves, all your size, are waiting on board the *Aquilon*. You will excuse me for the temporary discomfort. At the castle in Issyk-Kul you will have everything you need." He straightened up and in a more imposing tone, "Is fifteen minutes enough for you to get ready?"

"Should be," Sylvie answered curtly.

"Do you want to come up on deck by yourself?"

"Yes."

"Well then, I'll see you in fifteen to twenty minutes, mademoiselle." He bowed deeply, turned around and left.

Half an hour later the transfer was over and the *Aquilon* took off for Issyk-Kul, carrying the golden-haired virgin of Nostradamus' prophecies.

60

At the moment she dropped her white bathrobe on the sloop, in her swimsuit that was not too revealing, not too tight and had a knee-length skirt, Sylvie Mac Duhl didn't catch the fierce glare in Zattan's bloodshot eyes, but she did glimpse the Nyctalope's deep and reassuring gaze. Then she plopped down in the middle of the round buoy.

While the *Aquilon* was soaring off with Zattan and his precious prey, the *Taurus* hoisted sail to resume its journey to the Gulf of Adana.

The next morning, however, March 26th, with Sicily and Malta left behind, while Jacques Cervier was still asleep in the cabin, the crew's attention was fixed on a yacht surging out of the northwest and flaunting its speed.

"Caramba!" Geronimo exclaimed, "that's the boat we need to shake the barnacles off."

"I'll wager it passes us in three minutes," Tchicoz offered Ramuz who was at the helm.

Leaning against the stern crane Barbone watched the magnificent yacht without saying a word.

And almost immediately everyone on board the sloop was amazed except for the Nyctalope who had a gut feeling about what was going to happen.

"Right," he told himself, "Sylvie talked about a Gnô Mitang who wouldn't be able to rest if some twist of fate I cannot imagine made him suspect that the *Taurus* was stolen by Cervier. Oh, the yacht is slowing down for some reason. Strange, it's just sitting in the water. I'll bet it hails us and wants to board. If I'm not mistaken, I'm going to have some fun."

Indeed, what caused the amazement on board the sloop was the yacht slowing down and veering off its straight course to head towards the *Taurus*. Without a doubt, such a maneuver could mean only one thing: vocal communication between the captain of the yacht and the boss of the sloop.

This logical hypothesis was quickly confirmed.

Pulling up on the port side of the *Taurus*, the yacht, whose name could be seen now, *Fulgur*, was moving parallel at the same speed as the sloop. Fifteen or so men in white pants and sweaters were standing on the deck of the yacht. The wide bridge was occupied by three officers in white uniforms.

Del Campo and his four crewmates saw one of the officers raise a megaphone and right away these French words—an abrupt, forceful order:

"Ahoy, *Taurus*, stop immediately. We are going to board. Any resistance will be met with force of arms. I'll give you two minutes to come to a standstill."

The minds of Barbone, Ramuz and Geronimo were no more at ease than Tchicoz'. What was happening at the moment scared them but was hardly a surprise. When you lead the life of a bandit and pirate in this age of enforced civilization, you're always expecting to run into the police on land or sea. It's fate. These four hooligans swore, turned pale, but didn't say a word.

Pedro Del Campo, however, had no fear of these people who were apparently not official police but civilian enemies of Leonid Zattan. "There's Gnô Mitang and Mathias Lumen on the *Fulgur*," he supposed.

And the Nyctalope was thrilled! The adventure was certainly getting more and more intriguing. But he wanted to play the role of ship's captain working for the Lord of Issyk-Kul until the last moment. So, he grabbed his megaphone and 30 seconds later after the authoritative demand from the yacht's officer, the captain of the sloop answered in French:

"Ahoy, *Fulgur*! Who are you and what right do you have…"

He didn't finish because the officer already had the megaphone to his lips and was responding.

"The right of the bigger and stronger! Stop immediately! Or I'll fire and turn you into a pontoon."

At the same time, with incredible agility, the *Fulgur* turned 90 degrees to the north and presented its rear to the sloop. The pirates saw a cannon on a big carriage rise up over the railing. Two sailors in white were handling it. They had it aimed in the blink of an eye and stood at attention while the yacht's stern churned up the water as it started backing up.

Now Del Campo had to obey. He dropped the megaphone, shrugged his shoulders and ordered his men to stop the *Taurus*, which was easy enough on a sloop of its kind.

On the *Fulgur*, however, they dropped a whaleboat into the water. During the night the wind had blown off, taking the clouds with it. What was left after the rough storm was a cool breeze, clear skies and a manageable sea. Putting a boat in the water and berthing it next to a stationary sailboat was child's play.

When the long rowboat was lined up beside the sloop Del Campo gave the appropriate orders. Two well-secured rope ladders were dropped from the gangway and held fast by four of the ten sailors in the whaler. Two of them were officers who'd been seen before on the bridge of the *Fulgur*. They jumped on the ladders, climbed up and scrambled onto the sloop's deck. And they stood before a little guy in pajamas with bedraggled hair and his eyes still puffy with sleep. The hoarse voice of this little man shouted, "Messiers, I protest this…"

But Gnô Mitang and Captain Marc Ayol both recognized his face. They had seen it so often, this traitor's face, in the newspapers and magazines! Plus, they knew—Gnô through the letter from Ramon Bastos to Mathias Lumen and Ayol from what Gnô had told him—that Jacques Cervier had embarked on the sloop in the Bay of Roses.

Marc Ayol cut him off. His gold teeth sparkled in the brief, furious smile that sprang from his mouth. "Silence, traitor! Jacques Cervier, eh? Don't move or I'll squash you!"

He shook his left fist over Cervier's head. With his right hand he pulled his Browning out of the holster on his belt. He looked up and turned towards the bridge.

"Ahoy, up there! Whoever's the so-called captain of this boat, get down here! Speed it up, would you? All right! Tie up this weasel so he can't move. Yes, Cervier! And I'm doing you an honor by asking you to do it. A weasel stinks and bites but never betrays as far as I know. Hey, Gnô, it's all good what I'm doing?"

"All good," the stoical Japanese said.

Then laughter broke out, fresh and full of joy, light and young, the merriest, most magnificently French laughter that Marc Ayol had ever heard. He and Gnô and the bandit crew all looked at the laugher who was none other than Pedro Del Campo.

The laughter died down and a calm, steady voice with the hint of a smirking prankster said, "Congratulations, captain. I am once again seeing that mix of Marseille and Paris and England that gave me so much pleasure on board the *Galapias* for many weeks. Do you remember?"

"Oh, Monsieur Saint-Clair... The Nyctalope!" Ayol was flabbergasted. After taking a deep breath as if the air had been knocked out of his lungs, he muttered, "You... you... is it possible? On board the *Taurus*? And with this Cervier? But look, Gnô (he turned trembling to the Japanese), look, Mademoiselle Mac Duhl is here and everything is all right... I..."

"No, my friend," Saint-Clair was very serious now, "No, Sylvie Mac Duhl is no longer on board. But I'll explain everything to you. Patience, Ayol. Monsieur Gnô Mitang, Sylvie told me about you. I'm glad to make your acquaintance. Would you do me the honor, along with your captain, of working with me. For a few days now we've been hunting the same prey. From now on let's do it together."

He held out his right hand. Gnô Mitang took it, shook it, bowed deeply, then stood up straight. His face and eyes displayed admiration, respect and joy. He spoke very clearly.

"The Nyctalope! Who hasn't heard of him? Who wouldn't be happy and proud to fight alongside him? I'm all yours! I feel relieved now. With you, Sylvie will be saved and Lumen avenged."

But Saint-Clair furrowed his brow, looked gravely at Gnô Mitang and Marc Ayol and whispered, "Maybe. I saw Leonid Zattan yesterday. He's a genius, but also a demon."

He shook his head and closed his eyes. A few seconds of silence followed. Coming quickly back to the present dilemma Saint-Clair opened his eyes and rearing up like a lion spoke loudly in Spanish.

"Barbone, Geronimo, tie this man's hands and feet and throw him in the hold. You, Tchicoz, get into the whaleboat. Ayol, leave it to your men to put him in irons on the *Fulgur*. You, Ramuz, get to the helm as usual. But stay at a standstill until further notice."

As dazed as they were by what they'd just seen and heard, these men had endured too much under Del Campo's stature over the last eight days not to automatically obey his command. Barbone and Geronimo grabbed Cervier without a second thought—this was not the first time in their life that they changed masters and, according to one famous example, burned the one they had once adored. Tamely, Ramuz went back to the helm without really understanding any more than his comrades. Only Tchicoz, with a start, showed a vague sign to revolt, but the Nyctalope stared hard at him. Subdued, the wretched murderer lowered his head and walked to the gangway. He took one of the ladders and climbed down into the boat where the sailors had already received Ayol's orders from the Nyctalope.

Gnô Mitang addressed Saint-Clair with respect, "Please, boss, go on board the *Fulgur* to do us the honor of assessing the situation with us."

"Yes indeed!" the Saint-Clair replied. "And also for a good breakfast. That magnificent yacht must have a ship's cook worthy of its image and provisions worthy of its cook!"

"By all means!" the captain said.

"Well then, let's get going. While waiting for breakfast, messieurs, you can enlighten me on the situation and I will fill in any blanks for you. I believe we have a lot to tell each other."

In Spanish he shouted, "Ramuz, watch out! The sloop is a bull's eye for that cannon over there. Any suspicious movement from the *Taurus* and I'll sink it to the bottom of the sea. Besides, the sailboat won't get far running from the yacht. I'm telling you this so that nobody gets stupid enough to think of mutiny because you'll pay with your lives, instantly!"

There's no need to say that Saint-Clair was welcomed on board the *Fulgur* as if he were an admiral commanding the navy and the yacht was a part of his fleet. Loved or hated, the Nyctalope was universally famous and admired. Not a person on board hadn't heard or read about one of his exploits. Marc Ayol, as we know, had sailed with him for a few weeks on board a patrol boat during the worst time of the Great War. Paul Guennec had seen him once in Brest. Saint-Clair asked to be introduced to the whole crew. He shook hands and smiled at the cook, telling him he hadn't had a really good meal in five weeks and therefore hoped to be "cured" very soon.

In the meantime, before the breakfast bell rang, the staff of the *Fulgur*, now presided over by Saint-Clair, met in the yacht's parlor.

The Nyctalope, Gnô Mitang, Marc Ayol, Lieutenant Paul Guennec, the chief mechanic Adrien Dantal and the deck boss Yves Lequic—these men on board the ship that sat almost motionless south of the Ionian Sea were holding the first of many councils of war that would take place during the unprecedented battle between Mathias Lumen and Leonid Zattan that was going to shake the very foundations of the civilized world.

CHAPTER V

It was on March 31st, at 4 pm, that the *Taurus*, leaving behind it to the southwest the eastern point of Cyprus, headed into the waters of the Gulf of Adana.

The Gulf thrust deeply into that southern part of Asia Minor that was the most untamed, with steep, rugged peaks from north to south and the desert valleys of the Anti-Taurus Mountains. The Gulf itself and its entire rim are scored by countless creeks and inlets where small ships can hide for months without the wind coming to ripple the surface of the calm water beneath the high cliffs, without another human appearing to the idle crew.

When the outline of Cyprus had completely disappeared from view, Leo Saint-Clair came down from the bridge and went to the helm.

"Marc, it's hard for me think that the sloop is going to be destroyed. From the moment I stepped aboard in Roses, I felt attached to it."

"The fact is that it's a good little boat," the captain nodded. "Gnô said Miss Mac Duhl cried when she learned what we'd have to do to her. I can understand. Still, Leo, over the last five days I've thought a lot about the plan we came up with, that we decided on, that we're going to see through. Well, as sure as I tasted my first drop of mother's milk in Marseille and I'll drink my last glass of whisky in London, there's no better, more reasonable plan than ours, as crazy as it is."

The Nyctalope laughed. He loved Ayol's casual intimacy. For five days alone on the *Taurus*, they had got to know each other better than they had on the *Galapias*. They still used the "formal you" because it seemed impossible for either of them to drop it, but they called each other by their first names and didn't hesitate to use slang.

The council of war held on board the *Fulgur* in the Ionian Sea on March 26th had these first results: the transfer of Cervier and his four pirates from the sloop to the yacht; the transfer of the chests of gold and precious stones replaced by compensating ballast from the *Fulgur*; the boarding of Saint-Clair and Ayol as the only crew across the Mediterranean to the Gulf of Adana; finally, the navigation of the sloop escorted at a safe distance by the yacht until in sight of Cyprus. In the waters west of the island, the *Taurus* had continued straight over the north of Cyprus, but the *Fulgur*, the "pleasure yacht of a rich and misanthropic Belgian", had made a stopover in the small harbor of Famagusta on the east of the island.

If need be, the chief mechanic Adrien Dantal, in fact originally from Anvers, would play the role of the hypochondriac Belgian. Paul Guennec was captain of the ship. As for Gnô Mitang, he and Mâh Ito played the role of servants. But there was little chance that the English authorities in Famagusta would bother the *Fulgur*, which would be for them only an object of admiration and respect, a sterling example of luxury yachting.

During the five-day trip, the *Taurus* and its very minimal crew were lucky—they had steady, favorable winds, clear skies, moonlit nights and a splendid sea. The boat sailed smoothly towards its death.

Yes, its death had been decreed unanimously on the basis of Saint-Clair's reasoned decision in the council of war. And here is how the death came about.

During the entire afternoon of March 31st, with a good wind from the southwest, the sloop sailed swiftly away from Cyprus and approached the coast of Asia Minor. At nightfall the wind picked up and the full sails drove the sloop even faster.

Soon, the moon rose and the sky was twinkling with stars. Marc Ayol had almost no need of the lantern to consult the chart. For his part, the Nyctalope was carefully watching the coast, which he could do as easily during the day as on the darkest and cloudiest night.

From time to time the two men exchanged some information or observation. They'd gobbled up some biscuits and cold meat that Saint-Clair had found in the galley, then swallowed two big cups of coffee without sugar or alcohol.

And the hours passed…

Ten minutes or so had ticked off after midnight when the Nyctalope announced, "I think it's time. There's the bishop's cap headland that Cervier talked about… Your calculations, Marc…"

"It matches. We're at the place."

"Let's get to work, buddy."

With a rope already prepared, the captain fastened the wheel in place and followed the Nyctalope below deck through the forecastle hatch. A few moments later the two men reappeared together but through the deckhouse in the rear. They went portside, facing the coast, which showed a clear, sharp line of mountain peaks against the clear, star-studded sky.

After a minute of observation the Nyctalope spoke in a controlled but gleefully mischievous voice, "If there are any of Zattan's lookouts in those eagle's nests, they're going to see the sloop go up in flames."

"Right," Ayol agreed. "And the land is close enough that they'll be able to appraise the damage, as an insurance agent would say in a fire. We'll have to work out our movements."

"Easy enough, Marc. When the first smoke appears, we'll hide behind the deckhouse so that we won't be seen too soon in front of the flames that will spread quickly. At the last moment, when we're really in danger, we'll jump over to the starboard side, run around like we're panicking, finally throw the dinghy into the water and then row like hell while the sloop blows up."

"Let's hope it doesn't blow up before the dinghy is in the water and we're in the dinghy."

"I measured the fuse very carefully and I think we confined the fire enough for the flames not to burn the fuse sooner. Still, the risk is there. We can't help it, we have to act so that an observant witness can say, "Hey, they sure are in a hurry to get into the water without helping their comrades or trying to put out the fire." Marc if they can see the damage in enough detail, our behavior won't be questioned, especially after our explications, we'll be "undetectable"."

"Right! Then we can go on as if no suspicion..."

"None whatsoever. Not a shadow of doubt. Look, there's the smoke! Back up and disappear. Be careful of that spot of light from the lantern;"

"Yeah, I thought of that."

And in the nocturnal shadows the two men slipped behind the deckhouse and went starboard. Like this they were facing the open sea and couldn't be seen from land.

However, the smoke was already billowing out of the forward hatch. Crackling could be heard on the deck and the air was getting thick with the stench of burning material and boiling oil. Almost right away, still from the forward hatch, a flame shot out, licked the bottom of the wind-stretched sails, then a second one, bigger, reached higher. One sail caught fire... After that it was like a stampede of flames from front to back—sails, rigging, yardarms and mast instantly ablaze because they were so dry from days of sailing in the sun and calm waters.

"Here we go, Marc!"

"Yes, boss."

And the two men looked like they were panicking, running from one untouched part of the deck to another. They were shouting names while trying (or so it appeared) to open the portside door of the deckhouse.

"Cervier! Tchicoz! Ramuz! Barbone! Hey, hey! Tchicoz!"

But the mainsail caught fire. The entire back of the boat had fallen prey to the blaze.

Then the two men stopped struggling with the door. They ran to the stern crane, jumped into the hanging dinghy, untied the knots, unhooked the clamps, grabbed the oars...

And heave ho! With all the strength they could muster they rowed hard, instantly in rhythm and speeding off.

They weren't 500 feet from the sloop when the deckhouse burst from the pressure of the volcano inside. Flames leapt up while an explosion drowned out the high-pitched crackling. The whole burning boat seemed to bounce out of the sea... and it blew up like a huge grenade, spewing debris in every direction along with flaming rays and billowing red smoke.

The stupendous fireworks lasted a good thirty seconds. Afterward, the water extinguished the last firebrands and it was back to the starry night, the serene sea and the smooth waves. Sylvie Mac Duhl's *Taurus* was dead and pretty much obliterated.

An hour later, two men jumped out of a dingy onto the sand of a small beach at the end of a long cove. The moon and the stars were bright enough for them to see what they were doing and for anyone who happened to be on top of the cliffs to see them. Standing on solid ground, they dried their faces with their shirt sleeves, making the same mechanical motion. One of them spoke to the other in Spanish.

"Marco Pampil, it's awful! We're the only ones who got out alive. We barely made it."

"Yes, Pedro," the other said. "A minute more and we'd have gone up with the boat."

"Well, it's over. What a nightmarish memory this is going to make, Marco. But I was thinking... they were expecting the *Taurus* on this coast. Maybe someone saw it. Maybe they'll hear us. Let's start shouting, eh?"

"You're right, Pedro."

Cupping their hands around their mouths Leo Saint-Clair the Nyctalope, called Pedro Del Campo, and Captain Marc Ayol, now Marco Pampil, started yelling towards the cliffs to the right and left.

"Ahoy! Hey! Ahoy! Hey, hey!"

"Bueno, bueno, silencio," a hoarse voice came from the back of the beach.

From one of the dark crevasses in the rock a man stepped out and walked quickly towards them. The Nyctalope saw that he was holding a Browning with a long tube attached to the barrel. He thought: "Automatic pistol with a spotlight. The Zattanics are modern and technological. The electric plane, for one... We'll have to play this one very carefully."

The man stopped, raised and pointed his right hand holding the gun. In an instant Pedro Del Campo and Marco Pampil were blinded by a bright flash that struck their faces.

"Quien vive?" the man growled.

"And they're polyglots," Saint-Clair thought.

He answered immediately in Spanish, "The captain and one of the sailors from the *Taurus*. And you?"

"Envoy from Issyk-Kul.

Pretending to be greatly upset, Del Campo said, "The boat caught fire, blew up... Did you see? We were sleeping. Ramuz at the wheel and Barbone on watch must've been drunk. They probably stole some brandy from the storeroom and fell asleep. It's Marco who woke me up. But it was too late to get the pumps working to drench the hold. Everything was burning. I have no idea how the fire started. We tried to wake up Cervier and Tchicoz, but they were probably already suffocated, maybe burned. There were three barrels of gunpowder and we knew we'd've die for nothing if we stuck around. So, we grabbed the dinghy and..."

"I saw," the man broke in after putting the Browning back in its holster. "The prince won't be happy. When the transport planes arrive tomorrow, they won't have anything to transport but you two. Because you're going to Issyk-Kul. I'll send a wireless message with what I saw and what you just told me. But the Lord will want details. You'll give them to him in person. In the meantime…"

He closed his mouth and thought for a minute, clearly worried. Then he went on.

"I was specially appointed to meet the *Taurus*, unload the cargo and then burn it. A fatality! It burned by itself but too soon. I was supposed to be your guide. You, Captain Del Campo, and your crew, I was supposed to take you down the coast to a schooner with an auxiliary motor whose captain died eight days ago. You were going to take his place and your crew join his. It's because I speak Spanish that the Prince chose me. You're all Spanish from Europe or the Americas, right?"

"Yes," Del Campo replied.

"But now I'm sure the Lord will have some questions for you. The schooner can wait. Captain, what's this sailor's name?"

"Marco Pampil."

"Huh? What'd you say?"

"Marco Pampil."

"The name isn't one of the five I was given as the crew of the *Taurus*."

"That's right," Del Campo answered naturally. "Marco's a new recruit. I took him on in Malta to replace Geronimo who was killed an hour after the Lord took off."

"Killed? How?"

"He slipped on the edge of the forward hatch and took a bad fall down the ladder, cracked open his head on the bottom. His brains spilled out. Died on the spot. There was a burial at sea… but I need four men to work the sloop safely. I went ashore on Malta and ran into Marco Pompil. I'd already worked with him and can vouch for him. I brought him on board pending approval from higher up."

"Fine," the envoy shrugged his shoulders. He thought some more, his surly face showing his dilemma about what measures to take. Grumpily, he decided, "The dinghy will be burned. Come on, we'll pull up to dry land and tomorrow burn it in the sun."

Hauling the light rowboat over the sand was easy. The three men were all able-bodied.

"Come with me now. You'll spend the rest of the night in hammocks at the wireless station. My name's Manoël Guerro. I'm Portuguese, but I've been running all around the world since I was 20 and I'm 38 now. I serve Prince Leonid Zattan as head of wireless communication at Issyk-Kul. It's a good job. There's always danger serving the Lord, but we're well paid. In 12 years I can retire and earn double what a general earns in my country. What more could I ask for since I'm not ambitious? Anyway, I love danger… I'm telling you this so you'll know something about me and since you're being respectful. Do with it what you will!"

"Thanks, Guerro," Del Campo held out his right hand to the Portuguese.

He shook it with a smile that the Nyctalope felt was a little wry, "Spanish and Portuguese, we're brothers, if wild beasts like men can ever really call each other such."

"You're a pessimist and a misanthrope, Guerro." Del Campo almost whispered back.

"No!" the other insisted. "I know life. But things happen. When they're on the same side and they hit it off, men sometimes manage not to devour each other... Be careful, it climbs up steep here. One wrong move, a little slip and you won't be thinking or gabbing ever again."

It did, indeed, climb steeply. While talking, Manoël Guerro, flanked by Del Campo and the so-called Marco Pampil, had walked to the end of the beach and entered the rising ravine, which was relatively easy thanks to the eastern light at the end of the beautiful, spring night. But when he stopped talking, he stepped onto the first stair carved out of the rock. Two men couldn't go up side-by-side, so the three of them walked single file. Without railing or ledge the stairs zigzagged up the steep cliff, sometimes very uneven, natural formations, sometimes dug out by skillful, patiently handled tools long ago when Zattan had set up his wireless station on this wild, deserted, Asiatic coast. Many of these steps were less than three feet wide with the sheer, nearly smooth rock on one side and an abyss on the other. Anybody who suffered from vertigo wouldn't make it a quarter of the way up.

Manoël Guerro was used to it. Del Campo and Pampil had sea legs. But they managed the acrobatic ascension without incident. And even though the moon was occasionally shrouded by clouds that a strong breeze was driving out of the northwest, Guerro never pulled out a flashlight or used the light on his gun.

When they reached the top, the wireless engineer turned left into a kind of gutter that looked naturally grooved out of the rock by the age-old, whimsical work of rainwater. Soon this gutter became so deep and wide that it was more of a trench. It turned abruptly to the right, then a jagged line until the three men suddenly found themselves facing a long, wide, barren esplanade.

"Here we are," Guerro said.

The Nyctalope had seen a lot in his life. He couldn't imagine that he could still be surprised. However, he couldn't help feeling a little astonished here. He figured it appropriate, to keep up appearances, to express it and even exaggerate a little.

"Caramba! Where is here? On a barren plateau? Where's the wireless station?"

The Portuguese chuckled and answered, "As you see, this esplanade is big enough for a plane to land on. In the eyes of any rare individual who might somehow stumble upon this place, it's just a big, empty plateau built haphazardly by nature such that it is inaccessible from land because it's surrounded by steep bluffs. From the sea you can only get here like we did. Now watch and don't move until I tell you."

Imagine how Pedro Del Campo and Marco Pampil did indeed watch. The first with his nyctalopic eyes that saw as clearly as day; the second in the moonlight filtering through the thin veil of clouds being scattered by the wind.

Manoël Guerro went twenty feet to the left, pressed both hands on a rock jutting out of the ground and stepped back, spreading his legs into a weird position—he was digging his heels into the ground. Then, less than twenty feet in front of him, a square section of the flat rock slowly opened up like a trapdoor. The Nyctalope and his partner figured that the hinges of the door must have been oiled thoroughly and often. When the huge slab, almost ten feet square and three feet thick was standing vertically, Guerro went back to his natural stance and then walked forward.

"Come on," he threw back at the other two.

Del Campo and Pampil obeyed. When they were next to Guerro at the open trapdoor, they could see the first steps of a staircase plunging into the dark hole. The Nyctalope's acute vision penetrated the darkness. He saw that the stairs turned after 14 steps and dove deeper to the right.

Guerro said, "There are four trapdoors like this on the plateau. You just have to pull a lever inside the wireless station and four columns rise up. It only takes a few minutes to hook up the electrical wires and you can communicate with the Prince of Issyk-Kul and all his secret or public stations that he's organized for his own purposes around the globe."

Pedro Del Campo expressed his wonder, "What a work! So, the cliff is actually full of natural caves? And this plateau was dug out to connect with the caves I guess."

"That's right," Guerro said.

"Still, what a work! The system must need a lot of energy to move the huge slabs so easily and lift the columns?"

"A huge amount of energy," the Portuguese replied. "We get it from an underground river with a really strong current. You'll see it. But before heading down to the station, turn around and you can see where we came from. That natural trench we came through is overlooked not only by this trapdoor but by the four others. You can install four machine guns that can shoot through the barely open doors and since you can only come up the cliff single file and at most three abreast in certain parts of the trench, you understand that this place is impregnable. Plus, if it's attacked by planes, the station is armed with long-range antiaircraft guns that fire rockets through all four doors."

"Incredible! Incredible!" the two others droned together.

"Well then, let's go down."

Guerro led the way. When his foot hit the sixth step, electric lights set deep in the rock lit up. Overhead, the heavy slab dropped slowly, noiselessly back into its airtight frame. Two minutes later, after 38 steps and a narrow corridor, the three men came into a rotunda where several tunnels of varying widths met. With a flick of his hand at a switch, one of the tunnels lit up. They went down it to the end. It was very short and they entered a rectangular room much longer than it was wide with a high ceiling. It looked like a wireless office but with more powerful and sophisticated instruments.

A clean-shaven, young man with red hair wearing white, flannel pajamas and red slippers was casually lying on a lounge chair in the back of the room. On their arrival he opened his eyes, waved briefly, closed his eyes again and apparently tried to get back to the sleep they had interrupted.

Manoël Guerro didn't seem to notice. The Portuguese sat at a table of transmitting equipment and pointed to two stools with his left hand. "You two sit there. I'm going to talk to the Prince."

He donned the headset, pulled over the mouthpiece and after flipping half a dozen ivory switches, he said, "Hello? Issyk-Kul, Adana station here. Yes. I want to speak to the Lord. Hello? Yes, himself. Two minutes? Very well, I'll hold."

He sat still, as if meditating, until a muffled crackling was heard from the switchboard. He looked up and saw a little red flag shoot up in a window and while it slowly disappeared, he started speaking again.

"Hello, hello! Adana station here. Manoël Guerro wants to speak to the Lord. Hello? Yes, Lord, right away."

In a slow but steady voice, in correct if not eloquent French, Guerro told what had happened in the Gulf that night regarding the *Taurus*. He faithfully recounted the explanations given by Del Campo about the sloop, its passenger Jacques Cervier, the rest of the crew and the cargo, as well as how Del Campo and Pampil, the newcomer from Malta after the accidental death of Geronimo, had saved themselves. In short, his account, which included no superfluous words, was strictly accurate.

When he'd finished, a few seconds of silence passed before his voice was heard again, saying, "Very well, Lord, your orders will be carried out."

And very calmly, like an employee just doing his job, he took off the headset. He swung around to the two sailors and said, "Well! The order of the Lord of Issyk-Kul is that you stay here without leaving until the plane shows up to take you to the castle. Like I told you, the Prince will question you himself. I should add, Del Campo, that I'll have the pleasure of accompanying you on the trip because I'll be returning to the castle on the same plane. However, I'm sorry to have to cancel my offer to visit the underground marvels of the Adana station. The Lord's order is to keep you confined. If you give me your word that you won't leave your room, which is very comfortable I might add, I won't lock you in or shackle your feet, which is customary in your case."

The Nyctalope and Marc Ayol didn't hesitate. It never occurred to Del Campo or Pampil that they were anything but guests. If they refused to swear to what Guerro was asking out of courtesy, the refusal alone would make them highly suspicious and they would truly deserve to be treated like dangerous prisoners.

Therefore, Del Campo laughed and answered, "Naturally, I give you my word not to leave the room. Pampil and I are here to obey the Lord's orders, if he deems us fit to receive them, and to obey yours unconditionally. If you want us to swear, we'll do it, but I think it's enough just to say, 'Your wish is our command'."

"Good enough!" Guerro stood up. "The matter is closed. Follow me. Are you hungry or thirsty? You want dinner? We can give it to you in the room. We've got everything here, feel free."

"Well," Pampil said, "myself, I could eat a horse."

"Me too!" Del Campo chimed in.

Fifteen minutes later they were sitting in one of the three rooms that Guerro had given to them: bathroom, a room full of clamps, tools and special bedding for four hammocks, and the third serving as living room, dining room and smoking room. Electric lights in the arched ceiling lit up the rooms that were side by side with a common wall pierced by a long, narrow, deep slot.

"This rocky wall is the outside cliff that overlooks the beach you landed on," Guerro explained. "It faces south. During the day there's plenty of light and air coming through the slot. You'll be fine here, even if you have to wait at least 48 hours, which I believe is the case. You've got books on those shelves in five or six different languages. If you want to do some work with your hands, we can bring you machines, relatively simple ones, to take apart. For now, enjoy the meal, then get some sleep. Later or tomorrow, if you need anything or want to talk to me, press that button there. The Hindu slave at your service will answer right away and you just have to tell him what you want... Oh, do you speak English? Because not only is it his native language, but it's the only one he knows."

"Yes," Del Campo replied. "I can babble enough to get by and I understand no problem."

"Then everything's set. I myself am pretty tired, so I'm going to my room to get some sleep. Good night."

Manoël Guerro shook hands with Del Campo and Pampil and with a brief smile that lit up his grumpy face, he nodded to them. Then he turned around and walked out, leaving the door to swing closed by itself behind him.

Having eaten and drunk heartily and liberally, if not zealously, Del Campo and Pampil let ten minutes or so pass before Saint-Clair stared at this partner so that the magnetism in his eyes made him look up.

The two men read each other's minds. They shook hands across the table and a big smile brightened their wearied faces. But they didn't say a word. What for? They knew what each other would say and the response they would give. But they were so happy that they couldn't help shaking hands and smiling at each other.

Then each of them went back to his own thoughts. Leo Saint-Clair was thinking of the flight of thousands of miles and imagining the fanciful castle of Issyk-Kul. He wondered, "What is Sylvie Mac Duhl doing? And Leonid Zattan, what's he planning to do with her?"

CHAPTER VI

Sylvie Mac Duhl and Leonid Zattan! Ah, the drama had already unfolded in the castle of Issyk-Kul!

During the flight from the sea around Malta to the isolated lake in the mountains of Tian Shan, the young woman had not said a word. She was sunk comfortably into a padded bucket seat installed in a kind of tiny, luxurious compartment in the middle of the plane's main cabin.

The prisoner excepted everything that Ali Soud and Zattan himself offered her so attentively. The electric heater for her feet, gorgeous furs for her body, the privilege to be alone in the next compartment with a private bathroom and a comfortable armchair—the young lady had nothing to complain about, not just concerning the necessities but for her mere comfort too.

Occasionally, Ali Soud gave her some tasty fruit or an exquisite perfume, Turkish pastries, jams, coffee, champagne or pure, fresh water, exotically flavored if she desired. The Lord of Issyk-Kul came in person to beg her to accept a box of cigarettes from the Orient.

Calm, stoic, her big eyes showing no feeling other than a cold assurance of her own safety, Sylvie Mac Duhl ate what she liked, drank as much or as little as she wanted, and slept. But waking or sleeping, not a word passed her lips. After Zattan tried asking two or three questions concerning their present circumstances, he understood that the will to total silence was firmly fixed in the prisoner's mind. He didn't press her.

Leaving on March 25th at 6 pm from the spot in the Ionian Sea where the *Aquilon* had joined the *Taurus*, the plane arrived at Lake Issyk-Kul the next day, March 26th, at a little past 4 pm. The 3,500 miles over Asia Minor, the Caspian Sea, the transcaspian countries and the western range of the Tian Shan was covered at 180 mph.

Safely and skillfully piloting the plane, Petrus Ivitch landed on the big aviation platform at the Issyk Castle. The huge windows were open so the plane could enter its ingenious garage. When lieutenant-secretary Woldski came running up alone as usual on his master's arrival, Zattan introduced his right-hand man to Sylvie Mac Duhl.

"Mademoiselle, please accept the honor of my hospitality in my castle."

Ali Soud had hurried to open the separate door in the hull to the prisoner's compartment. The shiny metal ladder was already waiting. Still stoic, fixing her willfully blank eyes at nothing in particular, she placed her bare hand on Zattan's gloved fist and descended gracefully.

Woldski bowed deeply. The Prince shot him an order as they passed by. "Follow us!" And without saying a word to Ivitch, who was busy anyway inspecting his machine, the Lord of Issyk-Kul went down corridors, across rotundas, up elevators and led Sylvie Mac Duhl to the south tower.

Zattan's own rooms were on the second floor of this tower. As soon as the capture of Sylvie had been reported from the Baleares Islands, he had sumptuously fitted out the third floor, which was connected to the second not only by the big tower stairway next to an elevator, but also by a smaller, spiral staircase dug out of the thick wall. Of course, this second staircase was never used by the servants and only rarely by Zattan or specially authorized personnel.

The rooms reserved for the prisoner had the exact same architectural layout as those below, meaning Sylvie's bedroom was directly above Zattan's. The study/workroom on the second floor had been replaced by a parlor room on the third, which could be quickly changed into a pleasant dining room. The smoking room below corresponded to a very elegant, oriental sitting room above. All the windows looking out over the lake and facing south were barred on the outside.

When the Lord of Issyk-Kul, still supporting Sylvie's beautiful white hand with his closed fist, reached the third-floor landing in front of the double doors that led into the antechamber, he stopped and motioned with his right hand toward the lieutenant-secretary.

Woldski stepped forward and opened the door with a key that was hanging on a big ring from his belt. He bowed deeply again, backed away and disappeared. Presenting the open door with a flourish, Zattan smiled gently and spoke courteously.

"Mademoiselle, I hope you will be pleased with the rooms I have prepared for you. If I miscalculated your tastes in one thing or another, please tell me what you prefer and it will be immediately remedied. Three servants are at your disposal. They know French and English. One of them is a compatriot of yours since she comes from Paris. You will meet them in a minute. You may question them at will so you can use them as you think best.

"I beg you to relax tonight, make any changes you want to the arrangement or decoration of your rooms. The day after tomorrow, only after you've had time to settle in, think about things and maybe make some decisions, I will come back to talk with you and perhaps the greatest dream ever granted a man might finally appear attainable."

After this casual speech, Zattan let her hand drop gently. Then, bowing low, he took three steps back.

Sylvie had listened, cold and calm, without turning her head even a fraction of an inch towards him. She was facing the open door. When the terrible but gentle man had finished talking, she showed no sign that she had heard a word he said. She just stepped gingerly over the threshold and entered the room.

Behind her, Leonid Zattan was standing straight again, watching her walk up to the three servants waiting at the back of the antechamber and with a slightly devilish smile on his face he leaned forward, arms outstretched, reached for the doors and closed them.

Of course, Zattan's discreet politeness was only a façade. In reality, he had organized everything and trained everyone so that not one gesture, not one word, not one movement of his prisoner would be unknown to him if he so chose to be informed.

With a scientific and very devious arrangement of mirrors and devices conceived and created along the lines of a periscope, with an extremely sophisticated system of microtelephones and acoustic tubes, the rooms on the third floor were, for the man living underneath, a veritable glass cage and no less veritable sound box. Not only was he able to see Sylvie at every moment, not only was he able to hear even the lowest whisper she might pronounce, but with the mirrors watching her when she thought she was alone and letting her eyes express her inner thoughts, the diabolical man could spy on even these most intimate moments.

Moreover, the three specially trained servants had their orders concerning Sylvie Mac Duhl. Knowing that their slightest slip up against their master would be punished with torture and maybe death afterwards, these three servants were spies who would see, observe and hear everything and give regular reports about it.

If Sylvie had any suspicions about the scientific installments that revealed everything to the Lord of the castle, or about the domestic spying she was subject to, she was wise enough not to let it show.

She systematically accepted the Parisian servant as her chambermaid. A svelte and pretty woman of about 30 years-old, unoriginally called Marie, who proved right away to have nimble hands, graceful movements, a lively intelligence and the professional qualities normally required of a chambermaid who must wash and clean, brush and comb, do the nails and even massage her mistress... For, the prisoner—on the advice of the Nyctalope—had decided to fight against the boredom of captivity and the distress of the looming unknown by fostering (with all the benefits of her athletic training) her natural powers of beauty and elegance with meticulous care. Furthermore, like this—the Nyctalope had added—her moral force and mental lucidity had a better chance to remain intact. There was no point in neglecting herself morally or physically— that was the rule of life she adopted in her captivity, which would probably have some very singular adventures that would demand that she be strong in every way.

The two other English servants—Edith and Lucy—were assigned less intimate functions than those accorded to the French Marie.

After closely inspecting the five rooms, Sylvie demanded only one change. The bedroom and the bathroom were connected by two doors separated by a hallway that was turned into a large closet. And respectively, the bedroom door opened onto the sitting room that itself led to the parlor and then the antechamber while the bathroom on the other side also opened onto the rotunda-like antechamber.

"Marie," the prisoner said, "let Monsieur Zattan know that I will not eat or sleep, I will force myself to stay awake and I will never talk to him until the bathroom door connected directly to the antechamber and the bedroom door to the sitting room are fitted with deadbolts on the inside. I want to be able to lock myself in when I'm sleeping and dressing."

Marie bowed and picked up the telephone in the antechamber that put the third floor of the south tower in touch with the rest of the castle and with the Lord's personal apartment. The maidservant spoke quietly, trying to transmit Marie's request in the same terms she used.

Five minutes later lieutenant-secretary Woldski was there, as formal as ever, followed by a black man in blue overalls who promptly installed the two locks. Asking Sylvie respectfully to verify the work, she turned the deadbolt open and closed.

"That's fine," Sylvie said, "thank you, monsieur."

The Lord of Issyk-Kul and Tian Shan must have been very well informed about Sylvie in advance because when she went into the closet she was surprised to find all the clothes and shoes not only to her liking and very elegant but they were all exactly her size. She didn't wait to try them on. They had left the *Taurus* with only a chest containing some modest jewelry, photographs of her mother and father, and some souvenirs of personal value only. She was particularly satisfied to see a wide assortment of silk and wool loungewear. She really appreciated feeling physically comfortable and nothing pleased her more than pajamas as long as she could use them freely and carelessly and change them often.

The detailed examination of her prison took all of March 26th until dinner, which was served in her parlor. Marie had shown her the menu from which the captive had picked out all she wanted since her fortitude, stronger than ever thanks to knowing that the Nyctalope was involved, was able to push deep down inside her any worries she might have had and therefore she could eat and sleep normally.

She ate and drank, thought everything tasted good and it was. When she got up from that table, she had a smile and a word of appreciation to the chef of Issyk-Kul. Marie promised to deliver the praise. After smoking two cigarettes and drinking a lemon verbena tea, Sylvie said goodnight to her servant and retired to the bedroom where she locked the door. She went to check the lock on the bathroom door, then got ready and went to bed. She was so perfectly calm and collected that she fell asleep almost immediately.

She spent the next day moving some of the furniture a little and organizing her daily routine with Marie: washing and dressing, meals, private strolls along the ramparts and accompanied walks by the lake, excursions into the nearby mountains, also accompanied, she thought about everything, found out about everything until she knew everything she could.

On March 27th she didn't leave her rooms. But the second night was not as good as the first. With the physical and mental activity of the day complete, with everything the young lady had to sort out settled, her mind got stuck on one single thought:

"Leonid Zattan will talk to me tomorrow. What's he going to say? What does he want from me? Will I understand the mysteries of the adventures that have battered me since the death of my father?"

On the morning of the 28th, before breakfast, Sylvie Mac Duhl took a cold shower and rubbed herself vigorously with alcohol, then she got dressed for a horse ride: soft boots with spurs, pants, a flannel shirt with a buttoned-up collar, a tight jacket and she put in plain sight the gloves, helmet and riding crop.

After breakfast she told Marie, "Tell Monsieur Zattan that I'd like to take a horse ride on this beautiful, chilly morning."

Five minutes later Marie came back with the answer. "The Lord asks the pleasure of accompanying you."

Sylvie thought his courtesy could be dangerous but her courage had not shrunk. Since today was to be their first conversation anyway, it was better to be out in the fresh air, in the mountains, moving, than in a stuffy room feeling too much like a prisoner. Plus, if she didn't want to answer a question or wanted to change the subject, it would be easy to pretend her horse was acting up.

She simply said, "He is the master and can do as he wants."

Impassively, Marie bowed and left.

Two minutes later Woldski showed up and in his naturally respectful voice without a hint of severity, even a little graciously, he said, "If you would be pleased to follow me, mademoiselle, I will take you to main courtyard where the Lord is waiting for you with the horses."

Between the high, crenelated walls, between the main buildings of the castle and the two huge towers standing over the portcullis and drawbridge, the main courtyard lay spotless under the bright sun in the dry, chilly morning air. On the steps, Woldski bowed and said goodbye. With her helmet fastened tightly, her gloves buttoned up, the riding crop in hand, the young lady stood still for a moment on the steps as the door gently closed behind her. There was only one man and two horses in the vast courtyard. He hurried over to Sylvie. He looked very martial in his equestrian outfit, but a little pale, too.

She mused: "I seem to be less nervous than he is. Maybe I am. It's because I know nothing about the role I'm playing in this game and I don't even know what's at stake. He knows! It must be extremely important."

All of a sudden, her heart skipped a beat and her throat clenched but she was fully conscious of her nervousness so by force of will she was able to fight against it.

"I have to be strong," she thought. "I have to act as if the Nyctalope was always watching me."

Recalling Leo Saint-Clair was a comfort to her. Casually, with a calm but serious face, her gorgeous blue eyes wide open and serenely inexpressive, she walked down the stairs. The bizarre tyrant was waiting for her at the bottom. He took off his helmet, which was almost the same as Sylvie's but more militant-looking, and he bowed slightly.

He smiled when he said, "Mademoiselle, allow me to congratulate you on your courage."

She raised her eyebrows, surprised, or pretending to be, as naturally as possible.

He continued, "But of course! You're a prisoner. You should be worried about your fate, tortured by anxiety and curiosity, it's only natural. Don't deny it! If your denial were real, you'd be a callous, coldblooded monster or else completely resigned to your fate. But I know too much about the upbringing of Sylvie Mac Duhl, the Parisian, daughter of a Scotsman and a French woman, to believe in this callousness or the resignation. Therefore, you must have phenomenal courage seeing that you look as fresh and rosy, as calm and alert as if you were leaving your villa in Saint-Jean Cap-Ferrat to take a ride over to Eze."

He looked at her with real admiration.

But she just took it in stride with marvelous poise, "You talk a lot, monsieur, without saying much. I hope the conversation you alluded to the day before yesterday won't be spent with you rattling off vain compliments that I can't respond to."

The Lord of Issyk-Kul wasn't used to such affrontery. But he was a good and able sportsman. If he bit his lip and had a flash of anger in his eyes, it was only for a second. He quickly put his helmet back on and shot back, "You're right, mademoiselle, and your response tells me once and for all what my attitude must be with respect to you."

He paused, smiled ambiguously, leered a little, and then spoke more plainly.

"Let's get on the horses. That one is for you. They aren't exceptional beasts. At the Paris Horse Show they'd make a sorry spectacle. But for walking or trotting, even galloping on the challenging paths of our mountains, these horses have no equal."

He held a stirrup for her and with a graceful spring she swung herself into the saddle.

He was no less graceful in his more virile leap onto his horse.

Right away, almost automatically, the portcullis rose up and the drawbridge dropped down. And the two riders trotted out of the castle of Issyk-Kul.

She had glanced over Leonid Zattan and noticed that he was carrying no weapon, at least in plain sight. His riding crop was exactly the same as hers. On the ground he seemed much taller than his prisoner but it was mostly in his legs so that on horseback their heads were at the same level.

In the wild environs around Lake Issyk-Kul, there were no roads. The lanes were nothing but mountain paths. But the previous year, the Lord of Issyk-Kul had dug out and built a real cliff road twenty miles long going from the biggest fishing village of the area, called Nadpoul, to the city or rather the town of Karakol, administrative capital of the "realm" of Tian Shan.

It was on this road, but towards Nadpoul, that the two horses were trotting after crossing the drawbridge.

With a physical joy that she reveled in, the athlete in Sylvie inhaled the fresh air full of woodland scents, bounced in rhythm with her horse and filled her eyes with the space, light and colors. Even though the weather had been nice and the sun shining for days in Issyk-Kul, there was still a lot of snow in the ravines and hollows and under the trees at the base of the mountain—the steep sides and the summit were, of course, still completely white with the winter snow. But the huge lake, with its rippling, glistening, blue water, with its almost tropical vegetation on the shores, with its pleasant coves where nearly greenhouse temperatures were kept up by natural hot springs so that the fruit trees were already blooming their white and pink flowers, yes this lake was a springtime wonder.

When the horses slowed down of their own accord, Sylvie couldn't help murmuring, almost unconsciously, how physically satisfied she was in the luminous, odorous vitality of this splendid morning.

"My God, it's so pleasant, so beautiful!"

"It's up to you, mademoiselle, whether all this beauty will be yours forever."

What a thing to say! How weird! And that panting, hoarse voice he said it in!

For Sylvie it was a brutal shock that shook her out of her reverie, hurt her, but also put her on guard, hardened her. She was back to herself in no time and abruptly thrown back into another reality, a reality represented by Leonid Zattan.

The young lady only hesitated for two or three seconds... Then with her mind made up, armed with all her strength, thinking once again about the Nyctalope, she reined in her horse and stopped. Turning her head a little, she said, "What do you mean, monsieur?"

But Zattan was already back in control of himself. A savage desire had inflamed him when watching the pure and pretty girl getting carried away in her equestrian joy, in the brisk air of the serene morning amongst this magical landscape. And this desire had provoked him into making that comment, which he immediately knew was unworthy of him. But come now! Wasn't this girl his prisoner? Whether she liked it or not, wouldn't she be a slave to his fancies whenever he decided to make her so? Was he going crazy, all of a sudden, giving her the right to choose, in a way? To decide for herself by telling her stupidly, childishly, "It's up to you"? What was she going to think of the omnipotence of the Lord of Issyk-Kul? He was humiliated by his loss of control. And this humiliation was flogging him. Right away he jumped back into his menacing, mysterious role. To her question he responded deviously, in his calm and habitually callous voice.

"Mademoiselle, if the decision you are soon going to make agrees with what I believe to be one of two alternatives for your destiny, all this beautiful country around you will be the grounds of your private domain, a domain that will extend over all of Europe and the vast expanse of Asia."

This was all completely incomprehensible to Sylvie. With the sincere naivety that was one of her strengths, she said, "I don't understand, monsieur. Please explain yourself."

Expressionless, eyes half-closed, he answered, "Not here, mademoiselle, and not on horseback. What Leonid Zattan has to reveal to you is so important that the most crucial speech of a statesman on the eve of war, for example, is childish in comparison. Please swing your bridle around. We'll go back to the castle. I will show you the documents and I will tell you what you are..."

Surprised but wary, she declared, "I am Sylvie Mac Duhl whom you have kidnapped and are holding prisoner against the law, both human and divine..."

"And you think that's all?" he asked with no hint of mockery.

"What else could I be?"

His voice betrayed a little impatience when he repeated, this time as a master giving orders, "Turn around, mademoiselle, we're going back to the castle."

She obeyed. She knew how absolutely futile it was to rebel. A well-mannered young lady with the clear, rigorous, quick and ready mind of a woman raised tough, she followed orders and without breaking her somewhat haughty calm, she spun her horse around.

The ride back was short because it was barely 10 am when they entered the castle. Standing in the courtyard at the bottom of the steps leading up to the main building, the man finally spoke again.

"Please accept my invitation to continue our conversation in my rooms."

"As you want," Sylvie shrugged her shoulders.

"Would you like to change your clothes?"

"No, I'm just fine like this."

"My turn to say 'as you want.' Allow me to show you the way."

The prisoner had already noticed that behind the medieval fortress façade, the interior of the castle of Issyk-Kul was as modern as a New York skyscraper. So, she wasn't surprised to see the doors open automatically just before they walked through them or to hear the warning bells at times or to enter an elevator.

When she was in the study/workroom of the Lord of Issyk-Kul, she admired the tasteful luxury, practical and comfortable, of the tapestries, carpets, furniture, bookshelves, all the various electric light fixtures, the electric telephone and wireless devices—all in the bright and cheery sunlight pouring in through the big bay windows.

Following his sweeping gesture, she sat down in a leather armchair at a corner of the huge desk that he sat behind. Of course, the young lady was agitated, burning with impatient curiosity. But she kept a calm face, a distant stoicism. She felt good to be in masculine clothes: boots, pants, a buttoned-up jacket, a riding crop in her gloved hands. Her legs were crossed with the helmet sitting on one knee. She felt strong, ready for a physical fight, let alone any kind of mental or moral battle.

Yes, for a physical fight. Because when she had stopped on the road to turn around and ask "What do you mean?", she'd seen an unsettling glimmer in Zattan's eyes that her woman's intuition and her young life knew from experience since she'd often seen it in Monte Carlo, for example. Therefore, she feared the worst and was ready to go on the defensive, if necessary, in an all-out battle. She feared the worst—but she was not scared!

Thanks to his adventurous life in which he had encountered the most refined societies of the civilized world as well as the feudal ways of eastern societies, Leonid Zattan was familiar with the countless facets of feminine psychology. Since that short scene that had been the excuse for coming back to the castle, he had been closely observing his prisoner. As willfully inexpressive as her big, blue eyes were, he could read her thoughts in them like an open book.

When they were sitting together, he slowly pulled off his gloves, put them on the table, leaned back a little in his office chair, crossed his arms and put on his solemn, sophisticated face that revealed nothing of the Kalmyk's savage severity.

"Mademoiselle, I'll get right down to it without any useless preliminaries. But I ask you, unconditionally, not to lie... Yes, not to lie! I'm going to have to ask you some questions. Either answer clearly and truthfully or don't answer at all. For my part, I give you my word to do the same if you have any questions for me. Playing games, trying to outwit each other is, first of all, unworthy of us, and secondly, it will make it impossible to explain this very serious situation that I know must be clarified..."

He paused. She was thinking. Then, slowly, looking straight into her enemy's eyes, she said, "I give you my word, monsieur. When I speak, I will tell the truth."

"Thank you." And right after, "Do you know, mademoiselle, what work all that wealth stowed away secretly on your *Taurus* was meant for?"

She raised her eyebrows in surprise, but she answered without delay, "What work? No, I don't know. My father had me swear to transport it secretly without giving me an explanation. My mission was to use the Taurus to take it to a certain place where I was supposed to give the treasure to a certain man. That's all I know."

He smiled, satisfied, and said, "The place is Ushant Island, the man is Mathias Lumen."

She showed no reaction.

He didn't let the silence drag out. Right away, he asked another question.

"Did your father ever talk to you about a certain prophecy of Nostradamus?"

Again she looked surprised and didn't try to hide it. "A prophecy of Nostradamus? My father never mentioned the name to me and certainly never spoke of any prophecy."

"So, you know nothing about it," Zattan was visibly upset.

"I don't even know what 'it' is, obviously," she said.

He uncrossed his arms, locked his fingers together, cracked his bony knuckles and with his head lowered and his brow furrowed, he pondered.

He pondered a long time, watched closely by the attentive and intrigued young lady. Once again, she felt—like with her father sometimes, like with the Nyctalope on the *Taurus*—that she was on the verge of a tremendous mystery that her fate would undoubtedly penetrate sooner or later. And her soul, despite the muddled torment, was more curious than frightened. Was she going to find out today? Were the doors of the Unknown about to open? This strange man knew something, certainly. Maybe he even knew everything. Was he going to talk? She desperately hoped so. And while watching the spirited, passionate, disturbing face of an obviously extraordinary man, Sylvie Mac Duhl awaited.

At last, Zattan looked up. He was calm, a little pale, his eyes hard and cold. He spoke bluntly. "In this case, mademoiselle, I have no more questions for you. And I have nothing more to say to you, at least for today. I'll tell you right now that I won't answer any questions you might have for me if they are in any way related to the formidable problem whose solution Mathias Lumen and I, irreconcilable and mortal enemies, have devoted our lives to. Now, if do have any other questions, feel free to ask—I'll answer with the truth or simply refuse."

Sylvie was crushed. She didn't even try to wipe the frown off her face, which revealed her disappointment. She was also annoyed. But she had the presence of mind not to show this too feminine oversensitivity. She shrugged her shoulders and without changing position (legs crossed with the helmet on her knee and gloved hands holding the whip) she said, "Monsieur, how long do you intend to keep me prisoner here?"

He answered briskly, "In truth, I really don't know."

"What do you get out of depriving me of my freedom?"

"A great deal."

"But what?"

"I won't tell you today."

"But some other day?"

"I hope so."

"You hope so!" she raised her voice.

He replied very coldly, "Don't press me, mademoiselle. I won't tell you the whys or wherefores of this hope."

"And if I try to escape?" she challenged.

He smirked and waved his hand, "Try! But rest assured, you won't succeed."

She was about to show her bravado, her defiance, but saw the childishness of it and stayed quiet. After a short pause, she said, "And if I ask you about Mathias Lumen, about your relationship with him, the reasons for your antagonism, about this mysterious work you referred to?"

"Mademoiselle, I'm sorry to say I won't respond."

"That's the problem?"

"That is the problem."

She grabbed her helmet and stood up. Icily, "Well then, monsieur, we have nothing more to talk about. Please have someone show me back to my rooms."

"I'll be honored to show you myself."

Three minutes later, Sylvie was locked in her bedroom, lying on the bed and surrendering every fiber of her being to unwinding her nerves, which she needed badly. She started crying, deeply, madly sobbing.

CHAPTER VII

What, then, were the plans and projects of Leonid Zattan with respect to Sylvie? On what upcoming events did a second and fruitless conversation with the young lady depend? The Lord of Issyk-Kul had all kinds of officers, collaborators, soldiers and servants, but no friends, no confidants. If he had any plans and projects, if he had anything specific laid out, he had told no one. He kept observing his prisoner, kept spying on her by all the means at his disposal. But he didn't interfere in the routine, monotonous life of Sylvie Mac Duhl who seemed to be patient and, in all appearances, very courageous.

The month of March came to an end without anything new happening at the castle of Issyk-Kul with respect to the prisoner.

The "delegate" from Moscow showed up. The visit was expected and, we remember, the subject of Zattan's menacing instructions to Woldski. But he left without incident.

And the Lord of Issyk-Kul waited for news of the arrival of the *Taurus* in the Gulf of Adana so he could send two transport planes to pick up the precious cargo from the sloop. But on the night of March 31st, Zattan was awakened by the officer on duty at the wireless and was told about the fire and destruction of the Taurus, the death of Jacques Cervier and the rest of the crew except for two men: Pedro Del Campo and a Marcio Pampil who were awaiting the prince's orders at the Adana station.

Zattan couldn't doubt the truth of this information sent personally by his service chief Manoël Guerro. He couldn't suspect that Pedro Del Campo was the famous Leo Saint-Clair the Nyctalope, that Marco Pampil was a cover for Captain Marc Ayol, that Cervier and his cohorts were locked up on the *Fulgur* under the command of Gnô Mitang, the former factotum of Gregor Mac Duhl and lastly that the *Taurus* had been emptied of its cargo and burned intentionally by the two men sitting in the Adana Station.

Therefore, the Lord of Issyk-Kul, as was fitting, believed the truth of the bad news being very respectfully communicated by Guerro. And so bad was this news that Zattan shook and turned white with rage as he listened to the nasal voice over the radiotelephone.

But Zattan knew how to rein in his anger when there was no one person to blame for a mishap, failure or other misfortune. On the other hand, he had a long-standing, well purposed habit of learning every detail of an event when he felt his personal involvement was called for. Therefore, he ordered Manoël Guerro to keep the two survivors locked up in the station until one of the planes could bring them back to the castle.

On his orders in the morning, one of his three spy planes at Issyk-Kul took off immediately. A little after sunrise on the next day, April 2nd, the plane returned. It was met by Woldski who introduced himself by name, rank and function. The lieutenant-secretary put a few questions to Pedro Del Campo and Marco Pampil, then he led them to the Prince.

Leonid Zattan was in a bad mood. He hadn't come to terms with the disaster, which was all the more serious because he had lost Jacques Cervier whose knowledge, zeal, activity, devotion and ingenuity had been so useful to him and would've been even more so in the near future. He was more affected by the loss of this man than by the loss of the great sum of money in the cargo of the *Taurus*. Nevertheless, since he had been counting on this money, the fact that he no longer had it was hard.

He was also thinking sourly about Pedro Del Campo who, as captain of the sloop, could be somewhat responsible for the accident that sank the precious ship along with poor Jacques Cervier.

In his horse-riding outfit, sitting in his rolling armchair at the big desk, Zattan stared coldly and severely at the two men standing side by side, hats in hand, across from him. Their rough, hairy faces—they hadn't cut their hair for at least two weeks nor shaved for several days—were both alert and respectful: faces of good old sailors after a shipwreck who have to face the all-powerful owner who had the indisputable right to be unhappy, to say the least.

Zattan recognized Del Campo's face. On the *Taurus* he'd taken note of its keen intelligence and calm energy. At this moment, right here, in the light of the sun flooding the room, he saw nothing less and nothing more in this face except, as to be expected, alertness and respect. But the face of Marco Pampil was unknown to him. Fooled by the naivety that the alleged sailor, allegedly hired in Malta, knew how to adopt when necessary, Zattan didn't pay much attention to him. "Just another sailor." Even a more astute man than Zattan would have been fooled.

Shifting his cold, hard eyes back to Del Campo, he said in Spanish, "How is it that you, whom I see as an experienced ship captain, let a sloop burn so badly that the entire crew perished? Being so near the coast, how come you didn't run aground on the reefs to at least save the cargo? Answer!"

"By the will of God and the Devil," Del Campo muttered.

And his voice immediately got louder, obviously grieved but without remorse or shame, he went through the story again, the same account he had given Manoël Guerro.

"It was the middle of the night. Ramuz and Barbone were on duty on deck. Cervier and Tchicoz were sleeping in their rear cabins. Me and Pampil were asleep in the forecastle—I preferred the hammock there instead of the bunks because I'm used to it and it's not so stuffy. Pampil woke me up. I must've been half-suffocated already. The place was full of smoke so me and Pampil went on deck. Flames were everywhere already. Ramuz and Barbone by the helm were dead drunk, still holding the brandy bottles they must've stolen from the storeroom or galley. How and where did the fire start? I have no idea. The *Taurus* had been painted and varnished recently. The whole stern was aflame. It was too late to get pumps going to spray the hold. It wouldn't have done any good anyway—the fire was already burning the framework. Me and Pampil tried to get into the cabins for Cervier and Tchicoz. Couldn't do it. The fire barred the passage. Plus, the door of the deckhouse was locked. I have no idea what or who Cervier was afraid of to lock himself in like that. Look, there were three barrels of gunpowder in the back of the hold. For me and Pampil to get blown up with the boat would've been easy. We just had to putter around for a couple of minutes before throwing the skiff in the water. I knew that our lives belonged to Your Excellency, señor, and might still be of use. And I knew Marco—he loves life as much as I do. Therefore, duty called us not to sacrifice our lives because there was no point in it. So, we flung the skiff as soon as I was sure Cervier and Tchicoz had been charred or at least suffocated... We weren't far from the burning ship when the gunpowder blew it up. He ahi, amo mio!" With this, "That's it, my master!", which was both sorrowful and respectful, but also proud, calm and decisive, Pedro Del Campo stopped talking.

What response could be given? What blame? After hearing this report, Zattan had no reason to doubt the tiniest detail. The guilty parties were Ramuz and Barbone for stealing the brandy from the storeroom probably and then dropping a lighted match or tipping over a candle. They were both dead.

But the Lord of Issyk-Kul thought of something. In the same cold, hard voice he asked further, "Why didn't you save Ramuz and Barbone? They were drunk, sure, but you didn't have to waste time waking them up or explaining anything, you could've just picked them up and thrown them into the dinghy. Answer."

"I thought of that, señor! But to do what Your Excellency just said, it would've taken two minutes: one for each drunk. The boat blew up right after me and Pampil left, less than a minute after... I calculated correctly. If we'd saved Ramuz and Barbone, we'd have died with them. And if they'd accidentally started the fire, I do believe God punished them for it. Amen!"

Amen! Indeed, there was nothing more and nothing better to say. Del Campo's somewhat solemn calm had appeased the impetuous though intelligent Kalmyk. He suppressed his bitter disappointment of losing Jacques Cervier and his regret for not possessing the Mac Duhl treasure. He spoke again in a less cold, less hard tone.

"Very well. I believe you have nothing to be blamed for. But I won't trust you, Pedro Del Campo, until I've put you to the test. Get out of here, you two. Orders have been given concerning you."

Del Campo put his hand to his forehead and bowed, but only slightly and very proudly as if he were a Castilian who was, through his ancestors, still a hidalgo. More a commoner and knowing it, Marco Pampil bowed more deeply and raised both hands. Then, the two men marched out, side by side, leaving the brooding Prince of Tian Shan to his private thoughts.

In the antechamber, Woldski awaited them in person. No special alarm bell went off. Therefore, the two sailors had been absolved and not sentenced to death.

Now, as ex-captain of the *Taurus* and future commander of the big, secret fleet of the sovereign prince, Pedro Del Campo had an officer's rank in Issyk-Kul.

Woldski held out his hand, smiled and said in French, "Monsieur, I'm going to take you to your room. You'll eat at the officers' table. A black slave from Cuba who speaks Spanish will be your special assistant. He'll sleep in front of your door. But if you want to keep this sailor as a personal servant, you may. Outside the duty hours you set he'll still take orders from the other officers."

The Nyctalope was thinking "Damn, there's order and discipline at the Issyk-Kul castle!"

He quickly responded, "At your service, Lieutenant-Secretary. I'll keep Marco Pampil as my assistant."

Woldski led them first into the "clothes store." What they were wearing was all that they had. It was expected. The regulations of Issyk-Kul stipulated different outfits for different ranks and special insignia for certain duties. Del Campo and Pampil received what they needed. For the officer the head tailor of the castle altered the clothes. The "sailor" had to make do with what they gave him, which fit pretty well. They also got towels and toiletries.

Then on the third floor of the main building where all the passageways to the other towers were closed and guarded night and day by armed sentinels, Del Campo was brought into the room where he would stay for the remainder of his visit to Issyk-Kul. The door was just like the twenty others lining the long, wide hallway except it had the number 13.

Saint-Clair thought, "Good, 13 has always been a lucky number for me."

Pointing to the deeply set doorframe Woldski explained, "Your servant will sleep here on a mattress that he'll carry up every night and take away every morning. His name's Toma." He opened the door.

The Nyctalope and Marc Ayol noticed that the lock, a simple latch, had no keyhole or deadbolt. "You can't lock yourself in," they both thought. "And the black will be a guard as well as a servant."

With a bathroom on one side, the room was huge, lit by two windows with small, square panes, no shutters but thick, iron bars on the outside. There was an iron-frame bed, a massive wardrobe of dark wood, a big table in the middle, a small bedside table, a wicker rocking chair, four other chairs and a very beautiful carpet covering almost the entire tiled floor. Such was the furniture.

No fireplace or radiator. Three electric lights, one on the ceiling, a lamp on the table and one on the wall of the bathroom, which was, incidentally, completely modern and immaculately clean.

Pedro Del Campo had just finished making the tour of his "jail" when a tall, half-dressed black man appeared in the doorway. He was carrying a basket full of clothes, shoes, caps, towels and various toiletries for his new, temporary master.

"Toma!" Woldski exclaimed. And turning to Pampil, "You, sailor, follow me. I'll take you to the room with your things. When you've finished setting yourself up, you can read the regulations about the officers' servants on duty, then come back here and await your master's orders.

With a relatively friendly smile, he held out his hand to Del Campo and said, "When you're ready, Toma can show you to the library. You have your choice of books, pen and paper, pencils, whatever you need to read and write. You're free to work there in the library or in your room."

"Bah!" Del Campo spit out as naturally as could be and shrugged his shoulders.

Woldski laughed and explained, "A lot of officers passing through here kill time by writing stories of their adventures. Some work on philosophy or history... Oh, there are all kinds of men, from all over the world, with all kinds of intellects passing through Issyk-Kul. For the few weeks you're here, you'll see... But I have to leave you. I have other duties outside of being your welcoming committee today. I'll see you again at lunch. You'll soon know what you can and should be doing here at Issyk-Kul. Ask Toma for whatever you need. The regulations are very broad and generous. Goodbye, captain."

He left with a beckoning wave to Marco Pampil who fell in right behind him.

A day later Saint-Clair knew what he could and couldn't do according to the regulations during his disguised captivity that was, for the moment, his goal. Reading, writing, playing cards, backgammon, chess in the library, in the smoking room or in his room, strolling along the circular ramparts or in the courtyards, playing tennis or "boules" in the specially designed areas, boxing, stick fighting, fencing, shooting, sleeping when tired, eating when hungry, drinking when thirsty, chatting with the officers or with his slave Pampil, smoking cigarettes, cigars, pipes and nargilehs and comparing the fifty different types of tobacco, and finally, horseback riding in the wonderful ring, along the walls or between the north and east towers—all this permitted.

But he was forbidden from going into the main courtyard, entering the towers or the donjon, going into the storerooms and cellars, crossing the drawbridge and leaving the castle. Moreover, the places off-limit were guarded by special troops, exclusively Kalmyks, from the elite corps of Prince Zattan.

Having learned all this and watching the "officers" who were his messmates, either passing through like him or assigned to Issyk permanently, Leo Saint-Clair considered, "Marc and I have no one to count on but ourselves. I've learned from the table talk that a pretty girl has been on the third floor of the south tower for a few days and Zattan lives on the second floor of the same tower. That's all. Nothing can be done during the day. A hundred eyes are watching and the guards, sentinels, lookouts and patrols are everywhere. So be it! But, by God, I'm not the Nyctalope for nothing!"

Saint-Clair told all that he heard, saw and deduced during the 24 hours of his voluntary confinement at Issyk-Kul to Marc Ayol on April 3rd at 2 pm. After a cup of Turkish coffee, the after-lunch ritual, the "captain" had called his assistant to practice fencing with him. The sailor was a good blade since he'd been provost in the navy on board a Spanish cruiser—or so he told his temporary comrades in the mess hall and barracks.

During this lazy time after the meal the fencing room was empty. While in a stance the two swordsmen could converse without fear of being heard by some invisible "rat" spying on them.

Marc Ayol scowled. "So, I'm completely useless to you."

"First of all, no!" Saint-Clair replied. "At night you're in your bunk and it's at night that I can act, meaning search the place, find things out, get things ready."

"Right."

"But then if I get in a really tough spot or chances are better for two to succeed, you'll come and help me. In the meantime, find a way to sneak out at night so you can join me if I need you."

"Okay."

"Also think about getting yourself a weapon: knife, axe, cudgel, whatever. I've got an excellent sword that I can get to."

"Good."

"Do you have any news for me?"

"No."

"That's all I have to tell you. En guard, Pampil!"

"All set, captain!"

Saint-Clair didn't know if his stay at Issyk-Kul, at least for whatever Zattan planned, would last three days or three weeks. When and what was this "trial" the prince wanted to put him through? It was imperative, therefore, that Saint-Clair act quickly to get in touch with Sylvie Mac Duhl, tell her about the sloop and its cargo, about the crew of thugs, to find out what she knew in case Zattan had talked to her, and maybe even reveal what he had learned from Gnô Mitang, which might shed a little light on the mystery surrounding the mighty battle in the making between Mathias Lumen and Leonid Zattan... and wasn't it necessary to get Sylvie out of here if her captivity turned into one of those dangers that many young ladies—and she was one—might try to escape through suicide?

So, he had to act right away and not waste another night.

Luckily, for this dangerous and daring operation he was going to undertake, the Nyctalope had a valuable document: a complete map of the castle. The father of Leonid Zattan had a learned ulama come from Istanbul to write the history of the castle. It was a beautiful handwritten book with plates in ink and watercolor depicting the different sides of the castle from different angles. There were appended to these little works of art a few geometric drawings—detailed maps of the main keep, the towers, the cellars, the whole castle!

But when you're Leonid Zattan, you can't foresee or think of everything. The unique book was one of the five or six thousand books in various languages in the library that was freely available to the permanent and temporary residents of the castle, with the exception, of course, of the soldiers and servants who were almost all illiterates.

It didn't take long for the eyes of a cultivated mind to scan the well-organized books. Leo Saint-Clair tracked down the tome. He knew the Turk but he really admired the watercolors and drawings. With nimble fingers he pilfered the map, which he hid away to study later in his room while pretending to read a book.

On the night of April 3rd, a stimulating game of chess with Woldski had been so tempting that the lieutenant-secretary and the captain of the erstwhile *Taurus* were the last to respect the curfew bell that rang in the castle at 10 pm. They almost violated the five-minute grace period accorded by regulation to turn off all the lights other than in the guard posts and officers' rooms. Pedro Del Campo, consequently, had hung around so nobody would suspect that he had other plans than sleep for the night, as if such suspicions (an unlikely hypothesis) could arise in some worried mind concerning the simple and cheerful, although dignified and somewhat pompous, Pedro Del Campo!

The captain saw Toma standing in the doorway to his room, the mattress rolled up in a corner of the frame.

"Go to bed and get some sleep," he said. "I won't be needing you tonight."

With the door closed and only a simple latch separating him from his servant/guard, he got undressed, filled a pipe, lit it and started smoking in his bed while reading a book. During the day he had told Toma that it was his habit to stay up for a while in order to get a good night's rest. That was why he had reminded his servant to never forget, when arranging the room for the night, to put out a bag of tobacco, pipe and electric lighter on the bedside table next to a glass of water.

How could anyone suspect subversive ideas from a sailor who, as soon as his feet were on solid ground, resumed the old customs of his ancestors who were country hidalgos—old habits that he couldn't enjoy on board a ship? Obviously, Pedro Del Campo intended to spend his forced layover in Issyk-Kul like a lazy, peaceful vacation.

Toma made his report; Woldski had written it down on one page and added his own observations; Zattan had read it that night. Leo Saint-Clair could rest easy because Toma fast asleep at his doorstep was a symbol—no one in the castle was keeping a special eye on Pedro Del Campo.

For half an hour, with pipe in mouth and back against a pillow, the captain looked like he was avidly reading the big quarto volume of <u>Don Quixote</u>. In truth, he was studying, line by line, the map of the castle. At 10:45—according to the hands of his watch sitting on the bedside table—Saint-Clair slowly closed the book after taking out the map. He left the tome on the bed as he slipped out of the sheets and stood on the carpet so he could fold the map and put it in the right pocket of his "American" shirt that he had not switched to pajamas. Then he quietly got dressed.

He had made note of Toma's sleep the night before—he didn't wake up before the morning drumroll; he slept like a log. Furthermore, there was no patrol in the officers' wing and no lights were kept on. Saint-Clair knew this from hearsay and personal observation. Anyway, he was the Nyctalope!

The night turned the hallway into a tunnel of darkness—this night that stretched its black veil over the courtyards, porches and doorways, broken only by the lights in the guard houses; this night full of heavy clouds in a starless sky that enshrouded all the buildings of the castle; this night was Saint-Clair's friend, his partner, his ally, his protector, his slave because the Nyctalope's eyes saw through the darkness better than X-rays through human flesh.

Opening the door and closing it noiselessly, stepping over the mattress with the sleep-numbed body—it was a walk in the park for Saint-Clair. And in the hallway, light and agile on his feet, the Nyctalope could move with ease.

He had one hope. Having learned that morning during breakfast at the officers' table that the "little prisoner" was being kept on the third floor of the south tower, he had bent the rules as much as he could to stroll as far as he could on the circular rampart that made half-circles around the four big towers at the corners. And he dawdled around the south tower, first doing some stretching exercises, then pretending to admire the view and finally making the complete round a few times. So, his hope was that Sylvie Mac Duhl had seen and recognized him... and that she was expecting some contact if not a visit from him.

"If she saw me, she recognized me," he convinced himself. "And in that case, she's awake. If I can do what I think I can, it won't be hard to get her attention."

The library was on the ground floor of the main building. It was a long, wide room, decorated with paintings, statues and busts all along the walls and aisles between the shelves that left little free space. In the very back, facing the main door, a complete set of 18th century armor stood on a sculpted wood pedestal. Nothing was lacking: iron sabatons with spurs, greaves and cuisses, gauntlets and bracers, hauberk and breastplate, bevor and helmet, a long lance, a broadsword, axe and mace, the besaques at the shoulders and the shield and the short, strong dagger called a "mercy blade".

All the armor was meticulously polished, a magnificent, exquisite, exemplary museum piece. But it was not the artistic or historical aspect that made Del Campo admire its authentic details. With the ironic joy of a duelist in a trial by combat who has just found chinks in the armor of his adversary he thought, "Surely, Leonid Zattan is too occupied with his lofty speculations to worry about small, material things. The Turk's book gave me the map and this Frank-ish armor will provide me with the necessary weapons."

When the Nyctalope had safely crossed the dark hallway, gone down the steps of the back stairway and silently opened the door of the library, he headed straight to the back of the pitch-black room. He stepped onto the pedestal and drew the "mercy blade" from its iron sheath and stuck it in the right pocket of his coat without worrying about making a hole. Then he left.

But not by the main door or by one of the side doors, all of which opened onto a circular hallway that led only to the front door, the only way in or out of the main building from the inner courtyard. Next to this main door, in the huge entranceway, was a guard post with a light on and an armed soldier standing watch. Getting out this way was absolutely impossible, even for the Nyctalope.

However, on both sides of the medieval Christian armor were two small bathrooms so the booklovers could wash their hands of the venerable dust from the old books or of traces of ink. Although all the windows in the library were fitted with thick, strong bars on the outside, the two little windows high up on the walls to let light into the washrooms were left unobstructed. No doubt these "portholes" were built more recently and they'd figured it was useless to defend them in these less militant days for the castle where the weapons room (now turned into a library) no longer had to withstand sieges or guard prisoners.

The Nyctalope went into one of the bathrooms, opened the glass pane of the window by flipping the electric switch and using a small wooden table that was the rare piece of furniture in the space, he reached the window, hoisted him-self up and slipped outside, legs first, then his chest and head, hanging by the frame with his arms stretched out. Then he arched his back, let go and dropped to his feet, bent his knees and turned around.

He was in the main courtyard on the east side. One hundred yards away, at the end of the building, stood the south tower, separated by a narrow walkway from the half-circle shadow of the rampart.

The Nyctalope walked fifty feet, then stopped and looked up on seeing the pale rectangle of light cut into the black wall. "Zattan is still awake. But the cur-tains are drawn. Is he thinking? Working? Reading? Or dreaming of the pure and splendid beauty of Sylvie Mac Duhl? Or maybe pondering the quatrains of Nostradamus relating to the Antichrist? Maybe all of these?"

Higher up, the windows remained dark. "If she doesn't know I'm here in the castle, she's gone to bed and is probably already asleep. But if she saw me or possibly overheard some servant's gossip and figured me for the 'sailor' who arrived yesterday morning, then she'll be waiting, listening, watching… but be-hind which window? There are four…"

He stood perfectly still for five minutes, sometimes staring at the lighted window, sometimes at the darker ones above. Then suddenly he convinced him-self, "Come on!"

But just then he heard a low whistle behind him. Faster than a cat pouncing on a mouse spied out of the corner of its eye, he spun around.

"Oh!" he managed to stifle a cry bursting out of his surprise.

Marc Ayol! Two feet away, hands out front like a blind man, the captain seemed to be sliding over the heavy, smooth cobblestones that covered the courtyard. He stopped, lowered his arms, smiled and whispered so low that Saint-Clair barely heard him, but he did hear.

A brief silence. Then, "Leo, you might have the eyes of a lynx, but I've got the nose of the blind man of Wardrop who could recognize people by their smell. Like a good bloodhound following its master without seeing him, I picked up your scent and here you are right in front of me."

Saint-Clair stepped forward and spoke no louder than a breath. "I know the story of the blind man of Wardrop and its genuine. But why didn't you tell me before that you had this powerful sense of smell? It might've been handy at the right time?"

"I didn't think of it. Sorry. Anyway, the right time is now. And here I am."

The two men shook hands and without letting go, the Nyctalope asked, "How did you get out?"

Marc Ayol gave a quick rundown, "Loose board, trapdoor, attic room, sky-light, roof, gutter... I may be a ship's captain and enjoy the cushy job, but I'm also a top-notch boatswain, Leo! And I've got a knife."

"A knife?"

"Yes, a good, big one. Look here."

From the right pocket of his pants Marc Ayol, full of surprises, pulled out a Spanish switchblade, closed for the moment but big enough for a butcher and as long as an Italian stiletto.

"How'd you get that?"

"The men I'm with aren't sheep. They don't like discipline much and they're not so scared of the rules. Almost all of them hide weapons. I borrowed this one discreetly, without asking, from the bed next to mine. That's it. Now am I handy? Or am I a bother? Should I stay or go?"

"Stay, Marc."

"All right."

In fact, Saint-Clair was glad to have his partner with him. The two of them would be stronger. They could help each other. The plan was a hard one and the Nyctalope could gauge the difficulties better than in the day. For, it was necessary to climb.

Not for an instant did the so-called Pedro Del Campo ever consider reaching Sylvie Mac Duhl through the inside of the tower that was forbidden to enter, guarded day and night and whose doors were probably mechanically locked and rigged with electric alarms.

On the outside, however, it was possible to climb. And here's how:

In olden times, the four towers were built as the four corners of the great wall surrounding the fortress, the wall being two-thirds the height of the towers. The Turkish book found by the Nyctalope gave a precise date, 1629, that the wall was torn down and the towers were no longer connected to one another except by the drastically renovated central building. Then they had built the ramparts that stand now with their cellars and completely independent of the towers and central building out of which rose the keep.

But there were traces of the old wall on the towers: huge stones built into their walls that stuck out and must have been some kind of support for the old wall. Rising two-thirds of the way up the tower these jutting stones looked like a cyclopean stairway. A very tough stairway to climb since every stone was separated from the one higher up by what looked like a ten-foot gap.

Well, during his afternoon stroll along the ramparts, Del Campo had noticed that one of the stones jutted out right under one of the third-floor windows. Squatting or standing on this stone and reaching through the bars to knock on the window...

"That's all it would take," he had thought, "to get Sylvie to come over and talk with her."

And if the window was to a servant's room or an empty room? If the climb made noises that could be heard on the second floor? If the wind blew away the clouds and the bright moonlight lit up the tower just when a patrol was passing by on the ramparts? Or, finally, if it wasn't possible to climb the stones because the gap was bigger than it looked?

As expected, Saint-Clair had thought of every possible objection. About the last one he had decided as follows:

"They left me my Spanish belt, the ten feet of wide, strong sash. Twisted tightly it'll make a fine rope. With my arms raised I can cover over six feet. So, if I hold the belt in both hands, I should be able to loop it over the stone just above me. I tie the two ends together so one end won't slip out of my hands and I pull myself up. Then I just scramble up on the stone, brace my back against the wall and get ready for the next one."

As for the other obstacles, they were purely hypothetical dangers. Saint-Clair would figure out how to avoid them or overcome them if they turned out to be real.

But with a climb like this and the possible dangers, Marc Ayol's being there to help was extremely useful. Saint-Clair wouldn't have hesitated to meet him at the south tower if he'd known about the escape route and especially about the special sense of smell of the Marseille anglophile. But he had come on his own. "All right!"

Side by side and holding hands, Saint-Clair in his sandals and Marc Ayol barefoot, the Nyctalope led his partner silently and rapidly over the dark cobblestones. "To the foot of the tower. Stop!"

Saint-Clair described the stairway of jutting stones. "You won't go up with me," he decided. "I won't need you to climb or when I'm at the window, so it's no use. You stay here. You can go back and forth between towers sniffing the air and if you smell or, of course, hear any men coming, give me two hoots like an owl and I'll freeze until they've gone. I know the patrols change their schedule every night, so a guard could pass by at any time. And it might just be when the skies clear up... Well, you being here means that I won't have to worry about all that. I can concentrate all my attention and energy on the climb and rely on you to watch my back."

"Got it. Is this the wall of the tower I'm touching?"

"Yes. Here you've got the courtyard we just crossed behind you and the path around the towers is in front of you."

"I know it. OK, I'm set. You can go now."

"I'm off."

They shook hands again.

The Nyctalope took off his belt, twisted it lengthwise, grabbed the two ends and tossed it back like when playing jump rope. Then he threw his arms up and forward. The rope made a semi-circle from behind his legs up to the first stone. He swiftly tied the ends together and clutched the two sides to hoist himself up by his arms. He reached the stone, grabbed on and pulled himself up, using the rope like stirrup for his feet. In no time, he was on his knees, then standing on the stone.

"It's narrower than I'd hoped," he mused, "but if I'm careful, with my back against the wall, I'll be fine. There we are. It's going to be tiring, but I'll manage."

He bent over, pulled up the rope and staying flat against the wall he flung the rope over his head again. It caught. A minute later he was up on the second step of the gigantic stairway.

The windows on the second floor were ten feet up the wall. The third step stuck out maybe a foot and half beneath one of these windows. Then the fourth was around the same distance above it. finally, the fifth—the last one the Nyctalope had to reach—was just under one of the third-floor windows.

"Going from the third to fourth step I'll have to pass that window that is certainly in one of Zattan's rooms."

And at that very moment, despite all his determination and courage, the Nyctalope shivered—not from the cold, although the night was chilly, but from the feeling that this second-story window was going to be a fiendish hurdle. But his rational thinking kicked in.

"Why? That's not the window I saw lit. Zattan is in a room on the other side of the tower."

But the subconscious force that is inside of us and that is often sensitive to the imponderable portents of the mysterious future, this force in Saint-Clair interrupted his reasoning and stated with categorical certainty, "Zattan will come into this room and turn on the light."

Nevertheless, even while thinking all this, the Nyctalope didn't stop his activity. He pulled up the rope and tossed it overhead. It hooked onto the third step. Saint-Clair hung onto it, hauled himself up and clambered onto the stone. But just as he was standing up, facing the window, it suddenly lit up...

And just as suddenly, he squatted down, tucked his head between his knees and waited, all his senses on high alert. The stone was barely wide enough to kneel on—his feet were over the edge, his chest and face against the wall—but he held on, frozen in a precarious balance, by some miracle of will.

And that was when...

And at this already dreadful moment, at this moment full of mortal dangers...

That was when two hoots of an owl came out of the right side of the courtyard.

Saint-Clair thought, "Zattan behind the window and a patrol down below." Then after a couple of seconds, "Luckily the clouds are still packing the sky. The rectangle of light will make the wall I'm stuck to even darker." And following this logic, "But if Zattan opens the window when the patrol passes by and leans out... I'll feel him breathing on my neck... How will he not see me? He will see me for sure. In that case, I'll jump on his neck. There are no bars on this one. Yes, I'll jump on his neck."

He stopped thinking. He heard the rhythmic footsteps of the patrol in the courtyard. At the same time, a latch creaked—and the window opened!

CHAPTER VIII

Saint-Clair was as still as the stone he was squatting on, as the wall he was plastered against. He felt someone sticking his head out of the window above him, leaning out, looking down…

Down below, the marching steps of the patrol echoed through the court-yard to the left, then between the rampart and the tower, then to the right. Saint-Clair saw a lantern dancing in the dark below. He couldn't move his neck to look up at the window to see the man, but he was utterly convinced that all his senses would warn him if the man noticed him.

"So, relax," he told himself. "Or else you'll lose your balance and break your neck when you fall on the cobblestones. Or I could grab the man's neck and pull myself inside…"

Never in his life, however full of perilous adventures it had been, never had the Nyctalope felt the fractions of seconds between his heartbeats tick off so slowly. It felt like his heart was going to wind down and stop. And his whole body started shivering, almost pushing him over the edge, when he heard the man move away from the window, walk across the room, open a door…

He waited with a sweaty brow and icy hands.

Down below the sound of the patrol faded away and disappeared. Above, nothing. Nothing else happened.

Nothing.

Silence.

Suddenly the Nyctalope thought, "The window's still open!"

His heartbeat sped up again. But he kept waiting, patiently, which was harder than any daring deed. He forced himself to count off 100 seconds. And then slowly, gently, he raised his head, slid his hands up the wall and his fingers gripped the windowsill. His head rose up to its level. Motionless, he looked.

There wasn't the slightest breeze. The white curtains were open, hanging straight down on either side, their long folds completely still.

The room that Saint-Clair saw was lit by electric lights hidden in the opaque shell on the ceiling. It was a big bathroom with a bathtub-pool in the marble floor and all the modern conveniences.

"Nobody!" Saint-Clair observed. "I heard a door open and close to the right. It could only have been Zattan who'd come in here. Where'd he go? Well, I'll risk it. I didn't want to stop on the second floor but this window is too tempt-ing. Let's go! And don't forget your belt."

He grabbed the sash with one hand, stood up straight and like a gymnast vaulted into the room. Standing between the curtains, he untied the knot in his belt and put it around his waist normally. Then he walked in.

The huge bathroom was deserted. To the right, another open curtain revealed a door ajar. He walked over to listen and peek through. No sound. A bedroom. Saint-Clair pushed open the door gently until there was just enough room to sneak through.

"Nobody! Keep moving!"

He walked into the room that was also lit from the ceiling. But right away his attention was drawn to the bedside table.

"Now that's a fancy nightstand!"

The piece of furniture was placed on the left side of the head of the bed in a corner in an alcove. An electric reflector lamp with frosted glass cast an even light on the table. And this table, much bigger than the one on the right, also a nightstand, was indeed very extraordinary!

A set of mirrors mounted on legs and pivots and arranged along lines intersecting at different angles, a microtelephone device with a mouthpiece, a panel of ivory switches, another telephone device with a movable transmitter and receiver and wires, grouped together or separate, plugged into a flat backboard that fit the table up against the back wall.

"Ho, ho," Saint-Clair breathed softly. "Do I get it?"

Next to this table, the covered bed showed the imprint of an individual lying down with their elbow on the pillow.

"If I lay down in this position, my right elbow in the pillow there, my hand supporting my head, I would be looking at the mirrors and listening to the microtelephone and could easily reach the switches with my left hand. If I..."

He didn't waste another second. Instinctively making sure the mercy blade was still in his pocket, he crossed the room to the alcove, lay down on the bed, propped himself on an elbow and looked at the mirrors.

And if he didn't let out a cry of astonishment and triumph as loud as any human throat ever had, it was only because he had total and effective self-control. No, he didn't cry out, but looked on eagerly. And he listened very carefully so as not to forget what he was hearing.

He looked and listened. And it was like he was at a show where a director and a genius technician had brought all the latest inventions of color tele-cinematography and tele-phonography together in perfect synchronism.

The mirrors reflected a scene inside a luxurious, fashionable bedroom. There were two people in the scene: Sylvie Mac Duhl in pale green pajamas and red slippers and Leonid Zattan in a dark smoking jacket and blue leather sandals. Both were bare-headed. They stood face to face, separated by an oval pedestal table with a marble top but nothing on it. With her back arched in a position of defiance, Sylvie had both hands buried in her pockets; Zattan was holding a rectangular piece of off-white paper, probably parchment, at chest level.

That was the scene in the mirror.

And the microtelephone was providing the sounds.

Words and movements, gestures and silence, attitudes, glares, exclamations, retorts, all in perfect synchronism, all clearly visible and audible to Leo Saint-Clair the Nyctalope lying on the bed.

"Mademoiselle," Zattan was saying, "I've been thinking for six days. I received some information I was waiting for. With the heads of the most powerful revolutionary organizations in the world I signed some contracts that I consider indispensable to my plan. Everything will be ready within a month and the nations of Earth will start trembling on their foundations, which will soon collapse. Humanity will feel the ominous signs of the coming reign of the Antichrist… and so I now come to ask you to choose between life and death."

He went quiet. She burst out laughing. Her defiant arch relaxed into a shrug of the shoulders and her whole body loosened up like a cat. She took half a step back, then very calmly, rather softly, she said, "Are you a lunatic?"

Just as calmly, he answered, "It's all true. You know nothing. What I'm telling you, which you don't understand at the moment, might seem crazy to you, but you will soon see and then know that Leonid Zattan is saner than the most reasonable of men."

With his left hand, still holding the parchment, he motioned to the easy chair behind her.

"Please sit down. I, too, will take a seat. Please."

She turned her head a little, backed up, sat down with her arms on the arms of the chair. At the same time, the Prince dragged over a chair and sat down while putting the stiff parchment on the marble top table. As he smoothed the parchment with his hand it crackled a little.

As small as the image was in the mirror, the reflection was so clear that the Nyctalope lost the sense of dimension and believed he was actually looking at a "normal-sized" Leonid Zattan and Sylvie Mac Duhl.

The face of the young lady was attentive and serious without any apparent anxiety and nothing, neither physical fatigue nor moral suffering, affected her youthful and magnificent beauty.

With a wooden expression and icy glare, the enigmatic man was obviously in full possession of all of his formidable faculties.

As for Saint-Clair, he had the feeling that his entire body was hypnotized by the sight and sounds, by everything he was seeing and hearing. And he scolded himself silently for it. Until he accepted that it was just a recording device that was very good for spying and speculation.

"Mademoiselle," Zattan went on, "I give you my word that tonight, right now, it's a matter of life and death for you with no other alternative. Please listen to me without any of that useless show of stubborn ignorance and mockery. Listen and try to understand. Ask me questions if you don't understand enough. Because it's your decision and yours alone that will decide your fate. And in a way, to a certain extent, the fate of all mankind. It is crucial, therefore, that you make your decision in full knowledge of the cause."

He paused and stared urgently at the young lady. She didn't blink. Her face, however, had turned a little pale. She simply said, "Very well, I'm listening. I hope, monsieur, that I will understand."

After a brief smile of satisfaction, he took the parchment and held it over the marble tabletop.

"This, mademoiselle, is one of the most stirring prophecies of Michel de Notre Dame, known as Nostradamus, who lived in France in the 16th century and who was famous all over the world for his more or less hermetic works. One of these works, known under the title of 'Centuries', is a collection of prophetic quatrains. The specialists of the 'Centuries' have found, without any reasonable objection to oppose them, that many of these prophecies have come true. It is normal, therefore, to expect others to be fulfilled. Now, mademoiselle, the most serious, the most terrible, the most supernatural, perhaps, of all these prophecies concerns a young lady... who is none other than you."

Sylvie Mac Duhl shuddered at this conclusion. She sat up a little straighter in her chair, clenched her hands and stared a little harder at the man across from her.

Unaffected, Zattan said, "That's it." He said nothing more, just looked at the young lady. She was very pale, stiff, gripping the arms of the chair and he could see the surprise in her frightened eyes staring at the fateful parchment.

For a full minute, the room was utterly silent and still. Sylvie gazed at the parchment; Zattan gazed at Sylvie.

It was Sylvie who made the first move. She felt a sudden shiver and her eyes shifted, meeting the scrutinizing gaze of Zattan, and she blinked. Her face looked totally bewildered.

The man broke the silence, "Do you understand?"

With her face regaining its color and her eyes becoming calm and proud again, she shot back, "Truthfully, I may understand some of your mysterious statements, but others I don't get at all..." She coughed quietly and went on more firmly, "Anyway, all prophecies can be interpreted differently. I'm curious, I admit, to know how you interpret this one."

"You're wrong, mademoiselle, concerning the interpretation of this particular prophecy. The words, the phrases are very clear and can be understood in only one way. I'll explain so that you may understand completely. I see that I don't need to remind you..."

In the room beneath them, Saint-Clair shrugged and thought, "Well now, she understood. The golden virgin! And me too, just like Mathias Lumen and Gnô Mitang. But she's right, smart girl, to refer to alternate interpretations. And I'm no less curious than her to know what the Lord of Issyk-Kul thinks!"

Neither Sylvie nor Saint-Clair had to wait because Zattan was already explaining.

"You, mademoiselle Sylvie Mac Duhl, are indeed the golden virgin indicated by Nostradamus. You are Scottish by name; your mother died shortly after giving birth to you; your late father was a close friend of Mathias Lumen who bought a house that an Englishman had built on the island of Ushant; this Englishman had died by being stabbed in the throat; in the wells dug under the house Mathias Lumen, for years, buried gold and precious jewels that came from his gambling establishments; your father helped fill up those wells and we can guess that the cargo of the *Taurus* came directly from them... Your hair is golden and in certain light, the skin of your neck and arms have a golden hue... All I've just said is in the prophecy and points to you, Sylvie Mac Duhl, as the golden virgin. I know, I know, *I know* that there is no other woman on earth, no other virgin that fits the words and meaning of the prophecy like you."

He took a breath. She looked unruffled. Her arms were crossed over her chest and she was leaning back comfortably in the chair. She watched Zattan with eyes that showed no expression except for polite, somewhat aloof attention.

But he wasn't fooled by this attitude. He admired it and became even more desirous of this woman who had such self-control. He knew that the virgin had crossed her arms to hide her heaving chest in which her heart was throbbing with emotion.

He took a breath and in the same narrative voice went on, "It is the year *'one and nine and twenty-six,'* yes, as the calendar shows it's May 3, 1926. Now, mademoiselle, with all this understood, listen again to the prophecy whose meaning I haven't yet explained to you."

Without looking at the parchment, he recited from memory, "The Golden Virgin will arouse with love the great brown male... To the Antichrist the male is opposed... Victorious if the woman gives birth... Otherwise the..."

But his words were cut off by a burst of hearty, mocking laughter full of wonderful mischief! And before he could control his outraged surprise, Sylvie stopped laughing just as suddenly and shouted out, vibrant and taunting, "Oh, no, monsieur, no, this isn't fair. You're cheating! I have a good memory and I know, almost be heart, your prophecy of Nostradamus. Your first remarks have a certain clever logic, but don't you know I see where it's going? Golden virgin, love, brown male, etc. Bravo! A six-year-old child could see through you! The golden virgin is me, the great brown male is you, and for Leonid Zattan to triumph over the Antichrist, Sylvie Mac Duhl has to marry Leonid Zattan on whom victory will fall when God blesses the happy couple with a lovely baby daughter or son! Ha, ha, ha, that's a good one! Are you scowling? You look pale, are you angry? Don't be, monsieur, because, as I said, you're cheating and this isn't fair. You can't leave out anything of the prophecy or change the words around.

"It is said, if I'm not mistaken: 'The Golden Virgin will arouse with love in the time one and nine and nineteen.' Now, you yourself said this is May. The Virgin, therefore, has seven months to arouse with love. Seven months! Who knows the future? Nostradamus, sure, maybe. But us? It's possible that in seven months I will love you, but you'll have to start right now to make yourself lovable. And the first lovable act you could do would be to set me free. In seven months, if you want, we'll talk again about Nostradamus and love, the brown male and the Antichrist and the nursery. Until then…"

She stood up, jumped to the side, backed away, trembling, along a dresser whose marble top was at shoulder level—and as her eyes expressed an invincible will, her cold voice said, "Oh, no, don't touch me! If you make one move toward me, I'll crack my head on the corner of this dresser!"

"The corner of this dresser" was the long, sharp horn of a gilded bronze seahorse whose decorative head supported the marble top. If Sylvie dashed her desperate head against it, the horn could easily penetrate her brain.

There are looks and words that don't lie. Zattan had a vision of the sudden suicide. He slowly lowered his arms, got control of his humiliated fury, his enraged passion, his unnerved desire. His strong jaw clenched and his teeth gnashed. He closed his eyes. And he stayed there, standing up, using all his strength to calm down. His mind was stronger than his instincts. Suddenly he whirled around and was standing in front of the table.

He put his strong, fine hand on the yellowing parchment and declared with a kind of passionate solemnity, "Mademoiselle, in a way you're right. All prophecy can be interpreted freely. Well, in honor of you and in the name of my love for you, I'm going to interpret it like this. You are the Golden Virgin, for sure. The wells in the Ushant house will be filled whenever I feel like it with the gold from roulette tables, horseracing and baccarat—gambling. This will be one more fact added to all the others in the prophecy that have already come true.

"But then, oh then, Sylvie Mac Duhl, it's very simple. Either you marry me before a Catholic priest who will come to Issyk-Kul whenever you want and when I've had a child from you who will be the symbol of my love, of your own gift and of our prophetic union, then I will be victorious over the Antichrist whose imminent arrival has been heralded in the world by so many horrible signs over the past dozen years.

"Or else, Sylvie, you refuse to give yourself to me. Then, according to the alternative recorded by Nostradamus, '*the time will be long postponed.*' The time no doubt being when humanity will know peace and happiness by destroying the symbol of the Antichrist. So, through me, the supreme master of all the cursed, all the rejected of the earth, there will be '*blood with the dead in dreadful piles.*'

"And I will begin with murdering you with my own hands. The '*otherwise*' of the prophecy gives me every right without going against what was written. And after killing you, there will be no one and nothing that can prevail against my fanatic despair.

"Imagine it, think about it, evaluate the alternatives, Sylvie Mac Duhl."

He had nothing more to say. With one last wave of his hand he indicated the parchment left on the table. Then he spun around and marched toward the door.

Downstairs, Saint-Clair rose agilely from the bed, murmuring, "He'll be here in thirty seconds."

He crossed the room, the bathroom, reached the window, swung out, holding onto the sill, got his knees on the jutting stone, bent down and crouched against the wall.

His alert hearing caught the sound of a door opening and closing. He knew the place now. He heard Zattan coming and going. The window above the Nyctalope slammed shut.

The Nyctalope was thinking, "He'll go to bed but stay up for a long time spying on Sylvie through his hellishly clever system of periscopes, mirrors and microphones. When she's gone to bed, when she's turned out the lights, only then will he probably turn out his. Then I can act. But how to make sure I don't act too hastily? I can't see the windows of their bedrooms from here. From down below, I could. Should I climb down? And then back up? Well, yes, of course. Better than getting stiff and numb here, maybe losing my balance and falling off."

He took off his belt. It was easier to go down by the same procedure, only in reverse, than it had been to climb up. Just when his feet touched the cobblestones, he heard a voice whisper behind him, "Well, Leo?"

He turned around and saw Marc Ayol. "Well, I saw and heard some very interesting things. This Leonid is a tough bastard and pretty smart. And passionate! All the fires of hell burn in Zattan! Let me tell you. Come over here so we can see their windows. Right now we should see them lit up, unless they've closed the shutters. Over here. Good thing it's dark out. I don't want the moon coming out from behind the clouds. Here we are. Bravo, they haven't touched the shutters. Marc, when those two windows go dark I'll climb back up there."

"Yeah?"

"Yeah. Listen, since Gnô Mitang has already let you in on Mathias Lumen's secret and the prophecy of Nostradamus, I have nothing to hide from you. Here's what I heard and saw up there."

Concise, precise and intriguing, Saint-Clair told of his adventure.

Marc Ayol remarked, "Yeah, he's a tough one, all right. What are you going to do now, Leo? Because I think…"

"Shh! Not another word. I'm going up."

One after the other, the two windows, first the upper, then the lower, went dark.

The Nyctalope thought, "Time to climb, to get Sylvie's attention while Zattan is asleep. As long as he doesn't turn on his infernal spying device again. Let's hope. Anyway, I have to risk it."

And paying no more notice to Marc Ayol he went to the foot of the tower. He scaled up the wall more effortlessly but no less cautiously than the first time. At the window where he had just spent a few harrowing seconds, he listened for a long time. The shutters were not closed so the Nyctalope could see into the bathroom where nothing was moving. And not a sound.

"Let's keep moving!" And he tossed his belt to the higher stone.

When he was standing up, his knees and thighs against the wall, his belly and chest pressing against the bars on the outside of the third-story window, the Nyctalope strained his eyes to see inside. The shutters were not closed here either and the part in the curtains was wide enough to see most of the room. And by chance, the window was cracked open.

"Bathroom like below," the Nyctalope recited to himself. "So, the bedroom is on the right. If the door is closed, a noise loud enough for Sylvie to hear might also be heard by Zattan if the devil's not asleep yet. But if the door's open, just scratching over and over will be noticed if Sylvie's awake. She certainly can't be sleeping! After eight days as Zattan's prisoner and just thirty minutes after getting his ultimatum, she won't be able to sleep before the gloomy dawn...

"But I, too, face an ultimatum. Destiny gives it: talk tonight to Sylvie or give up. Because maybe tomorrow Zattan will demand the life or death of the 'golden virgin'. And above and beyond Sylvie Mac Duhl, humanity is living with hope and, despite some strife, in peace. Can I let this Zattan wreak havoc on the world by fire and sword?

"I know, I could've killed him earlier. I just had to hide in the bedroom when he came back. He shows up, I jump out and slit his throat or stab him in the heart. Any idiot could do it. But I know that killing the man means nothing if you don't kill the idea with him. How do I know that Zattan is the only one harboring this demonic dream? He himself said the web has been woven and he holds all the threads. By killing the leader, would I be cutting all the threads? Wouldn't there be another mad radical ready to take his place?

"And then, and then, damn, I have to admit—Zattan, Lumen, Sylvie Mac Duhl and this prophecy of Nostradamus are the important pieces in this game of chess that's fascinating me. I don't want to interrupt it. I want to know the mysterious rules of the game and what's at stake. I want to join in and win! Therefore, I was right not to kill Zattan. And I have to talk to Sylvie tonight. No more debating, my mind's made up. Let's take the chance."

Holding onto the bars with his left hand, he stuck his right arm through two bars and with the fingernail of his index finger he scratched the window rhythmically while counting to twenty, almost at the speed of the beating of his heart. Then he stopped and listened for around a minute. Nothing. Everything still. Silence.

"Let's start over."

He started over in the same way at the same rhythm for the same amount of time. Again he listened. Nothing. Nothing in the night but the monotonous ebb and flow of the lake against the rocks.

A third time he did the same thing.

Then, finally, Saint-Clair was sure he had been heard—by Sylvie. Clearly through the bathroom door left ajar, Saint-Clair heard the faint squeak of a mattress, the soft rustling of sheets and a blanket thrown back, then other rustling sounds.

"She heard. She's coming. God, if only Zattan on his bed doesn't find out through his machine. Oh, let him be sleeping and stay asleep!"

His eyes searched the darkness beyond the window to his right. And he listened. He caught some muffled sounds.

"Yes, yes, she's coming. Does she imagine it's me? There she is!"

A white shape, ghostly, appeared between the curtains. The Nyctalope saw the pretty, pale face and the big, blue eyes. He thought: "It's pitch black. She barely sees my dark outline against hazy shadows. But she'll hear me even if I whisper softly."

Sticking his face between the cursed bars, in a voice barely louder than a breath, he said, "Sylvie, it's the Nyctalope. Do you see me? Do you hear me?"

In the same, barely audible voice, the young lady answered, "I don't see you but I guess you're standing on that rock right outside the window. I hear you fine."

"Good. When Zattan was up here I was lying on his bed downstairs. He's set up a remarkable system of mirrors and microphones so he can hear and see everything said and done up here in your rooms. I took advantage of it and spied on your meeting. I know everything. Moreover, Gnô Mitang confided in me everything he knows about you, Mathias Lumen, the gold cargo and the prophecy of Nostradamus. Gnô's in Cyprus with a good, fast yacht. The gold's on board. The *Taurus* is no longer. The pirates are all our prisoners and Zattan, their master, thinks they're dead. I'm here with one of my friends. Zattan believes we're two good sailors he can make use of... Now you know everything.

"As for yourself, hang tight. But open resistance is risky. Stall. Ask for time. Be devious, flirt, whatever it takes! Yes, whatever it takes! My friend and I are planning your escape. But if you get in imminent, mortal danger, kill Zattan with this dagger I'm going to give you. Or else if you're given a couple of hours of grace, tie a white ribbon or something to these bars. Please, don't kill Zattan unless absolutely necessary. I value his life, in a way. I'll explain why some other time. Nevertheless, if your honor and your life, Sylvie, can only be saved by the death of Zattan, kill him.

"Reach out your hand. Good, here's the dagger, it's a good one. I hope you don't have to use it, but you can consider it your last resort. That's all I have to say. Anything you have to tell me?"

She replied immediately, "Thank you, Leo Saint-Clair. I'll do exactly as you say. You've just saved me from despair. When things get bad, I'll just think of you to stay calm and be strong. Thank you. But it's too dangerous for you stay here a minute longer. Thanks again."

The Nyctalope saw and heard her hesitating in the dark. He could say nothing more. But he appreciated the willpower, perhaps instinctive, behind the charming gesture made by the "golden virgin" as she hesitated bashfully. Then Sylvie's right hand withdrew, armed with the dagger. But her left hand reached out. Saint-Clair held it between the bars and brought it gently to his lips to give it a long, silent kiss.

Instead of going down he stayed there, not moving, watchful, also troubled by a feeling that surprised him to the depths of his soul. Torn between analyzing this feeling, not without some self-mockery, and catching the slightest sound to make sure that Zattan had heard nothing and that Sylvie was safely back in bed, Saint-Clair remained a good five minutes on his perilous perch.

When he was absolutely sure, if not about his personal emotions at least about Sylvie's safety, he got back to the gymnastic descent. When he was on the ground he told Marc Ayol, "All's well. I saw her and told her what I had to. And I gave her the mercy blade. That's enough for tonight. Let's get to bed, captain."

Fifteen minutes later, without anyone in the castle being alerted, Marc Ayol, alias Marco Pampil, was back in his room and Leo Saint-Clair the Nyctalope was in his. He got undressed, went to bed and closed his eyes because he was tired and wanted to sleep. But as he was quickly dozing off, he thought:

"My game has started on the Issyk-Kul chessboard while I wait to see if there are other boards I know nothing about, neither the pieces nor their positions. But I do believe that the player who will get his enemy, right here, in checkmate, will be the master of the future... The master of the future? This sounds more astounding to me than everything I've seen in the past. Master of the future! The Antichrist conquered or put off for a long time to come... Zattan defeated... Sylvie... Sylvie..."

And that night, Saint-Clair thought no more about it.

CHAPTER IX

That was the night of April 3rd.

Time had passed quickly for Leo Saint-Clair and Marc Ayol since March 26th, the day the *Fulgur* had boarded the *Taurus*, the day the Nyctalope and the captain had renewed their acquaintance, the day, finally, when the traitor Jacques Cervier and his crew of bandits had been taken off the sloop and put in irons on the yacht in separate compartments built in the hull of the *Fulgur* under the personal supervision of Gnô Mitang as "detention rooms."

The six men imprisoned there reacted like this: Jacques Cervier silent and defeated, sweating in fear at the thought of the capital punishment he had earned twenty times over; Geronimo, Ramuz and Barbone submissive, resigned, even repentant and ready to become honest sailors again, with the proviso of strict discipline to back up the return of their good intentions; Tchicoz stone cold furious and stubbornly mute.

While sailing away from Malta to a well-protected harbor on Cyprus, their attitudes persisted—so genuinely that Gnô Mitang promised Geronimo, Ramuz and Barbone to put them to the test and if they proved themselves worthy, he would consider taking them on his crew.

Two sailors from the *Fulgur* took turns refilling the water pitchers and food bowls for the prisoners, supervised a half-hour walk every morning on the foredeck of the ship and took care of what was necessary for their survival. These jailors kept the holsters of their Brownings continually unfastened so that the guns were always ready to be drawn. The prisoners had been warned once and for all that the only law that ruled on board the *Fulgur* was martial law. The slightest sign of revolt from them would earn them a bullet in the body. Of course, the five criminals had been meticulously searched when they were completely undressed. Gnô knew the ways a man could hide a little file in certain secret recesses of his body and a little file can be used for many things in the hands of a prisoner!

At night, while the jailors slept, two armed guards were on duty at either end of the long corridor that stretched along the cells.

Thus, any escape, any attempt to escape, any hope of escape was impossible!

But can the word "impossible" be applied to a prisoner ready to die instead of being locked up?

Jacques Cervier dreamed of escape. He had great cunning and imagination but he lacked moral energy. He loved life more than anything. He was scared of being caught and killed. He dreamed; he didn't act.

Geronimo, Ramuz and Barbone only wanted to mend their ways and get back to a life at sea, hard as it might be, honest even, but free of perpetual imprisonment.

As for Tchicoz, he wanted to escape. He wanted it with all the force of his savage soul and brawny body. He wanted it because he knew certain things that meant freedom for him would almost immediately bring him wealth.

Lying on the plank, both ankles bound, he told himself 100 times during the day and twenty times at night, "There's only two options: the penal colony or worse. I know what the penal colony is. I'd rather die than go back there. As for worse..."

The first day the *Fulgur* was anchored in a safe harbor, on his morning stroll Tchicoz recognized the port and town of Famagusta on Cyprus. At one point in his adventurous life he spent two months on this island. Moreover, he had recently learned some important things about this island's connection to Zattan.

"So be it," he told himself, "tomorrow I'll be free or dead."

Every morning the prisoners "took their stroll" around the deck in the front of the ship. They circled around in a single file in the middle of which stood a jailor with his Browning in hand. The other armed jailor stood outside the circle and with the two nightguards formed a triangle so that no prisoner was ever out of sight during the half hour exercise, which was usually pretty sluggish and gloomy. Furthermore, during this half hour, the sailors on deck proceeded to clean the ship.

If one of the prisoners was crazy enough to break the circle, jump in the sea and try to swim away, he would be snatched by strong hands or else shot down. Even if he managed to dive overboard, ten sailors would jump in after him and five or six others would drop in a dinghy and chase him down long before he reached the shore. This was obvious, so obvious that you'd have to (like Tchicoz) prefer suicide to the penal colony if you tried to "escape" this way.

But for all of the prisoners of Gnô Mitang, this was the only possible, the only feasible way.

If the prisoners could have talked together, made plans and worked together to escape one morning, maybe one of them, thanks to the confusion caused by the others, would have had a chance to reach the shore half a mile away. But from the moment they were transferred from the sloop to the yacht, the five of them didn't have one second alone together. Completely isolated except during the half-hour stroll, they couldn't say two words to each other or make the faintest sign. No planning possible. Therefore, no other option but to act alone.

Still, this multitude of difficulties didn't discourage the Mexican Tchicoz who was pretty sure he'd get a couple of bullet wounds when he jumped into the sea.

It was on the evening of March 31st that the *Fulgur* dropped anchor in the waters of Cyprus facing the small port of Famagusta. And it was at 6 o'clock in the morning on April 2nd that Tchicoz figured, "Tomorrow I'll be free."

But on the next day it rained buckets all day long and the open-air stroll was replaced with a march up and down the interior corridors. The same thing happened on April 3rd.

On the morning of the 4th, when Tchicoz woke up, with macabre and desperate irony but also with brutal resolve, he told himself, "I only have one chance—getting hanged but the rope will snap. The gallows ropes are generally new and strong, so a one in a thousand chance of it snapping. But things happen, even a hanged man's rope, as new and strong as could be, might snap. Even a man shot by a dozen soldiers might survive and be saved by a gravedigger. Even a prisoner in my situation might get free. In less than an hour, if it's not raining like yesterday and the day before, I'll be free... or dead!"

The routine was the same as any other day without rain. At 5:45 the two jailors came down the corridor of cells. One was holding his Browning, the other his bunch of keys. First Jacques Cervier, then Tchicoz, then Geronimo and Ramuz and Barbone, the five captives were unchained and lined up in the corridor under the watchful eyes of the two guards. Then with one jailor in front, the other behind and the two guards on either side, the small procession went up the stairs that took 42 steps and two landings to arrive on deck through the square opening of a big hatch. And the stroll started right away.

Cervier was lethargic and gloomy as usual. Geronimo, Ramuz and Barbone seemed rather jovial—yesterday during the daily visit that Gnô Mitang made of the prisoners, he let them understand that they had less than three more days in chains before their trial of trust to see whether they'd be used on board under supervision, which would serve as a stage of clear-cut reformation. For Tchicoz, head lowered and grim, he was just like the day before and the day before that and all the other days...

All around the *Fulgur*, from the port side to the coast side to the side facing open waters, the sea was empty, as usual at this hour. While pacing in circles, Tchicoz looked up from time to time and gazed at the sea, the coast, the port. He had done the same every morning. Neither jailors nor guards could have found anything different on Friday, April 4th, from what they'd seen every day during the stroll.

And like all the men busy cleaning the ship, Tchicoz saw three small fishing boats with lateen sails gliding slowly out to sea, a rowboat pulling in a net laid the day before a cove, four skiffs bobbing by the rocks while fishing for sea urchins close to the shore... Nothing and no one that could be of any help to aid his escape.

The jailors and guards and sailors milling about on the deck of the yacht anchored in the vacant sea half a mile off the coast—Tchicoz knew all this. And yet, in the course of his circular stroll made as casually as ever for around ten minutes, he desperately dared the impossible.

When the jailor in the middle had his back turned and he was halfway between the two sentinels on the outside triangle, Tchicoz leapt.

"Ahoy!" someone shouted.

A shot rang out. Men ran forward. But Tchicoz had a ten-foot head start, total disregard for death and an unquenchable passion for freedom. The first bullet missed. He reached the edge, dove… and splash! He disappeared into the sea. Three other shots were fired.

"Stop shooting!" someone ordered.

A few sailors dove into the water one by one.

"Enough!" the voice of Paul Guennec, interim captain, shouted. Then, "Get the dinghy in the water! We'll bring him back alive!"

As unlikely as it was, the possibility of an escape had been expressly prepared for. Forgotten for a moment, the orders were applied in an instant. While the deckhands dove into the sea, after the two jailors and the guards fired at the runaway, the first in the air, then the three others into the water, they rounded up the four stunned prisoners, pushed them toward the hatch, down the stairs, through the corridor and into their cells—and the chains snapped shut around their bare ankles.

Right away, the dinghy was dropped into the sea with Guennec and two men. The lieutenant was in command as the men grabbed the oars.

"Pull away!" Guennec ordered.

He directed the light craft toward the swimmers. There were five of them forming a group, twenty arms wheeling behind another swimmer who was Tchicoz. Standing up in the back of the rowboat, Guennec could see the fugitive clearly.

"Damn, what a swimmer!" he muttered, unable to contain his admiration for the courage, strength and athleticism of the bandit.

Tchicoz was swimming with long, regular strokes that took him farther away from his pursuers every second. He was heading straight for the nearest point on the shore. He must have thought that once on land, the men from the *Fulgur* would give up the chase lest they run into the English authorities since Cyprus belonged to Great Britain. And he knew enough of the "bush" on Cyprus to imagine he could escape any border control officers that might be in the area. The *Fulgur* was too far from the port for the gunfire to be heard. Moreover, the fishermen were simple folk little inclined to get mixed up in the affairs of a pleasure yacht owned by rich and powerful people.

While swimming away fast and steady, Tchicoz told himself all this and more, "I've already saved myself before by jumping overboard. Sure, it was the *Taurus* and a girl all alone and exhausted who couldn't chase me. Who cares! I saved myself. And I'll save myself today."

Even the approach of the rowboat, which he could easily see by turning his head a little, didn't crush his hope. He'd always considered the boat when he thought about escaping. He'd thought about the boat and the men in it. And he figured that at the crucial moment he'd choose between a half-dozen different ways of fighting and hopefully winning.

Still swimming, he thought, "What I feared most was the bullets and getting grabbed on deck, which I evaded... I don't care about the swimmers coming after me... And this rowboat with a few guys in it, ha, let 'em come since I can't stop them or outswim them... We'll see who has the last laugh... I'm not scared for my life. I already sacrificed it. It's my strength. I resolved to die before being put back in chains. Today I will be free or die. And I'll kill to be free..."

The dinghy didn't take long to pass the five swimmers who kept going, putting more effort into it since they got no orders to turn back. They thought they might be of use after capturing the fugitive in the water.

Everyone thought this capture would be as easy as it was inevitable. On the *Fulgur*, Gnô Mitang had come out of his cabin as soon as he heard the shots and the shouting. Leaving Paul Guennec to take command, he went up to the bridge where he had a good view of the manhunt. And he reckoned that in four or five minutes the dinghy would cut off the fugitive who would quickly be reached by his pursuers. Counting the men in the boat there would be seven strong sailors to deal with Tchicoz. Try as he might to dive down or slip away, the bandit would be chased and blocked in, mobbed in the water. With no axe or knife or any weapon whatsoever, he would quickly be overpowered despite the fury that would double his strength.

Gnô Mitang's conjectures, the same as all the silent crew of the *Fulgur* watching the dramatic chase, at first seemed justified.

Indeed, the dinghy quickly reached the fugitive and rowed past him. The planned, logical move was carried out, meaning that on Guennec's orders, the dinghy was turned 90 degrees in the middle of Tchicoz' direct line to the coast. If the fugitive turned to swim around either side, a couple of strokes of the oars would put the dinghy back in his way to give time to the five sailors chasing him to catch up. Besides, since they were each eager to be the first one to nab the pirate, they were all swimming faster.

Tchicoz knew he was lost if what he was about to do didn't work out as planned in his most optimistic speculations... "Freedom or death!" he told himself again.

What was he about to do? What was his ploy?

Paul Guennec and the sailors, both in the dinghy and in the sea, wondered about this when they saw Tchicoz suddenly dive down under the water.

"He's going to go under our keel," the lieutenant said aloud. "But what's the point when a couple of strokes will put us back in front of him? He can't believe we'll play this hopscotch all the way to the reef..."

A little way beyond the rowboat the Mexican resurfaced, swimming harder and faster than ever.

Guennec had to laugh. "This time I'll rope him in since he doesn't want to give up." Then, to the two rowers, "Get up close to him but don't go past." Dropping the rudder he picked up a line that was about ten feet long and fashioned a slipknot.

At every arm stroke Tchicoz turned his head just enough to see the dinghy. He saw the officer and his rope and the slipknot. And he understood. He pretended to make desperate efforts to outswim the dinghy as if he'd lost all sense of inevitable reality in his frenzy. Then he started diving like a dolphin, going so fast that the rowers had to push hard to keep up. Tchicoz swam even harder—they could hear his breathing. He plunged into the water, rose up in a wave, flying over the crest like an airplane, then vanished into another wave, reappeared, breathing hard...

Without warning, with that suddenness so typical, especially in swimming, of the utter exhaustion of human strength, he collapsed and floundered, just floated, then rolled over twice like a madman and was about to sink headfirst, overwhelmed by a cramp or maybe fatigue...

But Paul Guennec was on guard. He tossed the slipknot and it wrapped around his leg and arm. The officer pulled hard. The leg slipped out of the knot as it cinched, but the arm was caught above the elbow, tightened, squeezed...

Less than a minute later the two sailors dropped the oars and leaned over while Guennec moved to the other side as a counterweight to balance the dinghy. They grabbed the arm and head of the fugitive who was lifted up and dragged into the dinghy. They put him on the seat with his back against the chest of the sailor loosening the rope.

"Lay him down," Guennec ordered, "with his head lower than his body."

The three men thought Tchicoz was unconscious after swallowing too much water, half suffocated already, and they were about to try to revive him when...

When Tchicoz opened his eyes, he jumped up and in a calculated move pounced on the tiller, swung around and with one, two, three, four, five blows of his improvised weapon—the hard wood turned into a serious arm wielded expertly by the strong sailor—he knocked out Guennec and the two rowers. The officer tumbled overboard. The two sailors collapsed in the rowboat. Tchicoz grabbed their hands and strained his muscles to throw them one by one into the sea.

Then he laid up the two oars in the prow, grabbed the other two and turned the boat to head straight for the nearest shore.

The five sailors had to stop and tread water while keeping Guennec and the two unconscious men from drowning.

On board the *Fulgur* Gnô Mitang had seen everything. With his usual calm and detached manner, which seemed as if nothing in the world could disturb or inflame, he told the bosun, "Put the speedboat in the water. First pick up the lieutenant and his men, then go after the rogue."

He thought about getting a Lebel rifle to shoot at Tchicoz. He must have been less than 1,000 yards away and the Japanese was a first-class marksman. But at this moment three fishing boats from Famagusta, sailing slowly out to sea, were in the line of fire, even though a little farther off. Moreover, between the dinghy and the coast, closer to the former, a net fisherman was drifting closer. Obviously, the fisherman had noticed the weird scene and was curious. Obviously, too, the Cypriot would take sides with the "deserter" against the luxury yacht... Observations and deductions that prevented Gnô from putting a bullet in Tchicoz' hearty chest. Besides, such an act—a murder, in fact—could definitely make the English authorities from Famagusta want to investigate. Thinking of this as well, he was sure he could get by with an honorable "dismissal", but it would still be an unnecessary delay and unwanted publicity. Better to avoid all this that in these circumstances could have sudden and serious consequences.

With the speedboat, they would reach the dinghy before Tchicoz could get to shore, capture him and bring him back on board, wrapping up the matter without involving the English authorities.

The "speedboat" of the *Fulgur* was a kind of whaleboat with a half-deck and a gas engine and easy to navigate. It was always kept ready, well-oiled and with a full tank. As it was being put to sea, a mechanic started the engine, checked the idle and waited. As soon as it touched the water with its crew of four men and its boss, an officer and petty officer, the speedboat could rapidly get up to 20 miles an hour.

But getting the swimmers, Guennec and the sailors from the dinghy into the boat was not so easy since the former were out of breath and the latter dead weight. It took some time. Time that was passing since the first stroke of the oar given by Tchicoz in the rowboat he had appropriated with brains and brawn.

When the speedboat got back to the chase, the fugitive had given himself one more advantage: he had maneuvered so that several fishing boats coming from the port were between him and his pursuers. Now he could head straight for shore again while the speedboat had to make a wide turn to avoid the fishermen. When the speedboat finally had open water in front of it, the dinghy was at the reef.

There was no question of continuing the high-speed chase among the reefs if they didn't want to risk smashing the boat and possibly sinking. The bosun at the tiller wouldn't take the risk and therefore the responsibility.

"Come about, boys!" he said, "The scoundrel's home free." And secretly he thought, "Good riddance!"

But he had no idea what dire consequences the escape of a man like Tchicoz could have on the insidious mysteries he knew nothing about. So, he ordered them to abandon the chase and return to the *Fulgur*.

Half an hour later Lieutenant Guennec was waking up in the yacht's infirmary. His forehead was bandaged and his head ached. The first thing he asked about was the two sailors. They were lying on cots on either side of him, eyes open, smiling at him.

"And the prisoner?"

"Got away," Gnô Mitang answered impassively. Then he bent down, put his mouth to the officer's ear and whispered very quietly, "The English are usually very curious. They'd want to know the whys and wherefores. We're not exactly legal in locking up men, wanted or not, from various civilized country on board the yacht. And I believe Cervier has some contacts in the Intelligence Service in London. So, first I've given up on Tchicoz. And second, I've given orders to lift anchor immediately. Famagusta is no good to us now if we don't want the authorities getting involved in our affairs, as honest and admirable as they might be."

"You're right," Guennec said. "So, where are we going?"

"To Latakia since it's the second port we agreed to meet at with Saint-Clair. We'll stay a few more hours here, safe in a nearby cove that's out of sight of Famagusta. I'll decide after I go talk with Cervier."

"Very well."

But Pedro Tchicoz had abandoned the dinghy and hopped over the reef to the shore, climbed up a short cliff and was suddenly grabbed by two English border control officers who had spied him. This, too, had been expected by Tchicoz. He didn't put up a fight. And since he spoke English well he said:

"You can take me to your boss and then bring me to the Maritime Commission. I have nothing to hide. I'm part of that yacht's crew. They worked me like a slave, abused me, didn't feed me. I asked to quit but they didn't want to let me off, so I jumped overboard. I'm a technician specializing in airplane engines. I don't have my papers but you can put me in any workshop and my work will speak for itself."

"What nationality?" one of the officers asked.

"Mexican."

He spoke frankly and calmly like anyone within his rights and with nothing to fear. They just had to look at him—empty-handed, khaki pants and wet shirt stuck to his skin—to know he wasn't a thief. Besides, dealing with this guy would be a lot of trouble and paperwork for the two officers. They looked at each other.

One of them said, "All right."

The other agreed, "Yes."

They turned around and left Tchicoz. He understood. Gladly, he asked for nothing more.

And he thought, "The sun will dry me off."

Now free, he hurried down the path that led to Famagusta. He was used to walking barefoot. The skin on the soles of his feet was as tough as shoe leather. He walked fast. Before entering the fisherman's quarter he saw the *Fulgur* pushing out to sea.

"Bon voyage!" he snickered. "The game goes on. I won the second round. The final round is coming up and I hope to win that too…"

When he was in the narrow streets or on a stretch of the ramshackle dock, no one noticed him. His clothes were dry. He looked just like any other native. He went straight to a small square that separated the fishermen quarter from the first buildings of the modern city.

In the northeast corner of this square was a single-story house painted pale pink with balconies and wide awnings. Doors and windows were shut. Tchicoz stopped in front of this house and stared at it for a moment, then he went straight to the door on the left, smaller than the one in the middle or on the right, and he knocked. People passed by in the square, paying him no attention. The door opened and a servant, an old mulatto woman, showed her ugly troll face.

In a restrained but commanding voice Tchicoz said in English, "Go tell your master that an envoy from the 17 has to speak with him." The "17" was the number that those affiliated with the mysteries of Issyk-Kul knew signified Jacques Cervier.

The woman bowed her head and stepped back. Tchicoz entered as the door closed behind him. At the far end of the arbor lined with colorful rose bushes soft light shone on an interior garden. The servant motioned for Tchicoz to go there. It was a vast, open-air patio with four tall jujube trees, the whole space suffused with refreshing shade and scents. There were rocking chairs and a hammock.

Tchicoz was tired. He sat down, thinking, "If I have to wait a long time, at least I can get some rest."

But he didn't wait long, barely three or four minutes. In the tall rectangle of the entrance to the arbor a man appeared, bald-headed and dressed in white with an open-collared shirt. Tchicoz stood up. He went to stand before the man who waited and studied him from head to toe. Tchicoz examine the man in turn. Skinny with the severe face of a Turk, small, black, piercing and suspicious eyes.

"Who are you?" he asked in English.

Tchicoz looked around before answering in the same language, "Can we speak freely here?"

"Yes, I'm alone. My servant woman left to do some shopping."

"Well, excuse me for asking permission to sit down. I'm completely exhausted even if I don't look it. Then I'm going to ask you for something to eat and drink or for some money to get a snack somewhere. See, I'm really hungry and thirsty. But first I have to talk to you. It's more urgent and more important than anything else."

"Very well," the Turk entered the garden, pointed to a rocking chair, sat down in another and with his elbows on his knees, his chin cupped in his hands, his eyes bore into those of his unexpected visitor.

"Speak. I'm listening. Of course, don't raise your voice. The roofs and trees, even the clouds have ears.

Tchicoz smiled and spoke softly, "I know through Jacques Cervier, number 17, that you're the Turkish ex-captain Ismaïl Kadeuy, number 33. I see a pen and pad in the front pocket of your coat. Would you please write down what I tell you and send it at once to Issyk-Kul by wireless in the secret code, which you know but I don't."

Ismaïl Kadeuy showed no sign of surprise. Obviously, he'd seen many other men working for Zattan. He took the top off the pen, opened the pad and muttered, "Talk, comrade."

Tchicoz dictated slowly:

"The *Taurus* has been captured by the yacht *Fulgur*. Pedro del Campo is Leo Saint-Clair the Nyctalope. He teamed up with the Japanese Gnô Mitang, owner of the yacht, and Marc Ayol, the captain. The sloop's cargo was taken. Saint-Clair and Ayol left alone with the *Taurus*. Cervier, me and the three others from the sloop were put in chains on board the yacht. I escaped in the Famagusta bay. The *Fulgur* lifted anchor and went directly out to sea. I await orders. Pedro Tchicoz."

He stopped talking.

Kadeuy stopped writing and said, "I see now that it is, indeed, more urgent and more important than eating and drinking, even if you're dying of hunger and thirst. But you're not dying, comrade, unless it's of indigestion. I'll go send this right away. Make yourself at home. Go to the kitchen and eat and drink whatever you want. There are three bedrooms. Choose whichever pleases you. Lie down and sleep if you're tired. Otherwise, smoke and read or just think about things if you prefer. I'll be back by noon. We can eat together then if you want. Dorah will make a bouillabaisse like I had in Marseille in 1916 when I was a prisoner of war... Don't thank me. Your message is invaluable. It's me who is in your debt. Til noon, comrade."

Without another word Ismaïl Kadeuy hurried out of the garden.

Tchicoz laughed silently. His savage face blossomed into satisfaction. He stood up, went down the passage and saw a door open on the right into a huge kitchen.

At Issyk-Kul on the morning of April 4th, the Portuguese Manoël Guerro, head of the wireless service for the "Prince of Darkness," as Leonid Zattan calls himself, was personally checking the equipment on the top floor of the West Tower when one of the eight men on duty received a message whose secret code was known only by three people at Issyk-Kul: Zattan, Guerro himself and Woldski. So, the employee got up to give his boss the pale pink paper on which the message had just been automatically typed. On the dotted line used for the sender's location there was simply this: G. F. 33.

"Hey, this is coming from Cyprus and good old Kadeuy," Manoël thought to himself. "What's happening over there? Dreamy old Ismaïl's got a cushy job because it's usually so quiet in that sector. Let's see."

In his personal office on the fourth floor, right under the huge wireless set-up, Guerro got down to translating the message into clear and simple French. When he was finished, he had turned white.

"Caraco!" he swore. "This Pedro del Campo who tricked me good, who fooled the Prince even better, this guy's the famous Nyctalope! If Kadeuy hasn't suddenly gone mad, if this Tchicoz exists and isn't lying, if this message tells the truth, the Prince is going to be grateful... Quick!"

With the elevators and moving walkways, the wireless chief took five minutes to get from the West Tower to the South. He was met in the Supreme Master's vestibule by Ali Soud.

"Ali, is the Lord in?"

"Yes."

"I need to see him. Hurry. Utmost importance."

"He's sleeping," the valet said.

"Wake him up."

"You'll take responsibility?"

"Yes, yes, a thousand times over, yes."

"Very well, I'll wake up the Lord."

Ten minutes later, his face refreshed with ether, his supple body in thin, wool pajamas, bare feet in slippers, Leonid Zattan met his high-ranking servant, Manoël Guerro, in his workroom. After a deep bow received with a kindly wave of the hand, the pink slip of neatly typed paper passed from Guerro's right hand to Zattan's.

He read it.

And he turned pale... but he remained silent, pensive, looking down.

Then he looked at Guerro and spoke quietly, "Swear on your life that you'll forget this message. I know very well that you won't talk about it, but for your own sake, forget about it so that even your eyes won't betray you to your fellow officers or especially if you're with Del Campo... The Nyctalope! Saint-Clair! The most daunting hero of modern times! Him involved in this great adventure of the Antichrist! Him, my prisoner now in Issyk-Kul! Him, dead in five minutes if I choose! Manoël, go, go, and forget if you want to live... Forget!"

After an even deeper bow than the first, the chief of the wireless turned around and left the room without a word.

When the curtain fell back over the closed door, Zattan started pacing from one end of his vast lair to the other, arms crossed but holding the unfolded paper that he read over and over.

"Good!" he burst out. "Now I know it by heart."

A wood fire was burning in the big fireplace because Zattan liked real fire, but the room was also heated by a hidden network of air ducts. The Lord of Issyk-Kul threw the paper onto a burning log. It flamed and was consumed.

"I'll think about it some more, examine my idea inside and out," he muttered. "I have to control my impatience. In an hour my decision will be final... and then... oh, Sylvie, the only reason the Nyctalope's here is to save you, I know!"

He rang for Ali Soud. It took him one hour to get ready, dressed for horse riding, and have breakfast. Then he went back to his "studio", lit a cigarette, sat by the closed window—it was pouring rain this morning—and sent for Woldski.

The lieutenant-secretary entered with a red leather briefcase under his arm. "Lord, I'm honored to see you this morning."

"Hello, Woldski. The mail?"

"Nothing important." And he opened his briefcase.

"Good!" Zattan said. "You answer them and I'll sign. Write down my orders."

Woldski took a pen and notepad out of his briefcase.

"Secret!" Zattan enunciated. After a brief pause he continued, "First: Urgently send Petrus Ivitch in a plane to Famagusta. Manoël will go with him. A man is waiting at Ismaïl Kadeuy's house. His name is Pedro Tchicoz. Bring him back to me. Right away, posthaste, as soon as possible. Send a message before the plane with what I've just said. Stop."

"Got it."

"Second: assign the four best spies to watch Pedro Del Campo and put two on Marco Pampil. They'll report to you every two hours with every word and movement of those two. You'll report to me at noon and 6 pm. But if anything seems to you—do you hear me?—anything at all seems connected in any way to the South Tower or to me or to the prisoner, don't wait to come to me right away. I won't be leaving the castle. If you can't find me in three minutes, have me called. Stop."

"Got it."

"Read it over and memorize it. Then burn it."

The secretary read what he had written, then again slowly, tore the page out of the notebook, walked over to the fireplace and tossed the paper into the flames.

"That's all," Zattan said. "Go!"

The secretary left.

"Now for Sylvie," the Kalmyk mumbled.

The cigarette that he'd only touched twice with his lips gone dry from suppressed emotion was dropped into an ashtray and he went to his bedroom. Without bothering to take off his boots he lay down on the bed that Ali Soud had just "made" as promptly as always. He flipped one, two, three, four switches. Lights lit up, mirrors titled and the telephone horn bent down.

Leonid Zattan was surprised, disappointed, even humiliated. He was expecting to see his prisoner up and about, in the throes of insomnia, assailed by gloomy, unsettling thoughts, maybe in tears and sobbing. But in the dim, greenish glow of an electric nightlight, Sylvie was sleeping in her bed, peaceful as could be, even smiling a little as if she were having a pleasant dream.

"So be it!" he sat up. "She's mine no matter what happens. I know the truth about the *Taurus* thanks to Tchicoz. Plus, there can be no enemy more dangerous to me than Saint-Clair the Nyctalope and this formidable man is in my power, especially since he doesn't think I'm aware of it and watching him... In ten days, April 14th, the European and Asian delegates will come to get my orders. On April 15th at the latest the fate of the Nyctalope and the destiny of Sylvie will be sealed... And I, me... Oh, the days are going to be long for my pride and love and ambition!"

He flipped a switch and the lights went out, the mirrors turned dark and the horn straightened up again.

"Now we're going to watch the man I'd seen only as Pedro Del Campo but it's the Nyctalope I have to be observing!"

CHAPTER X

In Famagusta, Tchicoz had figured wrongly when he'd seen the *Fulgur* lift anchor and head out to sea. He was sure the yacht was leaving Cyprus to go wait in some port in Turkey or Syria. At most he could only have made a rough guess about it.

Gnô Mitang, however, who was the real captain on board the *Fulgur* had decided the yacht's direction would depend on what Jacques Cervier had to say during the conversation they would have on April 4th.

After sharing this decision with Lieutenant Guennec, the Japanese let the ship sail slowly away from Famagusta after he'd given orders for the speedboat to return immediately. Then he went to his cabin, a big sitting room/bedroom in the back of the yacht.

"Feraud," he said to the sailor he'd taken on as an orderly, "take this paper to petty officer Lequic." And he scribbled on a notepad: "*Order to bring prisoner number 1 to my cabin on April 4th at 7:48 am. Gnô Mitang.*"

For, the two sentinels and two jailors in the stockade could only obey orders that were signed, dated and written within five minutes of receiving them. And only Gnô Mitang and Paul Guennec were authorized to send such orders.

A few minutes later Yves Lequic brought prisoner number 1 who was none other than Jacques Cervier. With a wave of his hand Gnô Mitang offered the ringleader a swivel chair that was bolted to the floor. He himself was sitting behind an American desk in a corner in front of this chair.

Although only eight days in, the captivity had fully brought out the shifty weasel in him. His eyes blinked in the sunlight pouring in through the open portholes. Dressed only in grey pants and a blue jersey, his head shaved, barefoot, his hands fidgeting since he couldn't grab onto a vest or put them in his pockets, the traitor was in a sorry state.

With his inscrutable, cold, Asian eyes, Gnô Mitang stared at the contemptible but formidable criminal who couldn't stand it and looked down. After a few seconds of this the Japanese spoke.

"Monsieur, the most dangerous of your men has escaped. He's reached Cyprus. I need to know whether there is somewhere on the island where he can find one of those secret stations that Zattan has so cleverly set up around the world, particularly around the Mediterranean. Through our master Mathias Lumen, God bless him, I know about a lot of these stations. But I don't know if there's one on Cyprus. You're going to tell me." He stopped there.

Jacques Cervier looked up, set his dreary eyes on the Japanese, shrugged his shoulders and shook his head. This could mean either "I don't know" or "I won't tell you".

.

Gnô Mitang went on in the same icy voice, "You're going to tell me. And you won't lie because one of two things: either there's a Zattan station in Cyprus or there's not. Listen carefully. If there is and you refuse to give me the name, address and all the details, for me it would be like there wasn't. Then I'll have you shot and thrown into the sea with 100 pounds of lead strapped to your chest. That's how you'll pay for your silence or for Zattan's negligence to set up a post in Cyprus."

Cervier turned white as a sheet. His shifty eyes twitched. He grunted, his throat constricted. "But I don't..."

"Wait, I haven't finished. If there's a station and you want to have a chance of survival, tell me where it is, the name of the chief, how many people are there..."

"But, monsieur," Cervier raised his trembling hands above his head, "I don't know..."

"You don't know? Too bad for you. In five minutes you'll be shot because the life of an enemy who knows nothing is worth nothing. Besides, you've committed crimes that the laws in many civilized countries would punish with death."

Cervier straightened up as if he'd been lashed by a whip. "There's not... there's not..."

"I told you," the Japanese cut him off. "If there's a station there and you know it and refuse to tell me... or there's a station and you don't know about it... or there really isn't one. These three cases mean the same thing: you're completely useless to me. You're just a petty criminal who disgusts me, who's a burden to me, whom I'll kill in the name of the law of civilized countries whose authority I will assume."

There was a silence during which Cervier slumped again in his chair.

Gnô Mitang wrapped up, "So, that's your final word? There's not?"

His legs stretched out, arms hanging down, his head buried in his hollow chest, the criminal was panting. Maybe he didn't have the strength to answer.

"Very well. Too bad for you."

Gnô pressed one of the buttons on the left of his desk. Yves Lequic came through the curtain over the door. Gnô snapped out the orders. "At once, the firing squad, a plank, 100 pounds of iron and a rope. Then summon the whole crew to the quarterdeck. When everything's ready, come and get this man. I'll tell everyone why he deserves to die and I'll give the order to shoot. They'll shoot him and toss his corpse overboard. Go on!"

But before the arm of Yves Lequic could part the curtain again, Jacques Cervier raised his head, showed his fear-contorted face, his teary eyes and twisted mouth, and he muttered, "There's a station. I'll talk... but... you can't ever hand me over to Leonid Zattan. Swear you won't give me to him. If you don't swear, rather than taking the chance of falling into his hands after... after betraying him, even if I'm forced to by your appalling abuse of authority... Yes, exactly, I'd rather be shot right away than face Zattan... There's a station, there is, but swear to me, swear it..."

"Lequic, I'm cancelling my orders. You may leave but stay close in case I need you." And to Cervier, "I give you my word to never hand you over to Leonid Zattan. Speak up and don't lie. Otherwise, we'll be back to square one when I learn the truth."

The traitor made a motion of resigned despair. "Under these conditions, you're holding my life and freedom in your hands. I'll tell you about the Cyprus station and others and about Issyk-Kul and whatever you want... I won't keep anything to myself. I can see I'm caught in a trap that only you can unlock. Squeeze it all out of me like a lemon. Then drop me off in some port where there's an English bank. I swear on my life that no one in the world will ever hear of Jacques Cervier again and that I'll stay in some little town as the most innocent renter with an old servant, drinking coffee at the local café and playing a game of boules when the weather's good... I..."

He stopped talking, looking stupid, his eyes staring into space.

"That's nice," Gnô had listened thoughtfully with both scorn and surprise. "If what you know and tell me is useful, it's possible that I'll allow you to retire with a radical change of lifestyle. God alone can make you atone in this world or the next. But for the time being, you have to give me details about this Zattan station in Cyprus. Talk."

And Jacques Cervier talked.

At 1 pm in the garden patio of the pale pink house on one of the old squares in Famagusta, the Turkish ex-captain Ismaïl Kadeuy and the Mexican scoundrel Pedro Tchicoz had been sitting at a table for a few minutes and Dorah the servant had just put a huge bowl brimming with a Marseillaise bouillabaisse when the rusty old doorbell coughed out five or six convulsive rings.

"Oh, what's that about?" Ismaïl sounded very surprised. "At this hour?"

Tchicoz flinched nervously.

But Dorah smiled unexpectedly with all her 32 teeth, magnificent even with her trollish wrinkles. "It's a surprise for dessert. I got the idea coming back from the market. I ordered something to be delivered." And she scurried to answer the door.

It was indeed a surprise. But not dessert.

Men came rushing in through the open door. Two, five, six. The last one closed the door, shoved the old servant to the ground, straddled her back, gagged her, tied her hands to her neck and said in English, "Don't move, dear Dorah." Then after locking the door, he leaned back against it, took out a twist of black tobacco, gave it a hearty bite and started chewing with great satisfaction.

Before Tchicoz and Kadeuy had time to throw back their chairs and stand up, the five other intruders were on them. Four grabbed their arms while the fifth just stood in front of them, empty-handed. It was Gnô Mitang, the Japanese dressed all in white, a yachtsman hat on his head. His five men were wearing peacoats and white twill pants, espadrilles and marine berets with red pompoms whose red ribbon bore gold letters that said "the yacht *Fulgur*". Tchicoz' hawk eyes saw everything. The thought, "Gnô must be pretty sure of himself not to take off those identifying ribbons!" He forgot to remember that at this time of day, in this season, the streets of Famagusta were as empty as the streets of Toledo in July. At 1 pm the Cypriots and English were eating or taking a siesta. Gnô Mitang and the five sailors from the *Fulgur* had crossed town without seeing a living soul nor been seen by any shopkeepers whose doors and windows were shutting out the light and heat.

As soon as they were seized, Tchicoz and Kadeuy were tied up. They didn't gag them. What was the use? This precaution was needed for Dorah, however, who could've foolishly yelped in fear. But the Mexican knew that a scandal always weighs against the reckless one who causes it if he doesn't have a clear conscience. It's one thing to swagger around in front of two lazy border control officers or to concoct a story for a sleepy-eyed policeman in the little port town, but when you're Pedro Tchicoz, you don't call the police for help against a man who looks and acts and obviously possesses the moral force and social influence of Gnô Mitang, captain of the *Fulgur*. As for Ismaïl Kadeuy, he was a fatalist and a fatalist rarely cries out for help.

There was no struggle because the four sailors got the two victims under control before they had a chance to react. And there was no shouting or yelling because Tchicoz and Kadeuy were not idiots.

Tied up but with enough play in their legs to keep their balance, they were standing now.

"Very good," Gnô Mitang said in French.

Kadeuy, with sincere (and therefore all the more ludicrous) regret, spoke softly in the same language, "Since Allah willed that you come, monsieur, contrary to the reasoned opinion that Tchicoz gave me not ten minutes ago for the second time, Allah could've at least brought you here an hour later... This divine bouillabaisse shouldn't go to waste!"

Gnô smiled. He liked the spirit, understood the fatalists and, among all the peoples of the world, had a soft spot for the Turks, at least for their character before the opening of a Parliament, the closure of the harems, the abolition of dogs in Constantinople and the habit of wearing hats instead of the fez or turban. Ismaïl Kadeuy amused him.

"Very good," he repeated. "But cheer up, monsieur. For you, at least, and for me, this delicious smelling, beautifully red, splendid bouillabaisse will not go to waste. It's still steaming. My men already ate before leaving the yacht, but not me. This savory spread whets my appetite. If you please, monsieur Kadeuy, I will replace Mr. Tchicoz at the table."

"My word," the Turk was a little embarrassed, "I'd be honored and even pleased provided that you don't try to trick or force me to betray my duty before we've finished the meal, had coffee and smoked a few cigarettes. It'd be a waste, a dishonor, a disgrace to ruin such a pleasure. But afterward, I'll be your prisoner again and I hope I will earn your respect if not your good favor."

Tchicoz didn't miss any of this. It was the first time he caught a glimpse of feeling in the cold, impassive face of the Japanese. Indeed, Gnô Mitang was smiling, his eyes sparkling, his whole face open and cheerful.

"Bravo!" the master of the *Fulgur* exclaimed. "Here's a Turk after my own heart, an old-fashioned Turk, in the good old French style. How's it possible?"

Kadeuy responded simply, "Before being diverted in my life by the will of God, the smile of a woman and the baccarat tables in Monte Carlo, I spent several years as the military attaché to the Ottoman embassy in Paris. I have remained, I believe, a man of honor and good taste."

"I only ask to see your handywork," Gnô said.

The Turk jumped in again, "Whoa, monsieur! I don't doubt you'll enjoy my taste in food, but I fear the man of honor will prove more difficult for you..."

"Well, let's talk about that after the coffee."

Gnô made a gesture. The sailors had heard and understood. In the blink of an eye, Kadeuy was untied. As he turned questioningly toward Tchicoz, Gnô declared coldly:

"Boys, put this villain in that rocking-chair over there. And tell the other to let the servant go so one of you can bring her to her boss." Then to Kadeuy, "Monsieur, I want Tchicoz to witness our one-on-one. He'll see and hear everything. I want to avoid any outrageous accusations even from a scoundrel like him. During and after the meal, nothing will be said or done between us that he won't know about."

"I was going to ask this very thing," the Turk proclaimed. "Fate put Tchicoz and I together under the same master. I only met him this morning. I don't know if he's a scoundrel or an honest man. And I don't want to know. I know my duty. He ought to know his." After a moment of silence and with a snide little smile, "Luckily, Tchicoz, you drank and ate this morning when I wasn't here. So, I'm not too sorry that you can't share this bouillabaisse."

Tchicoz shrugged, grumbled a curse, threw his head back on the rocking-chair and pretended to go to sleep, or maybe he really did—appearance or reality didn't seem to bother the two diners at all.

Dorah showed up both outraged and astonished. But the doorbell rang.

"This time it really is the surprise dessert!" Ismaïl declared merrily. And he sent his servant off to her kitchen duties.

Soon, Gnô Mitang pronounced that the bouillabaisse was "first class" and he had seconds imitating the fatalist gourmand Kadeuy. Then Dorah served roast chicken and salad. Finally, the dessert—the surprise was ice cream with strawberries. It was topped off with Cypriot wine from the back of the cellar. Afterwards they had coffee—Turkish, of course!—and cigarettes.

The watch on Gnô's left wrist showed 3 o'clock when Kadeuy finally slipped out of the hammock he was lying in, stood before his guest sitting in a rocking-chair and spoke simply and solemnly:

"Monsieur, now that I've fulfilled all my obligations to you as a host, I would like to protest strongly against the violation of my home and against this abuse of power that you have committed not only by holding me under guard but also by threatening me with a gun. And then by tying up Monsieur Tchicoz who was my guest before your intrusion. I respectfully demand that you free Monsieur Tchicoz, whom you have no right to deprive of his liberty, and that you and your men leave immediately. If you refuse, I will be forced to…"

"Monsieur," Gnô Mitang, cut him off brutally, "one more word and you'll be joining your accomplice. Sit down! Good. Now first of all, do you know who Tchicoz is and what he did to deserve your hospitality?"

"I don't have to know and I didn't ask," Kadeuy answered with dignity.

"You will know now. He's a traitor and a killer and a kidnapper. He's also a thief and will continue to be so if I set him free. Are you friends with scoundrels like this?"

Kadeuy replied. More and more his attitude and tone of voice proved that this intelligent, brave and probably honorable man was not playing games. "I am neither friend nor enemy to him. He is my guest and as such I defend him."

"Very well. But he is my prisoner, just like you. I want to know certain things from you two. Therefore, I'm going to ask you both some questions. But first, be warned. I know my actions are illegal. I know that others can result that at first glance a judge would consider criminal… I know all this but it's not going to stop me. Because I also know that you and Tchicoz are both, knowingly or not, serving the plans of Leonid Zattan who is plotting nothing less than the destruction of the entire world by fire and sword!

"Now, me, I also serve a man, Mathias Lumen, who fights against Leonid Zattan as the principle of good fights against the principle of evil. Right now this war is secret, private, local, but it will soon become public and spread over the globe if Zattan defeats Lumen.

"And in this war, if Tchicoz had me in his hands, he'd torture me or kill me, whether he felt it more useful to make me talk or to shut me up forever. That's an example that makes a rule for both sides. I warn you, therefore, both of you, that once and for all I'm done with the normal laws of civilized countries and against Leonid Zattan and his troops I recognize only one law: martial law.

"Today we're in English territory, tomorrow we'll be in French territory or Italian, Spanish, German, maybe Japanese… If I happen to fall under the jurisdiction of one of these countries during my private, secret mission, I'll do what I can to respect them, but in the meantime, I can only follow my conscience. And my conscience, you understand, will not flinch at any means to achieve my goal: the victory of Mathias Lumen, the principle of Order and Good, over Leonid Zattan, the principle of Anarchy and Evil.

"I've spoken. And now, Monsieur Kadeuy, you have the honor of being the first interrogated."

Silence. Tchicoz opened his eyes and stared at the Turk. One of the sailors was guarding the closed door at the end of the hallway with Dorah, gagged again and tied to a chair. The four others were posted at the four angles of the patio in which Tchicoz sat tied to a chair with his back to the empty table and Kadeuy stood free to move. Facing the Mexican and the Turk, the cold and terrible Japanese stood up and leaned the back of his thighs against the edge of the well. He crossed his arms and still in a cold, calm voice said:

"Monsieur Kadeuy, will you tell me everything that Tchicoz has done and said since he entered your house?"

"No, I won't," the Turk answered curtly.

"Will you tell me what you yourself did and said as a result of Tchicoz being with you?"

"No, monsieur."

Gnô Mitang reminded him, "Consider that I am the law and justice here and I won't hesitate, if I think it necessary, to use the most violent means of persuasion."

"As you wish. I won't talk."

"So be it! Maybe the search I'm going to make of your house will compensate for you silence, which is very bad for you, as I said, but of course very noble and brave too..."

While speaking, Gnô Mitang's keen eyes were watching the thin, pale face of Ismaïl Kadeuy. At the word "search" he saw the face get flushed.

"Good!" he thought. "He's got documents here. It'll be a useful find, but it probably won't reveal to me what Tchicoz has been doing here. Kadeuy won't talk. He is, as he said, a man of honor. There's probably more like him working for Zattan. We'll have to take them out when we have the chance—it's a lot harder to fight against an honorable, courageous man than against a reckless scamp. Let's get Kadeuy out of here and deal with Tchicoz. No kid gloves with him."

Out loud he said, "Monsieur Kadeuy, I'm going to lock you up in a room where you won't be able to see or hear what is said and done here. Do you give me your word that you won't try to escape or harm me in any way?"

Stiff and even paler, he answered, "Monsieur, I cannot give you my word."

"Very well," Gnô didn't press him. He turned to two of the sailors, "Feraud, Blanchard, take him to the farthest room in the house and tie him to the bed, tightly but not cruelly. Blanchard, you stay there with the door closed. Feraud, you come back here."

While his orders were being carried out, Gnô remained silent, staring at the lowered eyes and worried brow of Tchicoz. When Feraud came back, the Japanese told the Mexican, "You heard. So, I have one question for you. Here it is: are you going to tell me what I want to know?"

Tchicoz barked out, "I get you. I'm sure you won't hesitate to torture me to get me to talk and to kill me slowly if I refuse. Well, I don't like to suffer for no good reason and I value my life. But I have to protect it, my life I mean, from the hatred of the man I will betray. Leonid Zattan has a long arm and an iron fist. It'll cost you dearly for me to get out of his reach, but I'll talk."

Gnô was still impassive when he replied, "We'll see. I'll respond depending on what you did here. And depending on how I respond, your life will be more or less under Zattan's threat. I will not, therefore, set a price. Speak and I'll pay what you need to start a new life, safe and serene wherever you want."

"You swear?" Tchicoz didn't trust him.

"I never swear. I said yes or no and it means yes or no."

The Mexican studied the unreadable Japanese face. Then he shrugged. "OK, whatever."

He spurted out, without omitting the slightest detail, what he'd done and said from his run-in with the border patrol up to being caught in the garden-patio. It didn't take him fifteen minutes to utterly betray Zattan. His betrayal was unrestrained, straight to the point, factual and precise. With a strange pride coupled with the love of life that formed the backbone of his character, he concluded:

"This morning, I proved my courage to you by escaping. Now, by obeying your wishes I've proved to you my intelligence. This morning I got more out of escaping than out of getting caught. Now I'm getting more out of talking than out of staying silent since I've got your promise to set me free and let me enjoy my freedom. You know everything. Act on it. I'll wait. No need to guard me, I won't try to escape this time—what would I get out of it?"

A thin, fleeting smile crossed Gnô Mitang's lips. "Maybe you won't get anything out of it, but maybe circumstances will change and you'll deem it more profitable to change sides again. Your courage and intelligence, Tchicoz, make you too unstable. So, I'll watch you just like I do Cervier, your equal in intelligence. You'll be set free later today, tomorrow, whenever I feel that your courage and intelligence can do nothing against me. Feraud, handcuff this man and chain his ankles. Then take him to Blanchard who can guard him along with the Turk."

"As you wish," Tchicoz shrugged his shoulders.

Twenty minutes later, with the help of Feraud and Bonnet, the methodical Gnô Mitang had finished searching the house of ex-captain Kadeuy. The search ended in the Turk's own bedroom and in this room was a chest hidden in the wall behind the bed. Ismaïl had locked the chest before going to breakfast but had neglected to spin the four number dials. With the keys taken out of Kadeuy's pocket, the chest was opened easily. Gnô immediately saw that their find was rich, plentiful, precious and extremely useful.

Then, for the third time he reread the wireless message dictated by Tchicoz and sent a few hours before to the Lord of Issyk-Kul.

"The *Taurus* has been captured by the yacht *Fulgur*. Pedro del Campo is Leo Saint-Clair the Nyctalope. He teamed up with the Japanese Gnô Mitang, owner of the yacht, and Marc Ayol, the captain. The sloop's cargo was taken. Saint-Clair and Ayol left alone with the *Taurus*. Cervier, me and the three others from the sloop were put in chains on board the yacht. I escaped in the Famagusta bay. The *Fulgur* lifted anchor and went directly out to sea. I await orders. Pedro Tchicoz."

The "orders" were found on a sheet of paper attached to the message. Kadeuy had written on the sheet the answer that came back from Issyk-Kul. It was short and clear since Gnô had found out from Tchicoz and Cervier what the numbers meant:

"3 to 33, direct. Tchicoz waits there for urgent plane. Z."

On a memo pad, which Kadeuy kept meticulously up-to-date, Gnô learned that the electric planes from Issyk-Kul, like the six-seater *Aquilon* with a "convertible body", flew at an average speed of around 185 miles per hour. He made a quick calculation and figured:

"From Issyk to Cyprus, around 2,200 miles. So, roughly a 12-hour flight. Leave around 10 am, the plane will be here at 10 pm. Here at Famagusta? Obviously not! But on the water nearby. Will an envoy come to pick up Tchicoz in the house? Yes, certainly. The order said to wait in place. Moreover, it's common sense that Zattan's planes never land in exactly the same place... It's 4:10 pm. I have less than six hours to wait for the envoy from Issyk-Kul. So, I have time to examine in detail the documents we've found, to talk more with Tchicoz if he has anything more to say, to think and make two or three different plans depending on the circumstances..."

Thinking all this to himself, Gnô, still in the bedroom, had sat at the table on which the documents pulled out of the chest were piled up. The chest had been closed again and the bed put back in place. The sunny room was as neat as ever. Feraud and Bonnet were at the door on guard for any sign or word from their boss.

Gnô Mitang was looking at a map he'd unfolded. An unusual map because it was printed by the private cartographic service of Prince Zattan. On a scale of 1:2,000,000 it showed the Mediterranean Basin and Western Asia, the Dardanelles at 80 degrees longitude east...

All of a sudden, his thin lips cracked a smile, his eyes sparkled and he muttered a thought so low that Bonnet and Feraud heard only an indistinct mumble.

"Seize the plane, go to Issyk-Kul, sneak in, free Sylvie, the Nyctalope and Marc Ayol, and capture Zattan. Then gather up all archives, burn down the castle and denounce the anarchic organizations to each government and to the general public. Now that's a preventive plan while waiting for Nostradamus' prophecy concerning Sylvie to come true... But what a chaos of obstacles... No matter! I'll have to take a closer look at it before adopting it for good. For the moment, however, I've got to rectify the consequences of Tchicoz' message on the Nyctalope and Marc Ayol. Let's think about it!"

He unbuttoned his white pea coat, pulled out of an inside pocket a thin case that he popped open and took out a long, flat cigar of blonde, very dry tobacco.

"Feraud, a light!"

The yellow wick of a lighter flamed in the hands of the sailor. With his feet on the edge of the table, leaning back, balancing the chair, the Japanese said:

"Feraud, Bonnet, leave. Go keep Sylvain company and make sure he's not having too much fun with the maid in the hallway. At the slightest sign of trouble, come and tell me. Go on."

The two sailors left, the last to go closed the door. In the silent bedroom Gnô smoked, eyes half-closed, his supple body rocking slightly, his brow furrowed a little in deep and methodical thought...

Thanks to the documents from the chest, Gnô Mitang knew of the wireless station set up in the foothills of the Kyrenia Mountains, about fifteen miles from Famagusta. He knew that Ismaïl Kadeuy had a farm there with goats and a goatherd and that the main occupant of the farm was another Turk named Ibrahim Denver, the telegraph operator and guard of the station. He had found out that to go back and forth from the pink house in Famagusta to his farm, Kadeuy used a small, fast van parked in a locked shed at the end of a road that was more or less accessible for the rural properties in the mountainous regions. He also had the key to the different secret ciphers and the code for the calls and signals used by Zattan and his Mediterranean agents. In sum, he was well armed to act.

But what action should he take? And where should he target first?

Diving into his meditation at 4 o'clock, Gnô didn't come out of it until 6, after smoking four cigars. He looked at his watch. "Good. I have four or five hours before the arrival of Zattan's envoy. That's more than enough time for me to set everything up."

He stood up, left carrying Kadeuy's keys and went to the room where Feraud and Blanchard were guarding the Turk and the Mexican.

"I'll be gone for half an hour at most," he told them. "Keep watching them and don't leave the room."

He went down the hallway to Bonnet and Sylvain who were lying on a mat watching the gagged and bound Dorah in her chair. At the sight of their boss, the two sailors sprang up.

"I'm going out," Gnô told them too. "Stay on guard. If anyone rings, don't answer, but if he persists, let him in, grab him and get him bound and gagged. I'll figure out later what to do with him. If it's two or three people, don't hesitate to use your blackjacks to knock them out if you need to. Got it?"

"Yes, monsieur," they chimed in together.

And Gnô Mitang left the house.

Nineteen minutes later he was back, but with Kadeuy's van. He parked the vehicle right in front of the pink house, jumped out, rang the bell, identified himself and entered.

In the van he was carrying three big, canvas sacks that he'd found in the shed. It only took fifteen minutes to bag the three prisoners, bound and gagged, and "load" them into the van. Feraud got into the driver's seat behind the wheel. Bonnet, Blanchard and Sylvain sat in the back on the bags, which were not air-tight so the captives could breathe. Gnô Mitang locked the front door of the pink house and slipped into the passenger seat next to Feraud who started the engine.

Only a few Cypriots were out on the square. For a couple of minutes there were a soldier and an English sailor, but they barely gave an uninterested glance at the van and the sailors inside. Since there were ships from various countries in the port, the brief sight of the Japanese was nothing out of the ordinary to the locals or the English in the small square.

The van left the city without a hitch. It rode along a bad road that led northeast not far from the coast for twenty minutes. It stopped in a deserted area, wild and desolate, only 500 yards from a chaos of rocks cascading down to the sea. And there, in a round cove, the *Fulgur* was anchored, all geared up and ready to go.

Gnô leaned forward and inspected the landscape. "No border patrol. If they're hiding and decide to come out, too bad for them. Sailors, stay alert to my orders! Get out your blackjacks. We'll bring them on board with us, at least for a few hours."

Silence.

And then, "Feraud, you watch the van. Blanchard, Bonnet, Sylvain, empty the sacks."

In no time, Kadeuy, Tchicoz and Dorah were standing next to the van, ankles unchained but their hands still tied and their mouths still gagged.

Gnô spoke to them in English so that Dorah would understand. "I invite you to follow me calmly, otherwise we'll have to carry you. Any futile resistance is a waste of energy for all of us."

Down through the chaos of rocks by a track used by goats and smugglers, they reached the sandy beach. A dinghy was waiting there with two men. The newcomers climbed in. Once on board the yacht, Ismaïl Kadeuy, Pedro Tchicoz and Dorah were put in rooms and treated in whatever way Gnô deemed both convenient and necessary. The Japanese talked with Paul Guennec for a good 30 minutes. Then the dinghy went back to shore with Gnô, Bonnet, Blanchard, Sylvain and the first mate Yves Lequic whom the boss figured was good to bring not only in case he needed someone to command the four other sailors, but also just to increase his small gang by one more intelligent, clever, strong and brave man.

Feraud drove the six of them back to Famagusta and the pink house as tranquilly as they had come. The van was left in front of the door to serve as a kind of screen. Gnô had given orders to bring enough food for the six of them to eat well for four days. And thus the three canvas bags were brought back into the pink house and the provisions taken out, which Blanchard and Sylvain put away in the kitchen or the pantry in the basement. Was the Japanese planning to use the bags again as prisoner removal?

When everything in Kadeuy's house was set up as planned, Gnô Mitang ordered a simple but refreshing meal to be prepared quickly with a little wine and a lot of coffee.

"Because it's very likely that we won't be sleeping tonight," he explained.

Once the meal was done, Gnô assigned his men: Feraud and Blanchard at the front door, Sylvain and Bonnet at the kitchen entrance to the hallway, and he kept Lequic with himself in the garden-patio. The five sailors had their black-jacks conveniently hanging from their belts next to a long, broad dagger in a sheath. All of them were furnished with rope and special gags with little balls. As for the Japanese, he carried no weapon. He figured that his best weapon, since the eventual confrontation had to make as little noise as possible, was his skill and strength in jiu-jitsu.

When everyone was in place, Gnô thought, "Even if Zattan's envoy arrives at the earliest time we've estimated, I've still got plenty of time to smoke a cigar."

On board the *Fulgur* he had taken the precaution of refilling his case. He took it out of his inside pocket, removed a cigar, split the end and lit it... and the scent of the Havana mingled with the odor of the trees and flowers on the patio, which was shrouded in twilight shadows...

JEAN DE LA HIRE
LA CAPTIVE DU DÉMON
LA PRINCESSE ROUGE

A. FAYARD ET Cie ÉDITEURS PARIS

LE VOLUME

PART TWO: THE RED PRINCESS

CHAPTER I

They said in the age of Abelard, they proclaimed under Louis XIV, they repeated every day since the beginning of the 20th century: Paris is the intellectual capital of the world. And in fact, it does seem that no idea has ever prevailed and prospered coming from the depths of Siberia, Alaska, Africa, Patagonia if it hadn't been born or at least nourished in the intellectually fertile ground of Paris. Since the fall of the Roman Empire, it's been at Lutetia, at Paris that, in hidden seeds or in public deeds, all kinds of revolutions have been created that civilized humanity are pleased to consider the essential elements of progress.

It was, therefore, logical, and in a way fated that it was in Paris that on April 4th, 1926, the congress of "Agents of the Revolution for Mankind" (A.R.M. as they called themselves for short) took place. An ultra-secret congress unknown to even the leaders of the numerous revolutionary organizations that would obey the decisions of the congress. And was it fate that the initials were also the first letters of the words, "arms", "army" and "armament"? War! And what a war! The one, certainly, whose supreme leader was named in the Apocalypse as the Antichrist.

There were twelve of these agents. They represented the twelve biggest countries that made up the civilized world on Earth. Or more precisely, they represented the most extreme revolutionary factions and hordes of these countries.

For the past two months in particular, the twelve agents had been corresponding actively with one another. All the respective organizations of which they were, to all appearances, delegates but in reality the chiefs, had given them full executive powers. And the continual correspondence between the A.R.M. led to this secret meeting in Paris on April 4th.

Now, in Paris there's a place that is well suited to the most clandestine meetings. There is no risk of being seen, heard or caught by surprise, provided that you use it only at night when it's not open to the public. This place is called the "Chapelle Expiatoire". This monument was built by Louis XVIII between 1815 and 1826 in memory of Louis XVI and Marie Antoinette who had been buried there (the old Madeleine Cemetery) and remained so until they were moved to Saint Denis in 1815. It is located on Boulevard Haussmann.

A revolutionary conspirator would have to be really inexperienced to have any problem taking the place of a normal guard at the monument and the little park surrounding the Chapelle. And everybody knows that be he policeman or citizen there are loopholes in the administrative regulations so that the public monuments are sometimes visited outside of official opening hours.

Therefore, no one was surprised or took any notice on April 4th at 8:30 pm when an officer in his kepi opened one of the entrances to the park and let in eleven visitors, including one woman, and followed after them. He closed the gate, went to open the door of the Chapelle and the guide and his visitors disappeared.

The so-called officer led the way while the others followed single-file. Clearly, he knew the place because he guided the procession without hesitating after turning a knob that lit up several electric lights. The guide was the first to sit directly on the floor. He took the kepi off his head, placed it in front of him and spoke in French:

"Here we are, comrades. Do as I do. Let's talk freely because I can assure you without a doubt that no other living being can see or hear us."

He was thin, with short, red hair, clean-shaven, prying eyes and an intelligent brow. He waited for his eleven colleagues to sit in a circle. He had a slightly ironic smile on his face, probably from the thought of this spectacle of the twelve A.R.M. in this devoutly royalist chapel commemorating the horrific revolutionary glory—it was a spectacle rife with romantic contradictions.

He continued, "We all know one another. The Chinese, Hindu, African, Italian, English, Spanish, Danish, American, Argentinian, the Russian and me the French, we've met somewhere before. And we recognize one another, don't we?"

Each of them looked around and gave either a resounding or a muffled "*oui*" as a unanimous response.

The "guide" had spoken casually, not without a barely perceptible hint of mockery. He was obviously one of those people who always saw the comical side of the most tragic events. But he became completely serious and solemn when he resumed his speech.

"Comrades, one of us here is the spokesperson for Leonid Zattan, whom we have acknowledged as the master of us all. This person is not me. Let him now speak up without further ado."

Then the only woman in the gathering stood up and spoke in a firm but lyrical voice, in French but without the accent characteristic of aristocratic Russians, which she was in blood, spirit and wealth.

"I'm the one, as well as the delegate of the Neo-terrorist Russians. And here's the proof."

With a kind of grace that was both simple and majestic, she took the glove off her left hand, which she held up in the light of the nearest electric bulb. On her ring finger sparkled a magnificent ruby set in two golden eagle's claws.

Diana Ivanova, Princess Krosnovief by her marriage with the last heir of a grand Moscovite family settled in Paris before the war, had been a widow for three years. She was 32 years-old. Tall, slender, supple and spirited, dressed with refined simplicity but expensively, she was very beautiful, with sensual lips and magnificently dark eyes, with a faint saffron tint to her skin. Long before the death of her husband, she was affiliated with the secret organizations of the Moscovite Neo-terrorists and had given grisly proof of her loyalty, courage and merciless self-control. No one knew why this woman, once one of the idols of the cosmopolitan aristocracy, hopping between London, Paris, Monte-Carlo, Venice, Rome and Cairo, was living a double life, using her intelligence and talents and fortune on behalf of the global revolution. But the fact was that her outstanding services were justly appreciated by the A.R.M. and a few other leaders in the know. But they never found out, at least from her, why she did what she did. They called her the "Red Princess" or "Pretty Diana". They never knew her to have a lover. She held such prestige, born of admiration, respect, desire and a little terror, that none of the members of the gathering were surprised that she was the representative of the mysterious, powerful and formidable Lord of Issyk-Kul.

At the sight of the fateful ruby the eleven men bowed deeply. When they raised their heads, Diana Ivanova Krosnovief was sitting back down while putting her glove back on.

Then the "French" delegate, sounding humbler than before, said, "Comrade, it is your turn to speak. We're all ears."

Diana had put her gray leather handbag on the floor beside her. She leaned her elbows on her knees, clasped her hands together and leaned forward a little. "Comrades," she said softly, "first, please provide me with updates, in the usual order, on the state of your sectors about what is immediately relevant. Afterward I'll transmit the orders of the supreme leader."

The first who "updated" was the Chinese, the delegate for China, Japan, the French colonies and protectorates in the Far East, the Dutch East Indies and Australia. He spoke slowly with extreme precision and used Esperanto, which was even better known than French among the A.R.M. His colleagues paid close attention to what he said but remained totally impassive.

He wrapped up by saying, "A report was sent eight days ago to Issyk-Kul."

"Right," Diana said. "Next."

The Hindu took the floor, also in Esperanto—all the others would do the same. He represented the revolutionary organizations in India, Persia, Afghanistan, Turkey and Arabia. He used poetic language full of superlatives. He, too, concluded by announcing that he had sent a report to the supreme leader.

"Thank you," Diana remarked.

Then the African spoke. He was a sickly-looking black man, but his eyes and his entire face exuded a forceful determination that was not lacking in treachery. He had once been imprisoned by the French government when working as a colonial official in the Congo. He was the revolutionary representative of the whole African continent, Madagasgar, Comoros and La Réunion. He had not yet finished his report and would send it to Issyk-Kul in a few days.

"As soon as possible, please, comrade," the Red Princess demanded with severity in her eyes.

Then it was the Italian's turn. He smiled, spoke fast, used his hands a lot. He was the delegate for Italy, Greece and all the islands in the eastern Mediterranean. He had sent his report.

"Perfect," Diana concluded.

And the German, a short, skinny, blond man with glasses and a beard, gave a three-point account in a croaky but sometimes squeaky voice. He was there for Germany, Austria, Hungary, Switzerland and the Balkan countries. He had sent his report in duplicate.

"Congratulations," Diana smiled. "Now you, John Bolton."

The Englishman's report was short and to-the-point, riddled with numbers. He represented Great Britain, nothing else. He had sent his report, very succinct but complete by wireless.

"Excellent, next," Diana nodded.

The Spaniard recited solemnly. He was delegated for Spain, Portugal, the Azores, Madeira, the Canary Islands and Cape Verde. He had sent his report that very morning.

"Right," Diana said.

The Dane sounded like he was constantly twisting his words but miraculously came out making sense. He represented Denmark, Sweden, Norway and Iceland. He didn't know he was supposed to send his report. He had it in his coat pocket.

"A mistake!" Diana scolded. "You will send it tomorrow by the usual route."

The American from the United States appeared to be competing with his English colleague in brevity and arithmetic. He spoke in the name of all of North America including Mexico and the small republics that stretched down to the Panama Canal. He, too, had sent his report by wireless.

"Congratulations," Diana repeated.

Then the turn of the Argentinian who proceeded with questions that he answered himself. He was the delegate of all the countries in South America and the Antilles. Had he sent his report? Yes, of course, before leaving Buenos Aires for France.

"Very good," Diana said.

The Frenchman represented France, Luxembourg, Belgium and Holland. He was rapid, a little snide, but clear, precise and modest. He had sent his report.

"My turn," Diana muttered.

And in her lyrical voice, which put sensual accents on certain words, pent-up anger on others, she explained the situation in all of Russia, from Riga to

Kamchatka, from the Caucasus to the northern limits of Siberia. She had sent her report.

Then with her potent memory, with tremendous intelligence and clarity, she summed up the entire global revolutionary situation that had just been divulged in twelve successive fragments.

And she concluded, "In short, the situation is favorable to our projects, to our hopes, to the realization of the plan worked out by Leonid Zattan. The countries that like France, Italy and Spain, seem more resistant, will be swept into the global conflict by the force of example, by the pull of the worldwide revolutionary movement. It will start in Asia and turn into a maelstrom with Europe at its center. Therefore, all goes well."

Silence. The eleven men sat unmoving, unmoved. They were waiting. So far, they had said and heard what each of them knew or foresaw. Now they were hoping to hear something new: the orders of Leonid Zattan.

Diana Ivanova Krosnovief let them wait. The silence only lasted 30 seconds. Without changing position, elbows on her knees, hands joined, her chest leaning forward a little, three-quarters of her beautiful face lit by the electric light, she spoke again but with a firmer and more authoritative voice.

"Here are the orders that I bring from Issyk-Kul where I have to return on April 14th to get them confirmed or canceled and to bring you the final decision with the date set for the most likely outcome of acting out in the open."

She took a breath before continuing.

"All of you will leave tomorrow for your respective regions and alert the sectors in terms of the 'final preparations for direct action'. You know what this means."

"This" meant that they would take the necessary measures so that when the final signal came, statesmen, generals, judges, heads of conservative organizations, bishops, leaders in finance and industry, publishers, newspaper editors, and many famous men and women among the cosmopolitan aristocracy were to be assassinated.

"This" meant the preparation for burning down the palaces and public buildings in every capital in the world; the storming of the barracks; the destruction of highways and waterways; railways and train stations seized or sabotaged by fire and sword.

"This" meant arousing all the catalysts, all the desires, all the hatred, all the anarchic powers in the world, not to mention the merciless, calculated, ferocious passions of individuals.

"But one of us," the Red Princess went on, "will not leave right away. He will have a mission to accomplish beforehand. A mission of utmost importance, whose success Leonid Zattan will consider a guarantee of victory but whose failure will be an omen of defeat. This mission is urgent. It's difficult and life-threatening. There are two parts: the first alone involves the utmost importance I mentioned, the success of the second is desirable but not absolutely necessary.

This means that if, to accomplish the first part of the mission, the agent has to put his own life at risk to win or lose everything, the second part will only be undertaken if there's no risk of perishing. Do you understand me?"

Not a word was said, but 11 heads nodded affirmatively.

"Good," and Diana's beautiful black eyes flashed when she announced, "It's a matter of killing Mathias Lumen and secondarily taking his treasure that's hidden in the wells of his house in Ushant."

"*Per Bacco!*" the Italian exclaimed.

And the ten other delegates arched their eyebrows, narrowed their eyes, frowned, shrugged their shoulders or simply shivered depending on what they felt and how they showed it. But all of them, just like the Italian, were astounded. They all knew, at least by sight, the enigmatic old man. They all knew the prophecy of Nostradamus by heart. They all had seen the house in Ushant, either up close or at a distance.

And they were all mystics.

For them, Mathias Lumen represented a superhuman entity just like they saw a kind of demonic emanation in Leonid Zattan. Killing the hermit of Ushant seemed as fantastically impossible, *morally*, as assassinating the Lord of Issyk-Kul.

Furthermore, they had the feeling, the intuition, the conviction, the certainty that, *physically*, Mathias Lumen was mightily defended on his island, even if the defense was not visible and its means were unknown to them.

Killing Mathias Lumen!

Yes, of course, the death of the mysterious hermit would in fact be of utmost importance for the global Revolution—if they weren't already in full swing, on the threshold of victory, it was because Mathias Lumen, day after day, in Europe, Africa, Asia and America, was patiently tearing apart, piece by piece, the web woven by the henchmen of Leonid Zattan. If the Lord of Issyk-Kul was in danger, the danger could only come directly or indirectly from Mathias Lumen... Yes... Yes!

But to kill him!

It was the black, the African, the former colonial official called Ouala who, out of shock or fear, expressed what the others were forcing themselves not to admit. In French, his voice a little choked, he asked, "Is this the direct order of Leonid Zattan?"

"Direct orders!" Diana Ivanova barked back.

Silence. It lasted a full two minutes. Diana watched her colleagues through half-closed eyes.

The Hindu finally spoke up in Esperanto, "How are we going to decide who gets the mission?"

"Draw lots," the young woman answered curtly.

"Do we all have to participate?"

Diana smirked briefly and her half-open eyes looked cruel as she replied bitterly, "No, Ouala. With his knowledge of men, Leonid Zattan foresaw your terror… yes, your terror! So, he leaves it up to each of you whether or not to participate in the lottery. Let's not beat around the bush. Who refuses?"

Ouala didn't hesitate for a second. His colleagues now saw him as a coward, he whom they believed to be insanely brave! And he made this revelation, dare we say, bravely. For, not only did he not hesitate, but he added enthusiastically:

"I, Ouala, I refuse. I won't take part in the lottery."

"It's up to you," the Red Princess uttered with no apparent contempt. Directing her wide-open eyes around the circle of colleagues, she added, "Anyone else want to take advantage of Leonid Zattan's considerate precaution?"

A short wait while all the faces resumed their impassive expressions.

"No?" Diana smiled. Not a mouth twitched. "Very well. Let's draw lots. Your marbles, comrades."

Each A.R.M. always carried a small ivory ball. The dozen marbles had the same diameter, the same weight, the same polish, all perfectly round. They differed only in color in order to identify, when needed, the men themselves. Thus, 11 marbles glimmered in the fingers of eleven hands.

Diana muttered gravely and ceremoniously, "Ouala, your hat. You're not part of the fateful lottery, so you can pick."

The African wore a flat-brimmed, felt hat like artists wear. He took it off and held it out upside-down. 11 balls fell into it. The ritual was familiar. The two A.R.M. next to Ouala blindfolded him carefully while Diana shook the hat in his hands. After the two were sitting back down, Ouala dug one hand into his hat, stirred the marbles more, without taking one out, under the watchful eyes of his colleagues, and suddenly his hand shot out holding…

"Purple!" Diana pronounced.

"Purple, that's me!" a voice acknowledged firmly.

The African ripped off his blindfold. Everyone turned to the Dane, Bo Gerrak—big, tall, blond, pale-skinned, with bright, blue, boyish eyes, but whose bushy eyebrows were separated by a deep line and his square chin looked carved with three swipes of an ax to support his tremendous jaws. At the moment he was faintly paler than usual. His eyes sparkled with a kind of wild joy.

"You're happy, comrade?" Diana asked curtly.

"Yes, very happy," Gerrak shot back.

"Too bad," the woman said.

"Huh?!"

Everyone had the same reaction to the Red Princess' extraordinary comment. It was her they were now staring at inquisitively.

Very calmly, with a velvety gaze into Gerrak's eyes, she continued, "Yes, too bad because if you're happy to be chosen for this mission, then there's little chance that you'll grant me the favor I'd like to ask of the chosen…"

"What favor?" Gerrak stammered in confusion.

"Oh, quite clear and easy. Give me your luck, Bo, your dangerous prize as a gift. Let me take your place. Pretend and let me pretend that it was my white marble that was picked."

"Oh, princess!" the Dane was much paler now, "you want to kill Mathias Lumen yourself?"

She smiled and with inexpressible elegance responded, "Yes, dear Bo, yes... but don't be too surprised or for too long. Later, if you want and I survive, I'll explain. Tonight, however, time is pressing. It's April 4th and I have to be in Constantinople on the 10th to catch a plane for Issyk-Kul. I have six days, therefore, to go to Ushant, kill the old man, make a decision with Ignace Kiewicz in Brest about the treasure in the well, then go to Constantinople. So, you see, every second is precious and I can't give you an explanation."

"But I haven't said yes!" Gerrak exclaimed.

"You're going to, Bo. Please. Do I have to beg you? Or if I can give you something in exchange..."

Then the Dane spoke earnestly, even tenderly, "I understand, Diana, that you've already given me the best and most beautiful gift you can offer—your friendship over the past two years." He choked back a tear and continued sincerely, "I offer my place to you, Diana Ivanovna. Go kill Mathias Lumen. And keep in mind, if you don't come back, I will get revenge or die trying, like you."

The young woman held out her two gloved hands and the big guy took them, squeezed them, and she was beaming when she replied, "Thank you."

This unexpected scene was obviously incomprehensible to the eleven men. What reason could Diana have for wanting to risk her life on a mission that had less than one chance in a hundred of success? That Bo Gerrak had passed on the honor and danger, they understood. Besides, it was in compliance with one of the articles of the statutes that governed the twelve A.R.M under the supreme control of Leonid Zattan. But that this woman had pleaded for his place, this woman in the full splendor of her life, with all her beauty and success in everything she did—her demand astounded the Englishman John Bolton, as well as the American Dickie Klopp, and even the Chinese Yeo Fi, who was famous in many quarters for not being surprised at anything. But none of them had the nerve or the guts to ask for an explanation.

Consequently, they looked like they had taken no particular notice to the amazing incident when Diana slowly unclasped Gerrak's hands and turned to rest of the group as it was standing up.

She smiled, "Well, farewell, comrades. We all have our orders and nothing else to discuss. Let's go, Namur."

"As you wish."

Fifteen minutes later the eleven visitors to the Chapelle Expiatoire gave their guide a tip after he closed the gate and they all scattered down the seven or eight streets and avenues branching out from the monument.

An automobile was parked on the square with a driver at the wheel. A powerful, convertible, two-seater touring car that was remarkable only to a real car-lover; flat, gun-metal gray paint; there was nothing strange or luxurious about it. But, being low and wide it must have hugged the road at high speeds. Diana Ivanova hurried toward this car and put on a big coat that the driver was holding for her. Then she wrapped a long veil around her hat, sat down and slipped her handbag into the pocket on the door.

She said, "Nicolas, let's go to Brest. And step on it."

The man didn't answer. He started the car, pulled away from the curb, turned around and headed toward Etoile to leave Paris through the Bois de Boulogne and then to Versailles. The car sped up or slowed down depending on the condition of the road.

From Paris to Brest by way of Versailles, Le Mans and Loudéac is 400 miles, covered at an average of 50 mph. The morning of April 5th had just risen when the gray car stopped on Rue de Siam in Brest at an old-style carriage door. It stopped just long enough for Diana to step onto the sidewalk before it rolled off, turned the corner and disappeared.

The carriage door was open in the morning for the milkman and newspaper deliveries. The woman entered, went down the wide path, crossed a tiny garden and climbed the six steps of the two-story detached house. The index finger of her right hand pushed the button of the electric doorbell. Nobody in the garden. Windows closed on the upper stories of the big house facing the street.

"Maybe they didn't see me come in," Diana mumbled to herself. "All right, I'll go out the other side."

The slot to the peephole slid open. Two eyes glowed behind the strong grill. The slot closed again and the door opened.

"Hello, Nadine," the visitor said. "Is Ignace awake?"

"Hello, barinia. The master hasn't rung yet."

The woman answering did so with profound respect and cheerful eagerness. She was blonde with green eyes, braided hair, dressed so that she looked like both a servant and child of the house. In fact, Nadine was the servant and slave lover of Ignace Kiewicz who lived in the little house alone with her, as was indicated by the brass plate on the wall to the left of the door: "Ignace Kiewicz, translator of French, Polish, Russian, German, English, Italian, Hebrew." But behind the polyglot façade was something else.

"Let's go wake him up, Nadine," the princess smiled at the friendly girl. "I have to talk to him right away."

The translator's house had two doors: one in the garden of the house facing Rue de Siam, the other in a narrow alley between the walls of old convents where barely three people a week passed by. On the ground floor, to the right of the entrance, was the Pole's bedroom that took up the whole side of the little house from the garden wall to the alley behind. At the end of the hallway were the stairs leading up to the first floor next to the back door with another peephole. From the outside, the door looked dilapidated, like it hadn't been used in years. But it opened as easily as the door to the garden. Off the hallway to the left were the dining room first, then the kitchen lit from the alley by a narrow, barred window. Upstairs were two "guest" bedrooms and Nadine's private room accessible to Ignace's below by a small spiral staircase, custom-built not long ago.

Such was the house where the nocturnal voyage of the Red Princess' car finally came to an end.

At the bedroom door Nadine pressed a floorboard in a certain way and almost immediately a muted ring was heard coming from, apparently, upstairs. Then she announced, "Master, number nine." A short wait before she herself opened the door.

"Thank you, Nadine. See you later," Diana said. "Can you fix me up some chocolate, I'm famished."

"It'll be ready in five minutes, barinia."

"Thanks."

The princess stepped familiarly into the room while the door closed automatically behind her. She headed toward the bed, narrow, low and very long, sitting in the back of an alcove between a bathroom and a closet. An electric light was on the ceiling of the alcove. A man in pajamas was sitting up in the bed, rubbing his eyes, not bothering to straighten his disheveled hair.

Diana's laughter was like wind chimes in the air, "I woke you up, Ignace. Sorry about that, couldn't be helped."

She held out her right hand after promptly taking off her glove. He got up, took the hand, kissed it and dropped back onto the edge of the bed while his visitor sat on a stool from which she had raked off some clothes.

"Come on, my friend, are you completely awake now? Can I talk?"

His laugh was boyish and carefree. "My word, you caught me before I could even get out of bed. But it only takes me a minute to come out of nirvana. Sure, I'm all ears."

Ignace Kiewicz was 28 years-old with the body of an athlete and a mind like an encyclopedia. Polyglot, doctor, chemist, engineer, sailor, philosopher and theologian, he was one of the great hopes of the worldwide revolution and a top-ranking agent with reasoned, calculated and willful devotion to Leonid Zattan. With all this he was also gifted with a childlike personality that made him joke and laugh in his work that could, for example, result in the deaths of many people. Some thought he was crazy, others a cold, calculating genius, others still a simple but very educated upstart.

In truth, Ignace Kiewicz had a mystic soul with the mind of a mathematician in the body of a young athlete.

"Hey," he said, "you were in Paris yesterday. Did you spend all night getting here? Why?"

With a deadpan face, her dark, passionate eyes staring into the intelligent blue eyes of the young Pole, she answered, "Destiny, Zattan and my will have imposed a mission upon me."

"What is it?"

"To kill Mathias Lumen."

"Huh?" And he winced.

"To kill Mathias Lumen," Diana repeated slowly.

Now Ignace was frowning, "You said 'Destiny, Zattan and my will', why your will?"

She explained, "The twelve Agents met last night. Zattan's order had reached me in the afternoon. We drew lots, as usual, but only eleven of us because Ouala bailed…"

"That's no surprise. I don't trust him. We've got to keep an eye on him."

"That's why I'm telling you he bailed. So, the purple ball was picked."

"Bravo!" Ignace cheered. "Bo Gerrak the Dane. Fate made a wise choice. But then…"

"I got Bo to let me take his place."

"Oh, why?"

"It's my secret."

"It'll be your life, Diana."

"I know."

"Barinia, my dear friend, Diana, may your will be done and your wishes come true!" He bowed his head, then looked up. There was no more emotion in his eyes or his voice when he went on, "You will or you won't kill Mathias Lumen. I'm no Nostradamus and I don't know the future, even just five minutes from now, but I must and I can be at your service. What do you need?"

"Good," a flicker of a smile crossed Diana's face. "First, I'm in a hurry. I have to be in Constantinople on the 10th."

"It's the 5th. You have five days, not much time."

"It'll be enough, I hope… Ignace, I need a motorboat this afternoon and six fully committed men, two of them as sailors from the port and the others as English tourists."

"Easy enough. At 2 pm at our usual place in the outer harbor. Can I be one of the six?"

Diana balked, then she barked, "No!"

He smiled. "You hesitated, Diana. So, you were thinking yes. I accept your thinking. I didn't hear you speaking. I'll lead the six and be the interim captain of the boat."

She looked a little scared and pained by his decision. "Ignace," she begged, "don't come. It'll be your life at stake as well. And your life is precious to…"

"Less than yours, Red Princess!" he cut her off. "Don't press it. You were thinking yes… Let's move on. What else do you need?"

She accepted the inevitable. Back to her deadpan face she replied, "Three explosive charges…"

"Got it."

"And… that's all."

"Great."

"I have nothing more to say." She stood up. "Just that I'm hungry and tired."

"I understand," he laughed. "But Nadine is preparing some chocolate, toast, honey, everything you like. Upstairs you have your choice of two bedrooms. Shall we eat at noon?"

"No, at 11."

"And we shove off at 2."

"Yes."

"Alea jacta est! All right, the die is cast… It's in God's hands… Sleep well, princess… Your hand, for a kiss. Thanks. I'll get the door."

Half an hour later, Diana Ivanova Krosnovief was in bed upstairs while Ignace Kiewicz was leaving the house through the garden door with his translation portfolio under his arm. The Red Princess in the fickle dreams of sleep, the Pole in the realities of methodical action, both were henceforth headed down an inescapable path.

CHAPTER II

At 2:20 pm the half-decked motorboat *Saint Pol* was crossing the inlet of Brest. It was a beautiful boat for coastal tourism, strong and steady, that could comfortably hold twelve to fifteen people, the usual number of tourists that its captain/owner, the retired Guenolas, took two or three times a week from Brest to Ushant. For the last three days Guenolas had been laid up in bed with rheumatism. For an amount equal to the insurance value of the *Saint Pol* and for 200 francs a day in advance, he had agreed to rent his precious vessel to Ignace Kiewicz, the well-known translator from Rue de Siam, for three days or more if need be.

The inhabitants of Brest, whoever they were and whatever they did, who happened to see the curious spectacle of the seven people on the *Saint Pol* on the afternoon of April 5th would not have recognized a single one, even though six of them had lived openly in the city for months. This was because four of the six men, clean-shaven with blond or red hair, looked like real middle-class English tourists. The two others looked and acted like veteran sailors, old navy men who were good for any honest and honorable work that wasn't too taxing and who usually spent their savings on a small fishing boat. One of them was wearing a shabby engineering officer's cap without stripes or braids but decorated with a brand-new anchor. The other had a sailor's beret with a faded pompom.

As for the seventh "tourist", it was a woman. No one from Brest had ever seen her before. But Parisians and aristocrat globetrotters would have recognized her immediately because she had no disguise. She had just put on a comfortable tailored suit and a raincoat cinched at the waist. Her gorgeous black hair, which she never deigned to cut no matter what the fashion, was tightly braided, wrapped around her head and hidden under an elegant but practical southwester hat to match her raincoat. She wore gloves. Ignace Kiewicz (the owner with the engineer's cap) had noticed at lunch that she wasn't wearing the ring with the fateful ruby on her left hand, the sign of total trust and special appointment by Leonid Zattan.

During this lunch that Diana and Ignace had together in the house on Rue de Siam, the Pole tried to find out, unsuccessfully, the real reason why the pretty young woman denied the fate of the lottery and embarked on this extraordinary and dangerous mission to kill Mathias Lumen. But his hints and allusions, his sly, wily inferences hit an impenetrable wall of silence.

Diana might have revealed the secret of her impassioned soul to her curious comrade with the slip of a single word, so she kept quiet, dulled her splendid eyes and let her mind wander off…

Before the end of the meal, as short and frugal as it was, Ignace had to admit defeat and give up. He simply said, "Diana, thank you for doing me the honor of accepting me as your partner on an adventure that threatens our lives more than ever before."

"Very good, Ignace." The smile she flashed him was both melancholic and sensuous and she had those bewitching eyes that had driven many men to despair. And they said no more.

They didn't talk even on the *Saint Pol*. The sailor and his four tourists were quiet, too—calm, cold, impassive, but with a kind of fierce expression frozen on all their faces. They were all thinking, fearlessly, of the mission they were undertaking with the Red Princess. When signing them onto this expedition, Kiewicz had told them the objective. He had the right since all five men were young, Russian, smart rebels, thoroughly trustworthy. They would obey, diligently and selflessly, any order given by Kiewicz, number 11, head of the sector, without any further explanation or comment. But informed that they were accompanying Diana Ivanova Krosnovief as head of the mission, they were excited to go anywhere the woman might lead them, even unto death.

After passing Pointe Saint-Mathieu, the Saint Pol set a course for the northwest intending to avoid the islands of Béniguet and Molène. From Brest to the Bay of Lampaul on Ushant, following the curved trajectory of the motorboat, was 25 nautical miles. For the *Saint Pol* at full speed it would take three hours tops in good seas like today.

After all the foreseeable details of their action were settled, Diana and Ignace wouldn't say a word to each other until they faced the first of the many obstacles they had not anticipated.

They reached Lampaul without any incident at sea. The "sailor" stayed behind to guard the boat, but the woman, the four Englishmen and the "owner" of the Saint Pol got off and took long, rapid strides in the direction of the "Ghost Chalet".

Kiewicz didn't ask the natives for any information. In his current role he must've known where in Ushant was the house of Mathias Lumen. And the group of tourists with the captain didn't surprise anyone because foreigners often came from Conquest or Brest, especially in the high season, to see the "curiosity" of the Ghost Chalet. Of course, the curious had to be satisfied with seeing it from the outside. Two or three times a tour guide risked ringing the doorbell and asking permission to visit the inside. These brazen sightseers were politely but firmly escorted away. They would spread the story of their failure. And in Brest and Conquest as much as Ushant, they knew that access to the Ghost Chalet was forbidden to tourists, just like almost all private residences all over the world. And this prohibition was considered normal, logical and natural to everyone.

It was 3:45 pm when Diana, Ignace and their four companions were standing before the brick wall that marked the boundary, on the land side, of the two acres from Créac'h Point in the middle of which the tragic Englishman had built his chalet in 1899.

On April 5th, then, the five men and the woman stopped in single file at this wall that they had each, at one time or another, visited before out of curiosity or duty. They had seen the chalet but never with the eyes or ideas they had this time.

"Obviously," Diana muttered, "my plan A is feasible only if fate is wholly on my side... As for the other plans, they all involve the same problem: first, to get over this open land from the wall to the house... And I don't think the property is undefended—electronic surveillance, snares and traps, dogs unleashed at night, undetectable pits... who knows? We have no information about it."

"I personally have made twenty different investigations to find out," Kiewicz whispered, "with no results. The land is apparently just barren land, rocky, uncultivated, arid, nothing else."

What a strange oddity for the Englishman to give the name of "chalet" to this house! The term "fort" would have been more appropriate.

In the middle of the two-acre property on the arid headland, almost entirely formed of rock, the most desolate one can imagine, picture a gray cube, 100 feet square, twenty-five feet-high, topped by a low-sloping, black slate roof from which eight short chimneys stick out. On the east side, which faces the straight wall fencing off the property, there are two low, rounded doors fitted with iron-studded gates, four windows on the ground floor and six on the one floor above—all of the windows closed on this day, April 5th, with their massive shutters locked tight. As for the house itself, just one look at the veritable porches created in the cavities of the inset doors will give an idea of how thick the walls are, along with the diagonal support beams in the four corners of the roof... And everyone in Ushant knew from the day of its construction (were willing to tell anyone who asked) that under the house, amidst the cyclopean foundations, were very deep, very vast cellars and vaults and two wells that could hold huge amounts of water had been dug right out of the rock with dynamite.

The boundary wall, which was only around three feet high so could be easily be hopped over, but which had no opening or gap whatsoever whereby you could enter—another really weird aspect of the place—the wall went straight into the ocean, disappearing into the chaos of waves and reefs.

Standing in front of this wall, the woman and five men really did look like tourists listening breathlessly to their guide. In fact, so as not to raise suspicions in the likely case that someone was watching them through an unseen hole in the wall or doors or through a crack in the shutters, Ignace Kiewicz was speaking loudly in a Breton accent, telling the story of the Englishman murdered by his servant, the abandonment of the house, then the arrival of Mathias Lumen, the "great scientist and the most eccentric man on earth".

When he had finished and while normal tourists would be mulling over the stories, he whispered, "Diana, what do we do?"

"Go up, ring the bell and ask if we can have a tour of the house and see the landscape behind it, Créac'h Point and the sea. Didn't you say that other tourists have been refused permission?"

"Yes."

"Well, try to get it for us. It won't be pointless."

"Madame and Messieurs," Ignace said aloud, still in his coastal accent, "I'm going to see if we might be allowed to take this tour one step further."

And like an agile sailor he skipped over the wall. It was highly likely that the secret defenses, if there were any, would be active only at night. In the middle of the day they weren't working because Lumen certainly had taken precautions so that from sunup to sundown any individual stepping onto the property could be observed. Even a big group, in this case, couldn't do any harm to the Ghost Chalet because before they could cover the barren land between the wall and the house, all the doors and windows would be shut and the building would be impenetrable. At night, in the dark, especially during a storm when the waves and wind make a deafening ruckus, access to the grounds could only be protected by a system of exterior defenses.

Ignace Kiewicz had convinced himself of this. Therefore, he marched confidently toward the house.

A strange thing about the property, which the Pole noticed once again, was that there was no path anywhere. It proved that to leave and enter the area the usual and unusual inhabitants of the Ghost Chalet almost never went over the wall in the same spot. The rough, rocky ground, or at least very dry because of its mineral composition, showed no trace of footsteps. All around the house was a cement walkway around thirty feet wide.

Ignace, therefore, made the following assumption:

"If there are defenses that a man like Mathias Lumen has to set up around him, then it's possible to spot them, at least hypothetically. They're all over the place here at night. Or else nowhere. In the latter case the danger would only start at the cement walkway, right? Diana's crazy. We'll stay here all night... unless her plan A, as she says, becomes suddenly operable by pure luck."

He wasn't thinking at all about the public, police or legal consequences of an attack, successful or not, against Lumen. But for eight days he knew that an open fight by the revolutionary organizations against the established Society was about to begin. Everything was ready for Ignace Kiewicz (Polish but a French national and certified translator) to disappear completely and be transformed, in an area of Brest less bourgeois than Rue de Siam, into a new person. From what he told the Red Princess, this attack against Lumen was to be his final act before his carefully prepared transformation.

While thinking these things and remembering some important details about his life as an anarchist conspirator, the fake sailor made it to the cement walkway. He stopped and hesitated between the two doors.

"Which one should I ring?" he wondered.

One of them had an electric doorbell on the right, clearly visible in a porcelain frame set flush into the gray stone. Both were closed, dark in their alcoves, grim and forbidding with the dark red color of the wood and their black studs and hinges. No window was open. No sound could be heard. No one showed up on either side of the house.

"Could there really be no one here?" Kiewicz wondered. "The old hermit, as they call him, might be traveling? No, my man in Lampaul would've told me when he saw me. He pretended not to know me, so, no news."

He lingered for a few seconds.

"Bah, if nothing happens at one, I'll ring the other!" he decided.

And he stepped up to the door on the right. He pressed the yellowish ivory button poking out of its white porcelain setting. He heard no ringing from the inside.

"Not surprising," he thought. "The walls are so thick!"

He waited one, two, three minutes…

"Next!"

He crossed the twenty feet or so separating him from the door on the left. The same action, the same wait, the same negative result.

"Oh well," he sighed, "Let's take a look around."

He stalked all the way around the house. The four sides "looked out" on the four cardinal points. On the south side, like on the east, were two doors and four windows on the ground floor, six upstairs, all closed, all exactly like the others. On the west was only one door and two windows upstairs—also closed.

Finally on the north side was a bare wall with no opening except a kind of low, narrow archway with an iron grill right in the middle of the ground floor.

And everywhere was silence and solitude.

If it weren't for the pristine condition of the doors, shutters and doorbells with their white porcelain plates, he could've believed the weird, noiseless, eerie house was completely abandoned.

Back on the east side Ignace took a deep breath and pressed the doorbell again. Another fruitless wait.

"If the people inside are sleeping at this time of the day, we're safe doing whatever we want. If they're spying on us, our behavior won't look suspicious."

He walked away from the house, took off his cap, waved it high in the air and shouted out cheerfully in his strongest Finistère accent, "Ahoy! Ahoy over there! Jump the wall. There's no one here. We'll go out to Creac'h Point and see all there is to see."

These were, indeed, the words of a normal tour guide in such a situation. Over behind the wall, the "tourists" didn't hesitate. Visibly amused, giggling, they jumped the wall more or less agilely. One of the men played the gentleman and offered his hand to the woman. As a group they hurried over the land.

Now, in the house of Mathias Lumen there was an eye and an ear that never slept, night or day. Normally, three men and a woman lived in the Ghost Chalet: Mathias Lumen, his secretary Placide Bonnard, the sailor, engineer and all-round handyman Ephrem Lluch (a Catalan from Collioure) and his aunt Sidonie, cook and maid.

But it was neither the maid nor the three men who belonged to this eye and ear constantly watching and listening to everything outside the house. No, in truth, there were four eyes and ears. At every corner of the roof, between the top of the support beams and the support frame of the double layer of slate, a periscope and a microphone were hidden. If he could have visited the house of the Ushant hermit in person, the Lord of Issyk-Kul would have found it technologically and defensively as expertly, if not better equipped than his feudal castle.

And here's what the periscopes and microphones did: in the west, south and north corners for 200 yards and in the east for 500 yards beyond the boundary wall, if a noise *other* than the usual rumbling or roaring of the wind and waves was picked up—bird calls, bleating sheep, talking or walking people, idling engines, the scraping oars of a boat, etc.—the sound was instantly recorded on a special phonograph. At the same time the periscopes would continually project onto four screens the images of everything within the designated range.

The screens and phonograph were set up in a big room converted by Mathias Lumen into a laboratory, workroom and library, a room where the hermit and his secretary were almost always to be found. When a sound was *other* than the wind and waves, when what was moving or still was *other* than land and sea, an automatic alarm rang *in all the rooms down to the cellars of the house*.

Moreover, the schedule for work, outings, meals, rest and relaxation was organized in such a way that one of the three men or the woman was always up and about.

On April 5ᵗʰ, Mathias Lumen, Placide Bonnard and Ephrem Lluch had been experimenting on the hermit's new electromagnetic invention designed to finish the construction of a tiny but powerful and perpetual engine for an "individual" submarine, meaning a submarine occupied and piloted by one man or even empty and controlled remotely. This experiment was being made in one of the huge cellars that had been turned into a 15-foot-deep pool set into a 6-foot-wide platform on which the men worked.

Worn out by a stubborn migraine, Sidonie had been told to stay in her room and lay down in the dark and silence for the rest of the day. Lumen himself had measured out the dose of chloral for her... and so the three men ate meat and cold vegetables.

That was why all the doors and windows were closed.

Now, at exactly 3:42 pm the blaring alarm was heard in the pool cellar. The miniature model of the experimental submarine was gliding around in the water lit from below by lights in the pool as the three men looked on.

"Ephrem," Lumen said, "go see what it is."

The Catalan climbed up a spiral staircase, went down a hallway and entered the lab. On the east screen, on the usual gloomy landscape, human shapes were moving.

"Tourists," Lluch said.

Soon they had stopped before the sea. Then the phonograph recorded and repeated the words spoken there. Since the machine was extremely sensitive with the highly sophisticated microphones, the whispered conversation between the guide and the woman was captured, recorded permanently on reel and replayed clearly.

The tough Catalan sneered, "Fake tourists! Zattanists! Poor fools who think we don't see or hear them. Better call the boss. I think this deserves an interruption of the experiment."

Without losing sight of the spying screen, without turning down the volume of the revealing recorder, Lluch went to the telephone panel, pressed button number 8 and spoke.

"Hello, master, a group of Zattanists. They're saying some alarming things. I think it'd be better if you and Monsieur Bonnard were here. Right."

Three minutes later, Lumen walked into the lab. His gray-blue eyes were sparkling. He sat in an armchair in front of the four screens lined up next to the phonograph and the speaker. Ephrem Lluch quickly ran through what had already been seen and heard. Bonnard was standing behind Lumen, legs apart and hands in his pockets, his hazel eyes glistening with mischievous delight. Ephrem went to stand next to him in almost the same position. And without saying a word or making any movement, the three men listened to everything being said and watched all the expressions passing over the faces.

After the fake Breton sailor had hopped the wall, when he was a few feet from the cement walkway and his face popped up in the foreground on the screen, Placide Bonnard said, "Master, I recognize that man's eyes, nose and the shape of his mouth. It's Ignace Kiewicz, the translator from Rue de Siam."

"Number 11," Lluch added.

"Yes," the secretary agreed.

Mathias Lumen didn't flinch, but his eyes flashed briefly. He said nothing.

They saw the Zattanist's image go from the east screen to the south, then to the two others: Kiewicz making a tour of the house after his ringing went unanswered.

Then there was the shout inviting the "tourists" to come over the wall. Their front line approached, the woman a little ahead on the left. When she was next to Kiewicz she whispered softly, but still picked up by the microphones and recorded for the three imposing spectators:

"Really? Nobody?"

"So it seems," Ignace shrugged his shoulders. "It doesn't matter. We'll keep up the farce. The walls, doors and windows might have eyes. Let's go out to the Point."

"Let's first make a tour of the house... out of curiosity."

"As you wish."

In the laboratory Mathias Lumen spoke up. His eyes were hard and his face, usually as white as his beard and hair, was suddenly flushed with color. But Bonnard and Lluch were behind him and saw nothing of this. They just heard his voice speaking with an uneasily repressed emotion.

"Me, I recognize the woman."

But he didn't say her name. Did he know it? Or would pronouncing it have unleashed a sudden storm of emotions?

Not another word was spoken in the lab during the whole time the tourists outside were roaming around the Point, making another tour of the house, then disappearing on the Lampaul side. Screens and phonograph did their twin duties. When the one was silent and the other displayed nothing but the usual sight of barren land, jumble of rocks, incessant waves and cloudy, afternoon skies, Mathias Lumen put his elbows on the arms of the chair, shielded his forehead with his cupped hands and sat motionless in one of those meditations that was his habit. Behind him, the secretary and the sailor didn't budge. They knew they had to wait. So, they waited.

Five, eight, ten minutes rolled by.

Finally, Lumen spread his hands, raised his head and rose up in a single, smooth movement. He turned to the two men who were the only ones in the world aware of all the secrets of his actions, not to mention his most intimate thoughts and feelings. The dead-white face, the gray eyes and the Olympian brow all exuded a cold energy.

"My friends," he put his hands in the pockets of his coat, which was always buttoned up, "you heard. It's reasonable to expect that we'll be attacked tonight. These people are going to get back on their boat in Lampaul and pretend to head back to Brest, but they'll wait for dark, circle around on the sea and come ashore in some sheltered spot around Creac'h. We'll let them come. I want to capture at least two of them alive—the woman and the Pole. For the others... execution!"

He furrowed his brow while his eyes turned stone cold. After a brief pause, he wrapped up, "But we've got three more hours of peace. Let's get back to work."

At 7 pm the three men went back up from the pool-cellar. They were satisfied. The electromagnetic engine had met all their expectations. Mathias Lumen was confident now of putting into action several submarines that would be no bigger than a torpedo. He would have them built by Creusot, the secret of the new device being wholly in the engine, which he and Ephrem Lluch could make at the rate of two a month in the underground workshop set up in one of the big cellars.

They ate in the dining room, standing up: cold cuts, canned fruit and a cup of coffee. Then they waited in the lab, sitting in front of the screens: Lumen with his arms crossed, Bonnard smoking a cigar and Lluch puffing leisurely on a long, white clay pipe.

The night had come, a calm night lit by myriad stars but no moon, which was in its last quarter and wouldn't rise until one in the morning. A machine automatically started up and the nocturnal periscopic views outside were projected onto the screen as bright as in daylight. For the scientific eyes of the Ghost Chalet, the dark of night didn't exist. The lab itself was lit by two electric lights behind green, frosted glass.

An hour passed without anything appearing on the screens except the land, sea and sky. Lumen sat like a statue, his wide-open eyes deeply contemplative. Bonnard had finished his cigar and was penciling in rows of numbers and letters in a small notebook. Lluch looked like he was asleep, his pipe growing cold between his teeth… But he was the one who first spotted, at 8:37 pm, what they were waiting for. He took the pipe out of his mouth and with his usual curse in pure Catalan, "Tefoum! They're here."

Mathias Lumen shuddered and uncrossed his arms; Placide Bonnard closed his notebook and slipped it into his pocket; Ephrem Lluch kept talking:

"They must've come ashore in cove D. At this time of night, with the little wind blowing, it's the calmest place around Crech'h."

"The woman's there!" Bonnard remarked.

"And only five men," Lluch observed. "They left one on the boat and rightly so." When the Hermit stood up, his two close collaborators did the same.

"Go man the machines," Lumen said in a normal voice, "but do nothing until I give the order. I want to see what they're planning to do and I especially want to capture the woman and the Pole alive."

Bonnard and Lluch went to the back of the lab where there was a black panel, six feet square, full of glowing devices: dials, levers, gauges, small, brass wheels with four, six or eight porcelain extensions, etc. The panel was lit by a green lamp.

From there, turning their heads to the left, the two men could see both Lumen and the screens. The south one showed the approaching troop of the woman and five men, the same as in the afternoon. Three of the men carried some kind of package under their left arm, held tightly in their downturned hand. They walked a little ahead of the others, briskly and light on their feet. But the microphones still caught the sound of their footsteps.

When they got in front of the south side of the house, they stopped just before the cement walkway. The mics recorded the whispered words:

"Go on alone and make the tour."

"Right away."

And Kiewicz stepped onto the walkway. They saw him going from one screen to another, walking around the house, carefully examining the doors and windows, then coming back to the stationary group.

The speaker broadcast: "Nothing, Diana. I didn't see or hear anything. Do you think the house is empty? I don't think so. Highly unlikely since the whaleboat *Nostradamus* is docked in Lampaul. Maybe they're lying in wait for us. I feel something inside me telling me that we're about to be..."

"No wild guesses, Ignace. We're here to act. Beyond factual reality, nothing is to be assumed that might jeopardize our action... Give me your bomb, Dmitri. You take another, Ignace. You, Ivan, come here with yours. You three, Dmitri, Alexis and Nicolas, each of you to one side of the house with guns drawn. In five minutes we'll know whether there are people in the house or not."

In the laboratory Lumen said, "I've seen enough."

Now the Hermit of Ushant looked truly menacing. He seemed to have grown taller. His bearded face and divinely white hair became severely majestic and ruthless. He turned slightly to Bonnard and Lluch, narrowed his eyes and ordered in a cold, hard voice:

"Ephrem, the KR waves!"

Immediately, he looked at the south screen. The woman and two men were approaching the house while the three others stayed beyond the walkway as they separated to the right and left. Lluch turned a wheel and lowered a lever. The four screens flashed together and for ten seconds blurred the images. Then the screens were clear again.

On the edge and on the walkway itself, six human bodies lay still, as if dead.

Lumen's calm, cold voice ordered again, "The woman and the Pole, in here! The four men in the dungeon!"

Without a word, faces turned pale and expressionless, Bonnard and Lluch bowed, went to the other end of the lab and disappeared behind a heavy curtain of Cordovan leather.

Less than a minute later Mathias Lumen saw them on the south screen standing over the bodies of the woman, the Pole and Ivan lying on the walkway. Both of them, strong and fit, picked up a body; Lluch lifted the woman in his arms; Bonnard dragged the Pole by his shoulders. They walked back to the house and disappeared from the screen.

An instant later the curtain parted. Lluch came in first.

"Over there," the Hermit grunted.

The unconscious woman was posed in a deep, leather armchair in the middle of the "library". Bonnard put the man in a similar chair almost right next to the first.

Lumen spoke without showing any emotion, "Pick up the bombs, which must have fuses. They would've lit them after setting them by the doors with enough time to get a safe distance away. The bombs are of no scientific interest. Toss them in the dungeon with the four men. Go on. And don't come back in here unless I call you."

"Master," Bonnard said, "we haven't searched these..."

"No need!"

But Lluch insisted, "Master, they're certainly armed, probably ready to sacrifice their lives to take yours... So, with a gun or a knife, secretly..."

The Hermit had lowered his head, "You're right," he muttered. "I don't have the right to sacrifice my life myself."

With a wave of his hand he let them search. The secretary and the sailor found a dagger and a Browning hidden in a belt under the woman's coat and two Brownings in the man's pockets. They left the room carrying the weapons.

Mathias Lumen stopped watching the screens. He knew his orders would be strictly obeyed and the three bombs and four "tourists" would be thrown where he had ordered them to be thrown.

He flipped some switches. A ceiling light and twenty lamps lit up the library. An opaque curtain stretched across the whole room, hiding the laboratory part. The microphones stopped recording the exterior sounds, which were only the wind and waves now.

Then Lumen examined the woman. He stood alone before her, next to the man. No one could see him. He let loose his emotions, his deep, violent emotions that had been forcibly repressed for hours since the moment he had seen the screen and said, "Me, I recognize the woman."

His face flushed, his eyes softened and misted a little, his hands trembled slightly as he gently touched her forehead, her temples, her wrists to feel for a pulse and her chest to check her heart. The coat was unbuttoned and spread open. The tight jacket of her tailored suit revealed her throat so that his hand could slide down to where her heart was. And beneath her silk shirt, his hand felt the heat and suppleness of her body...

And Lumen straightaway pulled back his hand and muttered, "Her! She's here! And to kill me! I always feared it but never believed it was possible. Oh, I have to be strong against myself, against her, against the past that is not dead... But am I able? God, symbol and the principle of good, the power eternal, give me the strength to overcome! Give me the uncompromising energy to be just towards her and cruel towards myself."

Lumen had only mumbled this prayer, but with such fervor, such passion, such noble and grievous sincerity!

He stood still, his head held straight, his eyes firm, his hands hanging down. He called upon all his calm, composure and lucidity. When he felt he was in total control of himself again, he did quickly and quietly what he had to do.

On a shelf in the library he opened a box hidden by the fake bindings of a half dozen books. He grabbed two metal mushrooms with porcelain stalks and walked back. Two electric wires attached to the mushrooms unrolled from two spools fixed to the box. When he was back in front of the passed out man and woman, he used the mushrooms on each in turn, putting one on the left temple, the other on the right hand. The two unconscious bodies quivered and opened their eyes. Mathias, meanwhile, put the mushrooms back in their box and with his hands in his pockets he stood and waited for the man and woman to regain full consciousness.

He stood four feet from the armchairs next to a short-backed wooden chair. And he watched calmly, curiously even, the woman and man sitting side by side before him. When he felt they were able to hear and understand and answer him, he shook them out their daze with a cold, hard pronouncement:

"Princess Diana Ivanova Krosnovief and you, Ignace Kiewicz, you can mentally say a farewell to your four comrades who came with you because you will never see them again. Extend that farewell even to the fifth who's guarding the *Saint Pol* because he will soon be joining the others."

"What have you done?" Diana stared at the impassive face of Mathias Lumen with eyes full of hatred, a hatred so deep and burning that Ignace Kiewicz, who was already keeping a keen eye on the proceedings, thought that the woman could not and would not ever feel any other sentiment towards the old man.

He corrected his thought: "Old man? With his white hair and beard, sure, but his build, his obvious vigor, the lack of wrinkles around his eyes—Lumen could be 40 or 80 years-old."

Paying no attention to the watchful eyes of the Pole, the Hermit answered the Red Princess coldly, "One of the many curiosities of the Ghost Chalet is that it has an artificial well that connects to the sea via natural excavations far below sea level at low tide. The constant ebb and flow create a kind of maelstrom on the bottom of the well. When the water rises, the whirlpool deepens and spins from left to right; when the water drops, the whirlpool turns convex and spins right to left. This alternation is as perpetual, as incessant as the flow of the tides. A body thrown into this well is immediately caught in the spiraling maelstrom. It spins and spins and spins, wildly fast. Plus, the walls of the well down below there are formed of sharp, very hard, rocky spikes. It only takes a few minutes for the bodies to be ripped to shreds. The crabs and fish get their food or the scraps of what was once human, animal or whatever are washed out into the wide open sea. Well, Diana Ivanova, I've thrown your four men and soon the fifth into the well, which I call the 'dungeon'. Furthermore, you and Monsieur Kiewicz would've gone first if I didn't have plans for you. But we'll talk about that later."

He smiled, wave his hand nonchalantly, sat in the wooden chair and continued just as coldly:

"No, don't reach for your belt, Diana, and Monsieur Kiewicz, don't bother with your pockets. We lifted all your weapons. As for jumping me, monsieur, don't even think about it. Diana can tell you how strong I was five years ago. I assure you I haven't lost an ounce of it. Even if no one comes to help me, you two couldn't beat me, supposing that I would let you attack me. You're in my power, with no help and no possible defense. Be happy that you're not already in the dungeon of the Hermit of Ushant."

"How did you catch us?" Ignace asked calmly while Diana turned pale, closed her eyes and clenched her fists on her chest.

"Child's play," Lumen shrugged his shoulders. "Electric shock. I could've hit you hard enough to kill you, but I didn't because you, Monsieur Kiewicz, have to return to Brest... and also because I have to have a very serious conversation with Diana Ivanova. I've wanted to talk with her for a long time. Unfortunately, I don't have the luxury to run all over the world searching for the Red Princess, who travels more than any other cosmopolitan noble. Thank you, Diana, for coming here yourself."

Without opening her eyes, she growled in rage, humiliation and dark pain. Mathias appeared to pay no attention to her. He stood with such grandeur that Ignace was astonished to find himself, out of awe and respect, standing up as well.

"Monsieur," Lumen said, as calm and cold as ever, "you're going to make Leonid Zattan understand that I have no more pity for my enemies than they have for me or my friends. That's why I, on my own authority and under the rights of war, am taking the lives of the five men you came here with to kill me, obviously. I am sending you back unharmed, firstly because I'd lose precious time getting the *Saint Pol* back to its owner—you can worry about that—and secondly because you will be my messenger to Zattan."

He paused as his whole face winced and a flash of superhuman anger lit up his eyes. He clenched his fists and managed to control the flood of passion. When he continued his voice was a little hoarse.

"Go tell Zattan... I could tell him myself because I've got control of a few of his wireless stations and I know most of his secret codes... but coming from you, who will be leaving here safe and sound, the message will be more meaningful and shocking. So, go tell Zattan that..."

His face turned so tragic that it looked like he was suddenly suffering some atrocious pain. But it only lasted a few seconds before he went on, emphasizing every word.

"If in five days, meaning April 10th, Sylvie Mac Duhl is not freed under safe and secure conditions, I will set free Princess Diana Ivanova Krosnovief."

"Huh? What?" Kiewicz stumbled backward. He was stupefied. He didn't understand. He was expecting the exact opposite of what he'd just heard. He thought he misunderstood. He stammered, "Repeat, monsieur, please, the message that... I..."

Lumen repeated icily, "*If in five days, meaning April 10th, Sylvie Mac Duhl is not freed under safe and secure conditions, I will set free Princess Diana Ivanova.*"

"Oh!" the Pole exclaimed. His eyes were dilated, his hands trembling. "I think I get it. I get it! Hold on!" He breathed deeply, wiped his forehead and looked at Diana who appeared mesmerized. "But if Leonid Zattan does send Sylvie Mac Duhl back safe and sound, what'll you do?"

"It makes no difference what I'll do. But I give my word that Diana Ivonova will be as good as dead to him."

With that said, he went to a table and pressed a button on a panel in the corner. A door opened and a curtain parted.

"Ephrem, take Monsieur Kiewicz to the *Saint Pol*. And get the man guarding the dinghy sent back here. Kiewicz is to be alone and the man thrown in the dungeon."

Ignace didn't ask for mercy for the fifth comrade, mercy that he might have got since the Hermit of Ushant didn't care one way of another about a petty henchman. But obviously Kiewicz preferred to be the only one to come out alive from this adventure. He didn't speak up on behalf of the fifth condemned man. He bowed silently before Diana whose face looked petrified in horror, then he said farewell to Lumen, turned around and marched towards Ephrem Lluch with whom he disappeared behind the curtain.

Mathias Lumen stood for a minute, deep in silent thought, his head lowered, his hands held behind his back. Then he looked up, turned his head and stared at Diana. As if shocked, she straightened up, her arms went stiff, her fists still clenched and a mask of anger and defiance froze on her face.

But the Hermit just nodded and said quietly, "Well then, it wasn't enough for you to make me suffer everything a woman like you can make a man suffer, a man who loves with all the strength and all the tenderness of his heart and soul... It wasn't enough for you to weave the most despicable plot to dishonor me, banish me, have me judged and shot! It wasn't enough, finally, for you to drive a man like me into such wild despair that he would consider suicide... Oh, if Placide Bonnard hadn't told me the truth, I would've killed myself... me... me, for you, for you!"

He was worked up and he realized it. He forced himself to stay in control, to calm down. Even more quietly than before he continued with an air of sadness and soon a fathomless sorrow in his voice.

"This wasn't enough for you, nor the crimes, the countless betrayals, your vile alliance with Leonid Zattan, the murder of my son... our son... Diana Ivanova... And you would come to kill the father like you killed the child!"

He raised his two arms, fists closed, and with a tremendous explosion of indignant anger, his face wracked with unspeakable suffering, he shouted, "Oh, you monster, you hellish monster!"

But she seemed to have recovered her usual self-control. At any rate she showed her mask of beauty, sad and passionate at the same time. She settled back into the armchair and spoke in a suave but firm voice.

"Never enough for me to avenge your murder of my lover."

"In a duel! He caused it!"

"You were jealous that I loved him and not you."

"Wasn't I right?"

"Yes, but what does it matter? I loved him, you killed him. Never enough revenge for me to get."

He abruptly moved away from the woman, from the table nearby and from the armchairs. He started pacing up and down the library with his hands in his pockets, trying to still his inner turmoil. He succeeded. But there were two or three minutes of silence during which the Red Princess, like a wild cat in the bush, glowered at the man with hateful, menacing eyes.

All of a sudden, he stopped right in front of her, let loose a wicked laugh, and in a cold voice he sneered, "You lie! It's been a long time since you got your revenge... But another love got hold of you... Who knows how many loves you've had, each new one making you betray the former? Now you love the Prince of Issyk-Kul and you think this new love is the most beautiful, the greatest, the strongest, the deepest, the one true love of your life, the final one! But Leonid Zattan, who fears nothing and no one, is scared of your love and of you. He's hoping you'll be killed coming here. And you accepted this ultimate crime in the hope of conquering him for good... Just try and tell me this isn't true."

She was petrified, stupefied and white with rage. She yelled, "It's not true!"

"You're lying and you know it," he replied vigorously. "And me, I know you so completely! I know you because I don't love you anymore. Coming here, you were telling yourself, 'If I fail initially, at least I'll see Mathias. He still loves me. Can anyone stop loving me after tasting my kisses? I'll take him back, sleep with him and then I'll kill him.' Ha, ha, you're not denying anymore. The truth is stifling you as well as the rage at being unmasked by me and therefore rendered powerless against me."

Another wicked laugh came out of him. Then he turned severe and almost whispered:

"Diana, you heard what I told Kiewicz. I thank Providence for bringing you here. If anything can influence the decisions of Zattan, it's knowing that you're alive here and that I'll set you free. I can't know how badly he wants to keep and probably seduce Sylvie Mac Duhl in his castle. If Zattan truly believes in the prophecy of Nostrdamus... I say 'if' because one never knows with that man. If he believes, he'll be more afraid of losing Sylvie than of knowing you're free. But if he doesn't believe, he'll prefer to release the girl than face your love, which is more dangerous and evil than hatred, Diana Ivanova! Anyway, you're a trump card in my game. Depending on the circumstances, I'll keep you in my hand or lay you on the table with the other cards. And I assure you that I'll play close to my chest, with ruthlessness and rationality because I don't love you anymore!"

He had said it all. He was breathing heavily. Sweat ran down his forehead. He stepped back until he was against a bookshelf. His calm, sad eyes stared at the woman.

While he was talking, she had gradually changed her attitude until she no longer looked like a crouching, lowering tiger but rather defeated, sad and sagging. When he had finished, she let out a long sigh, then groaned, threw back her head and two big tears sprang out of her half-closed eyelids. Ah, how beautiful she looked like this! With her face made more voluptuous by the look of sorrow, with her neck swollen by her throbbing throat... He was so affected that he, too, groaned, pressing his hands against his beating heart.

She muttered in a dreamy voice, "Mathias! Mathias!"

And it was so pathetic, so heartrending that he couldn't resist. He stepped up to her, leaned over, trembling, nervous, addled by the abandonment of all his energy...

But all of a sudden Diana sat up straight, her face hardened and her eyes flashed. She was holding in her right hand one of those long, hard stick pins used to hold down the wide lapels of a coat. The needle was aimed brutally at his left eye. He saw it. He understood.

He thought, "She wants to stab out my eyes and then kill me while I writhe in pain." As he was thinking this he snapped his head to the right. But too late to avoid pin that punched through the skin of his left temple and ear.

"You vixen!"

He swung his fist with all his strength and hit her. She rolled onto the carpet, then got on her knees, stood up and turned around, raging mad, her hands like claws and her teeth bared in a grin of demented hatred.

But he grabbed her wrist and twisted. She cried out in pain and fell to her knees. He let her go, stepped away and pulled out the pin that was still stuck in his skin. Blood flowed. He paid no heed. He tossed the pin on the table.

In a low, panting voice he said, "Reduced to fighting you or killing you or being killed by you, that's the fate of all men who let themselves get blinded by the sun of your eyes and poisoned by the kiss of your lips. You want me to say it? Fine, Diana, I love you, I still love you, I love you more than ever. But while never losing my love for you, I became a different man, a new man who will be stronger than the old love. And I'll prove it to you right now..."

He went back to a corner of the table and pressed a button. Ephrem Lluch came through a door. He saw the blood running down the left side of his master's face. He opened his mouth but said nothing.

The Hermit asked, "Is it done?"

"Everything's done. The bombs and five men are in the dungeon and the Pole is gone with the *Saint Pol*."

"Ephrem, come over here." When the sailor was next to him, he said, "Look at this woman. She's committed a hundred crimes. She's betrayed everyone who's ever loved her. She's abandoned every cause she's ever served. Her God, her country, her honor, it's all just her passion of the moment. And her passion of the moment today is called Leonid Zattan, the Prince of Issyk-Kul. She wanted to kill us tonight and burn down our house. Just now, she turned on the tears and then tried to gouge my eyes out with that pin there on the table... Get it?"

"Yes, master."

"Well, I'm putting this woman in your hands. Watch her and keep her alive. Lock her up wherever you want. Treat her as you want. I don't want to see her again. And just so you know how valuable she is to us, I'll say that this woman, Diana Ivanova Krosnovief, the Red Princess, is the ransom for our young Sylvie Mac Duhl."

The Catalan's savage face was as hard as stone. He said, "Very well, master." And to Diana, simply, "Get up, madame, and walk. Or else I'll carry you."

Quickly and gracefully she straightened up and passed by Mathias, saying ominously, "We will meet again."

"Maybe," he replied. "But don't look forward to it because I swear to God that if we meet again, it will be for your death."

"Or yours," she shot back coldly.

"Go on," Lluch ordered, pointing to the door. She went. He followed her.

Mathias Lumen watched them leave. When he was alone, all alone, he collapsed into an armchair, buried his face in his hands... and cried.

CHAPTER III

During the nocturnal return from Ushant to Brest, which he made alone on the *Saint Pol*, Ignace Kiewicz had plenty of time and opportunity—the sea was calm—to examine, reflect and decide. Actually, his decision had been made in a flash of revelation when he was with Diana and Lumen and cried out, "I think I get it. I get it!" His pondering at sea was only to reinforce this decision.

"And especially the method," he mused after leaving the boat with the night guard on duty along the same dock as all the other pleasure yachts. "Yes, the method. I can't waste any time."

He went straight to his house on Rue de Siam. As usual when her beloved master went out at night, Nadine was still up in the dining room, sewing or darning or embroidering because she was a perfect housekeeper.

"Nadine," Ignace said after mutual kisses, "my travel bag."

She shuddered and turned pale, the dear, pretty girl. She dared to ask, "For a long time?"

"I don't know. I'm going to Issyk."

He was already in his bedroom, followed by Nadine who got right down to obeying his order without another word. He opened an iron chest hidden in the back of the alcove behind the bed and pulled out a gray leather handbag with a silver lock, which the Red Princess had given him. It was locked with a key. Ignace didn't even try to open it. He fumbled in one of his pockets, brought out a knife, chose the sharpest blade and with one swipe, slashed open the bag. Straightaway, he pulled out a jewelry box that held a ring, the one with eagle claws grasping the ruby of Leonid Zattan. He slipped it onto his left ring finger and closed the chest, but not before throwing back the jewelry box in the bag and taking out a wallet that he put on a table.

Then he got undressed, washed off the makeup to be completely natural, put on a travel suit with a matching cap, grabbed gloves and stuffed a hooded raincoat under his arm.

"The bag's ready," Nadine said, pointing to the flat suitcase lying on a chair. With another indication she reminded him, "Don't forget the wallet."

"I was just thinking of it." He dropped it into the left inner pocket of his coat.

"Dear!" the woman sighed.

Was he going to forget? To leave without a word for her, a hug, a kiss? No, he bent down, hugged her tightly, then kissed her forehead, her eyes, her lips... And in a deep, caressing voice:

"Wait for me, Nadine. To anyone who asks, I'm going to Paris. If I'm not back in fifteen days, go to the Z station. You'll find news from me there."

He changed his tone and said, "And I'll tell you that Diana Ivanova is a prisoner of the Hermit. The others are dead. But to anyone who asks, you know nothing about it. In any case, you can't count on them, that's all."

Nadine showed no surprise at this brutal news. What did Diana or the others, their life or death mean to her? She loved only Ignace Kiewicz. She hung onto his neck, teary-eyed, and begged, "Don't put yourself in danger, Ignace!"

He responded with a very strange kind of violent, frantic reaction, "Oh, no, don't worry! I've got a specific goal now. You'll see me again, Nadine. And you will finally be able to offer the highest proof of your love… Just wait, Nadine, wait!"

He hugged her again, kissed her on the mouth again and pulled away, grabbed his suitcase and ran out the door.

Ten minutes later, while a bell in an invisible convent or church tolled 4 am, while the city was starting to wake up in the dark disturbed only by a few streetlamps, the Pole was pushing the "night bell" of a garage next to a small hotel. To the guard who peeked through the cracked open door he spoke with the kind of authoritarian gentleness that he used with people who could be considered, in one degree or another, his inferiors:

"Please wake up the driver Nicolas Topoff who arrived yesterday morning in a gray torpedo-sports car. I'm his boss. Get him on the phone right away."

"Very well, monsieur," the guard said. "Please come in."

The door opened wide onto the big entryway to a garage. To the left were glass-fronted offices; to the right a kind of cage with a cot and under a night light sat a telephone. The phone connected directly with the hotel next door where someone was always on duty.

The watchman there was informed by the guard that the chauffeur Nicolas Topoff was needed on the phone. Ignace Kiewicz didn't have to wait long. Two minutes tops.

"Monsieur," the guard handed over the phone, "your chauffeur is on the line."

"Hello? Hello, Nicolas?" Ignace said. "Good! Orders from madame. We're leaving. Hurry up. We'll get coffee on the road at the first bistro we find open… Very good."

He hung up and to the guard, "Where's the car?"

"Garage 22. Should I open it?"

"Yes, right away. I'll get it ready, put in oil and water if necessary while I'm waiting for Nicolas. That way I won't lose any time."

"As you wish, monsieur."

Nicolas arrived less than fifteen minutes later. He knew the Pole well enough, but this was as good as empty words to put the Red Princess' driver at his disposal. More was needed and Ignace knew it. He took off the glove of his left hand and while the guard was busy scribbling in an accounts book, he showed the ruby.

Nicolas Topoff gave him a solemn, military salute and said, "At your orders, monsieur."

"The car is ready," Ignace told him, putting his glove back on. "I filled it up with gas and oil. The radiator's fine. Get in. I'll pay the bill."

"Where are we going, monsieur?"

"Leaving Brest on Rue de Paris."

"Very well, monsieur. Going fast?"

"As fast as possible."

"Allow me to adjust the supercharger?"

"It's already done."

"Oh, very good."

Nicolas put on his leather overcoat (waterproof with a cotton-padded lining), strapped on his hat with earflaps and sat behind the wheel. When the bill was paid, Ignace Kiewicz sat next to Nicolas and wrapped himself in a blanket. The door was opened and the torpedo purred, rolled slowly out of the garage and took Rue de Siam to Rue de Paris, then the outskirts and finally the countryside.

At a sharp bend just before entering a town stood an inn with a coffee counter. "Stop!" Kiewicz commanded.

He stopped. A woman ran out. He gave her his order. Without leaving the car the two travelers could dunk their toast in a big cup of black coffee, extra sugar.

Afterwards, they were off again. They didn't stop again until Rennes to get gas and oil. At 2 pm, the gray sports car pulled up near Montsouris Park in the tiny, shaded, peaceful Rue Bruller. The street had only seven bourgeois residences, no shops or stores. Kiewicz went into No. 7, gave a wave, a smile and a brief greeting to the concierge at the entrance, and dashed up the stairs to the second floor. Only one door on the landing. The Pole didn't ring, but using two of the keys on a ring he pulled out of his pocket, he opened the door, went in and closed it behind him.

"Oh, Monsieur Ignace, what a surprise," a hoarse voice barked in Polish. "Monsieur Stanislas is going to be so happy! He was just talking about you."

"Telepathy, my good Handa, telepathy," Kiewicz chuckled as he gave a big, friendly hug to the tall, hefty woman in her fifties with big, blue, bulging eyes who was standing in the middle of the entryway with a scarf wrapped around her head and blue apron tied around her huge hips and holding a feather duster.

Straightaway, the visitor went into one of the rooms opening onto the entryway.

"Ignace, my brother!"

"Stanislas, big brother!"

Furnished as a study, the walls disappeared behind shelves of books of all sizes and colors (paperbacks, hardbacks, leather-bound), the medium-sized room was lit by two windows (wide open) that let in the slanted rays of the sun. In the middle of the room, next to a table piled with books and newspapers and facing a window, a man sat in a high-backed armchair with wings and wide armrests. Pale, gaunt, his face ravaged by burn scars, his nose bent, the mouth encircled by black, fleecy hair, the body visibly deformed—arms too long, hands too bony—this man was horrifyingly ugly. Big, rubber wheels were fitted to the legs of the armchair. The man was completely paralyzed in both legs, therefore piteously sick or crippled. But the pity, horror and other feelings, which an intelligent man is always ashamed or humiliated or resentful to inspire in others, could be instantly shaken off, snuffed out by one look from this man, a look that was always sublime no matter what other expression was on his face—arched eyes with long, silky eyelashes, bright eyes, deeply blue, which were ringed around the pupil with green—they revealed an ardent, passionate, domineering soul. And they could turn so soft, so tender, so childishly joyful!

And thus it was these divine eyes that welcomed Ignace Kiewicz.

The arms rose, spread and the long, bony hands softened as he hugged his brother. The two men kissed each other on both cheeks and took a few precious moments to look at each other, smiling cheerfully.

"Why'd you come, Igna?" Stanislas asked warmly in Polish.

In the same language (which the brothers always used when they were alone), after taking off his overcoat, hat and gloves, the traveler answered, "To give you great news, Stan!"

He pulled up a chair and sat directly in front of his brother whose own chair had turned 90 degrees. He continued fervently.

"The news I've been promising for three years…"

"Oh, Igna, are you kidding me?" The disabled brother tensed, straightened up, almost rose out of his chair, his hands trembling, his face elated, his eyes both spellbound and sorrowful.

Ignace took his hands and squeezed them. "No, brother, it's not a dream I'm bringing you, it's absolutely real. Don't forget! When I pulled you out of that fire you'd started and that was consuming you, when you listened to my pleas and agreed to live, I promised you that the hopeless love causing you to want to kill yourself and then after turning into hate, this love-hate the only passion of your life, I promised you that it would be fulfilled one day, that you would be able to satisfy your love and gratify your hatred. *For this*, I first became the man of the world that our ancestors, our name, our wealth and education justified in me and for a year there wasn't an elegant, cosmopolitan young man more fashionable than Count Ignace Kiewicz. *For this*, I then pretended to turn into a Neo-terrorist Russian. *For this*, I finally devoted myself body and soul, or so it seemed, to Leonid Zattan and his grand project of anarchy, ambition and autocracy. *For this*, so that the day would come when your honor, in fulfilling your love and hate, will be restored… Am I right?"

"Yes, brother, yes, you're right. And if I couldn't, deep down inside, do for you what you've done for me, I'd regret having occupied your life like this."

"Since that fatal night when our mother died of sorrow from the betrayal of our father and from your suicide, my life belongs to you. I couldn't bring back our father or revive our mother, but I saved you—for the future day of love and vengeance and justice. Well, Stan, my brother, that day has come."

He stood up, still holding and squeezing his brother's hands, and in a deep, rumbling voice pronounced, "Within two weeks Diana Ivanova Krosnovief will be your prisoner in Saint-Guilhem!"

There are joys that kill. Stanislas Kiewicz almost died, struck down by the joy that his brother was bringing him. His Messiah eyes flashed. He cried out, immediately fading into a groan. His hideous face turned pale. His eyelids closed. And he went limp in his big wheelchair.

But Ignace was not scared. He couldn't imagine that his brother would die from the news of what was keeping him alive. Indeed, with his fraternal attention Stanislas soon opened his eyes.

In a weary voice full of boundless bliss, he muttered, "I didn't for an instant lose consciousness, Igna, my beloved brother. Just my nerves couldn't stand such a sudden flood of pure joy. A few questions and you can take me to my bed so I can finally sleep knowing that you didn't save me for nothing."

Ignace giggled. He was kneeling on the carpet in front of his brother, still holding hands under the blanket that covered his knees and legs. He said, "Ask away, Stan."

"When did you become sure of it?"

"Last night."

"How is it that she came to you?"

"Listen up." And he told him the whole adventure from the arrival of Diana Ivanova in the house on Rue de Siam up to his leaving the house of Mathias Lumen. And he concluded, "Four times in two years I could've grabbed Diana and made her disappear, but I was afraid of both Lumen and Zattan. I knew that the first loved her and the second considered her his number one agent. I feared that each of them would go looking for her and with the means at their disposal they would've found her. We certainly could've killed her at the last minute, but that's not what you want…"

"Oh, no, no…"

"Well then, you get it too: neither Lumen nor Zattan will go looking for the Red Princess when the first will have unleashed her against the second who will think she's still in the hands of the first. Lumen will leave her to her fate, which he hopes will be catastrophic to Zattan. But Zattan won't be thinking of her after he hears what I have to tell him. And in Saint-Guilhem only the eagles will hear the cries of Diana Ivanova Krosnovief!"

"The eagles and me, brother. And you, too, if you want, you will hear the cries of this woman."

"I will hear them, too, brother. And I hope our mother in her grave will hear them with us."

The sick man leaned forward and hugged his brother, both of them crying.

Then Ignace pushed the wheelchair to a door, opened it, went through and stopped in the middle of a luxurious but sober and comfortable bedroom. As usual Ignace picked up Stanislas in his arms and lifted him effortlessly. The blanket fell off and the bathrobe dropped open: Stanislas Kiewicz' legs looked mummified; his knees were bent like a normal man sitting down, at a right angle to his thighs, but stiff, rigid because his skeletal knees had no living muscles, nerves, veins or arteries. When he was in bed, his back almost straight against the pillows, his legs remained bent at a right angle as they had been for years, as they would be until they decayed into dust after death...

"Soon, Stan," Ignace bent down to kiss his brother on the forehead.

"Soon, Igna. Bless you."

The sick man closed his eyes. The traveler went back into the study, put on his coat, hat and gloves, then into the entrance hall before going into the kitchen where the sturdy Polish servant was cleaning the silverware with Spanish whiting.

"Handa, I'm leaving. Listen, it's likely that my brother will want to go to Saint-Guilhem pretty soon. You don't have to inform me, I'll know."

"Very well, sir. Another trip?"

"Yes."

"God be with you, sir."

"And you, Handa, that he'll watch over you and reward you for my brother. Come here so I can kiss you."

They exchanged kisses, like a real nanny and child, strong and hard.

A few minutes later Ignace Kiewicz was back in the torpedo, which was waiting on Rue Bruller. He ordered, "Bourget airport."

Without a word, Nicolas Topoff sped off.

An hour later, in the second-floor apartment of 7 Rue Bruller, Stanislas Kiewicz, who hadn't slept, was pressing the button on a bulb hanging over his head. Handa rushed in.

"Nurse," he said, "we're leaving Paris tomorrow morning at 7 am. Tell Lang So that it's for a long time, maybe even forever. Get him to bring Belladone, Vladimir will drive the van. We'll go straight to Saint-Guilhem. Handa, I won't be eating today. Give me the opium. I'll smoke a little before going to sleep. And be glad, nurse, because I'm happy."

Saint-Guilhem-le-Désert is known to all tourists who have visited Languedoc and passed through the Rhône valley in the Garonne basin by taking the network of various river gorges that cut through the plateaus of Cévennes. If you're going from Avignon to Toulouse, it'd be better to get off the highways, which are often poorly maintained and therefore not very pleasant, and take the country roads. Through Remoulins and Pont-de-Gard, Nîmes, Quissac, Ganges, you go down into the Hérault valley to Gignac and then by Lodève, Saint-Pons, Castres, Lavaur and Toulouse. Wild country, picturesque, with dusky lowlands where farms and villages stay cool in the shade surrounded by the deserted plateaus. Between Ganges and Aniane the gorges of Hérault wind through the cliffs, in some places ominously steep, in others quite charming. It is there, at the entrance to a dead-end valley, which (because of its bleakness) they call "the End of the World", that you will find Saint-Guilhem-le-Désert.

A steep mountain rises above it and in spots looms over it. On the highest peak of this mountain feudal robber barons in the 17th century built a formidable castle defended by tiered walls on the side of the rocky mountain, furnished with deep cisterns. These plunderers were chased off by Saint Guilhem, the abbot of a nearby monastery whose warrior monks could meet force with force. The castle was demolished.

For centuries the summit was crowned with picturesque ruins that the region called the "Castle of Giants".

In 1916 a French writer, a reserve officer poisoned by gas and sent to one of the hospitals in Montpellier to recover, went to visit the Hérault valley and by a series of strange circumstances decided on a whim to buy the ruins of the Castle of Giants.

"By building up a few walls and putting a roof on it," he said, "I'll have a nice enough place for my fits of solitude."

But his destiny kept him far from the region. After a long conversation in a Paris salon in 1917, a bored American bought from him the ruins of Saint-Guilhem. This American set up the main office of his architect and construction manager in Montpellier. One year later the old feudal castle had risen from its ruins—exactly as it had been in the 17th century, at least on the outside, and as such was it in 1919. As for the interior, nothing could be more modern. A strong cable brought electricity from the closest power station into a diffuser post inside the walls to supply the lighting, heating and water pumps, which came from a deep spring discovered by drilling at the foot of the mountain almost at the edge of the End of the World.

English and French furniture of latest fashion, tasteful and comfortable; a French-English library of 3,000 books; in short, a 20th century luxury estate in a shroud of the hard, rugged rock of a medieval castle. A new, windy road led up to it, ending on one side in a garage with a guardhouse and on the other side in the castle's main courtyard.

The American stayed all winter in the Castle of Giants with a valet and cook. He hunted. He nurtured his hypochondria. He fended off ennui. But by the spring he was tired of it. He left one fine morning with his servants and dropped the keys off at a notary in Montpellier who immediately put the "estate" up for sale. The estate included the buildings, both old and new, with all they contained, the electric and hydraulic systems and 27 acres of mountain where rock and stone tolerated only a sparse growth of grass, gorse and scrub oak. This along with cataclysmic storms and obliterating winds, some rabbits, sparrow-hawks and a couple of eagles.

Withing a month the castle of Saint-Guilhem passed into the hands of a new owner: a man known only by the name and nationality he gave himself, even in Saint-Guilhem—Monsieur Reder, Belgian.

One fine day in Saint-Guilhem they learned that the new owner was living in his castle. He had come in the night. He stayed three weeks. No one saw him. But they often watched his car and chauffeur, his valet and cook, who went into Aniane to shop every day. The mayor, for local charitable offices, and the parish priest for the church and the poor, each got a donation, which would be renewed annually, of 5,000 francs. But the cook, valet and chauffeur passed through Saint-Guilhem without talking to anyone. When the so-called Belgian left after 22 days, he was as invisible as when he'd come.

But he left a guard up there who lived in the guardhouse next to the garage. He was a giant himself, six and a half feet tall, Chinese-looking, reserved, a fanatic of hunting and fishing whom no one ever got a word out of. When he went into the butcher's, the baker's, the grocer's, he asked for what he wanted in a raspy voice in very good French but only what was strictly necessary to be understood. He paid without ever haggling or questioning, just saying very politely "bonjour" or "bonsoir". And that was all.

One day when asked his name he had replied, "Tché Fah."

The Belgian came back a few times with his car and chauffeur, his valet and cook. He stayed for two or three weeks. He came and went during the day, but they glimpsed only a shadowy figure in the backseat. He never went out of the castle. If he strolled along one of the three surrounding walls, they couldn't see him because of the tiered construction from foot to summit and the walls were high enough to block the land behind them.

But since the notary in Aniane regularly sent the annual 5,000 francs in quarterly installments to the priest and mayor, from which the whole village reaped benefits, since the people's curiosity fades quickly when its not given not a shred of satisfaction, so in Saint-Guilhem they soon stopped thinking about the castle and its owner, except for a little idle gossip by the fire on cold winter nights.

However, there was talk, kindly for the most part, when they learned in the village that on April 9th Monsieur Reder had arrived early that morning not only in his car but with a van, probably full of baggage, which his valet was driving. They also noticed that next to the driver was a woman whose face was hidden behind veils. As for the well-known cook, she was, as usual, inside the car.

"With the guard that makes six people, including two women," they said.

No letter or telegram had arrived at the post office for Tché Fah. Nevertheless, the guard must have been informed because the first gate was waiting open for the car and as soon as the van passed through, the colossal Chinese closed it, jogged up to the rolling car and jumped on the running board.

The window was rolled down. "Hello, monsieur," he said in Polish. "Did you have a good trip?"

"Excellent, Tché" Stanislas Kiewicz smiled. "Is everything well?"

"All is well, monsieur."

"Good."

The two other gates were opened. After going through, the Chinese closed them. When the two vehicles were parked in the main courtyard in front of the front steps, he started unloading the suitcases, trunks, bundles and crates with his brother Lang So, the chauffeur-mechanic, and their colleague and friend Vladimir, the valet. Belladonna, Lang So's wife, went with Handa who carried Stanislas in her brawny arms.

This "Belladonna" had gotten her name six years ago because in Canton, with some belladonna tea, she had poisoned two Czech officers who had arrested her fiancé Lang So in order to have her. Using the same method she had poisoned the jailer, a soldier, one of the executioners in the prison and had managed to free Lang So who escaped with her to Saigon where Ignace Kiewicz met them, helped them and hired them. Thus, they were married. But since the Chinese name of Lang So's wife was long and hard to pronounce, Ignace called her Belladonna, for short just Bella. And this name fit her so well, in all languages, that her husband and brother in-law even called her by the Chinese word meaning Belladonna.

She was a short, stocky woman, full of invincible energy, who loved her husband, cherished her brother in-law and would have given her life for Kiewicz. Naturally and unconsciously cruel, feeling almost no physical pain, she was a very strange woman. When she was hired with her husband and brother in-law, Stanislas and Ignace had no idea how much they would later consider her fated to be part of their household.

Stanislas' own rooms were on the ground floor of the castle. A wheelchair (the same kind as on Rue Bruller) was waiting in the entrance hall with its soft padding on the seat, arms, headrest and adjustable back. When he was sitting in it with the customary blanket over his dead legs, he said with impatient joy, "Handa, you can go to the kitchen. I won't need you. I'll keep Bella with me and Vladimir will be back to his usual duties soon enough."

And she disappeared.

"Bella," Stanislas continued, "please take me to the padded room. The Chinese woman had taken off her veils, coat and gloves, which she left for the moment on one of the medieval bishop's chairs lined up along the walls of the entrance. She was dressed in a very short sheath dress of off-white linen that left her neck and arms bare. With all this, her Asian features and short, male haircut that plastered her black hair to her head, Bella was a baffling character. How old? 20, 30, 40? A mystery.

Without a word, without a smile on her lips, she obeyed. She pushed the wheelchair smoothly down the tiled and carpeted floor, opened and closed doors until she finally rolled her master into a very extraordinary room.

No windows, not a single piece of furniture. Lit by a red, electric, ceiling light that made the room more sinister than the uniform color of the carpets, cushions and padded walls—pale green. From floor to ceiling the four walls were completely covered in leather padding. In leather, too, were the round and square cushions scattered over the carpet. The whole thing made you feel like you were inside a giant jewelry box.

"Close the door, Bella," Stanislas ordered when his wheelchair was sitting in the middle of the room. And then, "Let's see if everything's working. I had Tché check it for a few minutes every day. Do what you need to."

The Chinese woman went to the back of the room and used two fingers (wiped clean with a handkerchief) to press one of the padded bulges. A door, completely invisible before, opened in front of her. She went through and the door closed behind her.

Stanislas waited, his hideous face with eyes half-closed looking eager and impatient. Not for long. Almost immediately his eyes opened wide and his hands started quivering. In a low voice he uttered a monologue:

"Ah, there's the air, the heavy, stinking, rotten air... A cellar closed off for a long time where a carcass is rotting and is next to a burning oven... Warm air, hard to breathe. Good! Oh, the change of light! Dim and dreary dusk... A November night with fog and soot... And this monotonous padding, so gloomy, so gloomy! Now the music... A cheap, second-rate jazz band, making noise with bad instruments... a phonograph... it'll have to be the same tune, if you can call it that, coming back over and over like an obsessive saw... Oh, oh, the buzz-buzz-buzz of the rusty drilling is wonderful! When I think that all this will be accompanied by badly cooked food with rancid fat and putrid grease... and drinks, sour wine and oily water..."

The sick man rejoiced in his wheelchair. His divine eyes glittered with diabolical joy, his shapeless mouth grinned bitterly, his bony fingers gripped the arms. Was he crazy? All of a sudden, he stopped mumbling, closed his eyes and mouth, froze his hideous, stitched up face and his right hand rose up, imposingly.

Immediately, the jazz band stopped, the light lost its color, the rancid air was cleared off by fans that hummed and purred. The hidden door opened and swiveled shut after Belladonna came in.

"Is that good, monsieur?" she asked.

"It's good, Bella. In two weeks, I hope, this room will have a tenant. You'll be able to smother the European beauty with care, remember? The beautiful Russian who was the force in Shanghai behind the Bolshevik General Fang Hog Fou, the murderer of your family?"

With these words, which Stanislas pronounced without opening his eyes, the wife of Lang So narrowed hers and her whole body quivered while her hands balled into tight fists on her flat chest. In a hoarse voice and in Chinese, she muttered, "The wretched woman?"

173

"Yes, Belladonna, yes, the wretched woman!" Stanislas repeated in the same language.

"Oh, monsieur, will she be here?"

"Here, yes."

"In two weeks?"

"I hope so."

"And all this is for her..."

"All for her, yes. Your brother in-law is a genius of torture, Bella. You can thank him. And also an expert engineer and decorator because he built and put all this together by himself. You can congratulate him... But stay calm, Belladonna, stay calm. For a few hours a day, I'll leave you alone with the wretched woman. But you must swear that you will obey everything I ask of you."

"Oh, monsieur," she fell on knees as if worshiping an idol, "I'll obey everything, everything, even if it's..."

"Don't imagine anything, Bella. Get up and not another word. Take me to my smoking room and bring me the pipes... one by one, slowly... and you can smoke, too..."

She had tears of joy. She grabbed his hand, brought it to her lips and kissed it devotedly three times, slowly, mumbling the religious chants for the immutable gift of every living being...

That was how Stanislas Kiewicz returned to his castle in Saint-Guilhem-le-Désert to wait for his brother Ignace to bring Princess Diana Ivanova Krosnovief.

Well, on April 9th, Ignace Kiewicz was arriving in Constantinople by plane after stopping in Vienna and Sofia to see the sector chiefs of the international Neo-terrorist organization whose supreme chief was Leonid Zattan. He showed them the fateful ruby. He talked and listened to them. And in Constantinople, in a grand cosmopolitan hotel in Pera, under the name of Count Ignace Kiewicz, he waited for the emissary from Issyk-Kul who was supposed to pick up, in the same hotel on April 10th, the Red Princess to bring her to Zattan... if, that is, she hadn't been captured on the mission to Ushant, a mission that she was initially only supposed to announce to the secret council.

He waited with complete confidence in the success of his plan and the fulfillment of his projects.

Maybe he would have been less optimistic—or would he have been even more so?—anything's possible, after all—if he'd known about the startling, secret events unfolding since April 4th that would have unforeseen consequences in the near or distant future!

In this whirlwind of events, would the two Polish brothers still have the power and privilege to play their own side-game of love, hate, vengeance and justice?

Neither Mathias Lumen nor Leonid Zattan were men who would overlook, willfully or by mistake, the different trump cards represented by Diana Ivanova, Stanislas and Ignace Kiewicz.

So?

In truth, though the Kiewicz brothers kept their eyes open, they were blind because they had not been in Cyprus or in Issyk-Kul since the night of April 4th.

CHAPTER IV

In Cyprus, on April 4th, around 11 pm, the sailors from the *Fulgur*, Feraud and Blanchard, on guard duty inside the front door of the house belonging to Ismaïl Kadeuy, heard the noise of scurrying footsteps in the small square outside. But instead of gradually fading away like the others had done, these became louder. Then they just stopped.

"Watch out!" the two men said together.

The bell rang softly.

Feraud had already tiptoed down the hallway. He came back, dragging his leg to the sound of a scraping shoe like Kadeuy's servant usually makes. Then he unlocked the door and hid behind it as it opened. A man came in. The door slammed shut. And Blanchard and Feraud jumped the man, bound his hands, gagged him and pushed him down the hallway where he was handed over to Sylvain and Bonnet who dragged him into the garden-patio and left him with Yves Lequic.

A lantern was lit on the table. Next to the table was a wicker rocking chair. In the chair sat Gnô Mitang who tossed away a half-smoked cigar to say:

"Manoël Guerro, I believe you can understand and speak French very well, so we'll use this language, if you please. I believe that you have no more desire than I to alert the neighbors or call for the help of the English. Therefore, do not scream. Lequic, ungag him."

It was done in a jiffy.

The Portuguese gasped in the fresh air of the small garden. He rolled his frightened eyes and stammered, "Who are you, monsieur?"

The Japanese chuckled and said, "Is it possible that you, the head of the wireless service for His Lord the Prince of Issyk-Kul, don't know about me? Come, come, Monsieur Guerro, don't pretend you haven't heard about the Japanese Gnô Mitang, the right-hand man of Gregor Mac Duhl and one of the lieutenants of Mathias Lumen. Now, I look as Japanese as they come, so you should have no problem identifying me."

He stopped talking and glared at Guerro who kept up his good-naturedly ruse.

Changing his tone, Gnô went on, "Enough with the pleasantries. You're my prisoner. Your life is in my hands. Do you want to redeem your life by serving me?"

Instead of answering, Guerro asked a question. He wanted to play dumb and he had regained his composure. "How do you know me, monsieur? I've never seen you before."

"I found your signed photo in Kadeuy's chest. It looks just like you. But answer my question, please."

"So be it," he shrugged. "But before committing myself, I have to know what it means for me to serve you."

"Very simple. Go back to the plane you came in and fly back to Issyk-Kul without delay. Give Leonid Zattan this message, which is more of an ultimatum."

The Portuguese didn't hesitate. With a great deal of dignity he said, "Monsieur, I see nothing there to break my solemn vow to Zattan. I came here only to pick up a sailor named Pedro Tchicoz. Can I see him and take him back?"

"No. I've gotten rid of him. Forever."

"I find myself, therefore, left with no choice since I'm alone, tied up, facing I don't know how many men and in a situation I know nothing about. I'll tell the Prince how I got into the house and how I left, because naturally I accept being your messenger."

"Wonderful."

Near the lantern on the table was a white, unmarked envelope. Gnô picked it up and handed it to the Portuguese. "Here's the message."

With his other hand he had made a sign to Lequic who quickly untied the captive. Guerro could then take the envelope and put it in his inside coat pocket.

"Is that all, monsieur?" he asked.

"That's all," the Japanese stood up.

"I can go?"

"In a few minutes, yes. Please follow me. Your photograph stayed in the room of good old Kadeuy. I want you to fully understand my good intentions for you because if Leonid Zattan ever found out that your picture and signature were so easily available to the first of Lumen's lieutenants to come along, he could very well accuse you of negligence. Go on up ahead of me, please, into Kadeuy's bedroom."

Being rattled, Guerro could do nothing but obey. But he didn't see the Japanese make a sign to the sailor behind him—right hand raised with fingers bent except for the index pointing up. Yves Lequic nodded in response and smiled, which obviously meant, "Good, good, I get it, let's have some fun."

While Gnô's improvised ploy was being played out in the Turk's bedroom in order to keep Guerro from seeing what was happening downstairs, Lequic went into the hallway and talked to Bonnet and Sylvain.

"Go outside. Hide yourselves on either side of the small square. When that guy comes out, follow him, but one by one. Whatever you do, don't get spotted. He shouldn't be suspecting a thing. Me and the boss and Feraud and Blanchard will be trailing at a distance. We'll follow whoever of you is second. Got it?"

"Yes."

"Good. This is the order: when you hear a whistle, jump the guy and don't let him scream. So, you have to follow as close as possible, of course. Without the whistle, you do nothing, no matter what. Still got it?"

"Yes."

"Good."

Then Lequic went to speak to Feraud and Blanchard. Afterwards he went back to the garden. A few minutes later he was joined by Gnô Mitang and Manoël Guerro.

"Well then, monsieur," the Japanese said, "I won't keep you any longer." And to Lequic, "Show him out."

Manoël Guerro left the house. He was so intrigued by the unexpected, enigmatic adventure that he didn't even think of the men in the hallway. He saw only two. Did he have any idea how many men had grabbed him and tied him up before taking him into the garden? He didn't have a clue that two men had just left and hidden in the square, waiting for him to leave, for him to walk, for him to pass by one of them so that they could shadow him discreetly.

It was Bonnet who got the lead. twenty feet behind him Sylvain started strolling. Then Gnô Mitang, Feraud, Blanchard and Lequic came out of the house one by one. The last one locked the door and put the key in his pocket.

At this time of night no one was out in the Famagusta district. A few scattered streetlamps flickered. They disappeared after the last house. But the sky was clear and cloudless, riddled with stars. Moreover, the moon had just risen, although in its waning quarter, providing just enough pale light on the land for a man to follow another at a distance and to see the loose rocks and ditches so he wouldn't fall or make a sound.

The trackers had to be careful, especially since they were completely unfamiliar with the goat trail Guerro hurried onto. The trail led north at first, then it veered west, made a hairpin turn into a jumble of rocks, stunted bushes and thorny gorse, and finally wound down to the sea. The plane from Issyk-Kul was waiting on the Famagusta coast across from the sheltered cove where the *Fulgur* was anchored.

As they got farther from the inhabited areas, Gnô, with Feraud, Blanchard and Lequic hot on his heels, closed in on Sylvain until he was only a few feet behind the sailor, who was maybe fifty yards behind Bonnet, who himself was around a hundred yards behind Guerro. In some places, at times, the uneven ground let the pursuers see the body of the walking Portuguese outlined in black against the sky.

Manoël Guerro had no idea that he was being followed so closely. Not once did he think of looking behind him. Since he didn't try to soften the sound of his footsteps, even this sound kept him from hearing the same sound, though fainter, that his stalkers couldn't help making despite their caution: dry nettles cracking, pebbles rolling down slopes, leaves brushing against each other. As a result, without a clue of being a guide, of the danger that threatened him, the Portuguese went directly to the still waters where the plane was waiting.

The moment came when Gnô Mitang glimpsed the plane for the first time when he was just about to reach the top of a rather steep hill that dropped down to the sea. At the same time he could see that Bonnet and Sylvain were twenty feet behind Guerro. Lastly, studying the lay of the land with his keen eye, he noticed that halfway down the hill was a ravine.

He thought, "The Portuguese will be out of the plane's sight in this ravine. That's where we have to jump him. But a whistle here might be heard on the plane. We have to get to him in that ravine."

The descending slope of the hill allowed the pursuers to close their ranks for a unified action. They were able to use the bushes and rocks to draw closer without being seen.

Consequently, Gnô first made a signal with his right hand to Feraud, Blanchard and Lequic to come and line up with him as he quickened his pace. They risked making more noise because the steep, rocky path taken by Guerro on his oblivious hike was full of loose rocks. Nevertheless, Gnô and his three companions reached Sylvain. They saw Bonnet sneaking from bush to bush ten feet in front of them.

"Get up to Bonnet," Gnô whispered to Sylvain, "and get as close as you can to Guerro. When you're in the ravine, which is hidden from the sea and the plane, jump him. Make sure he doesn't cry out!"

"Got it, boss." And Sylvain rushed off.

From that moment on, Gnô Mitang and the three others saw no more of Guerro, Syvain or Bonnet. The first because he was already in the shadows of the ravine; the two others because they were sneaking behind the bushes and rocks. The land was a real shrubland full of holm oaks, myrtles, strawberries and gorse, sometimes bunched together into tangled thickets, sometimes spread out in rows.

One or two minutes ticked off.

Gnô Mitang felt his heart beating faster and harder. He was playing a high-stakes game and the stakes were: probably the life and liberty of Saint-Clair and Marc Ayol; maybe even, as a consequence, the fate of Sylvie Mac Duhl and Leonid Zattan; and as a final result, the victory of Mathias Lumen over the catastrophic organization preparing the Dark Times symbolized by the prophesied Antichrist.

Yes, all this depended directly or indirectly on a series of logically connected actions: first, was knowing (now known) where the plane was waiting, second was to capture, without a sound, Manoël Guerro, and the third...

But Gnô's thought didn't have time to go further. The abrupt and brief noise of a heavy bodies crashing into a bush... A short groan... Silence.

"They got him!" And Gnô Mitang dashed forward, followed by Feraud, Blanchard and Lequic.

From a distance the ravine looked pitch black, not yet reached by the moonlight. But up close it was easy to distinguish everything thanks to the dim light of the myriad stars shining in the clear sky. The four men, therefore, had no problem seeing Bonnet and Sylvain in the middle of a round bush holding down Guerro who was already gagged.

"Very good," Gnô said. "Get him up and bring him over."

When the stunned Portuguese was standing in front of him, in the grip of strong hands on either side, his mouth stuffed with a rubber ball, Gnô simply said to him, "If you don't want to be knocked out, don't struggle. You won't get hurt. Agreed?"

Guerro would have been a real idiot to refuse. He nodded three times as a sign of total agreement.

"Thanks," the Japanese said. "Get undressed right now. No, don't take out that useless message. Its purpose was only to get you to trust me a little." Then in a different tone of voice, "You, Blanchard, are the closest to his size. Get undressed and put on the prisoner's clothes. It's only to look like him. I hope you won't have to talk. All of you, listen to me. There's only one guy on the plane. He's a pilot called Petrus Ivitch. Doesn't talk much. Right! Guerro's supposed to come back to the plane with Tchicoz, whom Ivitch has never seen. It's you, Bonnet, who will be Tchicoz. But it's likely that Ismail Kadeuy would come to say hello to Ivitch since they know each other. I'll be the Turk. I've got his clothes and straw hat here and I brought a cap that Tchicoz could very well have picked up. The cap will fit Bonnet for sure. But I'm a little short for Kadeuy's clothes. I'll roll up the sleeves and pant legs. From a distance, in the night, if Ivitch sees us coming he shouldn't suspect a thing."

Gnô Mitang patted the bundle hanging from Lequic's shoulder.

"You, Lequic, Feraud and Sylvain, stay here. Guard the prisoner. Keep him gagged. When you hear a whistle, go down to the little beach at the bottom of the hill."

While talking he had untied the bundle and opened it. In less than five minutes Gnô, Blanchard and Bonnet were disguised, the first two completely, the third by taking off his coat and exchanging his beret for the Cyprian cap.

"Your Brownings in easy reach of your right hand," he told the two sailors. "Ready?"

"Yes, monsieur."

"Let's go! Lequic, listen for the whistle."

Leaving the three men with their prisoner in the ravine, the Japanese started off again along with Blanchard-Guerro and Bonnet-Tchicoz.

His deductive reasoning resumed like this:

"The plane must be anchored a short distance from the shore. Guerro would've come ashore on a skiff like a "berton". Since the Portuguese has to bring back Tchicoz, the boat would normally hold two men. A third shouldn't overload it. That's why I can be Kadeuy. It'll be easier for the three of us to overpower Ivitch before he can do any serious harm, like kill one of us or smash some vital piece of the plane. The skiff should be dragged up on the beach or tied to a rock in still water."

Indeed, before even reaching the little, sloping beach, that bordered the cove where the plane looked like a huge seabird taking a rest, the three men saw the skiff on the sand. They went directly towards it. It was a "berton", top quality, so light a child could've pushed it into the water and so wide and well balanced that five men could've fit in it without danger of sinking, especially on a calm sea like this night on the Mediterranean off the coast of Cyprus.

"It can be broken down, of course," Bonnet whispered. "It takes up a lot less space when folded, which must be necessary in the plane."

Blanchard-Guerro pushed the skiff and they all jumped in. Bonnet-Tchicoz took the oars.

They were all fully aware of the gravity of the situation. Were they going to succeed and start a cycle of adventures that the boldest imagination would dread to think about? Were they going to lose, to die straightaway or be captured and wait for certain death in some dungeon of the Issyk-Kul castle?

But Gnô Mitang was braving the challenge with calm and composure. Bonnet and Blanchard would've been dishonored in their own eyes if they showed less serenity than "the boss". And yet, they didn't know, like him, the secret of the passionate struggle, in a way both divine and demonic, in which they were fighting like units of an uncountable army.

The plane was anchored a stone's throw from the shore. The distance was covered quickly. The night was clear enough for the Japanese to see the removable metal ladder on the left side of the fuselage leading up to the cargo door. During their short ride he had whispered detailed orders so Bonnet and Blanchard knew what they had to do.

When the skiff was stationary below the ladder, which Gnô Mitang had grabbed, Blanchard-Guerro wasted no time. He climbed up rung by rung, as bumbling as Guerro would do. The cargo door opened out to the right, worked by a kind of lever with a safety catch. The sailor saw all this. He didn't fumble or hesitate. He pushed the catch, pulled the lever and the door swung open.

The inside of the hold was lit by four electric lights of frosted glass. Six bucket seats, screwed down chests, shiny machines and instruments, the steering wheel, joysticks and control levers: the sailor saw everything with one quick glance, including Petrus Ivitch whose name Gnô had given him along with the orders in the skiff.

The Russian was sitting in his pilot's seat. When the cargo door opened, he turned to look. His sharp eyes saw a man whom his unsuspecting mind naturally accepted for a moment as Manoël Guerro because of his clothes. But that moment only lasted a few seconds. The man's face was the same as the Portuguese.

Ivitch was probably forming a question in his mind that would instinctively express his surprise... but it was already too late.

The fake Guerro had hopped into the cargo hold and was holding his Browning. Two other men, also armed, were standing up behind him. The last one spoke in Russian bluntly.

"Don't make a move, Ivitch, because none of us will hesitate to kill you. No! Don't do it or I'll shoot! Get up, hands where I can see them!"

The pilot-engineer stopped moving toward the lever he was reaching for, different from the others because it was strangely serrated. He stood up, hands raised over his head. It wasn't that he loved life for itself, but he loved the adverse twists and turns it offered. His mind was snickering, "What trap have I fallen into and how did Leonid not see this coming? Now it's getting interesting, if Mathias Lumen finally shows up himself to snuff for the battle!" And the new prospects of this adventure compelled him not to sacrifice his life, the plane or the three intruders, as he could have done.

Very calmly he said in Russian, "So be it. I surrender. But who are you and what do you want?"

"We're enemies of Leonid Zattan," the Japanese answered, "and we're taking control of this plane."

"You belong to Mathias Lumen?"

"Yes."

Ivitch laughed. "Finally! And right on time! The operations are under way. What'd you do with Guerro?"

"He'll be brought here. You'll leave the plane with him."

"Leave the plane!" Ivitch was outraged after he'd kindly let the Japanese put handcuffs on him. "But I'd rather stay and see what you're going to do. Obviously, you're going to Issyk-Kul. The adventure…"

"Sorry I have to disappoint you," Gnô cut him off sharply. "Unless you give me your word of honor as a Muscovite gentleman—because I know who you are, General Feodor Petrovitch Illine—your word of honor that you'll obey everything I tell you to do against Leonid Zattan."

"Oh, monsieur," the engineer replied, rearing up, "I've already given my word to Leonid Zattan against the entire world. He hasn't, he'll never give it back."

"Well, you'll have to be satisfied with knowing about events by hearsay. I'll be kind enough to tell you myself or at least to send someone to tell you. Let's wrap this up. So, you refuse to give me your word?"

"I can't."

"Too bad. You would've been very useful to me and probably would've really enjoyed the show. But you say you can't. Subject closed."

Gnô made a sign to Bonnet and Blanchard, who, like their boss, had holstered their Brownings, to take Ivitch and tie him up. The prisoner was smart enough not to resist. They took him out of the pilot's seat and tied him up in one of the two seats in the rear.

Then Gnô leaned out the cargo door and whistled three times into the night. He stepped aside and Bonnet climbed down to untie the skiff and paddle it toward the shore.

Leaving the door open, Gnô turned around and asked Ivitch, "I hope you're not too uncomfortable?"

"No," the Russian answered in good humor, apparently enjoying the prospects of an unforeseen adventure. "No, your partner was considerate and experienced. But if I give you my word not to do anything against you, seeing as you have the upper hand, will you untie me?"

"Certainly."

"Very well. It won't change the situation and I'll be more comfortable. I give you my word that I won't do anything to oppose you, monsieur."

"I accept. Blanchard, untie the engineer."

Handcuffs and ropes were quickly taken off and disappeared into the pockets of the fake Guerro.

Then Gnô said to Ivitch, "Of course, I won't ask you to explain to me how the plane works."

"I'd refuse, monsieur."

"I'm sure. So, I'll just ask you not to laugh too hard at me and my second-in-command for this if we don't fly like experts on our first go."

The Russian misanthrope laughed hard at that. This was great fun. He saw in Gnô Mitang a man of his intellectual class. They had opposite ideas about many things and served masters who were enemies, but they had the same higher sense of irony that put men above all the prejudices and all the human laws. He would've loved to switch places with the Japanese. Maybe he would've been more cruel straight off. In any case, if this is the Japanese they sometimes talked about in the secret meetings at Issyk-Kul, then it should turn out to be very interesting.

"Tell me," the engineer finished his bout of hearty laughter, "would you by any chance be Gnô Mitang, ex-captain aviator of..."

"In person," Gnô cut him off with a smile.

But the conversation ended there.

The Japanese had made a sign to Bonnet. The two men sat down next to each other in the forward seats, Gnô in Ivitch's place. One by one they examined the controls, levers, switches, etc., touching some cautiously while exchanging whispered reflections.

Fifteen minutes went by. Petrus Ivitch watched them with a smile and twinkling eyes.

"Well, monsieur," Gnô suddenly turned to the Russian, "I think we'll lift anchor, skate over the water, take off and fly almost as well as if you had done me the honor of remaining the pilot of this fabulous machine. A unique electric engine. Matching top-rate instruments. Wonderful simplicity. I believe you are the inventor and builder of this airplane—my compliments, monsieur. If Mathias Lumen wins the ultimate victory, as I hope he does, he will owe a lot to this plane that we're using on his behalf..."

He stopped. His narrowed eyes flashed, his thin lips pulled back into a feline's hungry grin and he went on, politely but wryly.

"There's no Russian from the old aristocracy that doesn't speak perfect French . You were part of that aristocracy, so I'm going to use this worldwide, diplomatic language since I want to be understood by both you and my second-in-command here, Charles Bonnet, an engineer-aviator and first-class soldier."

"As you want," Ivitch said. "I know French very well."

"I have no doubt."

Speaking slowly, seriously, his face turned to stone, his eyes turned hard, Gnô continued.

"I had three action plans I thought were all excellent. The one I started with wasn't bad since it worked, but an idea just came to mind that's compelling me to drop it. This idea is the start of a fourth plan. I'll tell you what you need to know. Are you listening?"

"I'm all ears."

"Well then, enjoy the ride, Petrus Ivitch, because you won't be getting off the plane. Guerro neither. I'm bringing both of you with me, yes, all the way to Issyk-Kul... whether you want to or not, you are going to play an important role in my plan. And thanks to you, Ivitch, thanks to your plane and also thanks to Guerro, I hope I can force Leonid Zattan to fall into a trap that he'll never get out of, bound in chains and brought back to the house in Ushant!"

Having said these ominous words, which might have sounded crazy to anyone else but Petrus Ivitch—who, as a Russian, believed anything possible, especially things that looked impossible—Gnô Mitang turned his back to the astounded engineer and in a different tone said:

"Bonnet, I hear the sound of oars in the water."

"Yes, boss, that's the skiff."

"Good. Blanchard and Lequic know what they have to do. Don't move."

Indeed, Lequic and Blanchard knew what they had to do. Before three minutes rolled by a visibly stunned man appeared in the frame of the cargo door. It was Manoël Guerro, legs free but handcuffs on his wrists. Blanchard pushed him so expertly that he fell directly into the second back seat next to Petrus Ivitch.

Behind Blanchard came Lequic who gave a military salute and said, "Boss, Feraud and Sylvain are off to the *Fulgur*. The skiff is moored and ladder folded. Should I close the door?"

"Yes."

Petrus Ivitch was over his astonishment and enjoying himself immensely. He gave Guerro a comforting pat on the shoulder since he was having a harder time pulling himself together. They heard Gnô Mitang speaking as calmly as ever.

"We won't be landing near the *Fulgur*, sailor. The situation has been anticipated. Lieutenant Guennec won't be worried or surprised. Besides, Feraud and Sylvain will tell him what's happening. We're going straight to Issyk-Kul. Everything ready?"

Cool and collected, Lequic and Blanchard sat in the two middle seats. Lequic, replied, "Everything's ready, boss."

"It's in God's hands!" He pulled a lever that worked a small electric winch to roll up the anchor. The plane skated over the water. The periscope mirror inside showed the anchor rising slowly into its casing where an automatic clamp grabbed it.

Then, working the flight instruments here and there, logically reasoned out, Gnô Mitang started the propellers, gave the engine more power, shifted the rudder and took off smoothly. The *Aquilon* soared into the sky to the obvious excitement of its inventor. Soon it was cruising at almost 200 mph toward Issyk-Kul.

CHAPTER V

After around 13 hours in the air, the Aquilon would land at the castle of Is-syk-Kul. What Gnô Mitang called his fourth plan would then either succeed or fail. He saw no other solution, no middle-ground between triumph or defeat. For, this plan was so audacious, depended on so many unforeseeable variables that Gnô wouldn't have dare it if he considered the outcome any differently from a coin toss: heads or tails, win or lose, life or death. And it was like this that he decided to present it to his men.

First, he wanted them to get as much rest as possible. After half an hour in the air during which he and Bonnard got wholly familiar with steering the plane (very simple by the way), he ordered, "Bonnet, Lequic, Blanchard, go get some sleep. In three hours, Bonnet, I'll wake you up so you can replace me and it'll be my turn to rest. Ivitch, I have your word. And you, Guerro, will you give me yours so we can take off those handcuffs?"

"What word?" the Portuguese asked, finally back to his calm and cordial self.

"Not to attack the plane or my men or me."

"Certainly, my word of honor."

"That's great. Blanchard, free the man's wrists... and now for some rest and silence."

The orders were obeyed.

After three hours Bonnet took the place of Gnô who fell asleep right away.

Three more hours passed during which, at certain moments, Gnô Mitang gave instructions to Lequic, Bonnet and Blanchard. Then, when everyone was awake together, no more sleep was needed but their stomachs were starting to grumble. They needed to be filled. There was plenty of food on the *Aquilon*. Ivitch himself did the honor of presenting the supply cabinet.

They were halfway through the trip, flying over the Caspian Sea, which they only saw occasionally through the patches of clouds beneath them at 10,000 feet altitude.

After the meal, pretty much without saying a word, there were fifteen minutes of silence. Bonnet was at the wheel. Gnô was meditating and they respected his meditation. But all of a sudden, the Japanese made a sign and turned in his seat so he could see the faces of his companions who had just turned toward him.

"Sailors," his voice was serious, his face emotionless, his gaze both bright and severe, "in five or six hours, more or less, we will be landing in Issyk-Kul. So far, we've only got dealt our hand, a good one, full of trump cards, but down there we'll have to play them. If we win, I don't know what that will mean for us but the victory will be something tremendous. If we lose, it'll mean death."

His hand chopped the air, followed by silence. Then in the same voice:

"Let me explain. This is my fourth plan. You have to know it and know the roles that each of you will play. Lequic, you're the size of Ismail Kadeuy so you and I will switch clothes and you'll be the Turk. You, Bonnet, will still be Tchicoz. Me and Blanchard will make ourselves look ordinary. Remember, we just have to fool them for a few seconds and probably just some grunts who have never seen Kadeuy or Tchicoz and who don't know Zattan's orders so they won't be surprised to see four passengers. That's our roles. Now, for our actions."

He paused to look at the weird smiles on the faces of Ivitch and Guerro who were hanging on every word he said.

He went on, "For your information, I've still got a good narcotic on me that takes effect immediately and for a period depending on the dose will make someone look like a corpse. Just before landing Ivitch and Guerro will take a few drops of it, by hook or by crook.

"I hope I can steer the plane well enough to land normally on the runway, which, I hope again, should be easy to spot thanks to the maps of Issyk-Kul I've seen in Mathias Lumen's possession...

"I know, I know, the man we suspect stole and delivered the maps of Issyk-Kul has probably been executed because Lumen stopped getting news from him. But he got the maps and I studied them. Therefore, the *Aquilon* will land at the automatic entrance, I imagine, of a hangar or underground depot and stop there.

"First, I'll open the cargo door. Men will be waiting. Lequic-Kadeuy will talk to them—in French, since French is the official language of the castle. Only one of the men needs to understand. I'll tell Lequic what Kadeuy should say. I'll bet my life that what I think will happen, will: they'll go get Zattan, he'll come into the plane and look at these two who will appear dead. But the cargo door will close and the only ones inside will be us four, Lumen's soldiers, and we'll grab Zattan. Then, oh, then, messieurs, depending on the circumstances, we'll have to accomplish two goals: get Zattan away without me being forced to kill him unless absolutely necessary and free Sylvie Mac Duhl, Marc Ayol, and Saint-Clair, the Nyctalope."

"What's that?" Ivitch almost jumped out of his seat. "What'd you say? What name did you just pronounce? Leo Saint-Clair... The Nyctalope?"

"Yes!" the Japanese said.

"But..."

"I see you didn't know the Nyctalope was at Issyk-Kul."

"Of course I..."

"Physically there, monsieur Ivitch. Perilously there for Leonid Zattan until a telegram from Kadeuy, who was told by Tchicoz, which Guerro should've told you about, alerted Zattan that the famous Nyctalope and Marc Ayol, the captain of the *Fulgur*, happened to show up at Issyk-Kul undercover as two sailors named Pedro del Campo and Marco Pampil."

"Oh!" Ivitch and Guerro expressed their astonishment in unison.

And the Russian said, "Pedro del Campo is Saint-Clair, the Nyctalope?"

"Yes. Enough said. Messieurs, calm down or I'll have to put the gags and handcuffs back on. Sit down. Control yourselves. That's better. Behave yourselves while my three companions and I, with your cooperation, Guerro, prepare our disguises for the roles we'll be playing for a few seconds or minutes on the Issyk-Kul landing strip."

They got ready, transforming themselves according to Gnô's plan. And they spoke no more. There were no more smirks or sneers. Everyone was serious, even grim. At the prospect of possible outcomes, Petrus Ivitch no longer looked like the cynical spectator pretending to be "above it all". He knew all about bravery. And the bravery of these men, in whose power he was now and forever fallen, filled him with stunned admiration. He might not ever have admired Leonid Zattan as much as this.

After an hour of silence, an idea popped into the Russian's head. He didn't bother to ponder it. He wanted to express right away.

"Monsieur Gnô Mitang!"

The Japanese was in the left front seat next to Bonnet who was acting as pilot. He turned around, and looked questioningly at Ivitch.

The Russian went on, "Monsieur, I have a request. Please understand that I am sincere and trustworthy, with no ulterior motives. And I swear that you won't regret satisfying my desire, my passionate desire."

"I believe you and I'm listening."

"Well then, don't put me to sleep. I'll play dead, but being able to hear and peek through my half-closed eyelids."

"I understand," Gnô answered with a smile, "but all your willpower won't make you look dead."

"Watch and you'll see."

Petrus Ivitch sank back in his seat, froze and closed his eyes and mouth. In less than thirty seconds his face changed. He turned pale, more than pale, he was waxen. His long, red eyelashes hid his eyes even though they were not completely closed. His gaunt face looked truly cadaverous. He stayed like this for five long minutes. Then little by little his natural, faintly tanned color came back. He opened his eyes, sat up straight and waited somberly.

"How'd you do that?" Gnô wondered aloud.

"It doesn't matter! I knew some fakirs in India. I can stay for hours like that in a trance."

"Okay, I'll grant your request. I won't put you to sleep. You play dead. I'll take your word for it. But don't come out of it until you're sure, really sure, that it's safe."

"I promise, monsieur."

"Agreed."

Then Manoël Guerro, "I'm sorry I can't do like you. I won't see or hear anything."

"I'll tell you all about it, my friend."

Those were the last words before the plan went into action.

Hours passed. The land rolled by under the *Aquilon*. They had crossed the vast plain of Turkestan and were flying over the western foothills of the Tian Shan mountains. Finally, they saw the lake of Issyk-Kul.

Without saying a word, Gnô Mitang suddenly thrust his open hand in front of Guerro. A black pill lay in the palm. The Portuguese tried to be the epitome of stoicism. He took the pill and swallowed. Fifteen minutes later, he was out cold, slumped in the seat, head thrown back, eyes closed, lips slightly parted—a dead man.

Petrus Ivitch watched on curiously. But he wanted to wait until the last minute to fake his death.

Trusting his word, Gnô Mitang and the sailors paid no attention to him. Blanchard and Lequic in the middle seats were concentrated on the wild landscape they could see through the windows. Above the lake of green water, the castle of Issyk-Kul spread its walls and towers and courtyards.

Gnô had replaced Bonnet as pilot. An observer would have spied no emotion on these four faces. Each in his own way was impassive, attentive, sort of acutely intense.

Soon the *Aquilon* had to spiral over Issyk-Kul. One of the inner buildings against the rampart had a wide balcony-terrace ending in a bare portion of the wall and it started extending over the lake. At the same time, a big storage bay opened in the side of the building.

"Perfect! Perfect!" Gnô muttered. "A landing platform ending in a hangar. Nothing more to expect..." Then more loudly, in a firm voice, "Watch yourselves now, Lequic, Bonnet, Blanchard!"

"We're ready," the first answered.

"Ready!" the two other sailors chimed in.

Only then did Petrus Ivitch throw back his head and quickly turn into a corpse.

Expertly piloted, with really admirable grace, the plane touched down its rubber skates on the long, wide platform. It bounced lightly and slid. The automatic brakes grabbed the skates, squeezed, slowed the slide while keeping the plane perfectly straight until it entered the hangar and stopped, gently, the skates fitting into long, deep, spring-loaded grooves.

Gnô Mitang and Bonnet, in this first, short part of the play, were only extras. They were calm and cool-headed enough to admire the mechanical system that took control of the plane inside the hangar as long as the pilot landed it correctly on the balcony-terrace.

But Lequic-Kadeuy and Blanchard—the former had to say certain things and the latter make certain signs—paid no attention to the technical marvels of the landing. They were already in their roles.

Without leaving their seat, Gnô and Bonnet put their right hands in their pocket and half turned to the cargo door, waiting.

Blanchard pushed the door, slowly, until it was wide open.

The four brave men saw a huge, vaulted rotunda. They noticed the back of another airplane sitting on a kind of base. They spotted half a dozen men grouped together, led by one man in front coming to board the *Aquilon*. Now he had come up the unfolded ladder and was halfway inside the cargo door when he realized he wasn't seeing the person he was expecting and then he caught sight of the apparent corpses of Ivitch and Guerro in the back seats.

"Oh!" and he instinctively pulled himself back.

But Lequic spoke quickly in French with beautifully faked emotion, "Monsieur, I'm Ismaïl Kadeuy, 33, Famagusta. These are three of my men that I had good reason to bring along. And those dead men are Petrus Ivitch and Manoël Guerro. Dead in extraordinary circumstances. I really need to report the responsibility and to clear mine. Please go immediately to the Master and inform him I'd like to see His Lordship in person to verify the state of these two corpses before they're moved and changed."

This formal language was what Gnô had learned from the documents he saw in Famagusta in Kadeuy's safe. He had soaked them up. During the first half of the trip, between his bouts of sleep, he had made Lequic memorize the phrases, word for word, that the fake Kadeuy would use in Issyk-Kul.

Lequic learned his lesson well. The tone, accent and emotion were a perfect fit for his character and the circumstances.

Someone more suspicious than Lieutenant-Secretary Woldski would not have been fooled by the tragic-comedy. Woldski, however, had no reason to be suspicious. He had walked into an unexpected, outrageous situation. But when you're the closest officer to the Lord of Issyk-Kul, these situations are not rare. Therefore, Woldski didn't suspect for a moment that he was the victim of a spectacular trick. Worried about incurring any undeserved responsibility himself, he immediately obeyed the polite but firm and definitive orders from the man of importance, Ismaïl Kadeuy, 33. Scrambling down the ladder faster than he'd come up, he almost ran out of the room.

Disciplined but without orders, the half dozen men gathered at the rear of the *Aquilon* just stood there, if not undaunted (since they'd heard and understood), at least guarded like soldiers on duty waiting for their chief.

Softly, Lequic pulled the cargo door but didn't close it completely. Deeply affected but under control, with cold intensity, they awaited the arrival of Leonid Zattan, Prince of Issyk-Kul, Sovereign King of Tian Shan, Grand Secret Master of the global revolution.

Specifically not to delay for one minute the interrogation of Tchicoz who was supposed to be on the plane, Zattan had not left his private rooms today. Naturally, the castle's surveillance post had called it in when the plane appeared in the sky, then its landing, entering the garage and the impatient wait. He had sent Woldski to bring this famous Tchicoz to him right away. But Woldski, to inform his dreadful master of the unimaginable incident, didn't want to use the phone.

When the lieutenant-secretary showed up alone in such a state of agitation, Zattan was surprised, he whom nothing surprised anymore.

"Whoa there, Woldski, what happened? Where's Tchicoz?"

"Prince," the officer spoke with reverence, described what he'd seen and repeated Kadeuy's request.

"Dead? Petrus Ivitch! Damn it!" Zattan shouted.

He did what the Japanese psychologist was expecting. He didn't hesitate for a second. He didn't even stop to think. Guerro's death barely affected him, even though he was the head of the wireless service, he was easily replaced.

But Petrus Ivitch, the inventor, the creative, prolific genius!

Plowing through Woldski as if he wasn't there, Zattan stomped out of the room. The elevators were too slow. More and more overexcited, he sprinted across the vast hangar.

Gnô saw him through a window. He recognized him from hundreds of pictures and portraits at Ushant. He made a sign. Lequic promptly opened the cargo door.

The Prince of Issyk-Kul leapt over the top rung of the ladder into the plane. The sunlight filtering into the hangar through the windows gave only a dim light inside the airplane.

Zattan first saw Ivitch and Guerro looking dead and swore "Karakov!" as his face was transformed by grievous anger. And he wanted to know immediately. He turned his head. The only face his eyes met was that of Gnô Mitang.

He had never seen this face before. The thought never even entered his mind even though he knew very well that a Japanese was the factotum, the right-hand man of Gregor Mac Duhl and that this Japanese had gone to Ushant after the death of the Scotsman.

For a second, he thought he was some menial servant and he wanted to see Kadeuy whom he knew well. He turned around to look for the Turk to talk to him, but the eyes of the Japanese held him as if hypnotized. His entire being had a bad feeling. He smelled a trap or at least something wrong. Automatically, instinctively, he demanded, "Who are you?"

Very simply, the Japanese answered, "Gnô Mitang, adopted son of Gregor mac Duhl and one of Mathias Lumen's lieutenants."

With the look in those eyes more than the words or names themselves, Zattan understood the danger looming over him. Instinctively again and automatically he swung around and saw the cargo door closed with three men standing

191

there holding Brownings. The eyes or these men also said more than their guns: they would kill him without a second thought.

Suddenly straightening and stiffening up, his face like a rabid animal, Zattan turned to the Japanese. Like in a murky nightmare he heard his voice, cold and sharp:

"Leonid Zattan, one false move, one sound out of you and you're dead, even if we have to die for killing you. Do as I say! Cross your arms over your chest and don't move. Obey me if you want to live." And then in a different tone of voice, "Sailors, on five you can shoot." And he started counting.

One... two... three...

Real virile strength is not to give in to the blind rage that sometimes possesses us, but to tame this rage, especially when its fed by humiliation, and to refuse it the death that all the frenzied passions of the soul would rush wildly into.

Leonid Zattan showed once again that he had this real virile strength.

After a shudder that shook him from head to toe, after a demonic flash of anger and hatred, after grinding his teeth and clenching his jaw to breaking point, he crossed his arms.

"Four!" Gnô pronounced.

He stopped counting. He saw that for the moment at least Zattan was submitting. Gnô had his two hands empty, hanging at his side. He raised his right hand and motioned politely to one of the middle seats.

"Please sit down."

"No!" Zattan barked. "We can talk standing up. I'm listening." Even in defeat (he was defeated now, wasn't he?) he gave orders.

"So be it. I'll be brief. I want to take off in a few minutes with Sylvie Mac Duhl and Saint-Clair and Marc Ayol and, of course, with you on board. Dumping the bodies of Petrus Ivitch and Manoël Guerro should give the plane plenty of space for all of us. We'll squeeze in if necessary. And I know the Aquilon can take off with double its normal load.

"Therefore, Leonid Zattan, you're going to lean out the cargo door, which we'll open, and call over your lieutenant-secretary Woldski. In French you'll give him the order to get Sylvie Mac Duhl, Pedro del Campo and Marco Pampil and bring them here. Once the order's given you'll step away and wait, silent and still. It's very simple.

"And this too: I'm playing for keeps. If you make one false move, if you make any attempt to escape, if you say one word that's not in French, if you don't give the order short and fast, I'll shout one word and these three men will fire at you point blank. I swear to you, we came here to do or die. The slightest indication that victory will slip away from us and we will all accept the consequences of your death. Because first things first, you will be killed. Do you understand and accept?"

Once again controlling himself, Zattan answered, "I accept."

Gnô Mitang was sure then that they had reached the climax of the situation. The Prince of Issyk-Kul was certainly in a tough spot that he apparently couldn't get out it except by submitting to the will of this surprise attacker. But justifiably, they had to beware the infinite resources of Zattan's intelligence, wickedness and indomitable courage. What might he cook up, at the critical moment, to turn the tables?

"Bah!" the Japanese told himself, "it's not imagination, intelligence, wickedness or courage that counts against three men armed with pistols and ready to kill. I'll shout, they'll shoot. Zattan is dead. And he knows it. What can he do against that? Nothing! Nothing? We'll see."

Then in a stern voice he said out loud, "Lequic, Bonnet, Blanchard, target this guy's back. Think of nothing but hearing the sound of my voice. Look at nothing but the target. If I shout, fire, empty your guns into him. Nine bullets each in three seconds ought to be enough to kill this guy. Afterwards we'll have to fight. They'll close the hangar and we'll be trapped in here. The castle's got over 200 men, so we'll probably die fighting. It's in God's hands! Let's go!"

"It's in God's hands, boss," Lequic echoed gravely.

With their left hands, Lequic, Bonnet and Blanchard crossed themselves.

"It's time!" Gnô decided. He looked at Zattan straight in the eyes. He saw only cold detachment. He reached over and pulled the lever to open the door. The oiled hinges made no sound as the cargo door slowly swung open.

Positioned as they were, Lequic, Bonnet and Blanchard couldn't be seen by the men standing around the plane whose interior, moreover, was darker than the light in the big hangar. What's more, the oval opening of the door was just big enough for a fat man to come through because the baggage, sometimes quite a lot of it, was loaded in a different cargo door located in the back of the plane. Consequently, if any danger were going to spring out, it would have to come from a word or gesture of Leonid Zattan. And Zattan *felt*, on his face, the piercing eyes of Gnô Mitang and two inches from his shoulders, his spinal column and his ribs, the three gun barrels held in steady hands controlled by the nerves and muscles of unfaltering minds.

Leonid Zattan leaned on the frame of the door with his right hand and in a completely normal voice, with his usual, dryly authoritative tone, said, "Woldski, go right now to ask Mademoiselle Mac Duhl to come back here with you." And since the lieutenant-secretary looked surprised and hesitant at this unexpected order, he barked, "Go on, then!"

Woldski turned around and left.

Then Zattan pointed with his left hand, "Hey you, sergeant, run off and get Pedro del Campo and Marco Pampil. Bring them back here double time!"

The officer obeyed without hesitation or surprise.

And to prove to Gnô Mitang his total acceptance of the present destiny, the Prince of Issyk-Kul added, "All of you, get out of here! Back to your posts!"

The dozen or so men grouped around the plane scattered in a hurry, some back to their duties, others to their rooms. Because the *Aquilon* had attracted not only the mechanics on duty in the hangar, but also some men just wandering around. In fact, all the work was taken care of at Issyk-Kul, like on a well-disciplined ship, by shifts on duty six hours at a time followed by the same amount of rest, which assured maximum results with a guarantee against over-work. Six hours daily of full sleep and six hours for eating and leisure is plenty for a well-balanced, well-fed man whose life is free of worries.

Having given the orders exactly as Gnô had wanted, Zattan stepped casually back from the door. Docilely obeying a sign from the Japanese, he stepped aside, along the wall of the hull, until he was backed against Lequic.

The three sailors were now huddled around in front of Zattan who was standing before the wall. To their right, a little farther in front and therefore a little behind Zattan were the two fake corpses of Ivitch and Guerro, still lying stiffly in their seats. Straight ahead and to the right of Zattan were the four other seats. And finally, directly across from him, the captive could see his captor. Leonid Zattan and Gnô Mitang were maybe four or five feet away from each other. On their left, the cargo door remained open.

Such was the situation of the seven people—the "corpses" on their backs and the "living" on their feet—crowded together in the airplane during the intermission of this drama.

Although still on their guard and coldly, lucidly attentive, Gnô, Lequic, Blanchard and Bonnet were, without really being aware of it, quite relieved and relaxed. The vague and lethal danger, which they had feared for a minute when Zattan gave orders in the doorway, didn't occur. The Prince of Issyk-Kul seemed resigned to his fate for the moment—even if it meant he'd already worked out or was now hoping for some terrible, imminent revenge whose ways and means were beyond the imagination of his captors.

They were just waiting for the arrival of Sylvie Mac Duhl, the Nyctalope and Marc Ayol. Then the order would be given to open the hangar doors so the plane could go from the prison hall to the open terrace. The four men were breathing freely. Their attention, their determination was no longer plagued by anxiety. If they once had doubts about their success, they were now convinced of its likelihood. Without realizing it, their bodies were affected by their state of mind, meaning their eyes were no longer fixed exclusively on Zattan and their nerves and muscles were relaxing. In short, the bow stopped being stretched to the maximum tension it takes to shoot a quick and sure arrow.

Nevertheless, the sergeant chosen by Zattan had gone in search of Pedro del Campo. He knew him. He had talked with him on occasion. For, using the relative freedom he enjoyed—a freedom that wasn't stamped with strict surveillance, entirely in secret, until 24 hours ago—the Nyctalope had visited every-where he could in the castle and had found countless reasons to talk with everyone he met, which quickly made him a very likable character. The sergeant happened to run into Marco Pampil first.

"The Lord wants to see you. You and your captain. In the hangar. Where's your captain?"

Marc Ayol was surprised, but he didn't show it. "What does the demon want with us?" he wondered. And aloud he said, "The captain is in the library. Is it for right now?"

"Yes, let's go get him."

"Sure."

Saint-Clair was even more surprised than Marc Ayol. Indeed, what could Zattan want with Pedro del Campo and Marco Pampil to summon them like this, urgently, in the hangar? Was he going to send them on a mission without warning? Weird! But the Nyctalope showed even less surprise than his partner.

"Let's go then," he said.

The two friends followed the sergeant.

But as they were entering the enclosed courtyard in front of the hangar, they both got a new and startling surprise when they saw Sylvie Mac Duhl being escorted through another door by the lieutenant-secretary. Marc Ayol had never seen the young woman, but from Saint-Clair's description he recognized her right away.

The two men looked at each other and both understood. They were thinking, "Sylvie was summoned like us, so there's some new development for sure. And its serious."

For her part, Sylvie saw Saint-Clair and guessed who his companion was from their conversation the night before last. She blushed a little. And her intelligent eyes let the Nyctalope know that she, too, was now on guard.

Taking advantage of the moment when the sergeant was staring at the prisoner who was famous now in the castle but seen by few people, Saint-Clair leaned over to Marc Ayol and whispered, "On your toes! When we're all together, if you see a chance to hit hard, take it!"

"All right," he panted.

Sylvie and Woldski were closer to the main hangar door than the sergeant, del Campo and Pampil. When they got into the entrance Saint-Clair intentionally dropped his handkerchief to slow them down for a few seconds. He picked it up, blew his nose... Of course, Marc Ayol slowed down with him. On the contrary, Woldski was eager to show how promptly he obeyed orders and was speeding up. Thus, the Nyctalope let Sylvie go in front of him. This gave him and Marc Ayol time to size up the situation before finding out why Zattan had summoned them here with Sylvie Mac Duhl.

Woldski was leading Sylvie with the sergeant a few feet behind them. Saint-Clair and Marc Ayol could see the plane straight ahead with the cargo door open and...

"Gnô."

They almost shouted out like Sylvie did since she had no reason to hide her great surprise or sudden hope, her rush of joy. Woldski didn't try to hold her back from running to the plane, arms out front...

"Run!" Saint-Clair bellowed.

Of course, he didn't understand. How could he? Zattan's summons and the presence there of Gnô Mitang, free and looking pleased, was so utterly unimaginable that he couldn't even guess what it was about. He could only hurry up to find out... He and Marc Ayol ran.

Now, in the plane the Lord of Issyk-Kul was waiting for the right moment, the exact moment when Sylvie Mac Duhl would get in the plane and reach out for Gnô Mitang...

Even though it was impossible to know how things would play out, the Nyctalope once again made good use of his exceptional intelligence and intuition: he understood that in this moment when the Japanese clearly had the upper hand over Zattan, this victorious control would make Gnô let down his guard a little. He saw this in Gnô's face.

Without hesitating, he yelled out in Japanese, "Watch out, Gnô! Be careful!"

Gnô shuddered, stepped back and his face froze while his eyes turned away from Sylvie and fell upon Leonid Zattan. At that very moment, the young lady stepped through the door. In her excitement she had bolted up the ladder and would have thrown herself into Gnô's saving arms if...

If the Nyctalope hadn't yelled!

And if the Nyctalope hadn't put Gnô on guard, the Japanese would have grabbed Sylvie's hands, squeezed them, kissed them, which would have given Zattan twenty, thirty, fifty seconds... the instant, the brief moment when he could duck down out of the line of fire and jump out of the cargo door and holler one word. It would take only one word, like "Treason!", for example, for Woldski and the others to attack.

But the Nyctalope had yelled!

And Gnô, remembering his duty, wasn't distracted. Zattan didn't get his break. And Sylvie saw Gnô back away, his face frozen and his eyes riveted. She froze, too, and followed his stare. Then she saw Zattan and the three men holding guns. And she understood that victory was not assured, they were still in grave danger. On guard now, she didn't say a word, just entered calmly, went towards the front of the plane and leaned against the wall so that she could observe the spectacle. But she hadn't yet seen the two so-called corpses.

She did see Marc Ayol and Saint-Clair climb into the plane. Each of them paused in the doorway for only a few seconds, time enough to take in the scene. Then they, too, went in between the first and second row of seats, but with their backs to the front seats so they could face Zattan and at the same time conceal nothing from Sylvie.

In a monotonous voice, his eyes cold and commanding, Gnô Mitang spoke loudly so that Woldski and the sergeant standing at the foot of the ladder could hear, "Lord, we're all here and everything's ready. Just give the order and we'll take off."

Then in a different tone, much more softly but just as firmly, "Boys, watch out!"

Everything had worked out well so far. One final point on the program still had to be accomplished: get the bodies of Guerro and Ivitch off the plane. But Gnô had just realized that getting rid of them was not really necessary, that it might be just enough distraction for Zattan to take advantage of the diversion…

They were holding Zattan! Sylive, Saint-Clair and Marc Ayol were there! It'd be better not to try fate. It'd be better not to wait. Leave, escape, get away from Issyk-Kul and fast, fast…

As for Leonid Zattan, he must have been raging mad at this point. He glared at the Nyctalope with eyes full of torture, murder, vampirism—if he got his hands on him, he'd tear him to pieces, roast him alive and rip out his heart! But he controlled himself. He was defeated. He wanted to live. In Gnô's falsely respectful request, he heard the inflexible order. Obey or be killed. He leaned over toward the door and in a voice that was first trembling with fury but abruptly, with a tremendous effort, turned calm, authoritative and relatively normal, "Woldski! The departure platform! I don't know how long I'll be gone. Until I get back, order number three."

He had said what he had to. He leaned back. And it was Gnô who closed the door. Then he turned to the Nyctalope and simply said, "Monsieur Saint-Clair, please watch Zattan for me. I have to pilot the plane."

But the Nyctalope raised his right hand, which stopped everything in its tracks and called for attention. He smiled. He looked at Sylvie, Gnô, Zattan. And in the most normal, mundane voice, "Gnô, my friend, where do you want to take us now?"

The Japanese answered, "On board the *Fulgur* first. Then, at least for Sylvie Mac Duhl, to Mathias Lumen's house."

"But no, no, my friend," Saint-Clair said with a sympathetic smile. "No, you're not going to sabotage your victory like that? Yes, I mean it and I beg you not to wince at the expression, a very French one, I might add. I'm asking you not to sabotage your magnificent, sublime victory. Right, I see you're listening respectfully, like I'm speaking to you, and you're trying to understand. Well, you will understand."

He shot a hard look at Zattan and continued more sharply.

"Don't get anxious, Prince of Issyk-Kul! Even as Gnô and I are talking, we haven't lost sight of you, nor of Mademoiselle Mac Duhl, nor have these three good sailors lowered their guns, nor has my friend Marc Ayol relaxed his attention and, if necessary, his fists. So, stay calm, monsieur."

Then back to Gnô Mitang, in his polite and friendly voice, "My dear friend, here you are in Issyk-Kul where you've accomplished the amazing feat of capturing the captor and freeing the prisoners. You're here in the eagle's nest, in the lion's den, in the viper's pit... You're in the very heart of the international Neo-terrorist organization, in the headquarters of the armies, past, present and future, of the Antichrist... You're here, finally, where Mathias Lumen would like to be, where you could ask him to come whenever you want... and you want to leave? We're going to leave? We're going to give up your real victory just to keep the deposed king? Come on, Gnô, my friend and brother-in-arms, it's not to the Ushant house that you should be going with Leonid Zattan, but simply to his personal rooms here in the castle of Issyk-Kul. We just have to take a few steps, speak a few words, get a few signatures from the Lord here and thanks to your amazing effort, to your great victory, we'll be able to prepare very quickly and pull off very soon the ultimate triumph. I mean it. What do you think?"

Obviously, Gnô Mitang, as well as Sylvie Mac Duhl and all the men there, including the self-comatosed Ivitch, but not Guerro who was really unconscious, all had listened keenly and closely to the Nyctalope. He answered right away with a smile and three simple words, "You are right."

"Thank you," Saint-Clair replied somberly.

And Gnô, just as somberly, added, "Please take command, monsieur. I'm just a soldier compared to you."

"No need for the monsieur. I'm your friend and partner. But I accept the authority you're offering me."

The Nyctalope was good-sized. He seemed to grow taller when he straightened up and looked around at his companions. And this look, sometimes hard for anyone to endure, came to rest on Leonid Zattan. There was a moment of silence. Everyone waited, struggling to restrain their emotions.

And Saint-Clair spoke in a very low, though still firm and domineering voice, "Prince, we have the victory in our hands just like we have you. In order not to lose it, we can't let you go. And yet, you must appear to be in control of us, to be our master...

"Seeing the attitude of the three armed men behind you, considering the present situation and what's happened, it's easy for me to see that for Gnô Mitang to come here and get us brought here, you and Sylvie Mac Duhl, myself and Marc Ayol, he had to risk his life constantly, along with the lives of his companions, and yours as well. You understand, therefore, that these people who are risking their lives in this deadly game won't hesitate to kill you if you don't obey to the letter, if you do anything at all that they might consider, rightly or wrongly, a signal to your men to revolt. Isn't that right, Prince? I'm asking you to be a good sport and answer."

Stiff and cold, very pale, with a blank stare, a distant voice, Zattan responded, "That's right."

"Well then," Saint-Clair said, "the awful game goes on. Since Gnô Mitang did me the honor of yielding to me his leadership, I will be giving the orders from now on and you'll obey. These three sailors hear me: if I yell 'Fire!', you kill Leonid Zattan. But that's not all. Gnô, if you're not armed, do so now. And get weapons for Mademoiselle Mac Duhl and Marc Ayol. For myself I'll take a Browning. I know there are a dozen of them with shells in one of these crates."

Silence. Gnô opened one of the crates and took out three loaded pistols, which he handed out. He himself showed the Browning he already had in his right coat pocket.

"Good," Saint-Clair continued, "but the guns can't be seen. Keep a firm hand on them, right or left as you want, but keep them in a pocket, finger on the trigger and always aimed at the Prince. Okay, let's get out of here. Gnô and I will leave first. At the bottom of the ladder we'll wait for the Prince who will come third and stay between us when his foot touches the ground. Behind him will be Marc Ayol, then Sylvie Mac Duhl, followed by the three sailors. You five will fan out behind him as he walks. Don't be stiff or awkward when you move, please. Act naturally. Looking around would be normal. Smile and sound curious and a little in awe. We need to look like we're following the Prince peacefully, cheerfully and respectfully.

"I'll be talking to you while we walk, Prince. Just small talk. But answer me. And we'll go all the way to your personal rooms. Do you hear me? Will you obey?"

Zattan, still with thee same attitude, shrugged his shoulders and said, "I'll have to."

"Good!" the Nyctalope said. "And now for a few details to consider. As soon as you get to the bottom of the ladder, Prince, tell Woldski that you've canceled the departure, that you've got enough information about Ivitch and Guerro and you're ordering them to bury the bodies right away as per regulations…"

"Stop!" Gnô interrupted with a smile.

"What is it?" Saint-Clair asked.

With a subtly amused look the Japanese explained, "Ivitch and Guerro aren't dead. They're just sleeping from something I gave that, as you see, feigns death. They can't be buried. They have to be put to bed. In a few minutes, hours maybe depending on their nature, they'll be waking up."

Zattan and Saint-Clair had seen other cases. The former showed no surprise. The latter had a brief smile cross his face. He was thinking: "Well done! Gnô will tell us about the adventure later. It should make for a good laugh for Sylvie and Marc Ayol and myself."

Then aloud he said, "Okay, then, Prince, instead of putting them in the grave, you'll have them put in a room. Then tell Woldski to stay in his office awaiting further instructions from you. As for us, you'll take us to your rooms but by the stairs and hallways, no elevators or moving walkways. Got it?"

"Got it," Zattan replied still in the same tone of voice.

"Fine." Whispering and more firmly he added, "Zattan, don't forget that Gnô and I are watching you. The slightest false move, I yell 'fire' and seven guns empty into you. You understand, eh?"

Finally, in a normal voice, "Gnô, are you ready? Open the door."

CHAPTER VI

This dramatic turn of events took place at Issyk-Kul on the afternoon of April 5th .

Now, it was on this same afternoon that, in Ushant, Diana Ivanova Krasnovief and Ignace Kiewicz were making their reconnaissance as false tourists around the house of Mathias Lumen. That night they came back, of course, and it resulted in the death of five terrorists in the dungeon, the imprisonment of the Red Princess and the return of Ignace Kiewicz with an ultimatum from Lumen to be given to Zattan.

It read: "If Sylvie Mac Duhl is not free and out of danger on April 10th I will set free Diana Ivanova."

Kiewicz left. And of course, after talking with his brother Stanislas in Paris, he went directly to Constantinople.

As for Diana Ivanova, the Hermit of Ushant had handed her over to the tough Catalan Ephrem Lluch, saying, "Guard this woman and keep her alive. Lock her up wherever and however you want. Treat her as you please. I don't want to see her. And just so you know how precious she is, I'll tell you that this woman, Diana Ivanova Krosnovief, the Red Princess, is the ransom for Sylvie Mac Duhl."

The Catalan's cruel face looked hard and grim. All he said was, "Very well, master." And to Diana, "Get up and walk. Or else I'll carry you."

The beautiful woman rose up gracefully and as she passed in front of Lumen, in a deep voice, very gravely, said, "We will see each other again."

"Maybe," he replied, "but don't wish for it, Diana. Because I swear to God that the next time I see you, you'll be dead."

"Or you!" she threw back one final defiance.

"Go!" Lluch ordered her through the door. She went. He followed.

The round room where they went first was furnished with only four stools standing here and there against the bare wall. Two black doors, two entrances to hallways, a stairway going down... An electric ceiling light diffused a harsh light.

"The stairway, madame," Lluch ordered tersely.

Diana took the stairs. After thirty steps she came into a bare, square room. Across from the bottom of the stairs was a hallway extending into darkness. To the right and left were black doors with white-painted numbers, which brought to mind monastic cells of penitence.

As the woman stopped in the middle of the room, Ephrem Lluch passed by her and pulled out of his pocket a ring of tiny keys, chose one, marched to door number 3 and opened it. He stepped inside and turned on the electric light.

"Please come in, madame."

She obeyed. She saw a basically rectangular room. An iron bed, a table, chair and a very simple, raw oak cabinet. In the back wall was a narrow alcove covered by a gray canvas curtain hanging on rod. Diana headed straight for the curtain and drew it aside: a bathroom half as big as the room, bare walls bleached with lime and perfectly spotless. Thick, straw mats lay on the gray tile floor in the middle of the bathroom and in front of the bed. The metal springs of the bed held a rolled up mattress, a bolster and a pillow. No towels or linens. Two lights were encased in frosted glass in the ceiling. All together it was thoroughly clean, neat, severe. It was neither cold nor hot.

In his naturally harsh voice, like a corporal giving orders with military clarity, the Catalan said, "Madame, you can use the light as you want. The water too—it's sea water that comes in distilled. I'll bring you sheets and towels, a pillowcase and blankets. Laundry every eight days. Every morning a bell will wake you up at exactly seven o'clock, but you're free to stay in bed and go back to sleep if you need to. In any case, breakfast will be brought to you at eight and left here. The other meals at noon and 6 pm. Some books will be made available to you. I'll bring a catalog of the small library and give you whatever books you request. Nothing for writing, it's forbidden. If you want to do some sewing, knitting or embroidery, you can ask for what you need. You'll get it the next day. Except on orders from the master, you won't be leaving here for any reason."

He stopped there. She had listened attentively. Softly, blushing a little with wonderfully imitated modesty, she said, "It'll be terribly hard on me if I can't change my underclothes more often. There's money in my handbag. Could buy in Brest, with the information I'll give you..."

She hesitated, embarrassed and ravishing.

The man waited, impassive, his cold, black eyes staring at the prisoner's face.

"Some bras, stockings, a pair of slippers, and such... handkerchiefs..."

"I'll relate your request to the master."

"Thank you." She looked around and muttered, "Isn't there a window. Fresh air..."

He cut her off, "The constant recirculation of air works through those grills you see in the four corners of the ceiling. Pipes of warm or cool water, depending on the season, wind through the walls. A constant, mild temperature. Regular ventilation..."

"That's interesting," she said. And then with a melancholy smile, "Thank you. Tomorrow I'll ask for books and hopefully my list of lingerie I'd like... For now, I'd like to go to bed and sleep."

"You'll have what you need for the bed in five minutes."

He left. The door closed without a sound. Standing in the middle of the room, Diana waited, thinking, her eyes blank. When he came back with blankets, sheets and towels, she shuddered frightfully, then shrugged her shoulders as if laughing at herself and finally settled into a sad, beautiful smile.

Ephrem Lluch put the things on the table. "There you go, madame. Please make your bed every day, it's the rules. Me, I'll sweep and scrub when needed."

"Oh," she said, "that shouldn't be needed very often. No dust can get in here."

The Catalan neither confirmed nor denied the insightful remark. He just grumbled, "Good night, madame." And he left.

She heard him turning the key in the lock two times, in the opposite direction after a brief horizontal slide. She thought, "A special lock, certainly impregnable without the right tools."

She hastened to the door, bent down and moved aside the small, metal cover over the lock and she saw strangely jagged edges inside. She stood up, put both hands against the door and pushed hard.

"It's like pushing against a wall. It's solid, all right. I'm locked in good. I don't and never will have tools in here... And yet he mentioned sewing. Would he give me scissors? No, they're not that stupid... And yet without scissors... I'll ask. We'll see. But right now, I need to sleep. I can't let myself get weak. Sleep, food, I'll do exercises by pacing the floor, some heavy-duty Swiss gymnastics. As long as Diana Ivanova is alive, she won't give up. Sleep! I mustn't think about Zattan and Lumen and their plotting over me. I must think about nothing. Sleep..."

Besides, she was exhausted. The bed made, the lights out, she didn't have to spend a long time using the method that had always worked for her: automatic repetition of a short, droning prayer that she had never forgotten since childhood. Within five minutes of going to bed, Diana Ivanova was in a deep sleep.

She awoke with a start. Her mind was alert. At once she was conscious of reality and her memory was clear. She felt sluggish and sore. They would bring her breakfast in an hour. She thought, "So, I can wake up but I'm still tired. I need as much rest as possible."

She changed position and almost instantly fell back to sleep. She hadn't even opened her eyes except for that brief moment when she snapped awake. When she did finally open her eyes, she realized she had spent several hours in her second sleep. She lay motionless under the warm sheets. Minutes passed. She remembered, reflected. At last, she reached out and felt along the wall for the light switch and turned it on. When her heavy eyes were used to the light, she saw the tray on the small table with a bowl, a piece of bread and a napkin. The unexpected creamy color of a spoon handle was poking out of the bowl.

She jumped out of bed and rushed over to the table. "Chocolate! Oh, the spoon is wooden and the bowl made of rubber."

Light and elegant, with a deep bowl, the spoon worked just fine. The hard rubber bowl was absolutely solid.

"If everything's like this, I won't be getting a knife for dinner or scissors for sewing. We'll have to see."

She tasted the chocolate. It was good but gone cold.

"What time is it now?" She shrugged. "Who cares?"

She went into the bathroom. She was so tired the night before that she had neglected to wash up. She made up for it this morning. Obviously at the same time as the breakfast, Ephrem Lluch had brought a big bar of soap and a huge sponge. Diana put them to good use. The straw mat was soaked with water running off her body.

"If he doesn't give me a tub," the prisoner mused, "he'll have to change the mat every day."

The cement tiles were sloped and striped with parallel grooves in one direction. The water ran down channel to the wall and disappeared into hole with a metal cover pierced like a sieve.

"Great, he'll pick up the mat and give me a wooden footstand."

With no more physical observations to make, her mind started the work it should never have stopped: figure out the possibilities, ways and means of escape.

"This Ephrem Lluch came in while I was sleeping. Did he look at me? They've told me so often that I'm "as pretty as an angel" when I sleep. The jailer is a man, after all! And a strong, healthy man at that! Did he look at me?"

But she noticed that the cement shelf sticking out of the wall above the toilet had no comb.

"No use asking for one, they'll refuse. A comb is a weapon."

After washing her hair with lots of water, she rubbed it and smoothed it, first with a towel, then with her hands. She had used up her four towels.

"I'll ask to change the towels every day. Great, no mirror!" She shrugged and smiled. "Ha, don't I know that I am beautiful? And that my skin needs no powders or makeup? All right, now I'm hungry."

She got fully dressed and realized that her hat and veil must have stayed with her handbag in the room where she'd had her dramatic meeting with Mathias Lumen. The most trivial details were magnifying her feeling of captivity. She needed to blow her nose, but she had no handkerchief. She had to use a towel.

"Trifles," she mumbled. "Later today I'll have everything I need... Tomorrow?"

Her two beautiful hands automatically started breaking the bread. The movement stopped. Her hands froze. She was staring at the wall.

"Tomorrow? Will I still be here tomorrow?"

For, an idea began to form in the clever mind of the daring and dangerous woman. An idea... and a plan.

Once after an unknown, very short-lived revolution in the Kremlin, she had been imprisoned for three days in Moscow by the Cheka. One of her cellmates, a repeat prisoner and escapee, had told her, "There's only one prison we can't ever escape from—the hole in the ground when we're dead."

Diana Ivanova Krosnovief remembered this perceptive saying. Despite being underground, her cell was not "a hole in the ground" and she was no corpse.

She smiled. She even had a little giggle, quickly cut short by her cautious mind... and she finished tearing off a piece of bread. She ate with a hearty appetite after reflecting: "I have to eat well every meal and get a good sleep. The game won't start until tomorrow."

When her breakfast was over, Diana made her bed with great care. Then she started walking, sometimes on tiptoes, sometimes normally, diagonally from one corner of the room to the other. A good, steady pace: healthy exercise. The air was pure with a faint smell of the sea. As Lluch had said, "Regular ventilation. A constant, mild temperature." But Diana was soon missing the daylight. The electric light, soft but gloomy, would become unbearable in the long run.

"I'll make it night and in the night my imagination and my eyes will see the most enchanting light of the countryside."

Indeed, when she was tired of pacing, she laid down on the bed and turned off the light but kept her eyes open in the dark. She started cooking up a plan that was already letting her picture the seas, plains and mountains... the mountains of Tian Shan around the lake and the castle of Issyk-Kul.

Time passed. One, maybe two hours.

All of a sudden, without any warning sound, the door opened, a switch was flipped and the darkness was replaced by the even light spread from the ceiling. Without getting up, the prisoner turned her head. The door was closed again.

Standing in front of the table so that he could keep his eyes on the Red Princess, Ephrem Lluch was taking a kind of covered dish out a basket, a square container, three plates, two spoons, a napkin, a cup and a short flask. Diana could see from her bed that the two containers were full of appetizers in one and dried fruits in the other. But it was only after getting up and going over to the table that she noticed everything was in rubber like the breakfast bowl. The spoons in wood, naturally!

She laughed. She had the strength to laugh.

"Hello, madame," Lluch had just grumbled.

"Hello, my friend," Diana shot back casually. Touching the hard rubber she added in a radiant voice full of good humor and surprising bravery given the situation, "You may give Mathias Lumen by warmest congratulations. As a dictator in the penitentiary of a despotic State, he would be top notch. He is the one, I imagine, who invented this rubber tableware and soft wooden utensils for prison cells! Congratulations again. And you can tell him one more thing: all these extra-careful precautions are useless for me. I don't want to kill myself or you, monsieur Lluch. For a while now I've been overworked and I need rest, solitude, silence and routine. I'll get all this here. So, for a couple of weeks, at least—the minimum time needed for a serious cure—I'll be thanking fate for this holiday."

Her exquisite, musical laughter rang out. Then quickly it sank, menacingly.

"But in two weeks, watch out, monsieur guard!"

Her eyes shot flames at the man. But his hard face was frozen. Not a single line or wrinkle budged. His dark, deep-set eyes didn't blink. And the man didn't say a word. However, with speed and skill his hands finished their humble task: putting into the basket the remains from the breakfast.

Diana sat at the table and said, "But I was thinking that there's no way I can call you. What if I get sick, say?"

He answered simply, "You are here in God's hands. Now, sickness comes from God and in this case man shouldn't interfere. As for the things you want, you can just ask me when I'm here. I come regularly, four times a day at the same time..."

"Four?"

"Yes. Three for the meals. One in the evening to clean, if necessary, and to make sure nothing in your cell is different from before."

"Great!" Diana chuckled. Right away while picking at the appetizers (radishes, sardines, butter and pitted green olives) she added, "Well, monsieur Ephrem Lluch, get some paper and write."

"Here's paper and pencil, you can write it yourself, madame, at your leisure after eating. I'll be back in an hour."

From one of his coat pockets he took out a small, soft-cover notebook and one of those pencils whose tip is not sharpened with a knife but unwrapped from the paper its made of.

Diana smiled and muttered, "Even the pencil is harmless."

The Catalan might not have heard this—he had already left.

When he came back, apparently an hour later, the list was ready. Underwear, slippers, extra towels, the "catalog of permitted books", things for sewing and embroidery, including a good length of different fabrics. Nothing was forgotten.

Lluch took the pencil back with the notebook. Emotionless but four feet away and clearly on his guard, he read. Only once did he cross out a word. Then he spoke calmly.

"That's fine, madame. Most of it will be brought to you today, the rest tomorrow."

"You crossed something out."

"Yes."

"What?"

"Scissors."

"But without scissors how I am supposed to..."

The man cut her off to explain without a hint of humor, "I'll bring you another pencil with thicker, softer lead. You can trace the fabric where you want it cut. I'll take them right away to be cut by Sidonie, the servant. She's a seamstress by trade and a very good one."

Diana was expecting something like this but still he pressed, "But the thread, the silk, the strings, how am supposed to cut those?"

"You have teeth!" And with this, still spoken with no humor intended, he left.

"Oh, you recognize that I have teeth," Diana growled to herself when the door had closed. "You don't know how true that is, idiot. As if I need any other weapon but myself to get the better of any man." And right then she decided to put her plan into action the very next day.

During the few minutes that Ephrem Lluch came into her room three different times—the first to bring the catalog of books and a few of the things, the second to bring her dinner and the third to give the prisoner the requested books (three "psychological" novels)—Diana was simple and friendly, even a little teasingly defiant.

And it was a long night.

But the next day!

When Ephrem Lluch entered, the cell he found a different woman from the one he'd known before.

Only half-dressed, bare legs and arms, she was sitting on edge of the bed, elbows on her knees and face buried in her hands. At the sound of the breakfast tray being put on the table she looked up.

What a beautiful and touching face of sorrowful weakness! Her face looked gaunt, her lips pale, her eyes sunken, those childishly fearful, imploring eyes with tears about to drop...

The Red Princess knew men! She had driven so many to despair, sometimes after believing or pretending that she loved them! In Ephrem Lluch she saw the fanatical partisan, the puritan Catholic that you see so often in the Catalan at sea or in the hills. Such a man would be unresponsive to the sensual seduction of this beauty. But it was not so rare that these tough, raw characters were sensitive to the weak and suffering—a child would get showered with attention, pulling all the heartstrings. And what was more like a child than a woman in tears?

The tears, the sobs, the shy and frightened plea from those watery eyes are physically unendurable to certain men. Even a brute ready to abuse, to beat, to kill a woman will feel unable to strike the vicious blow if the woman breaks down and cries. Since the time when men and women came out of the Stone Age, how many millions of these feverish pleas: "Oh, please stop crying, stop crying!" after curses, abuses and even a beating.

"If I'm not wrong about this Lluch," the Red Princess told herself, "this will be a show in which I have nothing to lose and he shouldn't look at suspiciously. It's only natural that after a day and night of brave defiance, I'm suddenly overcome by the inevitable certainty of my total defeat."

When Ephrem Lluch had put down the tray and looked at the prisoner, the prisoner was just a beautiful, young woman, helpless and beaten, who by a final effort of modest courage was still holding back the tears in those eyes of a terrified child.

He shivered. He took a step toward the woman.

And he who the day before had never let down his guard, never dropped his wary surveillance or distrust of this woman, he who, in all appearances, had been ready to jump aside and swing his massive fist to counter those sharp, nervous nails that wanted to strangle him and gouge out his eyes, he who had been ready to knock unconscious this sneaky, maniacal prisoner, he, Ephrem Lluch, forgot all precautions because his hidden sensitivity was suddenly touched by the grief-stricken face and the teary eyes.

They flowed, those tears, down the face that withered into a sob without losing any of its Our-Lady-of-Sorrows beauty.

"Oh, madame," he said. His voice shook but he babbled again, "Oh, madame, madame…"

He was bending over, holding out his helping hands. He spoke the words that every man feels at the sight of suffering that clutches his throat, weighs on his heart and tortures his nerves.

"Don't cry like that, don't cry!" And still able to think reasonably, "Come on, you were so strong yesterday. I was in awe of you myself, all the while hating you as my faith and my duty demanded. Yes, you were admirable! But now look at you…"

He was close enough to touch her soft hands, her trembling shoulders. He leaned over, his neck stretching out, chin first, defenseless…

"Now look at you crying like…"

Diana's right hand made a quick chop, striking his neck hard just above the larynx. It was a traditional jujitsu move, a crushing blow when delivered well because it caused a blackout that was always instantaneous and often lethal.

Without crying out, without even gasping, Ephrem Lluch teetered and slumped over. But before he fell to the ground Diana was under him. Her two hands wrapped around his neck and pressed the carotid artery and pharynx. One, two, three, four minutes she kept the pressure on. Finally, she stood up. Ephrem Lluch was dead.

"It's all or nothing," the Red Princess told herself. "If I get out of Ushant leaving Mathias Lumen alive, I'll be scorned by Leonid Zattan. Better off dead. And in order not to die, I can't spare anyone. This poor guy was in my way. It wasn't enough just to knock him out. He could've come to, jumped to his feet. Being dead, not only is he no longer an obstacle, but he can be useful to me."

While talking to herself like this, the terrible woman was hard at work. She undressed the corpse and put the boots, pants and pea coat on herself. In one of the coat pockets she found a Browning.

"Perfect! I was hoping for this!"

Only when he slept did Ephrem Lluch take off his sailor's cap with its patent leather bill. Diana put it on with her hair all stuffed inside and her face shadowed under the bill.

"Like this I'll have at least a few seconds of disguise to fool the people I'll have to kill to get out of this place."

All or nothing! The Red Princess was right. When a human being, especially a woman, decides to commit a crime of both passion and forethought, there is no more limit, number or quality to this crime. Diana Ivanova Krosnovief had come to Ushant to kill Mathias Lumen. She believed his death would earn her the grateful love of the Lord of Issyk-Kul and the fulfillment of all the dreams of desire, wealth, power and domineering grandeur that such love brought with it. For a moment she was captured and beaten, but now she saw her chance of coming out victorious. She only had to get through all the obstacles between her and Lumen and then kill the man. She was free now to leave her cell, walk around the house, look for him... As soon as she found him, she'd point the gun calmly and pull the trigger.

And then she'd try to leave the house. She'd use the secret wireless to send news of her victory over the enemy. And she'd go to Constantinople where a plane from Issyk-Kul would be waiting for her.

"Seven bullets in the Browning," she muttered. "I hope it's enough."

The door had been left cracked open. Diana was so exhilarated and focused on the dreadful goal she had to reach that she didn't even feel how heavy Lluch's big boots were. But at least the soles were soft and without nails. She could walk firmly and casually.

She left the cell, closed the door and went to the stairs. She remembered the route after Lumen's menacing speech, walking in front of Ephrem Lluch across a big, round room. She had crossed diagonally to get to the stairs. Therefore, going in reverse, she knew exactly what door led to Lumen's study. She headed for it directly, rapidly. With her left hand she grabbed the handle, turned it, pushed it open... and she was standing in the doorway, free, a gun in her right hand ready to fire...

But Diana saw no one.

The huge room was lit up through the three closed windows but with their shutters thrown open. They had immaculately white, tulle drapes. The big curtain separating the laboratory from the library was only partly drawn.

"Nobody," the Red Princess whispered.

She stood there for only three or four seconds before she made a quick and decisive move. She went in, closed the door and went to the half-closed curtain. Into the long, straight folds of the heavy fabric, she was able to hide herself completely. The curtain swayed a bit before falling perfectly straight and still again...

Well, on this morning, a little after 7 am, Mathias Lumen and Placide Bonnard had gone down into the cellar that had been changed into a research and experimentation pool for the "individual or single-seater submarine" with an electromagnetic engine invented by the Hermit of Ushant and built by him and his secretary with the help of Ephrem Lluch.

They were there to verify the upgrade of the rudder mechanism for horizontal movement.

Lumen was sitting in the mobile seat with the top open since the submarine only had to navigate on the surface for this experiment. The marvelous machine was cruising slowly through the calm water of the pool that was lit by a dozen electric lights under the roof from one end to the other. Sitting on the 6-foot wide, stone platform that encircled the pool, Bonnard was holding a notepad and pencil. Every ten seconds Lumen rattled off numbers that Bonnard noted down.

"3, 18... 4, 24... 5, 30... 6, 36..."

Between each pair of numbers the submarine coasted from one side of the pool to the other following various angles of direction.

"7, 42... 8, 48... 9, 54..."

And then, "Stop! That's enough. Your calculations are right. I'll use your corrections. No need to wait. Let's fix the rudder for good right now. This should be Ephrem's job but he's not here yet... What time is it?"

Bonnard looked at the small watch attached to his left wrist by a leather band. "8:20."

"Already?" Lumen frowned. "It's time for him to take breakfast to number 3. That should only take five minutes. Another five minutes to grab the tools I told him about last night, and then come here. Something might have happened? With that woman anything is possible. Let's go see."

While talking, Lumen had brought the submarine to the platform. The water in the pool was absolutely still. Moreover, the ingenious boat could be piloted from a certain distance by a device transmitting electric waves. There was no need, therefore, to moor it.

The two men were dressed alike in unbleached canvas suits like "overalls" of car or airplane mechanics and wearing Catalan rope espadrilles, which left the feet almost bare. No weapons on them. In the chest pockets of their suits were a handkerchief, notepad, pencils and a small wrench.

In this outfit, as little offensive as it was defensive, Mathias Lumen and Placide Bonnard walked out of the huge basement room, climbed the stairs, crossed the round vestibule, went down another flight of stairs and stopped in front of cell number 3. The door was closed. The signal light showed that the electricity in the cell was turned off.

"Door closed. Lights out. She's sleeping. And Lluch has left," Lumen uttered.

All of it was or looked self-evident.

"Let's go back," the master said. "Lluch must be in the workshop. If he leaves in the next minute or so, we'll hear him crossing the rotunda."

"We might as well look in the cell to see," Bonnard had a bad feeling.

Lumen kept his voice down, "I don't have the key. Besides, I swore I'd never see the woman again unless it was to kill her."

Quickly and decisively he marched up the stairs. Bonnard followed him. The workshop was at the end of one of the three hallways running off the rotunda. Telepathically, the secretary's bad feeling was affecting the master. They both dashed down the thirty feet to the workshop. Lumen opened the door, which automatically turned on the light.

"He's not here!"

"But the tools are…"

"Placide, the keys…"

In his own room next door Bonnard kept one of the four sets of special keys with master keys that were kept in the house for the four occupants: Lumen, Bonnard, Lluch and Sidonie.

While Lumen went back through the round room and down the stairs, Bonnard ran to get his set of keys and rejoined his master just when he was stopping for a second time at cell number 3.

Bonnard asked, "Should I open it and go in?"

"Yes."

And just as Bonnard was turning the key in the lock, Lumen grabbed his arm and whispered, almost gasped, "Do you have a weapon?"

"No."

"You'll need one. We haven't seen Ephrem since last night. This woman is terribly beautiful… and so diabolically, pervertedly seductive! Ephrem is just a man after all. If he's in there, dead or alive… Placide, don't forget that on my orders he was always armed with a loaded gun. Go get yours, fast! I'll wait here."

It didn't take two minutes for Bonnard to reach his room and come back with a Browning in his right hand.

"Placide, I won't come in unless you call me. And don't call me unless… unless the woman is dead or has to be killed. Be careful! She's a demon!"

Bonnard had stared at death a hundred times during the war. More than one wound had threatened to carry him out of the hospital in a coffin. Sometimes he was scared, but it never took him more than three seconds to overcome the fear and change it into noble bravery. This time, he stood there for a good thirty seconds with his left hand on the key. Finally, he let out a deep breath, turned the key and pushed open the door. He found the light switch immediately and entered the lit room.

"Oh, master, master, get in here!"

The anguish in his voice brought Lumen in like a magnet pulling iron filings.

"Ephrem Lluch," he cried. "Ephrem!"

With a single glance, like Bonnard had done before him, Mathias Lumen saw the empty bed, the deserted room… deserted by Diana Ivanova! But the body of the Catalan lying on the mat, legs stiff and arms akimbo. The light shone full in his face, illuminating the death mask—mouth gaping open, glassy eyes, pale skin…

"Ephrem! Dead! Dead!"

Placide Bonnard was standing at attention, watching the door, gripping the gun in his right hand. But Lumen was thinking of the danger. He was kneeling next to the body, mumbling, "Dead! Dead!"

Nevertheless, the will and the need to know forced him back to attention, to calm, to be clear and cool-headed. He felt the body from head to foot. He leaned over and examined the face, the neck…

"She strangled him!" he said. "The demoness! How could she overcome him when he was so strong and on his guard. How? Oh, he is dead for sure, but her? Where is she now? Not far, certainly. The corpse is still warm. Well, this time I'm going to kill her. She took his Browning. All the better. It'll be a duel!"

In one swift movement he was standing up. As in other tragic situations, Placide Bonnard saw before him a man around 40 years old, his prematurely white hair intensified his savage, powerfully young face, and the noble, vigorous maturity of his thin but athletic body. His gray-blue eyes had an unbearable glow. And his voice was firm and cold when he spoke.

"Placide, give me your gun."

Bonnard obeyed.

"And walk behind me or at my side but not in front, if you value my friendship. Understand?"

"I understand, master. I'll stay next to you."

"She's in the house. She can't have left. The corpse is still holding the keys in a pocket, I felt them. So, she can't get out of the house. Wherever she is, we'll find her. And Diana will kill me today or she'll die by my hand! I forbid you, Placide, absolutely forbid you to do anything to help me or protect me as long as I'm on my feet. If I drop, you're free to do as you please."

"Master, I'll obey."

"Good. Now, let's go."

Mathias Lumen was aware that he was risking being shot by surprise at point blank range. He thought, "Except for the cells here and the rest of the basement, all the doors inside the house are open. It's been probably ten minutes that she's been sneaking from room to room or hiding somewhere. She can see me coming. I might be standing right in front of her without knowing it. If she sees me first, I'm dead because she's most likely got Ephrem's gun."

He walked. He wanted to go the kitchen first to warn Sidonie. As he strode down the hallways, he scrutinized every corner, every doorway. The doors themselves he made sure were not cracked open a little and when he went through, he locked them behind him with the master key he kept in his left hand.

"If nothing happens on this round, we'll go through every room in the house, top to bottom, left to right."

"Right, master," Bonnard agreed.

They got to the kitchen. Sidonie was putting dishes away in a cupboard. On seeing the two men's faces and the guns in their hands, she shuddered with fear. Lumen didn't give her time to ask any questions.

"Have you left here yet this morning?"

"No, monsieur," she replied in a shaky voice.

"So, no one came in here."

Without another word, he turned around and left with Bonnard, locking the door behind him.

Next, he started the first methodical search of the house, but only in the hallways, the stairways, the vestibules, not entering any of the rooms. And he locked all the doors. When this was done, the two searchers returned to the round room, which was the center of the house.

Lumen told Bonnard, "From the cellars to the attic, no one. Therefore, she's inside one of the rooms. Which one? Except for the cells, the basement, the kitchen, it could be any of them, even the workshop. I'll go into every one. So that you don't get in my way, you stay at the door and let me enter alone."

"Very well, master."

And the dire search began.

First the bedrooms and bathrooms. One by one Lumen inspected each as meticulously and cautiously as a good police officer looking for a dangerous criminal who was armed, desperate and full of hate.

Nobody.

Next was the workshop, two storerooms, the dining room, Bonnard's private lab, the tool room of Ephrem Lluch, the arsenal, the archive and map room and the typing room.

Nobody.

There remained only the library/laboratory, the brains of the house.

Bonnard was thinking, "We should've started there. Why didn't the master think of that? She went straight there, by God! But maybe he didn't want to end it quickly so that she'd get anxious and annoyed while waiting and he'd have time to calm down."

Was this what Mathias Lumen was counting on? Maybe. In any case, the master did look much calmer, although no less determined, with a kind of wild austerity, to kill or be killed.

And the two men, side by side, step by step, came to the door of the last room of the house where Diana Ivanova Krosnovief must certainly be hiding with a gun in her hand.

For a moment, Mathias Lumen stood motionless.

Then, in slow motion, he grabbed the door handle, pushed and stretched out his left hand... He opened the door all the way. His right hand held the gun at chest level.

The dividing curtains were completely pulled back, massed together at the ends of the rods. The daylight, barely diminished by the bars on the windows, poured into the huge room and lit up every nook and cranny. Along the length of the library, under the tables on the bare floor and all the way to the workbenches, the glass-doored cabinets, the bookshelves and lab equipment, on the armchairs and stepladders, the keen eyes of Mathias Lumen and Placide Bonnard could find no trace of a human being. By chance the armchairs were arranged so that their wide, high backs, seen at an angle by the two men, could not be sheltering the woman from their view.

Only the curtains with their long, vertical folds presented a mystery.

And the two men were thinking, "She's there in one of the curtains. On the right or left?"

A terrible, menacing enigma whose solution could prove lethal.

Who would be killed? The woman hiding, spying on the man? Or the man searching for the woman?"

Lumen calculated coldly. And with telepathic correspondence, Bonnard calculated at the same time.

Going to the curtain behind which or within which Diana was not hiding, Lumen would be opening his side and back to an open shot. Going to where she was, it would be like Lumen offering himself wide open to death.

Either way, there was only one chance: that the hand of the Red Princess would be shaky or her aim unsure, that the bullet from the Browning, the first bullet, would miss. Lumen would fire blindly right away at his enemy hidden in the folds but who would necessarily have to reveal herself. Thus would be the duel. And Lumen trusted his aim and the steadiness of his hand.

But was the Red Princess so emotionally affected that she would miss a man two, four, six, even eight feet away? Or if she could wait, at point blank range?

Mathias Lumen believed in God. He knew now that God had chosen this hour of this day for his death or for the greatest victory he had ever known before the final victory over the occult forces of the near or distant Antichrist. Lumen believed in God. But he didn't pray to Him.

He simply mumbled, "*Fiat voluntas tua, Domine.*"

And he walked not to the left or to the right, but straight ahead, as if going through the middle of the room, an equal distance from each curtain. His eyes and ears were fully alert to pick up the slightest movement of the curtain, the faintest rustling.

He took four steps. He didn't finish the fifth.

Between two folds in the curtain on the left, a gun, a hand suddenly sprang out. And a shot was fired.

Pivoting on one leg, Lumen turned a quarter way, wobbled, straightened up and fired.

Another shot rang out, followed by another again. And Lumen, after firing only one shot whose results he probably never knew, collapsed on the floor.

Now from the doorway Bonnard dashed in, screaming, his hands outstretched, ready to strangle. But at close range, one after another, Diana fired two shots into his forehead. He dropped two feet away from his master.

Only then did the Red Princess step out of the curtains. She was pale, her whole body trembled. The gun slipped out of her shaking hand. She went over to Lumen, bent over, looked into his wide-open eyes and whispered, "Dead. One shot in the side, two in the chest... Dead! At last!"

She started a nervous laugh but it ended in a sob. She wobbled. If she hadn't grabbed the back of an armchair, she would have fallen.

"Come on," she coughed, "come on! Isn't this what you wanted, desired, hoped for with every fiber of your being? And now that you've succeeded, you're going to faint like a stupid little girl who killed her lover in a fit of jealous rage? Diana Ivanova, straighten up!"

And the dreadful murderess stood up straight, clenched her teeth, held both hands against her chest and arched her supple back into a posture of defiance. Thus did she conquer the emotion of her brain and flesh. She was back in control of her own life. And she felt as strong and clear-headed as ever.

Skirting around the corpse of Mathias Lumen, she stepped toward Placide Bonnard, pushed it with her foot and uttered a little scornfully, "This one was bound to be killed like every human being at this time, in this house... which should be nothing but a tomb and a safe full of secrets! Killed or seduced... His fate was to die with his master like Ephrem Lluch and like the woman, the servant... Come on! You have to finish it!"

She picked up the Browning and continued talking to herself in a whisper.

"Three more bullets left. More than enough. Killing that woman in cold blood without even having to defend myself won't be so easy, but, yes, it has to be done! I have to close all the shutters and stay in the house until nightfall. Then I have to leave by the front door and lock it behind me. Finally I have to take Lluch's whale boat, the *Nostradamus*, in Lampaul and get back to Brest... And the Ushant house will stay locked up, guarded by the respect and superstition it emanates. Our affiliate in Lampaul can keep an eye on it. The corpses will rot while the treasure in the basement will wait for Leonid Zattan to come and get it... I'm sure even Lumen's affiliates won't dare violate his house. The thought won't even cross their minds since they'll think that Lumen, Bonnard, Lluch and Sidonie are traveling on the continent like they do sometimes. Therefore, a tomb. Only the dead don't talk. If this woman is left alive, she'll talk. A man, Bonnard for example, I might be able to seduce, to tame, but this woman... I have to kill her. It's horrible! In cold blood, with no hatred against her, no provocation from her, no, I couldn't... Provocation? That's the way. It's me who'll provoke her. I'll tell her I killed Lluch and Lumen and Bonnard. She's tough and strong. She'll be seized not by paralyzing fear but by vengeful rage. She'll grab some kind of weapon. She'll attack me. Then I'll be forced to defend myself. Yes... but if she doesn't react violently? If she's scared, if she trembles, if she faints? No, that would be the opposite of everything we know about her. Come on, you have to do this!"

Sixteen hours later, meaning a little after midnight, a series of knocks were heard at the door of a little old cottage set apart from the others on the seashore of Lampaul. These knocks were rhythmic. After two minutes of silence, the same knocks were made in the same rhythm.

The door opened, letting a person enter, then closed again.

In the only room of the little cottage, the man who had opened the door stood in gray flannel pajamas holding a flashlight in his left hand. "Oh, it's you, Diana Ivanova," he said.

The Red Princess was dressed like on April 5th, the day she went to Ushant with Kiewicz and the other men.

"Yes, Nikitch, it's me," she replied without a trace of emotion. "Get dressed quickly, we're going to Brest with the *Nostradamus*."

"Hey, Diana Ivanova, the whale boat of Ephrem Lluch is chained to the dock with two special padlocks. Even at this time of the night, in this fine weather, there are always sailors at the port. Sawing through the chains will take a long time and breaking them would be noisy."

"Get dressed! I have the keys. It'll only take a minute and for this minute, so that no would-be night owl get any suspicious ideas that might cause us any problems, put these on instead of your own clothes."

She pointed to a wrapped package that she had tossed on the stone floor when she entered the cottage.

Nikitch was a very Frenchified Russian, an affiliate of the international Neo-terrorist network, connected to the Brest sector with residence in Ushant. He passed himself off as a former sailor of the Russian fleet who'd turned misanthrope and wanted to retire in Ushant, settling in Lampaul like a hopeless man in the desert. He had come to Brest in a second-hand little boat, had rented the abandoned cottage, fixed it up and lived a simple life off his fishing. That was for appearances. In reality, he was constantly spying on Mathias Lumen, his companions and any visitors he had. He was in his forties and looked like a real sailor.

He put the flashlight on a wobbly table so that the beam shined horizontally across the room and he hurried to put on the outfit over his pajamas. It was the pea-coat, pants, boots and cap of Ephrem Lluch. When he was fully dressed, he asked, "Will I be coming back here?"

"Yes, on a public boat."

"So I should bring my own clothes for when I come back."

"Yes."

He rapidly fixed up a bundle and grabbed the flashlight. "I'm ready."

"Let's go!" Diana ordered.

Despite the fine weather, despite the moon and the stars, despite the enchanting calm of the Ocean shimmering in the moonlight—very rare meteorological conditions in Ushant!—there was nobody wandering around the small port of Lampaul.

The nocturnal boarding of a woman "from the mainland" and the fake Ephrem Lluch on the Hermit's whaleboat had no witnesses and therefore caused no surprise, which might have started endlessly repeated stories, changed and explained during the day from one end of the island to the other. As it was, the dreadful secret of the Red Princess would be well guarded by the mysterious house with doors and windows shut tight.

The *Nostradamus* was always ready to cast off to sea. Once the padlocks were opened, the moorings unfastened and the anchor lifted and fixed in its slot, all that needed to be done was to start the engine and open the throttle. Diana sat in the back, wrapped in her coat. Nikitch stood at the helm, which was near the engine. And the *Nostradamus* headed out towards Brest.

At 4 am the whaleboat came into its usual place in the merchant port. It was moored and locked up. From now on the boat would be guarded, watched and taken care of by a sailor working for the Nautical Society who lived in a small wooden house right on the docks.

At this hour on April 8th, the guardian was asleep, naturally. But when he would make his first round, he would see the *Nostradamus* and would say, "Well, someone from the Hermit's house is on the mainland."

And "someone", in the sailor's mind, could mean plural as well as singular, could signify four people or just one, and they could be gone for weeks before returning to the island. So, the guardian was not surprised because this was not the first time it had happened.

During the trip Diana Ivanova had talked a little with Nikitch, certainly not to tell him what she had done in Ushant but to give him precise instructions on what he had to do over the next few days.

On the dock, however, there was a customs officer making his rounds. He recognized the *Nostradamus* and the figure of Ephrem Lluch. He only gave a brief, sleepy glance at the woman whom Lluch was bringing back from Ushant so early in the morning.

Diana and Nikitch left the dock without anyone else seeing them. They walked quickly to Rue de Siam. There, in the solitude disturbed only by rag-pickers at work and a few morning dockworkers, they stopped in a doorway.

The Red Princess held out her hand to the Neo-terrorist, "Goodbye, Nikitch, perhaps forever."

"Goodbye and farewell, Diana Ivanova."

They shook hands and the man disappeared down a side street while the woman went up Rue de Siam to meet her destiny. She didn't stop until she was at the door of the the house occupied by Ignace Kiewicz. She rang the bell. She waited. She was let in by Nadine in pajamas her eyes still heavy with sleep.

"Oh, Diana Ivanova!" the "slave" of Kiewicz yelped. And with strange change into a harder voice, "Are you alone?"

"Yes. Is Ignace here?"

Nadine paused, ever so briefly...

But if Diana had been on her guard, she would have noticed this hesitation and maybe picked up the vague suspicion that opens the door to bewilderment, questions, doubts, to defensiveness.

In fact, Diana was so ecstatic over her awful and astonishing victory that her very refined sense of the slightest incidental variations was completely turned off. Therefore, she didn't catch Nadine's hesitation and she trusted the answer that the slave-lover gave was true.

"Yes, Princess, he is here. He's even up. I know he's working in the lab. Would you follow me, please? He'll be happy to see you."

"Gladly," Diana said.

Watching pretty Nadine with a little contempt as she went first down the stairs that were lit with electric lights, she was thinking, "He didn't tell her anything about the day and night in Ushant. As for the message from Mathias to Leonid, he'll want to wait to deliver it until my imprisonment at the Hermit's house looks hopelessly permanent. Good! Kiewicz is smart and he's devoted to me. I won't forget him."

The stairs went down to the basement. The Red Princess figured it only natural that he had set up a lab—mechanics, chemistry and explosives—in the cellar. Thus she continued to have no suspicions.

And soon they were standing on a sandy floor before the rotten wood of the cellar door. Nadine turned the handle and opened it. An electric light high up on the wall lit the short, narrow hallway that ended in a padded door.

"Go on, Princess, enter," Nadine smiled and stepped aside with a graceful bow in the old Moscow style. "Just push the door."

Diana passed her and with one push of her right hand, she opened the padded door, but she saw nothing in front of her except a kind of dark void because at that very instant the light in the hallway went out.

All of a sudden, her blood ran cold. In a panicky fit of surprise and confusion, she heard a clanking that sounded like an iron gate. She swung around. She saw only blackness. She was stuck in the darkest dark. She took a step, two, three, hands held out in front of her...

"Hey!" she brayed.

Her hands touched the thick, close-set bars of a strong gate.

CHAPTER VII

That happened in Brest on April 8th.

And in Constantinople, on April 9th, Ignace Kiewicz, arriving by plane, had barely stepped onto the runway in front of the hangars and offices of the intercontinental airline when he heard his name pronounced with a question mark.

"That's me," he said in English.

An employee from the wireless office repeated, "Mr. Ignace Kiewicz?"

"Yes, that's me," the smiling traveler also repeated.

He was not worried. He had his reasons to fear nothing from the English and Turkish police who helped each other—or fought each other—on the cosmopolitan territory of the former capital of the Ottoman Empire.

The employee went on, "Would you be kind enough, sir, to show me your passport? I had a telegram for Mr. Ignace Kiewicz but only after verifying the identity."

"Well let's have it then!" He pulled out his passport.

30 seconds later his passport was given back to him along with the telegram. He signed the employee's book, paid the "duty on exiting the plane", and stood next to his light luggage while he read the message. He turned pale while reading.

"*Cellar filled. Nadine.*"

"Oh, already!" he gasped.

He was so affected that his hands were trembling. He read it again and again because he couldn't believe his eyes. Then he started laughing. And thinking to himself, "More than I hoped for. My hope, more an intuition, I had repressed it with all my strength. What madness to hope that Diana would escape from Mathias Lumen! What even greater madness to hope that she would do it so soon! It's only been four days since… Well then, I'll go to Issyk-Kul later. I've got better things to do now."

He stuffed his papers (passport and telegram) into his pockets, grabbed his suitcase and rushed over to the airline offices. He stopped at the first ticket counter.

"Please, sir, what time is the next flight for Paris?"

The clerk, a Turkish Englishman or an English Turk, answered in a detached monotone, "3:30 pm."

The clock showed 11:28.

"Perfect. Is there a seat?"

"One left."

"I'll take it."

He got his ticket, paid, left and hurried to the nearby restaurant that was recently set up for the airline personnel and the passengers coming from and going to Constantinople. He ate with a hearty appetite. After several cups of coffee (Turkish, of course) and two cigarettes it was 3:20. At half past he was taking off in a plane exactly like the one he came in. His return trip was uneventful. In Paris he retrieved the Red Princess' torpedo and the mechanic/driver Nicolas Topof.

The Pole still had the huge ruby ring on his finger. He showed it to the mechanic who responded solemnly and obediently, "At your service, monsieur."

"To my house, Rue de Siam in Brest, quickly."

And on the evening of April 13th, so seven days after kissing Nadine good-bye, Ignace Kiewicz kissed his charming and loving slave again, saying, "So, she's here?"

"Yes."

"How'd it happen? Tell me."

"I don't know, dear master. Last Thursday, very early in the morning, she showed up and asked for you. I followed your instructions. We didn't say two words to each other. She went into the cellar without suspecting a thing. Since then I haven't seen her again. I give her food and drink through the slot. She's been eating. That's all."

"Very good. I love you, Nadine." He gave her a big hug, kissed her again as she blushed and giggled. Then he said, "I'm going to see her. Give me the key."

"Be careful, my love," Nadine had suddenly turned pale. "She's probably armed. And you know better than anyone how terrible she is."

"Yes, I know," he rasped.

He thought he knew, but he had more to learn.

He added, "I'll send in some gas. I hope it's still working."

"It worked fine the last time it was checked."

"Perfect! And the first thing I'll do is take away any weapons."

Nadine hung onto the shoulders of her beloved master to plead with him. "Let me come with you. If there's any danger, I could be useful. And I'll do whenever you ask."

"Yes, come."

"Oh, thank you. You're so good. I love you."

The man left his small suitcase on the rug, took off his hat, coat and gloves and followed Nadine down the stairs.

For six days, six days of incomprehension, furious rage, heroic resignation and gloomy anticipation, one after another or mixed up together, Diana Ivanova was like a tigress captured by treachery in the jungle and straightaway caged within dark walls. For, it was really a cage of walls that the Red Princess found herself in.

Two cellars made up the basement of the small house. One was still used normally: small barrels of vinegar, bottles of wine, suitcases, scraps of furniture.

There was no humidity because the floor, walls and ceiling were all cement covered with cork tiles.

The second cellar had been refitted the same way but it could also be used as a cage, an iron cage almost as big as the cellar itself. Between the six sides of the cage and the six sides of the cellar there was an empty space about one and a half feet wide. The inside of the cage with its tight bars was also lined with wood planks that were covered with a thick layer of cork as hard as rock.

In this cage there was a day bed, a stool, a table and a toilet. It was less comfortable as a living space but a lot more solid as a prison than the cell 3 in the house in Ushant.

One wall of the cage had a door and next to this door there was a revolving hatch like for cloistered monks or nuns, what Nadine called the "turnstile". By reaching through the bars the prisoner could just barely grab what was left on the platform under the hatch. The light came from an electric bulb hanging from the ceiling of the cellar above the ceiling of the cage. As for air, it came from small vents, barely visible and fitted with sound absorbers, that were built into the only wall of the cage that was not detached from the cellar.

Diana Ivanova was only able to see and feel or deduce these things after a few hours of captivity. At first, she was a real "tiger in a cage", known by any big game hunter who provides all kinds of wild animals to zoos and museums.

Going from one prison to another was not something that scared the Red Princess. But until now she had been imprisoned only by her declared enemies. They were much less dangerous than treacherous friends.

"It's in the house of Ignace Kiewicz, my friend, that I'm being imprisoned... by betrayal!"

That was the first relatively lucid thought that Diana had after a long period of shock, rage and fright. Then her fright gradually turned into a more and more grievous anxiety that remained under all fits of violence and desperation.

Still she thought of not letting her watch stop. She wound it twice every 24 hours. Like that she could count the days. She managed to eat and drink what was given to her at set times. She examined her cage, bar by bar. She pondered. She imagined. She piled conjectures on top of hypotheses. And the days passed. No living thing showed up in the cage—unless you could call "living" the barely reachable hatch that made its regular, silent spins to give her food and drink.

She still had her Browning stolen off of Ephrem Lluch's dead body. This gun was her only hope. Maybe later she could fight again, come out victorious again...

But more than fighting and winning, she wanted to know, to understand, to talk about this.

"Why am I being held captive here in the house of Ignace Kiewicz?"

Soon this was the only question that filled her mind during the somewhat calmer hours of lucidity.

And the days passed.

In her handbag, which she had picked up before leaving the house in Ushant, was a small notebook and a mechanical pencil. She wrote the dates. It was on the evening of April 13th that the prisoner suddenly felt something different. Or rather she smelled something—the odor of ether. She sniffed the air. It was not pure ether, there was something else in it that gave her, when she opened her mouth, the faint taste of bitter almonds.

Her latent anxiety then became so intense that she screamed. She screamed like a madwoman. Her whole body shook with fear. She dropped on the edge of the bed and had the vague feeling that she was passing out. Her scream changed abruptly, becoming weaker and weaker, ending in a wheeze. And she fell totally unconscious.

The void...

And she was shaken out of this void by a feeling of coolness on her face, a momentary coolness that moved from her forehead to her temple, from one ear to her neck, from the other temple to her lips...

She opened her eyes, then closed them right away, blinded by a bright light. She tried to move her hands but felt her wrists being held down tightly, like in a vise.

Only then did her thoughts come back.

"I passed out. Gas was blown into the cage to knock me out. The light... My hands... Tied down... There's someone here!"

The mental commotion affected her body so strongly that she shot up and opened her eyes. She was sitting on the edge of the daybed and she saw a man in front of her.

"Ignace!" she shouted.

"In person," he said curtly.

"Finally! Explain this to me! What abominable mistake did your Nadine..."

She stopped. She understood with new horror that it was no mistake. The eyes and face of Ignace said enough: hatred, a savage and satisfied hatred was clearly expressed. She knew she was lost.

"But why? Why?" she coughed out, trembling, tormented.

He answered dryly, "You'll know soon enough. My brother will explain. I just wanted to get your gun, to search you and also to tell you that your life is not in danger as long as you are docile, very docile. Here, look, I'm taking off the handcuffs. Your hands are free to take your usual meals from the hatch. I'll come back in a few hours. We'll talk. Then we'll take a little trip. But if you want to live, you have to be docile, very docile, my dear, my precious Diana Ivanova..."

He stepped back, turned and left.

She wanted to jump up, run, grab him, beg him to explain, to help her understand, to free her from this dreadful anxiety of the unknown... but he was already out of the cage whose movable section clanged shut. And he was backing through the door.

Besides, she couldn't get up. Her legs were still too weak. So, she sat there. She held out imploring arms. She sobbed a little. She pleaded, "Explain this to me, explain it."

But he closed the door without any answer except a hateful, satisfied glare.

At the bottom of the stairs, Nadine was waiting for him worriedly. "Well?"

He snickered, "The tigress is tamed, I think. Keep doing exactly what you've been doing. I found a weird key on her, which is probably to the house in Ushant. This Browning I got off her isn't hers. The hem of her skirt is stained with something that looks like blood, as if she were standing over a bloody corpse. I want to find out without interrogating her. She might have come back from Ushant with only Nikitch. Or maybe he didn't even return. In any case, if he did come back to Brest he went to the office. I'll find out. See you later, Nadine. Thank you, congratulations and I love you."

He hugged her, kissed her, picked up his hat, gloves and coat and he left.

A stormy wind was hurling down Rue de Siam. The Pole said, "Ugh, if this wind doesn't die down I won't be able to go to Ushant tonight. I can just see it: the waves and current will toss me overboard. Well, we'll see."

The Neo-terrorist section of Brittany, of which Ignace Kiewicz was the head and was one of the most active cells of the international revolutionary organization controlled by Leonid Zattan, had what the affiliates called an "office" in Brest.

It was simply and ingeniously just a rented shop buying and selling used clothes. It had the very French name "Au décrochez-moi ça" or Off The Rack. It was run by a guy in his fifties, originally Italian now with French citizenship, helped by two "sellers", very young, said to be Alsatians, war orphans and totally innocent looking. There was a backroom and a cellar. The police had never poked their nose into the shop because there was nothing fishy about it. It was on a popular, very decent street. The backroom was flanked by a bedroom and kitchen that had a window and door onto another, less busy street. Therefore, double exit.

Many clandestine meetings were held there. Many changes of clothing and disguises were made there in order to throw off any suspicious police. Finally, the affiliates were brought there, in certain circumstances, to sign a special agenda.

It was in Off The Rack that he found, as expected, Nikitch who was usually assigned to watch the Ushant house but for the time being was on a break by order and permission of the Red Princess.

Kiewicz didn't have to show him the fateful ruby. More immediately and permanently here than the Red Princess, he was the chief. Nikitch talked. He couldn't say much. Diana Ivanova had drafted him to bring her to Brest on board the *Nostradamus* and told him to stay at the office until further orders. He was still waiting for these orders.

"Here they are," Kiewicz said, "As soon as the wind dies down, if the sea is navigable, we're going to Ushant, you and me, with the *Nostradmaus*."

The wind calmed down around 10 pm.

"Let's go," the Pole ordered. "Once out of the bottleneck, we'll see if we can risk it."

They saw that it was very risky, but Kiewicz had sailed in these dangerous waters in worse storms and on less reliable boats than the big, solid *Nostradamus*. Therefore, the two men headed for Ushant. Soaked and freezing cold but as undamaged as the boat, they arrived an hour before sunrise.

Leaving Nikitch to sneak his way back to his shack, Kiewicz hurried to the house of Mathias Lumen. He felt dark forebodings. But he wasn't afraid. Since he'd been chosen as special messenger for Lumen, wasn't he protected from any danger that might come from the mysterious house?

"For Diana to escape with the key to the house," he reasoned, "she had to have incapacitated the four occupants of the Ghost Chalet. How? And for how long? I could've asked her and she probably would've told me the truth. But that would mean talking to her. I don't want to talk to her. I'll leave that pleasure to my brother."

From Lampaul to the house Kiewicz saw no one at this early hour. He stepped onto the cement walkway only after calling out several times in vain since all the doors and windows were closed, making its silence even more sinister in the early morning mist.

Bravely but nervously Kiewicz went straight to one of the doors and tried it, but the key didn't work. In the next door, he put the key in and turned it easily. With a slight push, the door opened.

Of course, the Polish-Russian Neo-terrorist had seen, in Russia and elsewhere, scenes of horrible massacres. But none had ever made the impression on him that the quick and successive discovery of the four bodies of Lumen, Bonnard, Sidonie and Lluch did. At the thought of these murders being the work of the unarmed, imprisoned woman who was hated and distrusted by these four, (and rightfully so), Kiewicz shuddered and felt his hair stand on end, he got goosebumps and broke out in a cold sweat.

"She's terrible, terrible, terrible!" he repeated to himself as he went from room to room.

By sheer force of will he controlled his emotions, his horror, his fear and he examined the corpses one by one. After noting that Lluch had been strangled and Lumen, Bonnard and Sidonie shot, he reconstructed the drama fairly accurately.

Even though a meticulous search of the mysterious house was of great interest to the Neo-terrorist leader, one of the lieutenants of the Lord of Issyk-Kul, Kiewicz decided not to do it. Besides, *was he still, in truth, a lieutenant of the*

Lord of Issyk-Kul? Was he even a Neo-terrorist? Wasn't he part of this great adventure only to satisfy his individual passions, a personal and family hatred?

He left, closed the door, put the key in his pocket, went back to Lampaul and found Nikitch, who was wandering around the port now as ordered. Without raising any suspicions of the locals who might see them—because they were used to strangers getting off and on the *Nostradamus* and had often seen Ephrem Lluch use Nikitch as a handyman—the Pole got back to sea on the whaleboat.

In Brest he moored in the same berth as the night before. He gave Nikitch the same orders to stay at the office until further notice and he went directly back to his house of Rue de Siam.

Nadine had lunch ready. Noon bells had just chimed in the clocks around Brest. Despite his persistent agitation, he was hungry and thirsty. He sat across from Nadine and told her, "Basically, everything's fine. I'll tell you about it. I'm famished. And my throat's dry. Give me something to drink first."

When he had quenched his thirst and filled his belly Kiewicz gave a quick account of what he'd seen in Ushant. She was horrified.

"What are you going to do with this woman?" she groaned.

"Don't you know?"

"Yes, but how are you going to get her to Saint-Guilhem? She'll act up…"

The meal had invigorated the Pole. As usual the digestion made him forget about the recent past and think only of the near future: Diana in the hands of Stanislas. He chuckled and his eyes sparkled.

"I don't think I've ever spoken to you about the Yage?"

Nadine's face looked utterly surprised. "Yage? You've never mentioned it. What is it?"

"It's a plant. It's only found in the virgin forests of Mexico and used only in a brew, carefully measured It gives you the power see into the present and the future what is or will happen near or far in the issues around the life of the person who drinks the Yage. But even more marvelous effects can be had by combining the Yage with Peyote."

"Peyote?" Nadine sounded even more surprised.

"Yes. It's another plant of the same origin as the Yage. Whoever takes a certain dose of Peyote gets vibrant, colorful, very intense, enthralling visions. But if you mix correctly the Yage and Peyote, the intoxicated person falls into a state of *absence* that doesn't show on the outside but is absolute. He'll look awake, normal, but his will is controlled by whoever is with him. He'll hear and obey, not forcibly but with eager enthusiasm. And yet he'll be enjoying or suffering, with utmost intensity, not his immediate surroundings but either some purely imaginative heavenly visions or else infernal tortures caused by the visions of what will happen…"

"I don't really understand," Nadine said.

Ignace smiled. "An example will help. Diana Ivanova Krosnovief. Her lunch came with wine drugged by me with drops of Yage and Peyote. The wine will only taste fruitier. She'll drink it unsuspectingly. An hour later she'll be intoxicated. Then, thanks to the Peyote she'll start having a series of delightful, waking dreams. But thanks to the Yage she'll have a very clear vision of what is waiting for her and what she will suffer in Saint-Guilhem. Her heavenly visions will be entangled with the awareness of the physical and mental tortures that my brother has planned. All this without a trace left of her willpower.

"I'll get her in a car, in her own car with her own driver, that damned soul Nicolas Topoff. And when we drive to Saint-Guilhem, Topoff will see her calm, smiling, perfectly normal. But during those long hours crossing two-thirds of France, Diana will be seeing all the circles of hell that my brother will make her go through without mercy. And these mental sufferings, when they become real in Saint-Guilhem, will be so much more terrible because she'll be able to remember her heavenly visions.

"Can you imagine what an abominable horror for a human being will be this physical realization of a hideous nightmare that had been bizarrely mixed up with exquisite dreams? Well, that's what the Yage and Peyote will give Diana Ivanova, all the while making her a traveling companion as charming as can be."

Nadine closed her eyes and stayed silent for a moment. Then, raising her eyelids and looking with love at her master and lover, she said, "Everything you're doing is right. Besides, this woman deserves to suffer."

"Amen!" Kiewicz stood up and rubbed his hands together.

Nadine stood up, too, wrapped her pretty bare arms around his neck and tenderly said, "Can I ask you something?"

"Go ahead, dear."

"Once Diana Ivanova is in the hands of Stan, will you keep living this life of a conspirator and terrorist that constantly puts your life in danger? Won't the day come when we can experience the simple joy of living? Traveling, books, music, your Nadine... I know you've dreamed of it too. Will you make it come true when the work of justice will be accomplished for you? Answer your Nadine who would gladly give you her last drop of blood if you demanded it. Answer, my master."

The voice of this beautiful woman—and so deeply loved—was so heartrending that Ignace had tears in his eyes. He hugged her and said, "I'm leaving this afternoon, April 13th, for Saint-Guilhem. I'll get there on the 15th and stay only one night. I'll come back here right away. Or else, taking a different tactic, I'll go to the Perpignan airport and fly to Constantinople. I'll get there no later than the 18th. Send a message to the Boss and a plane from Issyk-Kul will come get me. Two, three, four days... Nadine, excepting some adverse twist of fate, I swear to you, at the end of the month I'll be back here. The month of May is wonderful on the island of Mallorca. We'll go to Mallorca, you and me, just the two of us. Traveling, books, music and my Nadine!"

"Yes, and your Nadine, my Ignace," the young woman thought, but she didn't say it. She closed her eyes, happy, and kissed him.

CHAPTER VIII

During this period between April 5th and 14th when the Red Princess had played her final hand and beaten Mathias Lumen, the Neo-terrorists all over the world, including France, knew nothing about the extraordinary events happening in the castle of Issyk-Kul.

Likewise, at Issyk-Kul the various, antagonistic players in the formidable drama knew nothing of the horrible tragedy at Ushant. The only man who could have revealed it was Ignace Kiewicz. Well, the Pole had his own ideas about the matter and he was waiting to either expose or keep his secret depending on the circumstances.

The heads of the Neo-terrorists weren't checking up on Issyk-Kul because they had a specific timetable: preparing for the sudden and simultaneous eruptions of thousands of revolutionary volcanoes being kept latent all over the globe and on April 14th going to Issyk-Kul for the last council of war presided over by Leonid Zattan.

On the other side, the various heads of the counter-revolutionary organizations under Mathias Lumen (many of whom were just representatives of the real, secret chiefs, kings, dictators or prime ministers of the nations of the world), weren't checking up on Ushant because Mathias Lumen was known to disappear for weeks on end when he would travel incognito to visit his powerful allies unannounced.

It was, therefore, no surprise that during this tragic period of April 5th to 14th the crucial events at Ushant and Issyk-Kul remained unknown to certain men who were the very ones most affected by them.

It is one of the games of Fate to maintain a kind of calm silence in the world while someplace, in secret, events are taking place with the most far-reaching and deadly consequences.

In Ushant a woman had killed Mathias Lumen, Placide Bonnard, Ephrem Lluch, Sidonie and had turned the house into a sealed, silent tomb, the house that was, in a way, the living brain of millions and millions of men. And only three human beings knew this: Diana, Ignace and Nadine. Of the three, two would never talk: Diana because she was as good as dead and Nadine because her love would keep her quiet. The third, Ignace Kiewicz, might speak up, but in his own good time, which had not yet come.

Meanwhile at Issyk-Kul...

Ah, there, we must witness the extraordinary series of contradictory incidents that were the consequence of the sensational drama played out on April 5th by Gnô Mitang first of all and then by Leo Saint-Clair, the Nyctalope, against Leonid Zattan. This drama, let's not forget, ended with the Nyctalope saying, "Gnô, are you ready? Open the door."

Gnô obeyed immediately. They left the plane following Saint-Clair's instructions, forming a kind of procession at the bottom of the ladder. Under the hidden but constant and ruthless threat of the seven Brownings held in pockets by right or left hands, Leonid Zattan, with admirable self-control, told Woldski what was to be done with Petrus Ivitch and Manoël Guerro. Then he marched. Avoiding the moving walkways and elevators as the Nyctalope had wisely demanded, he guided his vigilant captors to his rooms. They entered his "studio" together. And as naturally as could be he was going to sit in his armchair behind the luxurious worktable when Saint-Clair touched his arm and ordered:

"No, monsieur, no! There are too many devices that would make it easy for you to play a dirty trick on us. Please sit here and I'll sit in your place. Mademoiselle Mac Duhl, Monsieur Mitang, Captain Ayol, take those seats there to the right and left of the Lord of Issyk-Kul. And you three who I remember, Lequic, Bonnet and Blanchard, if I'm not mistaken? Right! Well, stand over there where you've got a good shot at our prisoner and a clear view of the door... Good. Now that we've all found our places, I'll sit down."

And sat he did, in Zattan's swiveling armchair. Then came silence. Zattan in anxious rage; Sylvie, Gnô and Marc Ayol burning with curiosity; Lequic, Bonnet and Blanchard in respectful admiration; everyone waited. Everyone felt that this game, so well played, was at an end and they were about to enter a drama, a formidable drama whose stage was the entire world. What was the Nyctalope going to say and do?

It's a long-standing, rather common game of wits to harp on this queen's nose or that tyrant's gall stones, on the grain of sand in the cogs of the great machine, on the tiny error of one number in the data of a long equation, an atom, a wisp, a trifle more or less and the face of the world is changed. Yes, this child's game has become common, but why? Because it represents an indisputable truth.

For weeks Gnô Mitang, Leo Saint-Clair and their companions had fought the most critical of battles against Leonid Zattan and his accomplices. From one phase to the next, little by little gaining victory, they had come to the point where they finally consider themselves the definitive victors. And Zattan saw himself as helplessly defeated.

Everyone ignored or just forgot about the grain of sand, the atom, the wisp, the trifle that brings down centuries-old dynasties—in this case, Ali-Soud.

Ali-Soud who had once been something like one of the twenty slaves of a pasha of Asia Minor; Ali-Soud, one soldier among thousands; Ali-Soud, a wreck among the wrecks of the Great War; Ali-Soud, presently the personal butler of Leonid Zattan at Issyk-Kul.

What was this humble creature compared to the Nyctalope, Gnô Mitang, even Marc Ayol? A trifle, nothing but a common human being, one among the 1.6 billion on earth.

He was the grain of sand in the machine.

When Zattan's procession and Zattan himself had entered the study, Ali-Soud went in also, to do his duty, but by another door. He had just opened it, was standing in the doorway, was about to part the heavy curtain and go in when he heard a voice, the voice of "Captain Pedro del Campo" commanding with authority, "No, monsieur, no!"

And through the narrow parting of the curtains, Ali-Soud saw the "Captain" touch the Lord's arm and stop the all-powerful master in his tracks.

Ali-Soud saw this! And he heard the words and names pronounced by Pedro del Campo! And then he saw the rogue sit in the chair of the Emperor of Tian Shan! He noticed that Sylvie Mac Duhl was free while Leonid Zattan was obviously under constraint, looking like a prisoner amongst suspicious jailers! Finally, Ali-Soud heard Pedro del Campo tell the three men standing in the middle of the room, "Stand over there where you've got a good shot at our prisoner and a clear view of the door."

Ali-Soud had no need or desire to see or hear more. He knew nothing, but he understood that his master (whom he loved, admired and venerated) was the victim of some despicable trick and had been caught in a trap, ambushed!

The Turk was neither stupid nor cowardly. Alone he could do nothing against all these armed men. He backed away. On the thick carpet of the bedroom, his soft leather sandals made no noise. He carefully closed the door. With the windows closed the bedroom was dark so none of the men or the woman had noticed the slight movement of the curtain behind which Fate, for a brief moment, had place the grain of sand.

"Obviously," Ali-Soud was thinking, "these people aren't thinking of my master's bedroom, otherwise they would've searched it and guarded it."

It was true. Saint-Clair, Gnô Mitang, Sylvie and their companions were, in a way, hypnotized by Leonid Zattan, unwittingly. It was necessary for them to be present and in constant control over their subject, a necessity that monopolized all their mental faculties. Keeping their eyes on Zattan and their immediate surroundings, they saw nothing else. A partial mental fog that would certainly only be momentary…

But this moment was enough for the grain of sand to fall into the cogs of the machine. Ali-Soud left silently from the rooms. He ran faster than the moving walkways, up and down stairs faster than the elevators and at the command center of the castle he asked for lieutenant-secretary Woldski. A system of telephonographic calls and signals made this center the ears and focal point of life at Issyk-Kul. In less than thirty seconds Ali-Soud was talking with Woldski who was at the infirmary handing Ivitch and Guerro over to the head doctor of the castle, Dr. Weilmann, an ex-professor of medicine in Hamburg.

"Lieutenant," the butler said, "orders from the Lord: please go immediately to office the commander of the guards. You'll find me there. I'll give you the confidential instructions from the Lord."

This order was no surprise to anyone. Ali-Soud was often the spokesman for Zattan.

At the guardhouse, as usual, there were fifty men sleeping or daydreaming or horsing around or just being stupid and lazy until the changing of the guards. At the entrance to the guardhouse, to the left, was a small room that served as the office of the officer in charge.

On this day and at this time the officer, the captain of the guards, was registered under the name of Punjaz, a Hindu.

Just like Woldski, Ali-Soud (personal butler and occasional representative of the Master) could speak and act with an authority that everyone in the castle had to bow before, even Colonel Karal Bey, the garrison major. Captain Punjaz made no objections, therefore, when Ali-Soud entered the office after knocking and simply said, "Captain, orders from the Lord. I'm waiting here for Lieutenant Woldski to give him confidential instructions."

One minute later Woldski came in.

And it was this very minute that begat the glory and misfortune of this man who until now had been the very devoted, very active but very obscure secretary of Leonid Zattan in his castle.

Modest and disciplined, Woldski was no less an intelligent man, clever and brave, highly self-controlled and always levelheaded. He was rarely seen otherwise.

What Ali-Soud was telling him was so bizarre that Woldski asked him to repeat it. After thinking calmly for a minute, he gave the order:

"Get Karal Bey here urgently."

Ali-Soud went to call him and waited for him to arrive before they went back into the office together.

Woldski made a sign to Karal Bey to pay attention and ordered Ali-Soud, "Tell him what you told me."

The colonel, tall and thin next to Woldski, who was rather short and fat, despite being strapped into his tight black uniform, listened with surprise, which quickly turned into alarm and then bewilderment. But the lieutenant-secretary calmed the head soldier of the castle with a simple phrase, "We have to act!"

"And without delay," Ali-Soud added.

"Damn!" the colonel swore.

Woldski again, "Ten men will be enough with us three, but we have to choose them well."

"Officers," the colonel said.

"Yes, the best."

"Punjaz, MacEorn, Wildorff, Baztev, Felgrau, Huan Chu, Magdolian, Zannatti, Milcent and Stoffmann." He named them without hesitating, counting them off on his fingers—this colonel-major knew his men.

"Good," Woldski approved. "Get them here double-quick. Armed with Browings and knives."

"Got it."

Karal Bey went to the telephone and communicated with the command center that immediately reached the nine officers scattered around the castle. Punjaz was waiting for them in the guardhouse. When the last one arrived, he brought them into the office, which was now filled up.

In a low voice to the ten officers huddled together with Karal Bey and Ali-Soud behind them by the door, Woldski gave a brief explanation of the paradoxical situation and concluded:

"No hat or gloves or boots, as light as possible, knives in one hand and guns in the other, you follow me. After me the colonel gives orders. After the colonel Ali-Soud's in command. After Ali-Soud, it's Punjaz… And so on by seniority. The goal is simple: get the Prince out safe and sound even if means killing all the men and the woman around him… I'll give you two minutes to get ready."

It was a hive of activity. Hats and caps, kepis and fez, boots and leggings, belts and suspenders, even their dolmans and pea coats—anything heavy or bulky was taken off and left on the floor.

"Let's go," Woldski barked.

The colonel had already given orders to his subordinates and soldiers: don't talk, don't move, wait for orders, called in or written, given to and carried out by Lieutenant Dervix, the second-in-command.

And the 13 men, Ali-Soud and Woldski in the lead, Karal Bey in the back, ran the shortest route to the south tower, second floor, the Lord's rooms. When they got there, they were about to break in and attack, a homicidal horde ready to massacre the woman and six men to save one, when suddenly Ali-Soud stopped, turned around, stuck out his chest, crossed his arms and became a human barrier that Woldski and the others close behind him almost ran into as they stopped their mad rush.

"What? What is it, Ali?" Woldski growled.

In the same low, impassioned voice he answered, "No, no! We can't go in! It'd be madness! Allah has just inspired me! Listen up! If we keep going, what will happen? We'll rush into the studio and kill or be killed. But who among us can guarantee that one of our enemies won't have time to point his gun at the back or in the face of the Lord and shoot once, twice, more? It would only take a few seconds! What good is it to kill the enemy if the Lord is killed too?"

Fate was very clever when it threw this grain of sand into the cogs. The progress of this grain into the vital gears of the machine was definitely well directed. For a moment this progress was almost diverted. "Allah inspired me!" is what Ali-Soud was thinking. Allah, God, Jehovah, Buddha, the Great Spirit, the Supreme Being—everyone has a name for Fate. This time the inspiration from the unknowable Divinity was practical, reasonable and logical.

"That's true," Woldski whispered.

"Then what do we do?" Karal Bey asked.

They stood there, motionless, silent, at the end of the hallway, twenty feet from the studio where their Prince was the plaything and maybe soon the victim of an unimaginable plot, an unthinkable defeat. Their Prince! The man who ensured their prosperity, their riches and the complete fulfillment of all their desires, of all their passions, all their vices! The Prince, Leonid Zattan, without whom hundreds of good men would be mere rogues, reduced to questionable or downright criminal devices that modern condottieri inevitably use when they are no longer in the military. Saving Leonid Zattan was saving themselves. This was the vital necessity of these thirteen burly, panting men armed with knives and guns, waiting for one of them, the least of them, to come up with an idea that would bring them victory and salvation.

But the grain of sand stood still for a long time, unsure. Fate blew on him and he started sliding once again into the vital gears, meaning that Ali-Soud had an idea and he told them right away. His face lit up and his eyes sparkled with hope.

"My lieutenant, my colonel, all you officers, please do as I say. Don't ask for explanations. My idea is as simple as one plus one equals two. It'll succeed with no risk to anyone. And I can do it by myself. But we must always plan for the worst. All of you, at all times, be ready to serve the Lord, but without anyone being able to see that there's a change in the daily routine of normal life in the castle. Go back to your posts or your rooms after picking up your things at the guardhouse. Live your life as usual. But at the first signal given by Woldski or myself, run here with your weapons... Excuse me for giving orders like this, me the butler, but it's necessary and Allah inspires me."

No matter what they thought of Allah's inspiration, the eleven officers obeyed. They left immediately. Eleven and not twelve because Ali-Soud held Woldski back with a hand on his shoulder.

When they were alone, he said, "Come. And from now on, not a word, not a sound. Come, look and listen. The more we know of the truth, the better we'll be able to act, sooner or later. Come! Let's go hide in the bedroom. We'll listen and maybe see something."

But they couldn't hear or see anything because the lapse of attention by the Nyctalope, Gnô, Sylvie and the others was only momentary. In the high, wide, long vestibule that opened onto the different rooms, Woldski and Ali-Soud saw above the main door, the one to the hallway leading to the studio, the warning light (red with a green cross) that meant strictly "Do not enter unless I call. I'm unavailable. In case of emergency, call me from the command center."

Often, to shut himself off from the whole world and to enjoy complete solitude in his private eyrie, the eagle of Issy-Kul would turn on the warning light. To ignore it, to disobey the order, to knock on the door was a grave offense punishable by death. To call if not absolutely necessary would result in very serious penalties.

But today...

"Today as usual we have to obey," Ali-Soud grumbled. "They've forced the Lord to reveal the device. Or not. The girl probably knows about the light and what it means. We can't get in—the doors are locked automatically."

"I know," Woldski sighed.

"What now?" Ali-Soud was demoralized by the predictable obstacle that they didn't predict.

"Now," Woldski was back to his customary role of authority, "we stay here. We have the right to. When the light turns off and the doors can be opened, I'll knock and go in. That's also my right."

"Mine too," Ali-Soud agreed.

"We'll pretend like nothing's wrong. We'll do our duties. And we'll see... But does this ruin your plan?"

"No."

"Can you tell it to me now?"

"Yes."

"I'm listening."

Standing there in the vestibule, looking up at the warning light, the two men had been whispering. But Ali-Soud thought this wasn't cautious enough. He pulled Woldski into the farthest corner from the door and holding him against the walls by the shoulders he leaned over and whispered into his ear. Woldski listened without interrupting, more serious as ever.

When Ali finished, Woldski murmured, "Your plan sounds good to me. It's easy to put it into action. It'll work if no unforeseen obstacles get in our way. So, you stay here. I'll go see Dr. Weilmann and ask him to prepare something. First, I'll go to the guardhouse and get my boots and coat. After the doctor I'll come back. I hope nothing else happens and we can be here together for the finale of this baffling scene that's playing out right now in the studio. See you soon."

And Woldski left.

The butler sat on one of the heavy oak, sculpted stools that lined the walls of the entrance hall. He knew that any reckless action would be in vain. The doors there were all padded. Behind them the hallways led to other doors (studio, dining room, bedroom, bathroom) that were also padded. Therefore, listening at any of these doors was completely useless. Even gunshots in most of these rooms wouldn't be heard. Only the bathroom, because of its bare walls with decorated tiles would act like a sound box and echo loud noises. But the other rooms with their many carpets, curtains, bookshelves and furniture would absorb sounds and nothing would reach the vestibule. Zattan had wanted it like this and rightly so. But under present circumstances this wise precaution worked against its creator and prevented his worried servant from learning anything about what he wanted so badly to know.

Fifteen minutes passed before Woldski came back. He sat on a stool next to Ali-Soud who hadn't moved an inch.

"Anything new?"

"Nothing. And the doctor?"

"He'll do what needs to be done."

"Good."

And they waited. They didn't talk. What for? Everything that could be done had been done. For the rest, they could only wait. But glancing every minute at the warning light, the two men were shivering with anxiety on the inside. What was happening in the studio? What were they talking about? How was this paradoxical situation, with the prisoner girl, Pedro del Campo and his mysterious companions holding the Prince hostage, how was it going to work out? And finally, would Ali's plan be able to be put in action?

During this wait (this torture) the lieutenant-secretary suffered more than the butler. He was less of a fatalist. He was more hot-blooded. He was furious that he couldn't use the brutal forces of the castle's garrison. Knowing that they had hundreds of fanatics, powerful technical devices, countless weapons from the old sword to the latest automatic pistols, and not being able to muster these armed men to attack in an invincible flood against the doors behind which was brewing, perhaps decisively, the defeat, the downfall, the annihilation of Leonid Zattan!

But at the peak of these furious speculations, Woldski had an idea. He shuddered. He put his hand on Ali-Soud's arm.

"Hey, Ali?"

"What is it?"

"What about knockout gas?"

"Huh?"

"Yes, knockout gas. Send it through the pipes bringing warm air into the radiators in the studio. It'll take fifteen minutes. If they try to leave, they'll be picked up by the guards at the door. If they don't leave, knockout gas. The Prince will also be knocked out, but who cares? The gas is almost never lethal. Everyone will be on their feet and normal in a few hours. And in chains, see, Ali-Soud? The Lord will be taken right away…"

"No way," the Turk broke in. "If it was feasible, I would've thought of it. Am I not, after you, the man must be devoted to the Lord? Who's to say that with the first whiff of gas, which won't take immediate effect, one of those men, even the woman, won't empty their gun into the Prince's head? When you've tried and succeeded at what these people have done, you won't balk at murder if you feel yourself threatened with death or even just failure."

"You're right, Ali," Woldski admitted with suppressed rage. "Let's wait then. And get your Allah to make sure Weilmann does a good job. That's my only hope now."

"For me too," Ali agreed.

From time to time the lieutenant-secretary had looked at the wristwatch on his left arm and was mumbling "six o'clock" when they heard a short beep and the red light suddenly shut off. Ali-Soud and Woldski jumped to their feet, ready for anything.

Silence. A long silence. A minute, maybe two. How long 60 seconds can be!

And the tapping of metal... One long, a pause, one short.

"It's for me," Woldski grumbled. "He's calling me."

"Go," Ali said. "And stay calm. You know nothing, you suspect nothing."

The two men looked at each other under the ceiling light. They were pale. And they were both trembling. The tapping metal came again, long, pause, two shorts.

"That's me," Ali said.

"Let's go together."

"By Allah stay calm."

"Yes, calm, calm," the Pole repeated.

They stiffened up, then right away relaxed, bringing color back to the faces by sheer willpower. Finally, almost normal, Woldski stepped over, opened the door, went down the hallway, pushed another door, parted the curtain and went through... Ali-Soud was next to him. They froze together.

In the big studio, the armchair behind the table was empty. Pedro del Campo was standing next to it. To his left, also standing, was Leonid Zattan smoking a cigarette. On the other side of the table Sylvie Mac Duhl and the Japanese were sitting on a couch and whispering to each other. Marco Pampil and three sailors, respectfully attentive, were standing at the back of the room. All the lights were on—the chandelier and the floor lamps spread a festive light. There was nothing more natural, more simple, more at ease than the attitude of this motley band gathered there. Woldski and Ali-Soud took it all in at one piercing glance. They snapped their heels together and saluted.

In his most friendly, most pleasant and captivating voice Leonid Zattan spoke, tapping his cigarette automatically:

"Ali, give orders to set the table for nine more. Mademoiselle and these men are my guests this evening. The ninth guest will be Petrus Ivitch. Woldski, go see if he's awake and tell him to come here. I'll be waiting. If he's not able to walk and talk, call me. Ali, make sure the dinner is the best. The best wines, etc., please... You will be waiting on us."

Woldski and Ali saluted again and turned around. But before leaving, they heard the Prince saying, "My dear del Campo, since you're an amateur of Burgundy wines, you should enjoy a certain Romanée that..."

The lieutenant-secretary and the butler didn't hear the rest. They understood nothing. But it didn't really matter. Understand? What for? The main point was to act. And how easy and successful the action was going to be!

"Come on, let's run to the infirmary," Woldski said. "Quickly!"

Dr. Weilmann was not at the infirmary but in his lab where Woldski and Ali-Soud went right away.

He was a typical dolicephalic blond from Northern Germany. Big, tall with an elongated head, a flattop haircut, blue eyes, an extremely intelligent face, a strong, clean-shaven jaw. No one knew why this "Herr professor", who had held important official posts in his country, was here in the headquarters of Leonid Zattan at Issyk-Kul. He never talked about it. He carried out his duties as head doctor with a kind of cocky cordiality but with devotion. He was polite to his two subordinates—a surgeon and a very young Chinese doctor. Towards Zattan he was always obedient but never servile, an admirer but no sycophant. In his ultra-modern laboratory he worked alone or with Petrus Ivitch on their secret projects. Thus, Dr. Weilmann was one more enigma among all the other enigmas at Issyk-Kul.

At the door to the laboratory, Woldski and Ali-Soud had to announce themselves through an acoustic tube. A light flashed to authorize entrance and the doors opened automatically.

Wrapped from chin to ankles in canvas overalls stained in every color, wearing rubber gloves and big goggles, the doctor greeted the lieutenant-secretary and the butler eagerly. He put the retort and test tube he was holding on the table and was obviously anxious. "Well, what's new?" he asked in German.

Woldski and Ali-Soud were both comfortable with the language of Goethe.

"There's a lot we still don't understand, but at least this seems clear: the Mac Duhl girl, the del Campo guy and his partner, the Japanese and the three sailors from Ivitch's plane have the Prince at their mercy. But it's just as clear that their power over him won't last, at least under present circumstances, if we can get him away from them. So, apparently acting of his own free will, but in reality being controlled by the girl and the six men, the Prince asked for nine settings for dinner in his personal dining room."

"Ha!" Weilmann guffawed, "we'll get them with no problem."

"No problem!" Ali-Soud echoed.

"But including the Prince, there are only eight of them. Who's the ninth guest?"

"Petrus Ivitch, if possible."

"It's possible," the doctor affirmed. "Petrus is awake. There, too, we need some explanations. Ivitch and Guerro were just in a peculiar hypnotic sleep that simulated death or rather catalepsy. There's nothing more I can do for Guerro even though his body is starting to lose some of its frigid stiffness. But Ivitch is awake and fine."

"Completely?" Woldski asked.

"Completely."

"Did you ask him about it?"

"Ach, yes, of course! But he said he knew nothing. And it's probably true. Partial amnesia often follows catalepsy. But it won't last. His memory of what happened will be back soon and then he can talk. Afterwards, it'll be Guerro."

"But at what point do the engineer's memories stop?" Woldski asked.

"At the moment Guerro got on the plane with Tchicoz and Ismaïl Kadeuy, going from Famagusta to Cyprus."

Woldski swore and then, "But neither Tchicoz nor Kadeuy were on the plane when it got here! Only Ivitch and Guerro, like dead men, and the Japanese and those three French sailors…"

Ali-Soud spoke softly, "Everything will be explained when Ivitch and Guerro can tell us the details. Doctor, I'm going to take care of the dinner. I believe you will do what you have to…"

"Of course, Ali. Come back in fifteen minutes. It'll be ready."

"Good!" Woldski said. "Me, I'm going to give Ivitch the Lord's invitation."

"Ha! He who laughs last, laughs best in this colossal mystery. In fifteen minutes, Ali, and see you soon, right, lieutenant?"

"Soon, doctor."

And they left Weilmann to his work.

Crossing the courtyard at the back of which was the doctor's lab, Woldski and Ali-Soud remained side by side.

The butler asked, "Lieutenant, where are you going to be during dinner?"

"In my office. I'll get some food brought to me and I'll be ready to run at the first beep."

"Listen, if there's only one beep, it's you alone. If there are two, you bring the colonel and the ten officers."

"Right. Good luck, Ali."

"I'll need it."

"We've sworn our lives and everything dear to us in life."

"I know."

"We have to win."

"We'll win!"

Equals before the mystery, the danger and their passions, the two men shook each other's hand firmly and fraternally. Then they went their separate ways, Woldski to see Ivitch who had left the infirmary and Ali-Soud to talk with the chef who was in charge of the Lord's meals.

An hour later the opulent silverware was set out for the nine guest in Zattan's dining room. Petrus Ivitch would be there. Given no special instructions, he was putting on a tuxedo. He had decided to "play stupid", as he called it, and keep pretending to have amnesia.

Ali-Soud brought the misanthropic engineer into the studio where Zattan and his guests were still oddly gathered, some in silence, others whispering together. Zattan was signing papers on the corner of the big table that Pedro del Campo was handing him one by one.

These signatures stopped when Ali-Soud announced, "Monsieur Petrus Ivitch." The engineer went straight in, bowed, shook the extended hand of the

Prince and listened to him introduce the guests one by one: Sylvie Mac Duhl, whom he had glimpsed once before, Pedro del Campo, whom he knew, Marco Pampil, whose name he vaguely recalled being mentioned by del Campo himself, the Japanese Gnô Mitang, whom he pretended not to know, and then the three French sailors about whom the Prince added with a smile:

"These humble sailors will honor us with their presence at dinner, my dear Ivitch, because they are true heroes."

Ivitch knew what was going on because he had seen and heard everything on the plane. He was having the time of his life.

"Lord, dinner is served!" Ali-Soud announced solemnly.

As usual at Zattan's table there were half a dozen servants, young and beautiful Circassians, to serve. Attentive and aloof, Ali-Soud directed them with his hands and eyes. The Turk's face was as expressionless as marble. He showed emotion only once, when two servants were pouring a new bottle of wine and the clear voice of Pedro del Campo broke the eerie silence of the meal, which was being eaten without even a whisper of conversation among the guests, and his voice said:

"The Romanée? The special wine you told us about? Yes? Well, I'm terribly sorry but neither mademoiselle nor Monsieur Mitang nor myself drink. We made a vow… Oh, it's a long story I'll tell you about some day… A vow to never drink a wine that's been named before the meal…"

Leonid Zattan stared at the Nyctalope and raised his eyebrows. And with a proud glare of defiance, a little annoyed, he said, "So, you're afraid of being poisoned? Look, I'll drink some myself."

He was sincere. Being unable to give orders of any kind to attack his secretly victorious enemies, he had only given the name of the wine beforehand so that Ali-Soud would serve it because the Lord of Issyk-Kul was very proud of the excellence of his wine cellar. By a strange but logical anomaly, this cruel and merciless man was hurt that they suspected him of poisoning them.

He got himself a big glass of the Romanée wine and drank it down.

"Just like Mithridates!" is all del Campo said.

It was then that the face of Ali-Soud lost, for a few seconds, its imperturbable mask. Until then his eyes had been open, cold, watching everything and everyone. After del Campo spoke up and with the Prince downing the glass of Romanée wine, Ali's eyes closed and his face briefly relaxed, even glowed a little with divine irony.

The quick-acting, powerful narcotic prepared by Weilmann was not in any of the wines but in the soup and all the other dishes. The "Giaours", the infidels, could drink the wine or not, the grain of sand was already moving through the gears of the machine.

CHAPTER IX

They were on dessert when Blanchard was the first to drop his face in his plate. Dr. Weilmann's narcotic was so fast-acting that he had felt no warning signs.

The Nyctalope, Sylvie Mac Duhl, Marc Ayol, even Lequic and Bonnet, all of them thought they knew. They jumped to their feet, Brownings in hand. But Petrus Ivitch, who had slipped off to the side, was already on the floor. And Leonid Zattan looked pale, frightened, teeth clenched, eyes wide open and bloodshot...

That the Prince himself should have addled the Nyctalope and his still conscious companions for an instant, but this instant was enough to incapacitate them in every way. Sylvie Mac Duhl collapsed against Saint-Clair's side while he suddenly looked dizzy and then just crashed on the carpet. They were like a bunch of broken puppets around the table. Marc Ayol, Lequic and Bonnet fell. The last to succumb was Gnô Mitang.

Stunned, then panicking, the servants ran around screaming, but Ali-Soud's commanding voice rang out, "Here, girls, over here! All of you!"

When they were together, trembling, staring at him, he spoke, cold and intimidating:

"Anyone who talks of this will die! You saw nothing. Nothing unusual happened. You did your duty and after the coffee left. So, go. You won't eat tonight. Go to your rooms, go to bed and sleep or pretend to. Tomorrow you will resume your duties like every day. And don't forget—torture and death for even one word of this. Go!"

They ran out of the room.

Well, unable to contain his delirious delight, Ali-Soud jumped and yelled and clapped his hands like a madman. After this fit of self-satisfaction, he was again perfectly calm and went to send the call, the double signal. Woldski and Karal Bey rushed into the room with the ten officers. They stopped and started laughing with joy at the strange sight of all these lifeless bodies.

Ali-Soud kept things simple, "Lieutenant, as is my duty, I'll take care of the Lord. You can deal with the unconscious bodies since in the Prince's rooms in his absence, you're in charge."

Indeed, under these circumstances, in the military regulations of Issyk-Kul, Woldski took precedence over Karal Bey.

The lieutenant-secretary thought for a few seconds before giving his orders, "Colonel, take Ivitch to his room. Officers, you take the six men and lock them up in separate but adjacent cells. Of course, you'll search them thoroughly before leaving them and take everything, without exception, that you find on them. I'll take care of the girl."

With a show of strength completely unexpected, Ali-Soud picked up Zattan's inert body and threw it over his shoulder and carried it into the room next door.

Karal Bey, on the other hand, cradled Ivitch in his arms like a child. Second Lieutenant Stoffmann, a giant, grabbed Pedro del Campo; Lieutenant MacEorne, just as brawny, hoisted Marc Ayol; the eight other officers, no matter their rank, paired up to carry away Gnô Mitang and the three sailors.

Ali-Soud had already come back. He gathered up the dropped Brownings and wrapped them in a towel. In the meantime, the officers left. Woldski alone stayed behind, standing there, puzzled, over the body of Sylvie Mac Duhl lying on her back on the carpet. At last he muttered, "Her, too? In a cell, right?"

"No, in fact," Ali-Soud replied. "In her room. The Lord would prefer it. I've called Dr. Weilmann. The Lord will make his own decisions, but we have, I believe, done the best we can."

"I believe so too."

Woldski bent down, picked up Sylvie Mac Duhl around the waist, held her against his chest and lifted her up. He left through the open doors of Zattan's rooms and went up to what had been and what would once again be the beautiful captive's prison.

An hour later everything was back to normal in the castle. With the table cleared, the dining room on the south tower was as calm and luxurious as before; the eleven officers were at their posts or in their rooms; Woldski was making his rounds after the curfew. But six cells in the bunker were occupied by unconscious prisoners and instead of working in his lab, reading in the library or sleeping in his bed, Dr. Weilmann, dressed very professionally in an immaculate white lab coat, was standing at the bedside of the Prince of Issyk-Kul. He had just given him a shot and was patiently waiting for the effects. In his left hand was a silver tray with a crystal glass half full of a pink liquid. His right hand was free and ready to act if necessary.

Ali-Soud was three feet behind him, also waiting but with much less composure and confidence because the Lord was taking a long time, Ali thought, to open his eyes.

And then suddenly his eyes opened without the slightest twitch in the rigid, death-like face. At once his eyes were alert. They stayed open while the rest of his face came alive.

Turning his head on the pillow, Zattan looked at the doctor and Ali-Soud. In a low, already assertive voice, he asked, "What happened?"

Weilmann answered, "Your propitious fate saw to it that Ali saw and heard everything right after you entered the studio. He understood that you were being threatened with guns hidden in the pockets of the people around you. He told Woldski, then Karal Bey and ten officers, then me. A strong narcotic was mixed into the food and all the guests were knocked out. I gave you an antidote to wake you up. It's 10:15 pm."

"Good." Zattan riveted his eyes on Ali-Soud and after a moment of silence, "So, you're the one who saved me?"

"By the will of Allah, Lord," the butler bowed very deeply.

"Sure, but you're the one who saved me. I won't forget it."

Then he looked at Weilmann, "Thank you, doctor, for the narcotic and the antidote."

Then back to Ali-Soud, "What'd you do with the girl?"

"In her room, on her bed, asleep."

And Weilmann added, "She won't wake by herself, just like the others, for ten to twelve hours."

"Very good. And the men, Ali?"

"Petrus Ivitch is in his room. Pedro del Campo and Marco Pampil, the Japanese and the sailors are all in cells in the bunker."

"Perfect. Doctor, when can I get up and get back to my normal life?"

"After your normal night's rest."

"Better and better. Leave me to Ali's care. He'll help me get ready for bed. Your hand, doctor. Thank you again. Please have breakfast with me tomorrow."

Such an invitation at Issyk-Kul was an extremely rare honor. Weilmann felt it and despite his fierce independence he blushed with joy. He bowed and left the room.

Half an hour later, in pajamas and warm under the electric blanket and sheets, Leonid Zattan had dozed off into his normal, calm sleep. Sunk in a deep armchair by a night light, Ali-Soud was fingering his Muslim rosary.

The next morning, at the usual time, to the cheery sounds of the reveille coming from the guardhouse, Zattan woke up. He waited a short while with his eyes half-closed, then opened them completely.

"Ali-Soud."

"Lord?"

"A Scottish shower right away."

And lashed by alternating hot and cold water, rinsed with alcohol, rubbed, massaged, shaved, dressed in horse-riding gear with spurs and all, a fur cap and tie, Leonid Zattan drank a big cup of burning hot coffee, lit a cigarette, then went down into the main courtyard where his favorite horse was waiting for him. He left, alone, to take a ride in the fresh air.

In the regions of Issky-Kul on April 6th, the weather was cold and gloomy with heavy clouds that the icy wind from the mountain gorges couldn't chase away. Pale and murky, the lake beat its angry waves against the dripping rocks and slimy cliffs. But Zattan felt nothing of the raging or dreary sadness of nature. When he found himself truly alone on the ledge path and far enough away from the castle, he let loose his savage joy and sang. He sang a warrior's hymn of fierce merriment that beat time violently with the horse's all-out galop. When the hymn was over, the Kalmyk burst out laughing, halted his steed, spun it around and trotted back to Issyk-Kul. He was calm, in complete control of himself, the clear-headed master with a will that he wielded without anger but in accord with higher aspirations that were over and above immediate and personal interests.

Back in his rooms, he got undressed and rubbed down by Ali-Soud. Now dressed in white silk and wool, with his hair shiny, his eyes sharp, his skin fresh, his neck bare and his feet shod in red leather, he rang for Woldski. Three minutes later the lieutenant-secretary came into the study. He had on his uniform and the usual expression on his face.

"Hello, Woldski," the Prince smiled. "I want to thank you and congratulate you on your conduct last night. In the end you made decisions that I approve of."

He held out his hand to the officer—a rare favor. Touched and pleased, Woldski shook the noble hand (so he considered it).

"Sit down, my friend," Zattan went on, sitting down himself. "I have two or three orders to give you and a few little things to tell you, which you'll like. But first the mail. Anything new or important?"

"Nothing unexpected," he answered, opening a register he had been keeping under his left arm and in which was noted all the messages received during the night. "I haven't brought any letters since they're all just administrative. As for the radio, the most important messages announce or confirm the departure of various Neo-terrorist delegates. Excepting any serious accidents or incidents, they will all be here in eight days on April 14th before noon."

"Nothing about Ushant?"

"Nothing."

"No news directly from Diana Ivanova?"

"Directly, nothing, but there are reports that the delegates met in the Chapelle Expiatiore in Paris yesterday, as Your Lord planned. Since the meeting took place the night of the 4th, Diana Ivanova should be in Brest, maybe even in Ushant today the 6th."

"Probably. Let's wait for the outcome of events in Europe that we can do nothing about so we can deal with the events here in Issyk-Kul, which are pressing and, if I may, tangible."

He smiled, took a minute, and continued in the same casual tone.

"Again, my thanks and congratulations, Woldski. But it's my turn now to show my enemies that I'm a good sport. You can put del Campo, Pampil and the Japanese or—since we know who they are—Saint-Clair the Nyctalope, Marc Ayol and Gnô Mitang in the same cell. Likewise for the three sailors. I want them to know that I'm strong enough not to fear them together... in prison almost like when they're free."

"Very well, Lord."

"Now, listen, Woldski, I'm going to tell you all about the trap from the beginning in Famagusta up to the final chapter, which was the decision to eat together in my private dining room. I know about Famagusta because Gnô Mitang told me so I might vindicate, in my mind, Kadeuy, Tchicoz, Ivitch and Guerro. As for the things here, I know all about them since if it wasn't for Ali-Soud I'd be the victim followed by the ruin of Issyk-Kul, including you, not to mention the tragic fall of the global revolution. From what slender threads hang the lives of men and the fate of the world! So, listen, Woldski, as a first thank you I'd like to satisfy your curiosity."

And Zattan painted a witty and vivid picture of everything he knew, which was accurate and complete, except that he thought the "catalepsy" of Petrus Ivitch was as real as Guerro's. On this point, Gnô Mitang had been careful not to reveal the truth, which would have kept Zattan from "vindicating" the innocence of Ivitch in the whole affair.

When the Prince had finished his story, which Woldski paid close attention to, he wrapped it all up lightly. "All's well that ends well. And thanks to Allah for creating Ali-Soud."

Then he got up to discharge Woldski who stood up as well, tucked the register under his arm and was about to salute and leave but stopped himself. He said, "Lord, may I ask a question?"

"But of course."

"What are you going to do with the Nyctalope and the others?"

Zattan stiffened, his face froze and his eyes flushed with blood. In a hard voice he replied, "Torture. For my Kurds and Kalmyks to have a little fun. Then death."

"When?"

"On the 15th of this month after the council of delegates.

"And until then?"

"Until then, Woldski, the cell and, as you no doubt guessed, Dr. Weilmann's talking device."

"Should I tell the doctor?"

"No, Woldski, you and I will work it together in secret so we will hear them alone."

"Thank you, Lord. I have nothing more. Your orders for the day?"

"Except for putting the prisoners into two cells, nothing but the usual."

"Good day, Lord,"

"See you later, Woldski. Oh, one last thing! You'll be eating lunch with me today along with Dr. Weilmann."

"Oh, Lord!" Swollen with pride, joy and gratitude, Woldski finally left after bowing deeply three times.

Zattan rubbed his hands together. Then he dashed up the stairs to the rooms of Sylvie Mac Duhl but before entering he pressed several buttons on a control panel...

CHAPTER X

Leonid Zattan burst into Sylvie's bedroom, but he stopped short. The bed, with all its luxurious lace covers, was standing in the brightness of all the lights turned on. There was no sign of life anywhere around it. In the adjoining bathroom and water-closet, not a sound. Zattan knew that on Woldski's orders no servant should have been in the rooms at this hour. The order was that they wait for a call. The lieutenant-secretary had correctly figured that the Prince would prefer to be alone with the girl when she woke up. This was all told to Zattan by Ali-Soud and he approved. But all the more reason why Sylvie should have been lying in her bed in the dress she wore the night before, a very simple tennis dress.

He called out loud, which reverberated through his whole being, "Sylvie! Sylvie!"

Silence.

Leonid Zattan dashed from here to there. The interior shutters were all closed, but the lamps and lights of the walls and ceiling were all lit. From one corner to another he searched. No one. Everything was in order like it was the day before when Sylvie came back from her walk on the ramparts and was asked by Woldski to go to the hangar.

Nobody. Nothing. The doors to the rooms were all closed and locked. Zattan turned pale. He suppressed his fear and rage and forced his mind to stay calm, although it boiled over with countless hypotheses. In the sitting room he grabbed the telephone and called Woldski and Ali-Soud.

He paced impatiently while waiting for them. On the phone he had ordered them to pass through his own rooms and come up by the interior stairs. He heard their double footsteps and they showed up together. On seeing the Prince's fierce and anguished face, they froze. But the dark, hard voice shook them out of it right away.

"Woldski, tell me again how you brought the sleeping Sylvie Mac Duhl here last night. How'd you leave her? How'd you close the doors? Were the lights on and the shudders closed? Tell me everything and leave out no details."

In a cold, clear voice the officer gave his brief but thorough report, keeping his calm.

"That's fine," Zattan said. "Ali-Soud, your turn! What'd you do last night after I went to bed. Speak up!"

And it was weird. The longer Ali-Soud spoke, the more he lost his composure. By the end of his report he was babbling. But he said nothing new. That morning, when his master woke up, he had already told him everything.

"Fine," Zattan said again. "But what's bothering you? You saved me, Ali, so you have nothing to fear from me. Tell me. Why are you upset? Did you do something wrong?"

Reassured and encouraged by these words, the Turk straightened up and his face took on his usual fatalistic tranquility. "Lord, I don't know if it was wrong. Nevertheless, a while after you fell asleep, I dozed off too. It'd been a long day, I'd worked hard to clean and shine all your silverware, then the emotion and anguish of the end of the day... In short, I was exhausted. I tried in vain to fight it and with every bead, murmuring the surahs of the Koran, the need for sleep... I fell asleep with the beads in my hand and I must have slept deeply."

"Ali," the Lord of Issyk-Kul interrupted him, "it wasn't wrong. I didn't tell you to stay awake. If that's the cause of your trouble..."

"No, Lord, no!"

"Then what?"

Ali took a deep breath and in a voice trembling with emotion, "When I woke up my beads were gone."

"Huh?"

"I didn't have my beads. They weren't in my hands or on my knees or on the carpet or anywhere in your room. My beads were gone, they'd vanished..."

Not knowing what significance, what consequence this strange incident might have, Zattan and Woldski stared bewildered at the poor butler who kept saying:

"They'd vanished, vanished! I looked everywhere... but it's stupid since they disappeared in my sleep and obviously in my sleep I didn't move from the armchair..."

Then Woldski looked at the Prince as if asking his permission to speak. Zattan nodded.

"Ali-Soud, do you know what somnambulism is?"

"Yes."

"Have you ever suffered from it?"

"No, never."

Woldski threw up his hands and said nothing more.

Silence fell over them.

Finally, Zattan spoke sharply, "Forget about the beads. I called you two, first of all, to hear you out. It's done. Except for the enigma of the vanishing beads, you've told me nothing new. But I also brought you here to tell you this: Sylvie Mac Duhl, whom you, Woldski, put to bed in this room and left after locking all the doors, who was sleeping upstairs here while I and Ali were sleeping below in a room that was also locked... Well, Sylvie Mac Duhl has vanished too!"

"Oh!" Woldski and Ali-Soud looked stunned.

"She's vanished," Zattan went on, still shaking with anger and fighting against it to keep himself from doing something rash. "Come with me and search everywhere."

And he stomped away.

"You put her on the bed, right, Woldski? On the lace sheets? Without touching anything?"

"Yes on the sheets... without touching anything," the secretary stammered.

"She's not here! She could've woken up earlier than Weilmann predicted, went into the other room... No, she's not here. Could she get out? No, the automatic locks only work from the outside. And if she left, she wouldn't lock them again. Could she have gone down through my rooms and left? No, for the same reason... unless, unless..."

Halting both his walk and his talk, Zattan looked at his butler. His eyes were aflame and bloodshot. His voice was hoarse when it utterly slowly, "Unless Ali-Soud opened a door and then came back inside... and she took the beads as a souvenir..."

He had a hideous grin on his face. Woldski was shaking. Ali-Soud opened his mouth wide, squinted his eyes and instinctively clutched his chest with both hands. Suddenly understanding everything, realizing the horror of the dreadful suspicion, he howled and howled, right there, tragic and shocking, he howled in grief. Then, abruptly, his hands fumbled for his belt, pulled out a long knife, held it aloft, then pointed the tip at his heart, vomiting words out of his contorted mouth, "This! To be accused of this! Lord, I must die... die here and now to prove to you..."

The point of the blade disappeared into the fabric of his livery coat and his eyes bulged... but Zattan had jumped. His hands grabbed the poor man's hands, pulled them back, first turned them aside and then snatched away the knife. A little blood welled up in the hole in the coat.

Zattan spat out, "It's all right, Ali, I believe you. Put this weapon away. Forget it... but understand that... Come on, calm down! It's all right! Your reaction affected me. It did me good. Now I'm back to my senses... Woldski, Ali, let's forget this. Let's look at the facts."

He took a deep breath and his voice turned cold as usual.

"Mademoiselle Sylvie Mac Duhl has vanished from here. But she can't leave the castle. We'll look for her and find her. She's a prisoner. And not the only one. Let's go see the other prisoners. Ali-Soud, stay here and search everything, examine the carpets, chairs and curtains. Maybe you'll find a clue. Woldski, follow me."

The Prince was no longer speaking so familiarly with his lieutenant-secretary. This was no longer a matter of passion but of duty. The officer saluted and without a glance at the butler, he followed his chief.

They went down the interior stairs. In his own rooms, Zattan quickly changed out of his pajamas and into pants and a dolman military jacket and tan leather boots. He put on gloves, slipped a Browning into his right pants pocket, grabbed a tie, threw on a Persian fur cap and went back into the studio where Woldski was waiting. He ordered, "To the prisons!"

The prison area at Issyk-Kul consisted of two bunkers dug into the rock or rather built out of natural caves next to the lake. The east bunker contained the "local offenders" from the garrison. The west bunker held the rooms, cells, dungeons and pits for prisoners from the outside. The two bunkers were separated by a three-room guardhouse and quarters for the head guard. This building and some of the rooms in the bunkers looked out on the lake through barred windows dug out of the rock itself. The cells and dungeons only got daylight from the lake through narrow slits, natural clefts in the rock. The pits had no outlets except for the trapdoor that the condemned were tossed through.

The six prisoners from the day before (April 5th) were locked up in cells 3 to 8 in the west bunker. (Cells 1 and 2 had been occupied for months by two bigwigs from Karakol who had the desire, not well enough guarded by themselves or their cohorts, to become a little Bolshevik and Soviet.)

The head guard, a Kurd named Djelmal, welcomed the High Lord in full military fashion. He grabbed the keys himself and led the way for the grand visitor and his secretary while the two guards, carrying iron rods in their right hands, followed at a respectful distance.

Thanks to the papers found on them, all the prisoners had been identified. Woldski named them. Cell 3—first mate Yves Lequic; 4—engineer Jean Bonnet; 5—helmsman Andre Blanchard.

"Why aren't they together in one cell like I ordered?" Zattan asked.

"I was about to do it when Your Excellency called me back to the girl's rooms."

"All right."

Lying on a straw mattress on one side of the cell, Lequic, Bonnet and Blanchard were still asleep, conked out by Weilmann's strong narcotic. A brown blanket was covering half their bodies.

Cell 6—Captain Marc Ayol; 7—the Japanese Gnô Mitang. They were sleeping like the three sailors under brown blankets.

Zattan said, "The three sailors in one cell with three mattresses. But Gnô Mitang and Marc Ayol, my dear Woldski, you can put in room 15, which is the most comfortable and, if I'm not mistaken, has three beds.

"Yes, Lord."

"Along with Leo Saint-Clair the Nyctalope, whom we're about to see."

These words were spoken in a tone and backed by a look that would have sent shivers down the spines of heroes.

The head guard opened cell 8 and stepped aside like he had done in the other cells. Leonid Zattan stepped inside, followed by Woldski.

"Karakov!" Zattan swore and clenched his fists.

"Huh? What is it?"

Woldski took a step forward, Djemal two steps. Together they saw the whole cell, top to bottom, back to front, the straw mattress, the stool, the clay jar, everything but Saint-Clair. No sign of the Nyctalope, nothing!

But there was someone else. In the corner to the right of the door, a big, tall man was sitting on the floor, his eyes open, his mouth gagged, his arms behind his back and his ankles bound.

"Stoffmann!" Woldski groaned.

It was, indeed, Lieutenant Stoffmann, the giant who the night before, after the narcotic dinner, had carried Pedro del Campo, i.e. the Nyctalope, from the dining room to this cell in the west bunker. Here, in the corner, Stoffmann was only half-dressed, with no boots and a pile of clothes at his feet.

The morning sun, still midway up the sky over Lake Issyk-Kul, cast its rays through the barred slits. Recently whitewashed (since grime was tolerated only in the pits), the cell was bright. The visitors, therefore, saw everything in detail.

Pale with rage, struggling to keep his calm, Zattan ordered, "Untie him!"

Woldski and the head guard got to work. When he was ungagged and unbound, Stoffmann stood up. He looked ridiculous but all the more tragic to the three men peering at him.

Zattan ordered again, "Djelmal, go back to the guardhouse with your men. Leave the keys with Lieutenant Woldski."

The head guard was trembling with terror. Wasn't he ultimately responsible? He handed over the ring of keys, saluted and left, grabbing his two subordinates by the arm on his way out.

"Woldski," Zattan went on, "close the door. Good. Now, for you, Stoffmann, talk."

The giant had taken the time to recover his composure. He stood stiffly in his corner. Without moving a muscle, looking glum, he spoke.

"I carried the man the lieutenant had pointed to in the dining room. At the guardhouse my comrades and I, under the command of the colonel, who had just come from taking Petrus Ivitch to his room, we searched the sleeping prisoners and we gave the colonel everything we found. Then we all picked up our load. The colonel opened the cells. I was in the back. I had to go a little farther. As I was putting the guy on the mattress, he grabbed my neck with both hands. I barely had time to react to the surprise fight. I got all tensed up, really painful, I was choking... And I must've passed out. When I came to, I was lying here, bound and gagged with the cut-up blanket. They were so tight I couldn't snap them or wriggle out of them or nothing. My uniform, my boots, my cap, knife and gun were all gone... and that's it, Lord."

Leonid Zattan knew this officer very well. He couldn't doubt his loyalty nor his courage nor the truth of his tale. "Fine," he was still pale and still in control of himself. "Stay here, Stoffmann. I'll send Woldski back with clothes and weapons for you. Then you can leave, close the door and give the keys back to

Djelmel. And you'll go back on duty as if nothing happened. But on your life, not a word of this to anyone. Give him the key to cell 8, Woldski."

Without another word Zattan left. In the bunker's guardhouse he made a sweeping gesture to all the guards who disappeared into the corridors of the prison. To the terrorized head guard, "Djelmel, on your life, not a word of any of this. Your two men with you, do you they know the prisoner? Answer!"

"Yes... yes, Lord. They heard and saw..."

"Did they talk with the others?"

"No, Lord."

"They're dead if they do. Tell them so. You have five prisoners instead of six. Or rather they brought in only five last night, got it?"

"Yes, Lord."

"Good." Once they were in the courtyard of the bunkers Zattan barked at Woldski, "You're going to start the search. For the castle, a state of siege right away. Send to me, one by one, every five minutes, the 11 officers, including Stoffmann and Karal Bey... finally, everyone you alerted yesterday. We have to find Sylvie and the Nyctalope seeing that they can't have left the castle."

And this was true. Orders were such, and so strictly observed, that leaving the castle without knowing the two daily passwords, without having a written pass and without being seen and questioned by the guard at the drawbridge was a truly impossible exploit, for "Pedro del Campo" just as much as for Sylvie Mac Duhl. Therefore, the two missing persons were within the castle walls. They would look for them. They would find them. For Zattan and Woldski there was doubt about this.

Yes!

But the Prince's inquiries and the lieutenant-secretary's search, then the corroborating investigation by Zattan and Woldski, then the visits and inspections of the buildings, storehouses, barracks and weapons rooms, then the calls and call-backs, then a drill for tracking escaped prisoners that dispatched 200 hunters into every nook and cranny of Issyk-Kul—all this filled the castle with monumental activity, but all this produced no results.

When the curfew bell rang on April 6th, Zattan, Woldski and Ali-Soud had found neither Sylvie Mac Duhl nor Saint-Clair the Nyctalope nor the Islamic beads. And they knew nothing more than they had in the morning.

Zattan couldn't sleep that night. He kept searching, not by material means but in his mind. He found nothing. When the morning call sounded, he dozed off, exhausted, into a world of nightmares.

He was startled awake by a touch on the shoulder. He jumped out of the armchair in which his fatigue had dropped him and saw his lieutenant-secretary standing in front of him, rings around his eyes, jaw clenched and flushed with anger, maybe fear too.

"What? What is it? What's happened?" Zattan growled, fully awake now.

"Lord," Woldski panted softly, "I've just found Djelmel in the corridor of the west bunker along with the two guards... bound and gagged. And... and... Gnô Mitang and Marc Ayol are no longer in their cells."

This time the Lord of Issyk-Kul could not contain himself. In a fit of frantic rage he snatched up the first thing he saw in reach—a bronze statue. He brandished it, howling, and threw it across the room. It struck a three-pronged lamp whose tinted crystal tulips were shattered.

The action and the noise calmed the Prince's nerves a little bit. He managed to get hold of himself by stomping from one end of the room to the other, swearing and shouting, biting his fists, pounding them on the furniture... Woldski stood still, waiting. He had seen these kinds of fits before. He knew that he shouldn't move or speak and that the wisest thing to do was to pretend, later, that he'd seen and heard nothing.

Gradually, Zattan calmed down. Gradually, his muscles relaxed, his nerves "died down" and this mind went back to working normally. He was red, his forehead covered in sweat, his eyes so bloodshot that even in his red face they looked like two open wounds in which his pupils sparkled.

One, two minutes of silence, of anticipation. Finally, the dreaded Lord could speak. His voice was piercing, metallic.

"Report, Woldski!"

What the lieutenant-secretary said was just a string of useless words after what he'd already said. Briefly: Djelmel and the two guards on night duty had been overpowered by unknown attackers. Gnô Mitang and Marc Ayol, just like Ali's beads, Sylvie Mac Duhl and the Nyctalope, had disappeared without a trace.

"In Issyk-Kul! In my castle! With me here!" Zattan yelled.

Was he about to fall into another fit of demented rage? No! He controlled himself, went to sit in the armchair behind the worktable. He pointed to a big leather armchair four of five feet in front and spoke in a normal voice.

"Woldski, sit down." Then, simply, "It's a mystery, Woldski. We have to solve it with our intelligence. Nevertheless, we'll use all material means at our disposal. But especially our wits, Woldski, our wits!"

During one full hour the two men talked. Point by point they examined the facts of the five-fold problem, or rather four-fold because the disappearance of Ali's beads was immediately set aside as insignificant in comparison to the human disappearances.

Once again, the question of leaving the castle was only posed as a formality. The order for a state of siege, by reinforcing the defenses and multiplying the precautions, made it impossible. On the other hand, this same order had tripled the guards, the rounds, the sentinels. Night duty in the bunker had quadrupled, the watchmen, in pairs, were replaced every half hour. The guards bound and gagged with Djelmel must not have put up a fight or made a sound because it was unlikely that the 14 guards in the guardhouse had all been sleeping during the half hour it happened.

Accomplices? One or more traitors in the garrison?

"I don't think so," Zattan said. "The troops? I know all the officers and all the men by name. The mass of servants is made up of mostly unthinking, ignorant slaves and they couldn't take twenty steps outside their particular section without being stopped by the soldiers on duty. I also know the heads of the staff by name along with their personal histories before coming here to the castle."

"Besides," Woldski offered, "no one—officers, soldiers, servants and their chiefs—knows what or how important is your global mission. No one knows about Mathias Lumen except Ivitch, Guerro and Weilmann. But the two sick men haven't left their rooms, the first barely conscious and the second still in a deep sleep. Weilmann checks them every three hours and the nurses are watching them. Weilmann is as trustworthy as me and Ali. And everyone, even these three, knows that the present peace is due to you and you alone and future wealth, power and pleasure depend on you. Plus, everyone knows what horrific death awaits anyone even thinking about betrayal. No one knows about Lumen, about the power, only potential, of course, of your enemies. How, then, could they ever think of betraying you? What's the point?"

"Exactly," Zattan agreed.

"As for the deliveries of food, supplies and mail and the work outside the castle, they are so strictly controlled and watched, so severely regulated and monitored that it's absolutely impossible that the key to the mystery could lie there."

"I think so too."

"So?"

"So, Woldski, let's think and discuss it some more. Have a cigar. Tobacco sometimes inspires... and always calms the nerves if you use it wisely."

For fifteen minutes the two men smoked and pondered without saying a word. They were no longer a prince with absolute power and his humble secretary, but simply two investigators who were pooling their experience, intelligence and various wisdom and ingenuity, struggling to find a solution to a tough and complicated problem, to discover the key to a series of enigmas whose scope, though obscure, was defined by the confines of the castle.

Suddenly, Zattan's voice cut through the silence, "We have to accept as fact that the four missing people haven't left the castle."

"Yes," Woldski said.

"So, they're hiding within the castle walls."

"Without a doubt."

"Where? You and I have known Issyk-Kul from when the deepest of its caves were changed into cellars and storerooms up to the watch tower being built on the central tower. But as much as we searched yesterday, we didn't go everywhere. There was some disorganization, little or no method. We have to organize methodical investigations, divide the castle into sectors, form search parties by sector, each one led by an officer."

"Yes," Woldski approved, "but then there will be no more secrets."

"Obviously." He frowned. He was irritated and a little ashamed to think that there would be endless talk in the castle among the officers, soldiers and servants about the disappearance of the prisoners. He had to admit that some people, more rebellious than others, might have, for the first time, the idea that the Lord of Issyk-Kul, the King of Karakol, the Emperor of Tian Shan was suffering a defeat, in a way.

Of course, there was no prison so well locked up and carefully guarded that prisoners can't escape, but this had never happened at Issyk-Kul.

Boldly, Zattan expressed his objectives.

Woldski nodded while listening. When the Prince had finished, he said, "Yes, of course. But we'll see results. There's no doubt that an organized, coordinated, all-out search will discover the missing persons. The hand will play out and you will be the winner. So, even if some men were a little doubtful during the search, your prestige will only grow afterwards since you will have triumphed over an obstacle so great that you were forced to make it public and ask for the help of all your men."

Woldski's point of view was optimistic and Zattan was too anxious for success not to share his optimism. Still, he didn't show it right away. He took a few puffs off his cigar and pondered some more with his eyes closed. At last, he agreed with what Woldski predicted and what the circumstances demanded.

"It's decided," he threw his cigar into a brass bowl serving as an ashtray. "Let's get to work at once. Pull your chair up closer and let's divide up the castle into sectors and assign officers for each at the same time."

The work took the two men until noon.

Ali-Soud had come back as usual to present the day's menu from which the Prince chose the dishes he wanted for lunch and dinner. Zattan added, "Yesterday I'd invited Weilmann and Woldski to lunch with me. That lunch will be today. In half an hour, Ali-Soud! In my dining room, of course. No one else present. You alone will be serving." And being a good sport, with a slight smile, "No news about the beads?"

"No, Lord, no," the butler answered sadly.

"All right," the master replied, "I hope they'll turn up soon."

Waving Ali out of the room, he started in with Woldski on reviewing the work they wanted to accomplish. 30 minutes later, Ali-Soud was back with Weilmann and announcing that lunch was served.

The three men went into the dining room where Zattan shared his plans with Weilmann and how they would be organized. It was only then that Weilmann learned of the extraordinary disappearances.

He had suspected that something strange had happened over the last 36 hours and didn't hide the fact that in the officers' mess there was some unrest, whispering, shifty looks expressing a kind of uncertainty in some of them, an uncertainty that is an unheard-of new phenomenon at Issyk-Kul that he, Weilmann, had never seen before.

Zattan thoroughly trusted Weilmann who, besides being a rather mysterious scientist and philosopher when it came to his own feelings, had always held himself above the routine problems. He was, like Petrus Ivitch, an original, almost independent character on the fringes of the garrison.

In brief, Zattan was thinking of calling another war council consisting of only four men: himself, of course, then Woldski, Weilmann and Petrus Ivitch. As for Karal Bey, the commanding officer of the garrison, the Prince considered him an excellent soldier but only fit for following orders and utterly incapable of real leadership.

In fact, this lunch was the first meeting, except for Ivitch, of the tiny but all-powerful general staff.

All the measures planned and organized in the morning by Zattan and Woldski were, so to speak, heartily approved by Weilmann. He made only one objection, already considered by Zattan, about the drawbacks of revealing some of the strange affairs they were involved in. So, Woldski repeated his optimistic argument and Weilmann conceded.

After dessert and coffee the three men got up and went into the study where Zattan finalized his decision so they could start right away on executing the plan. Colonel Karal Bey and all the officers appointed as sector chiefs were immediately summoned to the conference room, which was on the ground floor of the south tower.

The conference on April 7th, presided over by the Prince in person, had only one speaker—Woldski. Of course, of the events in question he told only what was strictly necessary for the officers to accomplish their mission. So as not to sow the seeds of unwanted suspicions in certain minds, he didn't ask the officers to keep anything secret from their men. He specified for them the complete system of organizing the sectors for the search.

"Officers and soldiers will be supplied with cold meals so that they can eat and drink on the spot at the standard time and only break off their search for half an hour. When the curfew sounds, they'll stay in place and spend the night. The officers won't have to worry about watches because the night patrols will be dealt with by others, to be assigned later, who will patrol the castle all night long."

When the lieutenant-secretary had finished giving these special instructions and supplied each officer with a small map of the sectors and, lastly, in the name of the Prince, appointed Karal Bey as head inspector to oversee all activity during the search, he said, "Messieurs, if any one of you has an objection to make or an idea to express, don't hesitate. Our Prince is here to listen to anything that might contribute to the success of the endeavor."

And he sat down.

Right away, it was clear that no one was going to say a word. At the start of his speech almost all the faces looked utterly stunned. A few, however, stayed firm, with an ironic twinkle in their eyes as if they had already guessed or maybe even knew what this was all about.

Then, as Woldski was speaking, the faces slowly became more dutiful as it were—soldiers receiving orders they would obey unquestioningly.

Coldly, calmly, Zattan and Woldski waited five minutes. When no one stood up to voice an objection or share an idea, Zattan stood up and in the firm, authoritarian voice that everyone knew, he said:

"Thank you, messieurs. Colonel, please do what needs to be done with Woldski so that the search can start at 3 pm. It will continue until its goals are accomplished. Woldski has my orders for the measures to take in case the search has to go on for several days. It's possible because to be meticulous and thorough, we have to work slowly and you know that the buildings, courtyards, gardens and cellars of Issyk-Kul, even though they can fit on a map, they're hundreds of acres to cover. And there are nooks and crannies, stairs and corridors, so many rooms that the missing persons might sneak in front of or behind the search parties, hide and then double back... So, let's expect the worst and plan to be out there for days. But short or long, it will succeed.

"I know that your sense of duty doesn't need to be motivated, but still, it's part of my philosophy of life that every effort crowned with success be rewarded. In life, luck is a virtue no less positive or profitable than good intentions. Therefore, I'll tell you that every prisoner represents a bonus of 10,000 piastres to be shared equally between the officer and his men who are favored with success."

With that, everyone stood up.

Every hour, as Woldski had instructed, a petty officer from each sector came to give a report that was forwarded to the Lord of Issyk-Kul. When the curfew sounded, the sum of all these reports was negative. They had seen nothing, heard nothing, found nothing, not a single trace of the missing.

The night shift followed the day shift.

All the electric lights in the castle were turned on, except for the very back of the cellars containing ammunition and powder up to the back of the cellars with stocks of wine and alcohol. The courtyards were bright and the constant, countless rounds of men with guns in hand made them as busy all night long as during the day.

Nevertheless, the buildings and walls surrounding the castle had so many angles that some places got only indirect light or none at all. Still, they were never completely dark because the light was diffused throughout the atmosphere and to some degree spread like the air itself into the darkest corners of the castle.

The big clock on the tower had just struck 4 am on April 8th when Ali-Soud became the hero of his very personal adventure!

Very tired, as to be expected, he had gone to bed early after eating alone with his master. At first, he slept deeply, but his agitated mind ran wild when his body got a little rest. That was why he woke up, his eyes wide open and his mind alert, a little after 3 am. He knew he wouldn't be able to get back to sleep, so he got up, dressed and felt a little sluggish. He wanted to get some fresh air. He opened the inside shutters, then the window, then the outside shutters of one of the windows in his second-story bedroom in the building with the south tower at one corner. There was a private hallway connecting his room with the vestibule of the Prince's chambers.

So, Ali-Soud was at the window, which had a stone balcony. He stepped out, leaned on the railing and after contemplating the star-studded sky for a few minutes, he looked down into the small courtyard lit up by lights on the doors of the low building across from him. Behind these doors were the stables housing the Prince's personal horses.

A patrol passed by, coming from the right and disappearing to the left at the corner of the stables. All of a sudden Ali had a start. He leaned over, rubbing his eyes and coughing out an emotional appeal, "By Allah! Am I dreaming? Is it a hallucination? Is this vision about to vanish?"

For 30 seconds he was enraptured before he yelped and stumbled back into his bedroom, then ran to open the door, scramble down the stairs, push a secret button that opened the outside door and rushed into the courtyard, immediately turning to his right. He stopped short, squatted down, then turned around to approach the wall of the stables more slowly. And there, right away, in the bright light, both dazed and delighted, he stared at the object he'd seen from his balcony. He picked it up and was holding it now in his hands...

His beads!

It was the long string of yellow amber beads that the pious Ali used for murmuring the surahs of the Koran.

"My beads! My beads!"

After turning them over, fingering them, tossing them up in the air, he kissed them and hung them around his neck. Then mumbling his heartfelt thanks to Allah, Ali-Soud walked slowly back to his room. The door of the building was protected by a very wide, very steep awning that was situated lower than the facing lights so that a dark shadow fell over the three steps leading up to the door. Ali-Soud took these three, dark steps slowly because his mind was waffling between surprise and joy at his find. And he wondered how the missing beads could miraculously turn up right after the patrol passed by, on the very ground it had marched over. His deep ad fervent concentration slowed his steps. But when he got in front of the half-closed door, where the shadow was darkest, Ali stopped again and stood frozen for a full minute.

At last, shrugging his shoulders with a silent admission of powerlessness, he went in, closed the door and reset the secret lock before going back up to his room.

Of course, the matter of going back to bed was out of the question. On the contrary, he was eager to see someone. Not just anyone but Leonid Zattan or at least Woldski to tell him about his extraordinary find. Therefore, he left his room almost immediately, telling himself, "Woldski is usually up very early. Today more than ever. Maybe even the Lord is up? I can't wait any longer to tell them what happened."

He was pleased to run into Woldski in the Prince's vestibule, sitting on a stool, legs crossed, smoking a cigar as calm as could be. At this hour of the morning? Yes, because the lieutenant-secretary, the big smoker, took advantage of every free moment to give his passion a little relief, which he could only do at times when the duty roster was fully organized and Zattan was busy or absent.

Almost right after Ali-Soud entered the brightly lit vestibule Woldski stood up and pointed his left index finger at the butler's chest. "Hey, hey, Ali-Soud, the beads? Really your beads? The ones that disappeared or different ones?"

Smiling, triumphant, the Turk replied, "They're the ones that disappeared. There are marks that make them unique. It would take months to make a bad imitation. These are certainly my beads."

Without waiting for any more questions, he told how he found them.

Woldski was worn out and tired but he felt his whole body, his whole being, buoyed up and filled with energy. He listened to Ali's moving tale and then, "You came to tell the Prince?"

"Yes."

"Right, wait here with me. He's sleeping or doesn't want company since the light's still on."

He pointed to the red light with a green cross over the door.

"All right, I'll wait, just like you, I guess?"

"Just like me."

The two men went to sit down. By chance Ali was ahead of Woldski. He felt a strong grip on his shoulder and Woldski spoke behind him.

"Hey, pal, what's on your back? Paper... a piece of paper pinned there. Hold on so I can read it."

But Ali-Soud swung around instinctively and the piece of paper ripped off the pin, left in the hand of the lieutenant-secretary. Side by side, the two men read the brief note written in black ink in big letters.

"*Soon I will make Leonid Zattan vanish too. The Nyctalope.*"

It's impossible to describe the stupefaction, the anger and even the deep, dark, irresistible fear that took hold of the two men for a few minutes. They just stood there staring at the paper.

Ten, twenty times they reread those dreadful words. Finally, by some kind of mental telepathy, the same questions came to their minds at the same time.

"How? Where? Who?"

They quickly came up with some easy answers, which they shared, and Woldski concluded by summing up, "It was when you stopped at the door of your building. You were in the shadows where someone could have hidden while you were getting the beads. Then, when you stopped, you were probably too preoccupied to hear their breathing and they pinned the note on your coat."

Fifteen minutes later Leonid Zattan was hearing the story of the beads and reading the note. Of course, the Kalmyk had lost nothing of his tendency to violent fits of rage, but the physical and mental conditions of his life over the past three days had tempered him so that he could resist his emotions with a more than ordinary detachment.

The episode of the beads quickly faded before the paper with the short note. The cold rage seething inside him was so deep that for a long moment he couldn't say a word. Woldski and Ali-Soud stood before him, side by side, waiting, trembling.

Finally, with little, jerky movements that betrayed his inner struggle, Zattan folded the note and slipped it into a wallet that he had taken out of his dolman jacket (the Prince had put on his horse-riding outfit when he got up in the morning). He slowly buttoned up his jacket and then shot the two men a cold, piercing glare like a steel dagger.

"Not a word of this! Not a word to anyone!"

Futile orders!

In fact, at the wake-up bell Woldski started on his usual rounds but he stopped in the first courtyard at the sight of a piece of paper nailed to a door. He walked up and read it:

"Soon I will make Leonid Zattan vanish too. The Nyctalope."

He tore it off and stuffed it into a pocket. But 200 yards farther down, on the trunk of a tree, he saw an exact copy. And he ran into Karal Bey who was silent and pale when he showed him the note he'd found a few yards away.

The two men made the official rounds together and in a short time they understood that there were at least 100 of these notes with the same threat, all signed the Nyctalope, posted in different parts of the castle.

Already every single soldier, officer or servant knew about the phenomenon. One of the prisoners they were searching for was called "the Nyctalope" and he dared to threaten Leonid Zattan with making him vanish in his own castle! No, everyone at Issyk-Kul knew about it because the notes were not written in the same language. The extraordinary threat was made in French, English, Russian, German, Italian, Spanish, Turkish, Arabic and Chinese!

From here on out, the atmosphere in Issyk-Kul was completely changed.

The sector-by-sector search started up again and continued all day long on April 8th. With no results. The two most recent mysteries, the discovery of Ali's beads and the Nyctalopian threats, provided no clues to clear anything up.

Zattan didn't show himself. But in the evening after curfew a very worried Woldski gave him a strange report that can be summed up thus: "the garrison is restless; rumors are spreading; there are some cynical grins; among all the search parties, in the guardhouse, with the servants, everywhere, we can't deny that the seeds have been sown for a lot of talk and maybe even insubordination."

That night passed without any new incident to trouble the already ruffled minds.

But during the hours of insomnia, interrupted by deep but short naps, the Lord of Issyk-Kul had ruminated on a counter-attack. It took the form of a hastily printed poster (the castle had its own print shop) hung in every place where the Nyctalope's note had been found the day before.

It read: "*In 24 hours, if everything is not back to normal, if the escaped prisoners have not given themselves up, the three French sailors still in prison will be tortured to death. Leonid Zattan.*"

Back to normal? Voluntary surrender and return to the cells? Ah, good, yes. The mysterious Nyctalope answered back and he pulled no punches!

On the morning of April 10th, meaning 24 hours after posting his ultimatum, Zattan noted that Woldski and Ali-Soud weren't answering his calls. An investigation discovered that they'd been abducted from their rooms during the night. Moreover, all the ultimatum posters were covered by another that said:

"*If you touch the three French sailors or even one of them, Woldski and Ali-Soud will be put to death. The Nyctalope.*"

This was too much for the Lord of Issyk-Kul to keep up his artificial attitude by sheer willpower. From now on he couldn't hold back his rage, his anger, his humiliation, his instinct for revenge and savagery, his diabolical pride of always being the all-out winner. And Leonid Zattan became the Kalmyk of the days of war, plunder and carnage.

Right after being sure that Woldski and Ali-Soud had disappeared and were probably as lost as the escaped prisoners, Zattan replaced his assistants. For lieutenant-secretary he took Captain Punjaz and as butler he appointed Yan Ten, whom he had noticed among his personal servants and whom Ali-Soud held in high respect. Punjaz was a Hindu and Yan Ten an Annamite from Vietnam.

Once these two men had been publicly inducted into their respective services, Zattan made another announcement that the three French sailors were to be executed at 2 pm.

On making this decision, which he related coldly to Punjaz and Karal Bey, the Lord finished with, "Colonel, muster the entire garrison, everyone except the guards on duty. The sailors will be shot."

Silence, then harder than ever, his whole being strained to breaking point:

"If the Nyctalope is strong enough, Woldski and Ali-Soud will be killed in the hideout where my enemy has defied me for four days. I'm fond of Woldski and Ali-Soud. I'll suffer from their death like losing brothers-in-arms on the battlefield. But I know them. They would be the first to sacrifice themselves if it served to make my cause triumphant. Colonel, you will soon find out how grand is my cause, which belongs to you and millions of men, and how worthy it is of sacrifice. Woldski and Ali-Soud will be forever honored in our annals."

Certainly, it was a pretty speech. Colonel Karal Bey was moved to tears—his warrior eyes lost their metallic gleam for a few seconds. The Hindu Punjaz showed no emotion, but he obviously approved because he was a merciless character. Besides, succeeding Woldski was a boost to his ambition, which he didn't show on the outside but it was insatiable.

"Go on, Colonel," Zattan said, "make all the necessary arrangements for the public execution of the prisoners."

Nonetheless, the sector searches were still operating throughout the castle. Most had already gone over every inch of their sector several times. But if Zattan could have been an invisible presence during the work, he would have been surprised and even terrified.

The spirit of the men, and so of the conversations and some insubordination, was making what Woldski had called "horrible ravages" in the garrison. There were men mocking their work and not at all shy about criticizing its foolishness with open insolence, to which the officers turned a deaf ear.

If Leonid Zattan had been able to see without being seen, he would have noticed that here and there, in the corners of some buildings, in the back of a cellar or behind a stack of boxes in a storeroom, men were huddled together, whispering, swearing, or giggling. Some groups, on the other hand, were displaying an odd flurry of activity and what was worse, there were only three or four officers who hinted at this strange state of mind in their reports. But this state of mind should have been a telltale sign.

When the whole garrison found out about the Prince's decision to execute the three French sailors, the least intelligent worker and slave could see the consequences of this decision. Based on the last note from the mysterious Nyctalope, the execution of the sailors would be followed (nobody doubted it) by the death of Woldski and Ali-Soud. Well, both of them were adored by the garrison and the servants.

Woldski was always fair, often being called on as mediator between officers and just as often exempted many men from certain rigors (probably too excessive) of the Issyk-Kul military code. As for Ali-Soud, the services he rendered, speaking to the Lord on behalf of some of the men and officers, had earned him the affection and gratitude of the castle. These sentiments, which Zattan hadn't even imagined, quickly materialized, troubled him and convinced him that something had changed in his "kingdom".

He was sitting down to eat alone, served by Yan Ten and two Circassians when the phone on the table rang. He picked it up. "Hello, I'm listening!"

He heard, "Hello, Lord? The officers mess here... Karal Bey speaking. I believe I'm doing my duty by telling you that all the officers, under pressure by their men, had formed a delegation of six captains and lieutenants. This delegation is asking to see Your Lordship at once."

The voice on the phone went quiet.

Of course, during his turbulent, often tragic life, Leonid Zattan, Prince of Issyk-Kul, King and Tyrant of Tian Shen, had seen and heard many things that had hardened him against emotions. But this time, it was too much.

In his moments of pessimism, especially over the last 48 hours, Zattan could picture the worst before capturing Saint-Clair the Nyctalope, but the blackest, gloomiest pessimism had not imagined what was happening at the moment, i.e. a kind of soviet movement in Issyk-Kul, secret meetings among the men, pressure on the officers from the troops and the officers uniting in a soviet, forming a delegation to come to him, even getting the colonel to announce it!

It was crazy, unbelievable! So unbelievable and so crazy that Zattan couldn't really, truly accept the reality of it.

After a moment's hesitation, he broke out laughing. "Come on, Karal, are you joking? Are you feeling all right? Or have you drunk so much it's gone to your head? Is this really you talking or some idiot imitating your voice?"

"Hello, Lord, the delegation is right here next to me. Their spokesman tells me that they shouldn't be kept waiting if you want to avoid a mutiny in part of the garrison. Many soldiers, even some officers, and a lot of the servants are ready for anything to stop the execution that will result in the death of Woldski and Ali-Soud... Hello?... I have the honor and the regret to inform you that I can, in no way, oppose the deplorable attitude of the officers except by violence, which will provoke retaliation and I will be the first victim... Hello?... The delegation has left and is heading for the south tower. I'll run over so I can die by your side if..."

The Prince heard nothing more. Someone must have snatched the phone out of the colonel's hand.

Livid, Zattan stood up. He couldn't doubt it now. But his natural courage, his unyielding personality compelled him to face every danger and challenge it with fury or calm depending on the circumstances. Which put the Prince in his studio, sitting in his armchair behind his work table, when, with his spoken permission, his lieutenant-secretary Punjaz let in first Colonel Karal Bey and right behind him, on his heels so to speak, the delegation of six captains and lieutenants.

The colonel hurried over to stand beside his master and in a simple but significant gesture he put his right hand on the butt of his Browning, which hung from his belt.

The six officers stood in the middle of the huge room in a front line, heels snapped together in strictly military fashion. The one at the right of the line, none other than Lieutenant Stoffmann, stepped forward, saluted and waited.

Staring at the blond giant whose gesture obviously meant he would be the spokesman for the delegation, Zattan gave him one of those glares that few men could endure. But the lieutenant's blue eyes didn't waver or blink.

"This is certainly going to be serious," Zattan thought to himself.

He remembered the time during the Great War when he had defied his general a few hours before deserting the Turkish army and setting himself up as the undisputed head of a troop of partisans, a small group of officers and rebels. He had succeeded.

But at present, faced with this memory, he thought proudly, "Yes! But I was better than this Stoffmann and my general was not Leonid Zattan!"

He met the challenge directly. Showing no emotion he said sharply, "Messieurs, I've just been informed by your colonel that you wish to speak to me. I'm listening."

Of course, the lieutenant was nervous, but his emotion, obvious from the pallor of his face, was barely detectable in this voice. He lowered his salute and spoke slowly but firmly:

"Lord, the lives of the three French soldiers imprisoned in the west bunker mean nothing to any of us, but that's not the case for the lives of Woldski and Ali-Soud. If their sacrifice were to solve the mysteries, to once and for all clear up the enigmas that have haunted the castle for four days, I'm sure they would be proud to sacrifice themselves. There's no one of us who wouldn't gladly pour out all the blood in our veins under such conditions. But that's not the case here. All we know about these enigmatic mysteries is that they're the work of a man whose reputation is universal—the Nyctalope!

"Your enemy, Lord, is not a rogue named Pedro del Campo or an old salt called Marco Pampil or even a Japanese however dangerous he might be seeing that he could take over Ivitch's plane without a shot fired. Despite their exploits they are, after all, only ordinary men and no better than many of us. But the Nyctalope, Lord! Right or wrong, fear has infiltrated the garrison, the fear that it's not a fair match between the Nyctalope and Leonid Zattan and in the end Zattan will lose."

At this last statement, which Stoffmann uttered with his whole body quivering, Zattan jumped up. A crazed impulse flung him at Stoffmann. But Stoffmann stood stiffly, his chest out, making his giant stature even bigger. He was like a impregnable cliff facing a storm-tossed wave. The storm-tossed wave here was a man endowed with keen eyes and a strong mind. So, once again, the Kalmyk managed to control himself.

He stopped, went back to his chair and in a sarcastic tone, "I see, Lieutenant Stoffmann, that you don't trust my destiny anymore. So be it! This kind of moral treason will be dealt with at the appropriate time. But go on because, obviously, you haven't finished your speech."

"No, Lord," the brave lieutenant replied without insolence but with purpose. After a short pause, he went on, "Lord, I've been overpowered by the Nyctalope, by two bare hands without weapons, me who no man has ever beaten physically. This first victory has been repeated for 96 hours against you. The men know it, see it, talk about it. They're not disloyal to you yet. They don't think about revolt yet. Not one of them has turned his weapon against you yet.

261

Us officers, if we wish to stay loyal to you, will be the first victims of the violence. No, there's no mutiny yet or even thought of revolt.

"Lord, if you can get together a firing squad from your Kalmyks that won't hesitate to shoot the sailors on your order, this same squad will be either completely wiped out before firing a shot or savagely massacred after the execution. There will be a fierce battle in Issyk-Kul between most of the garrison backed up by the servants against your officers and the few men who remain loyal to you."

Zattan didn't let this go unanswered, "Loyal!" he shouted. "The officers! Am I to believe that you six here and the comrades you represent..."

"Yes, Lord, yes," Stoffmann cut him off. "Yes, in spite of everything and even against the Nyctalope, we will be loyal to you. But if you don't want us, between 2 and 4 pm, to die beside you with a small number of men against the vast majority of the garrison, stop the execution order you gave, which will reassure the men about the fate of Woldski and Ali-Soud. On this condition alone will the sector search continue and the state of seige at Issyk-Kul will be respected. As for the fight against the Nyctalope, well, Lord, it will turn out as fate wills it or rather as the Nyctalope decides. We feel all the more honorable, I dare say, to solemnly renew our oaths of loyalty to you."

In a magnificent gesture, Stoffman raised his right arm, his hand open, and looking his comrades in the eyes, pronounced, "My friends, in our name and in the name of all the officers we represent, we swear to fight and vanquish or die with Prince Leonid Zattan, our chief!"

The five officers raised their right arms and in unison, loud and clear, they declared, "We swear it!"

This scene, which started as a mutiny and ended with the most courageous and noble affirmation of loyalty, this scene was more troubling than touching to Zattan.

Much of what had been said had been very humiliating to him but still didn't convince him of his so-called inferiority to Saint-Clair the Nyctalope. This humiliation, at least for the moment, was pretty much negated by their oath of loyalty.

After all, what Zattan wanted was not to spill the blood of three worthless sailors whose life or death meant less than nothing to him, but to wage the supreme battle, with a chance of victory, against the Nyctalope. This battle was about to enter a new phase. He would lead it in person. He would have all the officers and all his men behind him. And they would be all the more fanatical and grateful to him for saving the lives, as they wanted, of Woldski and Ali-Soud. Therefore, all was not lost. In fact, the chance of success was looking up.

Zattan ran through these thoughts in a matter of seconds. He stood up, turned to Karal Bey and in a benevolent but authoritarian voice ordered, "Colonel, take these officers back so they can resume their duties along with their men under your command. This morning's order is canceled. The three sailors will remain alive in their cells. Thus, the Nyctalope's threat against Woldski and Ali-Soud won't be carried out. But I'm telling all of you, I will blow up Issyk-Kul and bury myself with you under the ruins if the Nyctalope comes out the winner. If victory isn't mine, it'll take three seconds for my enemies and the entire castle to be reduced to bloody rags and a pile of smoking ruins. Go!"

When the officers had left, Zattan stood there for a long time, staring at the frozen folds of the velvet curtain before the door through which Karal Bey was the last to disappear. With his face and eyes reflecting a savage hatred, he growled, "When I'm on top again, they'll pay for today's humiliation."

Since Leonid Zattan was an uninjured, well-tuned human machine, the Lord of Issyk-Kul went back to finish his lunch. An hour later, flanked by Karal Bey and Punjaz, he took control of the searches himself. Inspired with renewed enthusiasm, all the sectors knuckled down as rigorously as ever.

It seemed truly impossible that they hadn't discovered the woman and five men anywhere in the closed castle, especially as one of the men, the strongest so to speak, Saint-Clair the Nyctalope, had left their hiding place several times—to give back Ali's beads and to post his insolent notes and finally to kidnap Woldski and Ali-Soud from their rooms.

But the curfew on April 10th sounded without the search teams marking one point to their credit. The mystery remained unsolved, wholly intact.

Saint-Clair the Nyctalope, Sylvie Mac Duhl, Gnô Mitang, Marc Ayol and Woldski and Ali-Soud had hidden somewhere within the castle walls for days. They'd searched day and night but no one, from Zattan himself down to the low-liest dishwasher of the kitchen slaves, had found the slightest clue to where or how they were living.

Of course, by his former exploits, known throughout the world, and because of his rare ability to see in the dark as if it were the middle of the day, the Nyctalope, "the Master of the Night", was capable of all kinds of miracles! But still...

At times when he realized the shocking gravity of the situation, Leonid Zattan wondered whether he, like a new Oedipus facing a new sphinx, wasn't going to be eaten alive as punishment for his inability to solve the mystery, to explain the enigma...

CHAPTER XI

Now, the loyalty of the officers and some of the department heads did not guarantee the loyalty of all soldiers and servants and slaves. When the chief being talked about doesn't immediately recover his prestige and authority by a daring and victorious feat, the spirit of the talk by underlings quickly degenerates into scorn and ridicule. And if he's not motivated by one of the grand and heroic and selfless sentiments that require faith and sacrifice, the mercenary is all ready to go over to the enemy as long as the enemy shows a little generosity to the defector.

During the days of April 11th and 12th Zattan found no opportunity for a daring move to assure a victory. Nothing because his searches yielded no results. The Nyctalope and Sylvie and the others were utterly untraceable.

Despite Stoffmann's noble speech on behalf of the delegation, it was clear that after the curfew on April 12th many of their colleagues didn't consider themselves duty-bound. It was easy for Karal Bey to see in their attitudes that they and their men were ready to rebel and to declare a mutiny.

It was true that after five days of searching and the state of siege, the officers and soldiers were exhausted. The physical fatigue aggravated their mental turmoil.

Especially on the afternoon of the 12th, Zattan could see for himself the state of mind of the garrison. He got angry about it, but hid his feelings. Still, it urged him to take a precaution that was reckless in the sense that on the one hand, by humiliating the officers, it rankled those who were still loyal in their hearts and on the other hand it revealed publicly that the Lord of Issyk-Kul was scared.

Here is what it was:

Leonid Zattan summoned to the castle fifty men from the Kalmyk cavalry stationed in Karakol. These horsemen were truly savage, attached by tradition (you can say from father to son) to the sovereign princes of Issyk-Kul. Their loyalty would be ironclad and they would be hacked to pieces and beheaded rather than betray an order coming out of the mouth of Leonid Zattan, son of Yark. These fifty cavalry men, led by a captain and two lieutenants, were housed on the ground floor of the building attached to the south tower. They formed Zattan's security detail, his 24-hour bodyguard. They assured his physical safety and security, at least to a certain extent.

Yes, but their presence proved that in the very midst of his castle and his garrison, the Prince didn't feel safe. What an insult to the loyal soldiers! What encouragement to the others who no longer thought their own safety was directly reliant on their chief's.

There was, therefore, a very troubling atmosphere on the morning of April 13th when the wake-up bells rang. The men were grumbling and slow when they got back to their assigned tasks: inventory and checking all the boxes and crates in the storerooms (could the missing people be hiding in partially empty crates? In boxes that only looked full?), tasks that had already been considered to be absolutely ridiculous by everyone.

All of a sudden, a special alarm called the entire garrison into the main courtyard. An order was read to stop the searches. The state of siege was lifted. Only the sentinels, changing often, were to remain posted at the entrances to all the buildings, towers, courtyards and bunkers with orders to detain anyone not wearing a special armband, white or red, stamped with Zattan's mark. These armbands were kept by Zattan himself in one of his chests reserved for exceptional circumstances.

The circumstances had arrived. The previously unknown armbands made their appearance. Of course, the number of armbands corresponded exactly with the number of men and women at the castle. Now all the left arms of the of the garrison, servants and slaves were decorated and under the command of Karal Bey the officers enforced the new order. Thus, they gave up the search and settled on very strict and constant surveillance.

Why? Because something new and very important to Zattan was happening at Issyk-Kul—it was the arrival of the delegates from the Neo-terrorist organizations from around the world.

In fact, this congress of all the delegates presided over by Leonid Zattan was supposed to take place on April 14th. On the 13th, at 9 am, they called from Karakol to say that three delegates had arrived and were being escorted to Issyk-Kul. These first arrivals were the Greek, Bulgarian and Romanian delegates.

The preparations for the crucial congress occupied all the attention and concern of Leonid Zattan because this congress was of global significance whereas "the Nyctalope affair", as Petrus Ivitch called it, not without a little hidden irony, was just an interior, local, minor problem.

For Zattan, the secret chief and sovereign leader of the global revolution, the adversary and enemy was not the Nyctalope but Mathias Lumen. After the congress, the formidable consequences of Zattan's decisions and orders would affect the entire world. The Prince would leave Issyk-Kul. And lighting the fuse of an ever-ready system of mines, he would send the castle crumbling into the lake, even if it meant losing forever the hope of possessing Sylvie Mac Duhl and the "prodigious male" prophesied by Nostradamus regarding the Antichrist.

"As for the bellyachers and deviants," Zattan was thinking of the garrison, "I hope to be leading them in a few days beyond my borders into battle, pillage and massacre... a good old bloodletting will knock some sense back into them, restore their discipline and the fear and love of their Lord!"

Weilmann, Ivitch, Karal Bey and Punjaz, who were listening to him, approved solemnly. They also approved the fifth "advisor", Captain Yeldaz, commander of the Kalmyk cavalry.

So again, on April 13th three delegates arrived: the Greek, Bulgarian and Romanian. Before noon five others were announced: the French, Spanish, Italian, English and Belgian. Then a trio: the German, Scandinavian and West Russian (Moscow).

Coming on horseback or on a litter from Karakol, escorted by Kalmyks, the revolutionary delegates were welcomed by Weilmann, Ivitch and Punjaz in the main courtyard, a few feet from the portcullis that was the third line defense of the drawbridge. After the greetings, Punjaz led the delegates to their individual, luxuriously furnished rooms in the central building of the castle.

And more delegates came after. The East Russian (Irkutsk), the Turkish, Arabian, Persian and Hindu came in a group. Then the three black delegates from vast Africa. On the morning of the 14th, the Mongol, Tibetan, Manchu, Chinese and Japanese were shortly afterwards followed by the Dutch and Australian. The delegates from North and South America were the last to arrive a little before noon.

In all, 30 delegates represented all the Neo-terrorist and revolutionary organizations around the globe.

Before lunch, in a lounge adjoining the huge dining room that had been prepared specially for them, the 30 delegates were introduced to one another by lieutenant-secretary Punjaz who showed, in this very delicate situation, as much tact and authority as Woldski would have.

Zattan was in the next room where he could see and hear everything thanks to hidden devices. He thought, "Woldski has been replaced well. This Punjaz is going to make a first-rate secretary."

So, already, the tyrant of Issyk-Kul had forgotten everything he owed to the wisest and most faithful of his collaborators. In his mind, Woldski and Ali-Soud were gone forever. For, the terrible Kalmyk had definitely decided to leave Issyk-Kul the next day for Karakol and blow up the castle if the missing persons had not been found or surrendered before the fateful hour.

To that end, furthermore, in certain parts of the castle where the delegates should have no reason to go he had posted a final ultimatum that bid the Nyctalope to surrender with his companions if they didn't all want to be buried under the ruins of the castle.

The first meal with all the delegates in Issyk-Kul was a simple cold buffet. Since the first and probably only session of the congress was to take place at 2 pm, it was important that the participants not be tired, groggy or sick from eating. With his usual sarcasm Ivitch had said, "the head cold, the belly free and the feet warm".

These three hygienic conditions, to guarantee a perfect congress, were met in the sense that the delegates ate and drank very little at lunch and the meeting room was heated, like all the rooms in the castle, not from the walls but from the floor.

At 2 pm sharp, when all the delegates were in the meeting room, lieutenant-secretary Punjaz pulled back a curtain and announced, "Messieurs, Leonid Zattan!"

There, before these thirty men who, in truth, represented only a consortium of individual interests and ambitions but who claimed to be the delegates of the worldwide proletariat, the regulation hypocrisy, the protocol hypocrisy, so to speak, raised Zattan to the genuine title of prince and to the very real power of absolute sovereign, potentate and tyrant. He was, however, just Leonid Zattan, elected head of the global terrorist organizations.

But no one was fooled. The thirty men gathered there knew very well that the success of the crucial revolution would give Zattan an empire. And they were each of them hoping for one of those honorary positions in which you can play at being almighty, what they call "the people's commissariat" but are, in fact, nothing but dictatorships. It was understood that in the room were only 30 proletarian delegates for all the peoples of the world and a democratic head recognized by these same delegates.

They all formed a semi-circle around a long, narrow, U-shaped table. Between the two ends of the U and facing the middle of the table was a square pedestal in front of an armchair.

At first Zattan made the tour while Punjaz introduced the delegates. He shook each of the 30 hands with the same cordiality. Then he sat in the armchair. Right away all the delegates sat in their own armchairs in front of their name cards on the table with fountain pen and paper.

A phonograph was fitted into the ceiling to record every word of the proceedings. It was better than the best stenographers since there was no risk of making mistakes or missing anything. Manoël Guerro was in charge of working it.

The doors were closed with an armed Kalmyk stationed at each. It was forbidden to enter the room under any pretext. In case the castle needed to get in touch with the room, Punjaz was there to deal with it.

When everyone was seated and each delegate had put his briefcase or satchel or file full of documents on the table, Leonid Zattan sat there for a full minute. Then, slowly raising his right hand, he spoke in French, the language that all the delegates understood.

"Messieurs, the session is open."

What this congress of global Neo-terrorism was, besides one of a kind, will some day be known to historians. The famous, occult meeting will enlarge beyond the mere story that is told here in summary, short and sweet.

It suffices to say that the delegates, in alphabetical order, spoke briefly, clearly, with their documents and numbers as support. When each had finished his report, he gave Punjaz a sheet with the recap and conclusions of his report and Punjaz handed it to Zattan. When all the delegates had given their reports, a lively discussion ensued between some of them and Zattan. The chief was asking them who would become his lieutenants for further information.

All this lasted a little over two hours. Finally, having gone through the agenda, the floor was reserved for Zattan to wrap things up. The chief spoke calmly, clearly and quickly. He itemized all the measures to be taken round the world to sedate the governments so the revolution could act fast and furiously.

In fact, whereas the terrorist organizations of all the nations of the earth were working to prepare the uprising of the masses, Leonid Zattan, through the very special and secret representatives he maintained close to the upper echelons of governments, had worked in the opposite direction, at least in appearance, meaning he had done all he could for the heads of state and their ministers, along with most of the big newspapers in the world, to be numbed, so to speak, with peace and trust and social optimism.

His short lecture was answered with applause, at first restrained, then more and more excited and loud. In the end, they gave Zattan a standing ovation that lasted for minutes, accompanied not only by shouts but by passionate outcries.

Unmoved, Zattan waited for their enthusiasm to calm down, then he stood up. At that moment his face took on a strange expression of intense gravity and deep emotion. His jaws quivered a little, his forehead seemed wider and brighter, his eyes flashed. He spoke:

"Gentlemen, it is now undeniable that we all agree, that the entire world, with just one signal, can be transformed into a raging social volcano. Well, I'm going to give this signal and set the time and date for this global eruption. I'll give you the date since you've already guessed it: Thursday, May 1st, so, in fifteen days. As for the signal, it has to be sent by wireless, by telephone , by cable to all the centers of action. It's a secret word that was communicated confidentially six months ago to all the heads of these centers. When they hear or read it again with my initials, they'll know that everything is ready, that the waiting is over, that on May 1st at 8 am, our revolution, messieurs, will turn the entire world upside down!"

He stopped talking and raised his right hand. For a few seconds he stayed like that, in control, then slowly lowered his hand, pointing his finger... and holding this finger hovering a few inches above a tiny, ivory button on the pedestal.

He said, "Gentlemen, I'm going to push this button and the signal, the secret word, the order will travel around the world."

Then something unexpected happened that for a second aroused a vague and fleeting feeling of fear in the Lord of Issyk-Kul. It was the abrupt and identical movement of two of the delegates—the West Russian and Japanese.

These two men stood up and made as if they were about to jump over the table towards or rather at Leonid Zattan. But immediately following their example and carried away by their fervor, all the other delegates stood up, some indeed jumping over the table, others running around it towards Zattan, their arms raised, shouting violently their flattering praises.

After hovering in the air for that incalculable moment of shivering fear, Zattan's index finger lowered onto the button and pressed hard…

The fatal click was finished by the time the Russian and Japanese delegates got to the pedestal first, shouting out like their colleagues what could have been fervent, revolutionary joy.

With the final gesture made, the button pressed, the signal, the word, the order had been sent out! In a few minutes or hours both hemispheres of the globe, the heads of the revolutionary centers were going to receive the terrible word followed by the initials LZ, which would be, in their eyes, in their minds, like the blazing bolts of lightning before the storm!

Ten minutes after the supreme gesture of their chief, the delegates had gone back to their respective rooms to get into their formal attire. A big dinner with music and lights was going to bring them all together again with Leonid Zattan and all the military staff of Karakol and Issyk-Kul. The program and the menu of the feast had been organized long before by the Prince himself.

In theory only one woman should be present: Diana Ivanova Krosnovief. But since the capture of Sylvie Mac Duhl, Zattan had crossed the name of the Red Princess off the list. Then, in moments of vainglorious dreaming, he thought the Golden-Haired Virgin would replace the Red Princess at the feast. We can only imagine what had become of such a tremendous hope in Zattan's mind.

Therefore, there would be no woman at the sumptuous table where the Prince of Issyk-Kul, future emperor of the world, would be surrounded by men who as viceroys, dictators or commissars would share the government of the earth.

The U-shaped table of the congress and been straightened out and extended. Many more chairs were brought in. Ceiling and wall lights and standing lamps, decoratively shaded, diffused a soft light. Beautiful flowers bloomed between the gold and silver baskets and platters full of the finest, tastiest fruits of the world. The opulence of the crystal, silverware and table setting was a sight out of the 1,001 Nights.

Obviously, after the austerity of the political congress, the Prince wanted to give his closest collaborators a foretaste of what their own tables might look like in their imperial palaces.

Now, this dinner, which in the mind of Leonid Zattan, some of his officers and almost all of the delegates should have been a kind of banquet for a modern Tamerlane on the threshold of victory, this feast was, in reality, like the feast of Balthazar. If there wasn't the prophetic "Mene, Mene, Tekel, Upharsin" written on the wall, it was only because it would've been very reckless to warn Zattan. *But the lightning strike was no less terrible.*

The dishes were as delicious as they were abundant. The authentic wines composed a symphony of the most famous vintages of the world. The service was carried out by a troop of beautiful young girls dressed as Turkish slaves from the time of Suleiman II called the Great. Lastly, an invisible orchestra softly diffused not music but much more voluptuous breaths of harmonious sounds as if carried into the banquet hall on a scented breeze.

Finally the time came to raise their glasses and give speeches of congratulations.

Zattan began. He spoke only a few words, quite cryptic, that everyone interpreted as they wanted. Then, one after another, the twenty-nine delegates gave a toast. None of them had drunk too much, so their voices were clear and steady.

The last to stand up was the Russian delegate from Moscow.

Contrary to his colleagues, he was not all smiles. His hand, still holding the half-full glass of champagne, wasn't making the reverential gesture of a vassal to the overlord Leonid Zattan. To start, this was a little surprising because all their minds were tense enough that nothing went unnoticed and therefore the mental state of the guests was instantly changed. Some maybe realized this and watched the Russian delegate in an attempt to understand his strange and confusing attitude.

It also created an atmosphere of nervous expectation that brought all the bodies to a standstill and the noisy room full of toasting and whispering automatically turned silent, completely silent.

This Russian delegate was a little taller than average, slender, but with a wide chest and a strong neck. He gave the impression of power and agility. He was probably 40 years-old at most. His clean-shaven, sharply chiseled face with pronounced cheekbones, thin lips not shadowed by a mustache and an almost brutal chin was weirdly lit up by his extraordinary eyes—huge and widely slit with a dilated pupil bizarrely tinted golden yellow that encircled a deep, dark, eerie black pupil like the eye of a sphinx.

So far, neither during the congress nor during the feast had those eyes been completely open. The Russian delegate from Moscow had always kept this eyelids half-closed, letting in only a thin streak of light under the long, full eyelashes. But now, having already caught everyone's attention with his sudden change in attitude and with his neglect of the ritual gesture to Zattan, the Russian surprised them even more with the fantastic singularity of his eyes. In the magnificently male and beautifully energetic face, the strange eyes recalled the piercing gaze of birds of prey that are masters of the night skies.

When Leonid Zattan saw those eyes staring at him, the apparently crazy idea rose up from the depths of his soul that this man...

But the man was speaking in a voice somewhat raspy with a heavy Slavic accent. "I drink to the regeneration of the world, to the triumphant sun rising out of the sea, chasing away the darkness, to the light of truth, to victory..."

He paused for a moment and the odd change was felt by everyone as he spoke now pure and clear with no Slavic accent at all.

"To the victory of the principle of good over the principle of evil! I drink, finally, to the failure of the herald of the Antichrist and the downfall of Leonid Zattan!"

And in the midst of the incomprehensible and horrified stupor of all the guests, he downed his drink. Then he threw the empty glass hard at Zattan and it shattered against his forehead.

But Zattan was already standing up, Browning in hand. The blood blinded him. He didn't hesitate to shoot but he missed. None of the three bullets he shot hit their target. Moreover, when the Russian delegate had pronounced the name Leonid Zattan, all the doors were thrown open and an armed horde invaded the room. "Saint-Clair! Saint-Clair!" they shouted on all sides.

Through a bloody haze Zattan saw the Russian delegate rip off his wig while the Japanese delegate tore a mask off his own face. Zattan figured it was the Nyctalope and he recognized Gnô Mitang. But at that very moment he was grabbed, thrown down, tied up and gagged.

The fight between the delegates in the room, mostly unarmed, and the horde of invaders was short. It ended in the victory of the motley crew commanded by Marc Ayol and led by Lequic, Bonnet and Blanchard. Sylvie Mac Duhl stood empty-handed between Saint-Clair and Gnô Mitang.

They could hear, more or less clearly, shouting and shooting all over the castle. Karal Bey, Punjaz and Manoël Guerro were the first killed, shot down by the soldiers from the garrison of Issyk-Kul. Then most of the officers fell, Stoffmann at their head. They kept their vow of loyalty. The worst massacre befell the Kalmyks from Karakol. Wherever they were found, they stood against their attackers (including the soldiers and slaves of Issyk-Kul revolting against their High Lord) as they now obeyed the new leaders who wore the distinctive sign of a thin white turban at the base of their black hats.

The battle for possession of Issyk-Kul lasted until dawn throughout the castle. It was commanded by the Nyctalope, Sylvie Mac Duhl, Gnô Mitang and Marc Ayol. Whenever possible the invaders tied up the partisans of the vanquished prince instead of killing them. At the first warning given by Saint-Clair in person, Dr. Weilmann and Petrus Ivitch surrendered.

In the morning when the reveille was sounded (a memorable detail: it was improvised fancifully with a lot of very French flourishes), the battle for Issyk-Kul was over. Dead, wounded or tied up, all the officers and all the men remaining loyal to Zattan to the last had been rendered harmless.

Marc Ayol, Gnô Mitang, Yves Lequic, Jean Bonnet and Andre Blanchard followed the orders given by Saint-Clair and organized all the survivors of the tragic night into equal sections, each of them taking command of one of them.

At 9 am the long, stormy night that followed the lightning strike of fate was over for good.

CHAPTER XII

Leonid Zattan was brought into his own studio by the man who had guarded him since the start of the combat. In the studio, standing side by side, Sylvie Mac Duhl and the the Nyctalope were waiting when Zattan walked towards them, his forehead cleaned and faintly scarred, his hands empty and unbound. They nodded and gestured to the vanquished.

Saint-Clair pointed to an armchair, "Please sit down, monsieur, we have to talk."

"We do, indeed, have to talk," the Prince was as calm as ever.

He sat down. His face bore the traces of long fatigue, hidden anger and the serious concerns of the precedent days and nights. He was extremely pale, thin, with circles around his deep-set eyes, but in those hollows his eyes were gleaming, hard and cold, alive with an energy that Saint-Clair and Sylvie couldn't help admiring and respecting in this indomitable fighter.

Zattan was as intelligent as he was energetic. He perceived the complex feelings of these victors towards him. He wanted to use it straight off to get an advantage over them, so the negotiator in him was already taking the lead. He still had a powerful ace up his sleeve that he was hoping would win the final round or at least get him out of the game alive, with his wealth intact and the means to start the fight again in a few years on a different level and with all the chances for victory.

Therefore, he didn't wait for the Nyctalope to speak again. When the young lady and Saint-Clair had sat down next to each other facing him in the other armchairs, which were as wide and deep as his own, he spoke. It was in the same calm voice.

"Monsieur, above all, I'd like to see clearly behind me, to leave no murky, messy terrain. If you will, let's clear up and clean up the past, the recent past. This will make it easier for us to speak about the future."

While Sylvie was self-controlled and impassive, a fleeting smile crossed Saint-Clair's face. He thought, "Here's an adversary. If I didn't know his real power, I'd judge him to be insanely smug. But he's fully aware of his importance and determined to use it until he dies. Bravo! It's a pleasure to go up against such a man."

In a very polite, almost warm voice he said aloud, "As you wish, Prince. If I understand, you want me to enlighten you about certain mysteries that have brought us to where we are?"

"Yes, monsieur."

"Well then, Prince, ask away. I'm ready to answer."

What a switch in roles, at least in appearance! The victor opening up to the defeated to explain to him what tactics and strategy had guaranteed his victory.

But Saint-Clair the Nyctalope obviously figured he was strong enough to lay his cards on the table before his enemy.

Zattan took some time to consider. Sitting back in his chair, crossing his legs, slipping his hands into the pockets of his dolman, he looked truly at ease, not just putting on a show. At last he said, "First of all, how did you escape the drug? Like me and Ivitch and mademoiselle and everyone else, you ate the food and drank the wine except for the Romanée. You alone didn't pass out seeing that ten minutes later you overpowered Lieutenant Stoffmann when he put you in the cell."

The Nyctalope answered softly, "When you said we were going to be served the Romanée, didn't I make a reference to Mithradates when I refused? I don't have to remind you, right, that the King of Pontus, the staunch enemy of Rome, was constantly threatened by plots and conspiracies from within his own court, which feared him. So as not to fall victim to some craven treachery from someone bribed by his enemies, he had studied drugs and poisons as well as minerals with harmful effects, at least what was known at the time, and he accustomed his body to the strongest poisons that he feared he might eat or drink. Well, my Prince, my allusion should've alerted you. I am, if you forgive a neologism taken from antiquity, I am mithridated.

"Near the end of dinner, when I saw one of Gnô's sailors bury his nose in his plate, my suspicions were raised. I just had to catch a brief scowl from Ali-Soud to confirm. Then I pretended to be drugged myself... But you know the rest, which Ali-Soud and Stoffmann must've told you in detail."

"Yes, monsieur, yes," Zattan said. "But after knocking out and tying up Stoffmann, what did you do?"

"Stoffmann was a lot bigger than me. The difficulty at that moment was to fit into his boots and clothes. I stuffed them with straw from the mattress and in less than five minutes I'd grown taller and fatter. Oh, sure, I wouldn't have stood up to close examination, even for ten seconds, but I only had to get past the jailers who were too busy with other things to worry about Stoffmann (me in disguise) closing up cell 8 and rushing out while tossing the guard the key he'd received a few minutes before from Karal Bey who himself had asked the head guard for the other keys. So, I left unmolested from the prison bunker shortly after the other officers. Once I got into the semi-darkness of the courtyard I had nothing more to fear."

"What do you mean?" Zattan spurted out, being caught up in the intriguing story that he listened to avidly.

"My dear Prince," the Nyctalope continued with amused civility and a little mockery, "don't forget that for several days and nights, under the name of Pedro del Campo and Marco Pampil, I and my friend Marc Ayol had free rein throughout Issyk-Kul. If you consider the various languages we know, we were able to talk easily with almost all the good men and some of the louts who came into the castle. Marco Pampil was a sailor and my subordinate so he mingled with the soldiers, servants and slaves and gave me reports every day. Pedro del Campo, the captain of your navy on standby, hobnobbed with the officers. Pampil was clever and generous with his promises. Del Campo had, I believe, knowledge of the human soul. We both did good work. It was during those relatively free days and nights that we sowed the seeds of revolt in the garrison and revolution in the palace without which, I have to admit, it would've been a lot harder, if not impossible, for us to defeat you."

"If you say so!" Zattan barked out. "But that doesn't tell me how you could hide and do things after leaving the bunker."

Saint-Clair answered quietly, "What I just told you about the secret actions of del Campo and Pampil should help you to understand the relative ease for the Nyctalope to act after the so-called Stoffmann left the bunker."

"I'm listening!"

"I can see that!" Smiling as Zattan bit his lip, Saint-Clair went on, "In Issyk-Kul one man before you, Prince, knew my true identity. I'd told him while I was still Pedro del Campo to you. He's the guy listed as number 789 in your register under the name of Horace Van Deulen…"

"My sommelier! The wine expert!" Zattan cried out, shocked and not even trying to hide his feelings.

"That's right. He's not Dutch and his name's not Horace Van Deulen. He's Belgian, from Brussels, and is called François de Veder. He was a second lieutenant in Ypres during the Great War. He fought under my command and I happened to save his life. In 1917, a woman had stolen his heart and he was on the verge of betraying his country for Germany. He recovered in time but he was compromised and exposed by two false documents sent by those he'd finally refused to serve. He deserted to avoid being shot. Young and passionate, he didn't give up and managed to become a traveling salesman partnered up with Horace Van Deulen. The Dutchman died in Java. With the dead man's papers in hand, François de Veder continued traveling the world. He was part of a caravan of Tibetan merchants that arrived in Karakol where your secretary Woldski found him. Now, François is the son of a big wine broker in Brussels. He is schooled, as you know, in the wines of France, Spain and Italy. By chance, in Karakol, Woldski became familiar with his knowledge of wine and that's how the false Dutchman, under the name of Horace Van Deulen, within three months was working in the very important job of head sommelier in Issyk-Kul. But the spirited traveler started finding life here monotonous and then Pedro del Campo showed up. The fake Dutchman and the fake Spaniard saw and recognized each other. François de Veder had not forgotten that Saint-Clair had saved his life."

"Destiny," Zattan muttered.

"Providence!" the Nyctalope shot back. "You can guess the rest. Your basements, Prince, are huge and have thousands of barrels, casks, kegs and two or three dozen vats. The caves over which your castle is built out of the rock, extend and branch out for miles. It was in these caves, sometimes hiding far away, sometimes in the empty vats for days at a time, eluding your searches and patrols. With the help of Horace Van Deulen, now on my side, I was able sway the workers and black slaves in the cellars. I made promises. It will cost me dearly. But the treasure of Issyk-Kul is valuable, isn't it?"

Overcome by his passions, almost forgetting he was defeated, Zattan clenched his fists and stiffened up. His bloodshot eyes glared hatefully at the Nyctalope. He grumbled, "Talk, keep talking. How did you take Sylvie Mac Duhl from her bedroom?"

Still as calm as ever, smiling occasionally, the Nyctalope continued, "Something else, Prince, that you must know. Something prior to your first defeat. You'll see, it should be very interesting to you. While I was still Pedro del Campo I came into your bedroom one night. I lay down on your bed. Thanks to your marvelous device I saw and heard your conversation with Sylvie Mac Duhl and a few minutes later I talked with her at her window. It was, I believe, the night of April 3rd, so 11 days ago."

"How'd you do that?" Zattan grumbled.

"I assure you, it was the easiest thing in the world. Am I not the Nyctalope? Don't I see in the dark as clearly as in the light?"

And Saint-Clair told how Marc Ayol was lookout as he climbed the wall of the south tower up to the second floor, then after an informative break in Zattan's bedroom, he had continued up to the third floor and talked with Sylvie through the bars of her window.

"Oh, oh," Zattan grunted. Then springing like a tiger he pounced on his adversary, hands out to grab his throat, squeeze, strangle. Sylvie had seen this coming for a couple of minutes, but before even she had time to get between them, Saint-Clair's right arm shot out like a piston rod in a steam engine and punched Zattan on the chin, throwing him back into his armchair.

It was maybe this moment that the Prince of Issyk-Kul best displayed the diabolical (and could very well be divine) strength of his character. He was fazed for only fifteen seconds. Then he pulled himself together and in a hoarse but firm voice:

"Thank you, monsieur. You just gave me a lesson in self-control and dignity. I deserved it. I acted like an angry child. Please continue. I won't be stupid enough to interrupt you with any impulsive assaults while you explain what I asked of you."

This time it was Saint-Clair and Sylvie who were stunned.

The Nyctalope couldn't help expressing his thoughts, "I say, Prince, congratulations..." And after a brief pause, "Well then, I'll continue. And I'll make it quick because everything that happened was just the logical outcome of what had happened before. Here goes.

"After the prison bunker I went straight to the main entrance to the cellars. The guard on duty let me in. I talked with the sommelier and got rid of my Stoffmann disguise. During the night, when Issyk-Kul had quieted down, I climbed the south tower again. Through the window of your bathroom, cracked open as usual, I snuck into your rooms. You were sleeping in your bed and Ali-Soud was dozing in the armchair. Using your stairs I went up to Sylvie's rooms. She was out cold from the drug, lying on her bed. I picked her up and tied her, yes, tied her to my back and shoulders. Passing back through your bedroom, I swiped Ali's beads. A little prank to spice up the mystery. It was no picnic getting back down the outside of the tower, but five minutes later Sylvie was safe inside an empty vat in cellar 22 on a cot set up by Van Deulen."

A short pause. Then in a more serious, harder voice, the Nyctalope continued.

"After that I figured you were beat, Prince. Your prestige hinged primarily on the belief of your officers and all your men that you were invincible, that nobody in the world could defy you for long and that every insult to your power, especially in Issyk-Kul, would be immediately punished with death.

"Well, this prestige started crumbling the moment I made your soldiers and servants aware, thanks to the seeds I'd already sown around Issyk-Kul, that in your own castle, in the very center of your so-called absolute power, one man, acting alone with only his intelligence as a weapon, could not only hold you off but could do it over and over and even strike back.

"You can imagine how easy it was, thanks to Van Deulen and his mates in the cellar, to get Kalmyk uniforms so that I and Marc Ayol, Gnô and Sylvie formed a little squad within your own guard patrolling the castle. Yes, on the night of the 6th, freeing Marc Ayol and Gnô was child's play for me. Then I spent the 7th preparing the posters to be seen as a threat to you and a defiance for the garrison so that you'd have to be victorious or else be ridiculed.

"On the night of the 7th, despite all the lights you flooded the castle with, I was able to use the shadows to put Ali's beads on the ground and since I was disguised as an officer, to pin the first of my messages on his coat. As for the others, Gnô and Marc Ayol had fun putting them up all over the place.

"The 8th and 9th were spent working to demoralize your garrison as much as possible. Marc Ayol, too easy to recognize with his 32 gold teeth, painted them black so that they looked like he'd been chewing betel like your soldiers. Disguised as a Chinese, he mingled with the other Chinese soldiers for two days and had a great influence. The masterstroke for us was on the night of the 9th when we kidnapped Woldski and Ali-Soud. They were both sleeping in their rooms, exhausted from all the work. Marc Ayol, Gnô, Van Deulen and I operated without a hitch. We were helped by three of your officers, the ones who forced a meeting with you on the 10th along with some of their men. I woke Woldski up and he willingly enough bowed to the compelling argument of hands wrapped around his neck in the dark—I saw him but he couldn't see me. I convinced him of my strength against himself and you. Ali-Soud was no less understanding faced with the fact that these events, as I proved to him, were the will of Allah.

"What more can I tell you? The only risk we ran at the start was being caught in the cellars, but it wasn't an issue after the 8th because we spent most of our time out in the open, disguised among your soldiers, at least those who had already decided to march with me against you. See, after my many triumphs and your repeated defeats, I had gained all the prestige you'd lost.

"I told you that from the moment I could get Sylvie out of your immediate reach, I considered you beaten. Events proved me right."

He stopped talking, a little out of breath from his hasty speech.

Zattan sat there stone-faced. Out of his mouth escaped these words: "One more question, please. How did you and Gnô replace the Russian from Moscow and the Japanese delegate?"

Saint-Clair smiled, "It was on the night of the 13th. Keeping to yourself the Kalmyk guards, whom it was impossible for us to even talk to, you had to put regular soldiers and servants at the doors of the delegates, whoever happened to be on duty. I'd already decided to replace two of the revolutionary delegates. Since we saw them coming in, we had our choice. The Russian from Moscow looked enough like me and unless you see them often it's hard for some people to tell the difference between two Japanese of the same build and same age. Gnô was a little taller than the real delegate but hunching over a little, drooping his shoulders, it was easy to shrink.

"Besides, you'd barely glimpsed most the delegates before the meeting. Some you'd probably never seen at all. So, it was unlikely that you'd recognize that the Russian had been replaced by the Nyctalope as long as I didn't open my eyes wide. As for the Japanese, I imagine that if you'd seen him for eight days, you wouldn't know that on the ninth it was Gnô Mitang with a little makeup and acting.

"Of course, the two real delegates were tied up and stuffed into an empty barrel for the time being. And the word had already been sent and spread among most of the garrison.

"One cannot take over Issyk-Kul without a fight, I know. Fifteen of your officers remained loyal. But they didn't know what was brewing because we were careful to keep a distance from those few officers and heads of service and anyone who was obviously too loyal to you. Like all the Kalmyks from Karakol were incorruptible. Therefore, the battle was unavoidable. But I gave strict orders to kill as few as possible, to capture and tie up more than stab and shoot. The tally of casualties and wounded hasn't finished yet, but I think I can assure you that there was a lot more noise than bloodshed and some of your officers and men and even your Kalmyks, a large number of your loyalists, survived just like almost all the revolutionary delegates.

"However, I do believe that Punjaz was killed. But I'll let Woldski and Ali-Soud go. In your exile or rather in the fortified town where, I think, you will be imprisoned, as befits your rank, Woldski and Ali-Soud will serve you, the former as a friend and partner, the latter as your butler.

"And that's it, Prince. I've told you everything I believe should interest you personally. But I'm ready to answer any other questions you might have."

The Nyctalope was quiet.

Leonid Zattan smiled. "Yes, one last question," he casually. "You didn't plan that to wrap up the pan-revolutionary congress I would push a button thanks to which the secret order of the global revolution would be launched to the ends of the earth and at the same time set the date of the inevitable upheaval for May 1st. No, you didn't foresee this! Because I remember now that when my finger was on the fateful button, the Russian and Japanese delegates made a move towards me. I thought it was out of enthusiasm like all the others, but now I see clearly. Your rushing me was a second before and was the cause of the commotion. So your movement was masked by the others. In truth, you were charging at me to stop me from pushing the button, right?"

"That's right," the Nyctalope said. "But you were too fast. Just as well since my orders in Issyk-Kul set the time of the revolt for the end of the banquet. My glass thrown to the ground or at you was supposed to be the signal, relayed immediately outside by your second butler, Yan Ten, whom you believed was devoted to you but was one of the first seduced by Marc Ayol's speeches.

"And by the way, Prince, give me credit. Any number of times I could've had you killed or killed you myself. On the night of April 3rd when I saw Sylvie Mac Duhl, I gave your prisoner a dagger stolen from the armor in the library. If I'd begged her, really simply asked her, she would not have hesitated to plant the blade in your heart or throat. She had many chances. Isn't that right, Sylvie?"

While pronouncing these final words gravely, he turned to the young lady. She nodded two times, staring at the Lord of Issyk-Kul with her big, blue, ice-cold eyes.

"Yes," Saint-Clair went on, "I could've killed you myself on several occasions, which I don't need to recount. Or I could've had the wine poisoned by Horace Van Deulen. Lastly, I could've had you strangled by Ali-Soud's successor... So, give me credit, you are alive and unharmed—I won't offend you by counting that little bruise from the broken glass on your forehead."

Without blinking, Zattan bowed his head slightly and said, "I will give credit. It would've been a lot easier for you to kill me than to succeed in the extraordinary feats that brought you here *to what you believe to be your victory.*" And the Prince of Issyk-Kul stressed these last eight words.

But when Saint-Clair just raised his eyebrows and looked strangely at him, Zattan repeated it, clutching the arms of his chair and leaning forward.

"Yes, monsieur, *what you believe to be your victory.*"

"Oh," the Nyctalope replied. "Would you explain, Prince? For me, I've never seen a more unquestionable and total victory. Even though there's not the slightest trace of arrogance in my mind, the facts speak for themselves: Issyk-

Kul belongs to me, the revolutionary delegates are dead or imprisoned and you cannot take a step outside this room without my permission. So, I don't get it."

"You will," Zattan snarled. "Go back to the little scene of my finger pushing the button. What does my castle, the delegates or even my own person matter! We could all die here, but events will continue their fated course. At 8 am on May 1st the proletarian masses led by revolutionary professionals will rise up over the surface of the globe. We here were meant to be not so much the directors but the spectators and inspectors of the universal movement. Well, you can kill us so we can't watch, but the global revolution still has its leaders and they will secure my victory on the ruins of the present society!"

He stopped there. With a quick glance he glowered at Sylvie Mac Duhl and Saint-Clair, who were looking back at him as calmly as ever. Obviously, Zattan's speech had no effect on them. Surprised on the inside but keeping his haughty, sneering attitude on the outside, he spoke up again.

"It is in my power alone to cancel the order for revolution and delay it for some future date. Only I can do this because only I know the secret word for it. Those who have received it around the world are, I am absolutely certain, ignorant of the counter-revolutionary led by Mathias Lumen, the Hermit of Ushant.

"But this counter-order, which I alone can give, you are right to think that I won't give it. You can torture me, kill me slowly, meanwhile parading before me the advantages of freedom, money and power compared to this torture and death—that should do it, right? To convince you of my iron will, of my determination that *Leonid Zattan will never give the counter-order*. Therefore, and I'll finish with this, Leo Saint-Clair, called the Nyctalope, your victory is only a personal one, man against man. But my personality disappears before my work and its the work that you're really fighting against. I'm sure you don't care at all me personally. Well, my work goes on and your victory doesn't exist!"

Saint-Clair stood up, instantly followed by Sylvie Mac Duhl, and spoke softly, very politely, "Prince, you've just expressed your opinion. You will allow me, without further explanation, to hold the opposite opinion."

In slow motion he pushed one of the buttons on the corner of the table. A door opened. Lequic, Bonnet and Blanchard appeared. They were holding not weapons but shackles for the wrists and ankles and a ball gag for the mouth.

"Sailors," Saint-Clair ordered courteously, "Please escort the Prince to cell 8 and lock him up." Turning back to Zattan, "Please go with them quietly."

The defeated man, who still didn't believe he had lost for good, turned to the door. He saw the three men. He saw what they were holding. He knew any resistance would be futile and end regardless in the humiliation of chains and gag, slung over a shoulder...

With dignity and pride he accepted the inevitable. He bowed before Sylvie Mac Duhl, gave the Nyctalope a military salute and marched bravely to the door. With Blanchard and Bonnet on either side and Lequic in the rear, the curtain fell back over the doorway.

CHAPTER XIII

The Nyctalope gave Marc Ayol responsibility for the organization and management, with some well-defined groundwork, of the liquidation of the principality of Issyk-Kul, the kingdom of Karakol and the empire of Tian Shan. It was done quickly. And these politico-historical events whose hidden significance was enormous, was received by the chancelleries and major newspapers around the world as a minor local news item. There was: "Republic of Tian Shan with so-called president-dictator, hetman of the Cossacks (i.e. Kalmyks) of Karakol". There was: "Prince Leonid Zattan deposed by his people", "Acquisition of Issyk-Kul castle, one of the most picturesque medieval sites, by Sylvie Mac Duhl, daughter of Gregor Mac Duhl, famous in Monte Carlo before the Great War". But we have just seen and will see more of the formidable—and diabolical and divine—designs hiding behind this petty official news.

In Issyk-Kul itself, the "arrangement" of everything was boldly handed over to Sylvie Mac Duhl because it required as much alluring tenderness as it did clever energy. Dr. Weilmann submitted along with Petrus Ivitch. The former was very helpful to the young lady in transforming the infirmary into a hospital to take care of the wounded. The latter took charge of the technical services. A German officer, a former colonel from Württemberg, reformed the garrison. With Lequic, Blanchard and Bonnet as adjutants, Sylvie Mac Duhl was a tactful, diplomatic dictator whose character and actions were as disciplined as they were fervent. It didn't take long for all the men of Issyk-Kul, more or less misanthropic or barbaric, to admire and obey her more and better than Prince Zattan.

All the able-bodied officers and soldiers who remained defiant got six months' pay and were sent to Karakol to be employed in the various branches of the budding republic of Tian Shan.

As for the twenty-six revolutionary delegates who survived the battle on April 14th, Sylvie threw them in prison like Zattan, Woldski and Ali-Soud until Saint-Clair decided what to do with them. The captives were well treated but so closely guarded that the fallen prince couldn't reasonably hope for the wheel of fortune to ever turn in his favor.

And yet, what hopes might he have had if he knew the dreadful fact, which Saint-Clair himself knew nothing about, that loomed secretly over the situation—the fact that Mathias Lumen was dead!

Because it was the life of Mathias Lumen and the actions emanating from it that the Nyctalope was counting on when he had replied to Zattan, "Prince, you've just expressed your opinion. You will allow me, without further explanation, to hold the opposite opinion."

While motivating and checking the work of Captain Marc Ayol and Sylvie Mac Duhl, which was limited to the region of Tian Shan and the castle of Issyk-

Kul, Saint-Clair was working with Gnô Mitang on a global level. This work started right away on the morning of April 15th. Being close friends and avid collaborators, the two men set up in the studio of the south tower, which became their headquarters. They quickly cleared away the insignificant issues and got down to the main problem. The conclusion of their two-man council was this:

"We have to talk to Mathias Lumen."

"It should be easy," Gnô added.

In fact, before leaving the house in Ushant to look for the *Taurus* and Sylvie Mac Duhl, the Japanese had got precise instructions from Mathias Lumen for Gnô and any collaborators he might let in on the secret to communicate by wireless with the house in Ushant.

Moreover, the first order of business for the Nyctalope that morning had been to replace Manoël Guerro as the head of the wireless service. He assigned a former engineer from Luxembourg who had served in the French Foreign Legion during the Great War. His name was Karl Menos. During Zattan's reign he had been one of Guerro's top employees, so he knew the wireless service thoroughly.

The Nyctalope and Gnô got in touch with Karl Menos by phone.

"Hello!" Saint-Clair said.

A metallic voice answered, "Menos here. At your service."

"Please send this urgent message." And he rattled off some letters in French and a few numbers.

According to the code brought from Ushant by Gnô Mitang this made four brief but explicit sentences informing Mathias Lumen of Gnô and the Nyctalope's victory over Leonid Zattan and the occupation of Issyk-Kul where they would await orders from Lumen, that he would immediately call and summon Gnô back to Ushant or that he would figure it more practical to come himself to the castle where he would be at the heart of the global revolutionary organization and from here set up the counter-strike destined to cancel out the order sent by Zattan for May 1st.

The coded message was bound to go across the official stations and lastly through the Eiffel Tower station which would wire it in such a way that it would get to Ushant as soon as possible.

"We'll have an answer in a few hours," Gnô commented.

But the 15th passed by with the two men organizing the details of their victory and no message came from Lumen.

"That's worrying," the Japanese said.

In the Nyctalope's headquarters Gnô Mitang was the only man who had certain information about Mathias Lumen and the house in Ushant. But for the powerful organization created and led by Lumen in person, except for the close collaboration of his secretary Placide Bonnard, no one knew anything about it.

It seemed impossible to Saint-Clair and Gnô to stand in for Lumen in any way whatsoever. But it was not in the Nyctalope's character to sit idle. Before going to bed on the night of the 15th he told Gnô, "It's simple. If we get nothing from Lumen tomorrow after the second message we sent and the one you'll send in the morning, well, tomorrow night Ivitch and I will leave for Ushant."

What worried the two men the most was the silence, not from Mathias Lumen in particular but the absolute silence. Gnô knew that when the Hermit of Ushant left his island with his very small staff, which happened on occasion, one of the main French affiliates would answer urgent messages for him. Now, this time, Lumen would have had to go away without making any preparations seeing that the three messages from Issyk-Kul went unanswered. And the two worried men were coming up with all kinds of wild theories.

At 3 pm on April 16th Saint-Clair told Sylvie and Marc Ayol about the situation. With the potent and profound intuition that women so often have, Sylvie kept their minds focused on the proper action to take.

"Don't you think that some misfortune might have befallen the house in Ushant? From what you two know, our master Mathias Lumen has so many terrible, bitter enemies! Zattan's just one among many!"

"So, I should go to Ushant!" the Nyctalope made his final decision.

And he went to invite Gnô to go along, which he'd already done the night before. But the Japanese spoke before he could open his mouth.

"No, chief, no! The situation might get really tricky here. We always have to fear a setback, a betrayal by one or several men. Some, who betrayed Zattan for us, might turn around and betray us for their old idol or maybe a new one who will rise up in their imagination. We need as many as we can get here, with Marc Ayol and our three sailors, to keep an eye on things. Go with Petrus Ivitch who knows the *Aquilon* better than anyone, yes. But instead of me take Sylvie Mac Duhl."

After a silence that his face saddled with rare gravity, he concluded in a most unexpected way: "The main character clearly designated by the prophecy of Nostradamus is Sylvie Mac Duhl. Basically, all our actions have been directed by the mysterious meaning of the prophecy. The key to the mystery is in Ushant. Sylvie must hear it from Mathias Lumen, who is the best man to explain it. Therefore, take her to Ushant!"

He stood up, turned to the young lady and bowed deeply with his right hand on his forehead in quasi-religious veneration.

Standing up as well, Saint-Clair and Sylvie looked at each other, she blushing in modesty, he turned pale, suddenly troubled. Their souls stared at each other through their eyes.

The Nyctalope said, "You are no doubt right, Gnô."

At the end of the afternoon on April 16th all preparations had been made for the Nyctalope's absence. With Gnô Mitang as commander-in-chief at Issyk-Kul, the fruits of the victory over Zattan wouldn't be destroyed or even damaged by any treason from the inside or attack from the outside.

Summoned and informed about the decision of the air travel, Petrus Ivitch said, in a tone that left no doubt about his loyalty, that he was ready to obey "with utmost pleasure". Obviously, the misanthrope was enjoying the spectacle of the battle between Zattan and the Nyctalope. He was thinking, "I want to and must be neutral, scoring the blows, serving whoever is stronger with the same passive loyalty. The Nyctalope orders, I obey him. If the Lord of Issyk-Kul gets the upper hand, I'll obey the terrorist prince. It's the only way I have to watch the fight until the final bell! Only then, if I choose, will I do what I want."

At 8 pm the *Aquilon* took off from the big terrace/runway at Issyk-Kul. Only Petrus Ivitch, Leo Saint-Clair and Sylvie Mac Duhl were on board.

Just to remember!

On the morning of April 7th in the Ushant house, Diana Ivanova Krosno-vief had killed Ephrem Lluch, Mathias Lumen, Placide Bonnard and the cook Sidonie. The Red Princess then left for Brest carrying the key to the house, which had been turned into a sepulcher.

On the morning of the 14th Ignace Kiewicz, warden of the imprisoned Diana and holding the key, went to Ushant. He had looked upon the four corpses with horrified surprise. The next night he left for Saint-Guilhem-le-Desert, bringing Diana Ivanova rendered unconscious by a carefully dosed potion of yage and peyote.

After the 14th, days passed in Ushant without anyone, except for a rare daydreaming stroller, coming in sight of the locked and silent Ghost Chalet. Days passed—from April 15th to the 19th.

Now, on the 20th at daybreak, in the clear, mild morning air in which the strong smell of the sea couldn't completely absorb the delicate Spring scents from the flowers and grass, two "tourists" stopped in front of the low wall surrounding the barren land on which the mysterious house stood.

The night before a plane had landed and anchored in a quiet corner of the Brest harbor. A rented speedboat brought the two tourists to Lampaul.

After fifteen minutes of mute observation, one of the tourists spoke softly, "Mademoiselle, the house looks deserted. We don't have a key. Should we leave without finding out anything?"

And the other, "We should make a tour of the house, monsieur, and go from door to door, knock or ring the bell."

"Of course, but if there's no one in the house?"

"Let's go anyway."

"Yes, let's go."

The Nyctalope hopped over the wall and held out his hand to Sylvie who grabbed it and jumped. They hurried over the land and then the cement walkway. At the first door Saint-Clair rang the bell and then knocked on the wooden door with his gloved hand. Nothing! They made the tour of the house, rang and knocked at all the doors…

But as Sylvie was ringing the door that directly faced the farthest western point of the island, something happened that caused them to blurt out, "Oh!" and "Finally!"

A kind of small panel had just opened, revealing a kind of opening in the door. There was no grill, no window. It made no hole of shadow or light inside the house. It was just a plain white enameled surface on which words were written in blue—an order: "Whoever you are / Say your name aloud."

For the past fifteen days, the Nyctalope and Sylvie Mac Duhl had lived through so many extraordinary adventures that they were ready for anything. So, their surprise didn't last long. Their decision was quick.

The young lady took a breath and hammered out the words loud and clear, "Sylvie Mac Duhl."

One, two, three seconds, maybe. With a click the panel snapped shut. One, two, three minutes went by. Nothing!

"Your turn, monsieur," Sylvie said quietly. "But I think you have to ring first to get it working."

Saint-Clair pressed the electric button. An instant later the little opening appeared again with the imperative inscription. The man reeled off, "Leo Saint-Clair the Nyctalope."

One, two, three seconds... With a click the panel snapped shut... Then there was a hushed but audible movement of a mechanism, a crackling ring and a shrill whistle. The heavy door swung silently on its hinges, opened slowly, slowly...

In a trembling voice that she didn't even try to control, Sylvie whispered, "You go first because you're expected."

No less effected but controlling himself, he held her long, gloved hand and said simply, "Let's go in together, please."

They entered. The door closed behind them. Then the electric lights turned on in the ceiling of the stairway in front of them. But as soon as they had climbed the twenty steps, all the lights went out together.

Almost at the same time, at the end of the hallway that widened into a rotunda, a door opened. The Nyctalope was the only one, of course, to see the invitation in the dark.

"Come on, Sylvie, walk next to me. I'll be the eyes for both of us."

The two of them felt like they were heading into something phenomenal where the modern Genius was allied to Unknown Forces lying hidden in the eternity of the Occult... But they didn't hesitate. They were ready to make split-second decisions and act on them. Their hands clasped together were trembling a little and squeezing each other. Side by side they walked forward.

No light turned on. There was no need for the master of the night since he was expected!

The darkness, what a symbol! What profound meaning! Saint-Clair the Nyctalope walked firmly towards his inevitable Destiny. And Sylvie felt called, supported, defended, protected absolutely. They kept moving forward.

They followed the hallway, crossed the rotunda and went through the open door, which closed automatically behind them. And the lights in the ceiling, on the walls and lamps on the tables, over the workbench, around the huge laboratory oven lit up...

"That's for you, no doubt expected as well," the Nyctalope murmured.

In the brightness from the electric lights, Sylvie and Saint-Clair saw what they were least expecting. They saw it and their throats tightened, choking their cries; they squeezed each other's hand so hard it hurt; their nerves first shook them from head to toe, then turned them to stone, pale, squinting—two bodies were lying on the floor, one with white hair and a full beard, the other with his face withering.

Saint-Clair didn't know Mathias Lumen or Placide Bonnard, but Gnô Mitang had talked about them enough and described them in detail. So, Saint-Clair and Sylvie could identify the corpses. And they couldn't take their eyes off them. They couldn't understand. They felt enshrouded in a tragic mystery.

But it was not an emotion that the Nyctalope couldn't overcome. The sight of the bodies drying out, mummifying, sparked a question in his mind, which cleared his head.

"Sylvie, don't move," he said.

Pulling his hand out of hers, he stepped away, approached the white-haired corpse, leaned over and examined it. Blood clotted, dry, staining the red carpet black along the body.

"He was shot," the Nyctalope said.

He went to the second corpse.

"Same here."

He stood up, in total control of himself now, and turned to Sylvie.

"Who could have...?"

But he didn't finish the question. In the back of the room, above a section of bare wall between two rows of symmetrically arranged instruments and devices, a small electric bell was ringing. It was like a call that the man and woman obeyed instinctively. Once again, they held hands, slipped between the corpses, crossed the library and stepped off the soft carpet onto the galvanized "tile" floor. They stopped in the middle of the laboratory because under the bell on the wall a small panel, invisible before, slid open to reveal an enamel plate like on the outside door. The fateful inscription was written on it: "Whoever you are / Say your name aloud."

There was no hesitation. They both understood that the two dead men lying there had done what they could, while still alive, to prepare for the foreseeable consequences of their dangerous life, and thus for their own sudden death. The man and woman both understood that these mechanisms had been designed and built in view of things that might possibly or probably happen.

Loud and clear he said, "Leo Saint-Clair, the Nyctalope."

Then truly began the extraordinary scene that decided the fate of the human race in this year.

The small plate closed up again, invisible once more. And above it the bare patch of wall slid open from right to left, slid and disappeared behind the instruments and devices. In the open space behind it, the black horn of a phonograph slid forward and stopped. A silvery tone rang out three times and a male voice came out of the horn:

"If you are really Leo Saint-Clair, the Nyctalope, say the name that, if Nostradamus predicted correctly, has been the only one living in your heart over the last few days."

The Nyctalope was expecting anything but this. His whole body shivered. He turned to his companion who was trembling, looking at him with her big blue eyes in a kind of sudden rapture. Then he knew the secret confirmation of what he was hoping, of what he'd known for days.

"Sylvie! Sylvie Mac Duhl!"

"Oh, Leo!" Her head dropped onto his shoulder while his right arm wrapped around her supple, yielding waist.

But the phonograph right away, "God willing then, I, Mathias Lumen, wasn't wrong about the interpretation of the two final prophecies of Nostradamus."

A short silence. Three more silvery tones and then:

"Nyctalope, whether you are alone here or with a young lady or other partners, everything will be explained to you, then you will receive my orders that you will obey. The Principle of Good will have once more vanquished the Principle of Evil. Once again, the Darkness will recede before the Light, of which you are the living symbol, you for whom there is no night. And the secular work of men will progress until... But the future is God's to know.

"Being absent, I'll speak to those present. Being dead, I will speak to the living."

In the ensuing silence, Saint-Clair and Sylvie heard their hearts beating. They squeezed each other harder. With almost religious passion, with inflamed fervor, with minds open to all wonders, they listened.

Three more tones, slow, clear, and the voice of Mathias Lumen, "I have always prepared for the possibility of my enemies killing me and Placide Bonnard and Ephrem Lluch before my work was finished. Therefore, a mechanical device was built in this house so that the Nyctalope, who was expressly named by Nostradamus as 'the man with the mark of the divine', enemy of the Antichrist, would see the doors open before him and receive my instructions. Thus, he will succeed me in knowing the cause of the current battle of the soldiers of civilization against the order of barbarous and anarchic hordes, a battle that is only a precursor to another battle, much more significant, in which the Antichrist will appear at the start.

"This mechanism has been ready for three years, designed not to turn on unless the Nyctalope says his name at the west door after pressing the bell, like anyone would do.

"If I, Bonnard and Lluch are only away for the moment, you will soon know how to reach me by radio. If we are dead, you already know it or will soon find out. In this case, you are the successor, in everything, of Mathias Lumen."

The voice went quiet. Saint-Clair and Sylvie were panting a little. But the silence didn't last long. Again after three bells the phonograph spoke:

"Nostradamus wrote:

"In the name of Scotland and orphaned of all
"Golden maiden with love will bring to life
"In the time one and nine and nineteen
"Great brown-haired male with divine attributes.
"If stone and gold by chance more than enough
"Fill the well that in Ushant Englishman made
"Death wretchedly by blade to the throat
"Against the Antichrist the male is opposed.
"Victorious will he be if the woman gives birth
"Otherwise, the Time will be long delayed
"Blood over one and nine and nineteen
"With the dead in dreadful piles."

A pause before Lumen's voice continued. "This prophecy was known to me, my immediate collaborators and to Leonid Zattan who managed to steal a copy of it from me one day. But the copy was incomplete. Here is the end of the prophecy that the only ones who know or have known are myself, Bonnard and Lluch:

"But this is not yet the Antichrist
"Zattan heralds it in male rage
"Vanquished by the fated brown-haired male
"With eyes that pierce the darkness."

Another pause and then another bell. "Now, Leo Saint-Clair, the Nyctalope, you whose eyes pierce the darkest dark, go to the big chest here in the library between two pillars. Say your name, slowly and clearly, three times, into the carved emblem on the entablature. The chest will open. In the upper compartment you will find all the documents necessary for you to effectively replace me."

Silence again. Then in a mellow voice full of true affection, the posthumous Lumen said, "Sylvie and Leo, be happy!"

A bell rang, a muffled squeak, five seconds later there was nothing but the bare blank wall staring at them.

Men of vast and profound intelligence are also mystics. Mysticism is but a certain understanding of the unknowable divinity, is it not? On the other hand, on another level, mysticism is love. Now, the Nyctalope was superbly intelligent and passionately in love. Therefore, he was a mystic twice over. He couldn't accept Nostradamus' prophecy with skepticism: the words, clear enough now, of the prophecy completed by Lumen's voice seemed to fit the past and present reality perfectly, so it was only natural that they would work for the future as well.

Moreover, Saint-Clair was well enough educated to know that other prophecies of Nostradamus, published centuries ago, had been verified by the course of events. For example, the one relating to the death of Louis XVI, to the destiny of Napoleon 1st, to the accession of the Napoleon 3rd to the imperial throne, to the invasion of Belgium by Germany in 1914, to the treachery of Ferdinand of Bulgaria, named by the wondrous prophet. Therefore, the Nyctalope had to give credence, with all his soul and all his heart, to the prophetic words that he had just heard.

As for Sylvie...

She expressed herself wholly and perfectly when Saint-Clair came back to her and stared at her with a kind of eager, questioning look. Pale and grave she said, "I love you. I'm yours."

For a few minutes Sylvie and Leo forgot all about the terrestrial world. They were living only in and for each other. A long embrace kept them pressed together. Their lips joined. Their gaze melted together in the fusion of their souls...

CHAPTER XIV

But the lovers, the engaged, the future husband and wife, were abruptly awakened from their ecstasy by a very unexpected sound that they recognized immediately: the sound of footsteps!

In the hallway, in the rotunda, someone was marching steadily, rapidly... As soon as they stopped on the other side of the door, it swung open.

Suddenly wrenched back to the outside world, Saint-Clair and Sylvie separated a little and each pulled out their Browning to face the stranger.

A man came through the doorway and started to make a gesture that was cut short because the Nyctalope boomed out, "Hands in the air, monsieur!" The two raised Brownings backed up the order. The newcomer obeyed as his face took on a look of utter surprise.

"Who are you?" Saint-Clair asked. "And what are you doing here?"

The man didn't answer right off. He looked down and stared at the desiccated faces of the two corpses, then raised his eyes to regard the armed couple. Only then did he speak.

"My name is Ignace Kiewicz. I came to check if anyone has entered the house in the last six days. And you, monsieur?"

"I'm Leo Saint-Clair, the Nyctalope, and the master here!"

"Oh." The man's face suddenly lit up with joy. He forgot all about the threatening guns. But the movement he made was not a threat. On the contrary! With his hands raised and open he took a few quick steps forward. Then he stopped short, clicked his heels together, took off his cap and said with utmost sincerity, "Monsieur, I pay my respects to you. I don't know your role you play in the work of Mathias Lumen, I didn't even know you were involved, but since you're here, it can't be..."

He paused, waved his hand as if to brush aside any useless words and very simply, pointing both hands at the corpses, said, "Do you know how these two men died?"

"No," Saint-Clair answered. "But I see integrity in your eyes. Promise me you're not hostile."

"Oh not at all, monsieur!"

"Very well." And the Nyctalope put the gun back in his pocket. Sylvie did the same.

Kiewicz gave a brief account of the events relating to the murder of Lumen, Bonnard, Lluch and Sidonie by Diana Ivanova Krosnovief, the Red Princess. He concluded with, "Neither my brother nor I serve Leonid Zattan for his sake. Through the global terrorist organization we were looking for the Red Princess to avenge our parents who were ruthlessly tortured and killed by her. Vengeful justice has been exacted for four days, hour by hour—my brother has seen to it. Me, I came back thinking I might be useful to Lumen's work, that maybe I'd find some documents that would give me the names of men I could contact... And you, the famous Nyctalope, are here. Let me repeat, I pay my respects to you and I am at your service."

"That's fine, monsieur," Saint-Clair said. "I believe you. I accept your loyal obedience. We'll work together. You visited the whole house six days ago?"

"No."

"Well then, let's find the bedrooms and put these bodies on the beds they used while alive. We'll do the same for the two others. Then we'll come back here and get to work."

Sylvie Mac Duhl knelt down, lowered her head and joined her hands together. During the entire time that Saint-Clair and Kiewicz were busy with their morbid but pious task, the young lady prayed. When the two men returned, she crossed herself and stood up.

The Nyctalope was saying, "The bodies are dried out, mummified, without a trace or odor of decomposition. I know the secret that must be what Lumen used, or something like it. The Brahmin of Ceylon brew drinks, as often as possible, with a certain sap that gradually saturates all the bodily tissues of the living flesh that prevents it from rotting after death... Mathias Lumen must've had made provisions for the unexpected, sudden death for him and his companions if immediate burial was impossible. He preserved the bodies as much as possible maybe for positive identification... but it doesn't matter! The dead Lumen spoke to me and Sylvie. His work needs to be finished. We're going to do it. But first, monsieur, you should know that Leonid Zattan is a prisoner in his own castle in Issyk-Kul under the supervision of my collaborators. Listen up!"

From the mouth of the Nyctalope Kiewicz was surprised and glad to hear the recap of the dramatic events that took place in Issyk-Kul.

When he was done, Saint-Clair paused a moment and then concluded, "And now for the chest!"

Ignace Kiewicz was amazed... and happy. After fulfilling his family duty (as he considered it) by capturing and delivering the Red Princess to his brother, he felt like he was now back in the flow of his own life, back to himself with respect to his logical destiny. He already had those feelings for the Nyctalope that certain educated, intelligent and fanatic soldiers had for Napoleon.

Standing in front of the chest, with Sylvie on his right and Kiewicz on his left, Saint-Clair pronounced his name. The chest opened.

Three bundles of documents and a register on whose white, parchment cover was written "Final Orders", were taken out of the upper compartment and placed on the big table in the studio. They all sat down. Sylvie and Kiewicz held pens over pads of paper while the Nyctalope opened the register...

And the living shivered as they wisely obeyed the orders of the dead.

The next day, April 21st, the main correspondents of Mathias Lumen, the affiliates and finally the members of the secret general staff set up in the five parts of the world by Lumen for the sacred defense of the Principle of Good against the Principle of Evil, all these important and powerful people received a long, coded message by radio or cable: in the name of the murdered Lumen Leo Saint-Clair the Nyctalope was warning them to carry out the plans to thwart the general outbreak of the universal revolutionary plot on May 1st. And the message was accompanied with a list of names, which Saint-Clair, Sylvie and Kiewicz had drawn up from the documents brought from Issyk-Kul by the Nyctalope and with the documents found in the big chest in Ushant house. The names were those of the heads of the terrorist organizations and the leaders of the global revolution.

At the same time, official statements were sent to the news agencies in every capital. Starting on April 23rd the big papers from one end of the civilized world to the other began publishing reports that immediately threw the terrorist organizations into turmoil, which helped the governments the duly accredited authorities. The reports were about the destruction of the "principality" of Karakol, the capture and arrest of Leonid Zattan, Prince of Issyk-Kul, along with a number of his important accomplices.

So, starting on this date, which could have been calamitous, the civilized nations of the earth saw only moderate commotion from failed strikes, harmless skirmishes and fruitless meetings.

The late Mathias Lumen was victorious thanks to the intelligence of a man. Without ever using any weapons, with no other power but his bright eyes and bare hands aiding his mind, the Nyctalope had constantly gotten the better of an armed enemy, surrounded by soldiers, equipped with all kinds of inventions of modern science and the master in a fortified castle where the victor had to enter as a prisoner.

And up until the first months of the present year, 1927, humanity remains ignorant of the peril that it faced.

But what became of the men who spawned this peril and the ones sustaining it? To this the author can only answer with partial accuracy.

Leonid Zattan, Woldski and Ali-Soud are living in colonies under strict and constant surveillance on a tiny island in the southern regions of the Pacific Ocean. Petrus Ivitch died last year in a surgical clinic run by Dr. Weilmann in a new city in South America. Ismaïl Kadeuy is enjoying a modest retirement around Monte Carlo.

Jacques Cervier and Pedro Tchicoz died pathetically like they deserved. On board the *Fulgur* where Gnô Mitang had put them on the night of April 4th, they got into a fight during one of their "strolls" on deck, accusing each other of "selling out". It came to blows. When the guards went to separate them, Paul Guennec ordered, "Let them be."

The two rats hit and kicked and bit each other. A bitter brawl claimed Tchicoz first, even though he was by far the stronger! It was Cervier who was more clever and vicious. He sunk his teeth into Tchicoz' throat, just above the

Adam's apple, so savagely that the Mexican was fatally wounded and almost immediately breathed his last. But Cervier had been punched hard around his heart and liver. The two organs were gravely injured and after a few days of agony on the *Fulgur*, Cervier perished.

Of Diana Ivanova and the Kiewicz brothers we know nothing. After May 1st Ignace bid farewell to Saint-Clair and went to Saint-Guilhem, to the Giant's Castle. But a week later, in the middle of the night, the castle caught fire, fanned by the wind, and all the modern structures burned down. Tourists passing through Saint-Guilhem can see up on top of the sharp peak a few dark ruins that resembled more the castle as it was before the renovations. Among the ashes and smoking debris they found no signs of human remains whatsoever. They figured that the mysterious owners of the tragic castle started the fire themselves and under darkness had fled in a car on the deserted roads. Is Diana Ivanova still alive? If yes, where are the brothers keeping her to exact their sophisticated revenge? Or has this vengeance already tortured her to death? A mystery.

Under the direction of Gnô Mitang and following Lumen's last will, the house in Ushant was razed to the ground, its wells and pools demolished, every last vestige carefully obliterated. Rocks, bare stone, patches of sparse grass and weeds—that's all that you can see of the house that the Red Princess turned into a sepulcher.

But to wrap things up, let's turn our eyes away from these tragic and gloomy sights…

What do you think became of Gnô Mitang? He is living in his homeland, Japan. Alone, taken for the humble philosopher of the village, he spends his days and nights in silent meditation. Sometimes he is gone from his small house. The people in the village believe he takes pilgrimages to old temples. In reality, Gnô Mitang, under a name that cannot be revealed, is welcomed with honor and even with great pomp, by his king who respects him most of all his secret advisors.

Marc Ayol is still captain of the *Fulgur* with Paul Guennec as second-in-command. Yves Lequic, Adrien Dantal, Feraud, Blanchard, Bonnard and Syvlain are officer-engineers and first mates. Among the sailors there are three, highly disciplined and devoted, who are called Barbone, Ramuz and Geronimo.

The *Fulgur* is a yacht used for pleasure, traveling and exploration by Leo Saint-Clair and his wife, Sylvie. It took them on their honeymoon under the stars of both hemispheres. It is where they live most of the time. Now and then Leo and Sylvie spend one or two weeks in Paris, incognito.

Love lives in their hearts as strongly as on the first day of their amorous vows. They are happy and their bliss is reflected in their eyes when they look at each other.

But when Leo and Sylvie look at the stars, which Nostradamus used to consult so often, they shudder with a kind of holy expectation at the thought that they are still children, at the thought that many of Nostradamus' prophecies have come true, and finally at the thought that the prophecy under the auspices of which they fell in love and got married contains these verses that are full of both hope and horror:

"*Victorious will he be if the woman gives birth*

"*Otherwise, the Time will be long delayed*

"*Blood over one and nine and nineteen*

"*With the dead in dreadful piles.*"

And the agonizing question is posed: For the Nyctalope to be "victorious" over a new human manifestation of the Antichrist, Sylvie has to have a child... will this child be born?

Let's hope so. Let's hope that the love of the man who is the Nyctalope "with divine attributes" and the woman who is the "Golden Virgin", let's hope that this fated love will not be sterile and that it will soon bear a child chosen as the herald and the pledge of victory.

LE LIVRE POPULAIRE

JEAN DE LA HIRE

LA CAPTIVE DU DÉMON

PRIX :
2 fr. 25
LE VOLUME

A. FAYARD & Cie ÉDITEURS PARIS

www.ingramcontent.com/pod-product-compliance
Lightning Source LLC
Chambersburg PA
CBHW060433030726
47495CB00003B/863